CRASH COURSE

STEELE RIDGE: THE BLACKWELLS

ADRIENNE GIORDANO

TEAM STEELE RIDGE

Edited by Kristen Weber

Copyedited by Martha Trachtenberg

Cover Design by Stuart Bache, Books Covered

Copyright © Adrienne Giordano

Print Edition ISBN: 978-1-942504-87-0
Digital Edition ISBN: 978-1-942504-86-3

DISCOVER MORE STEELE RIDGE

STEELE RIDGE: THE STEELES

The BEGINNING, A Novella

Going HARD, Book 1

Living FAST, Book 2

Loving DEEP, Book 3

Breaking FREE, Book 4

Roaming WILD, Book 5

Stripping BARE, Book 6

Enduring LOVE, A Novella, Book 7

Vowing LOVE, A Novella, Book 8

STEELE RIDGE: THE KINGSTONS

Craving HEAT, Book 1

Tasting FIRE, Book 2

Searing NEED, Book 3

Striking EDGE, Book 4

Burning ACHE, Book 5

STEELE RIDGE: THE BLACKWELLS

Flash Point, Book 1

Smoke Screen, Book 2

Cross Roads, Book 3

Crash Course, Book 4

End Game, Book 5

STEELE RIDGE CHRISTMAS CAPERS

The Most Wonderful Gift of All, Caper 1

A Sign of the Season, Caper 2

His Holiday Miracle, Caper 3

A Holly Jolly Homecoming, Caper 4

Hope for the Holidays, Caper 5

All She Wants for Christmas, Caper 6

Jingle Bell Rock Tonight, Caper 7

Not So Silent Night, Caper 8

A Rogue Santa, Caper 9

The Puppy Present, Caper 10

For the Love of Santa, Caper 11

Beneath the Mistletoe, Caper 12

ALSO BY ADRIENNE GIORDANO

Crossing Lines

Deadly Odds

HARLEQUIN INTRIGUES

The Prosecutor

The Defender

The Marshal

The Detective

The Rebel

JUSTIFIABLE CAUSE ROMANTIC SUSPENSE SERIES

The Chase

The Evasion

The Capture

JUSTICE ROMANTIC SUSPENSE SERIES w/MISTY EVANS

Stealing Justice

Cheating Justice

Holiday Justice

Exposing Justice

Undercover Justice

Protecting Justice

Missing Justice

Defending Justice

SCHOCK SISTERS MYSTERY SERIES w/MISTY EVANS

1st Shock

2nd Strike

3rd Tango

4th Silence

WOMEN'S FICTION

BY ADRIENNE WRITING AS ANNE DANO

The Money Shot

CRASH COURSE

STEELE RIDGE: THE BLACKWELLS

ADRIENNE GIORDANO

For Garry.
Thank you for proving that perseverance pays off. I love you.

1

_____

"Wake up, dumbass."

Cruz Blackwell opened his eyes and took in the pristine leather loafers that could only belong to his clotheshorse brother Phin.

What the hell?

A full freaking marching band erupted inside his skull, the pounding so fierce he closed his eyes, focused on not puking all over said loafers.

"Cruz."

Phin's voice. Definitely. To maximize his wake-this-fucker-up efforts, little brother added a not-so-subtle toe to his ribcage. But Cruz? All he cared about was the hardwood floor pressing against his cheek.

Apparently, he'd decided his suite's kitchen would be a good slumber spot. Man, his head hurt.

If he could stay here, or maybe crawl to his bed, in a few hours he'd be okay.

That's all he needed. More sleep.

"Get up," Phin said. "Zeke is on the warpath. You're

missing a meeting. And Christ on a cracker, did you seriously pass out on your kitchen floor?"

Meeting.

They had a meeting? He opened his eyes again, focused on the hem of Phin's dress slacks for a few seconds until the haze cleared. But that marching band? Brutal, those fuckers.

"As the song says," Cruz grumbled. "Jack Daniels kicked my ass."

Phin let out a sigh. "Yeah. I see the bottle there next to you. The fucking floor, dude? Are you in college again?"

Gathering every ounce of strength, Cruz lifted his head. Big mistake. The room whirled. His stomach along with it. If he'd had any food in his belly, he might have blown chunks on baby brother's fancy shoes.

What kind of an asshole misses a meeting when he's employed by his family?

Jesus, he needed to get his act together. Lately, everything was changing. Even his drinking habits. Considering he'd gotten wasted on a Wednesday night.

What kind of an asshole does *that*?

Rolling to his back, he stared up at the ceiling, concentrating on stabilizing his rioting system.

Phin's head appeared over him. "Grab a shower. We're all waiting on you."

Ha! Good one. He could barely lift his head and now he was supposed to attend a meeting? This was the problem that came of cohabitating with family and having their workplace just steps away. Sure, each lived in separate suites with full kitchens, but they were all under the same giant roof.

All. The. Time.

Today proved if he didn't come out of his suite, someone

would bang on the door and check on him. A friendly gesture, but could a guy not sleep in?

Cruz cleared whatever kind of muck clogged his throat, blinked a few times, and said a silent thanks when a spot on the white ceiling came into focus. Lord, his body despised him right now. "When did this meeting get scheduled?"

"Zeke texted last night. We have a recovery. Last-minute deal in Nashville. And it's happening today."

Today?

I don't think so.

Maybe, if he hydrated all morning—what the hell time was it?—and power napped, he might be functional. At least he had a plan.

He inched himself to his side and levered up, pausing with each infinitesimal movement to steady himself. To his left sat the empty Jack Daniels bottle. *Some friend you are.*

Once upright—no chunks blown—he slumped back against the lower cabinets and his head flopped forward. In his current condition, he considered it a win.

"The fridge," he croaked. "Gatorade. Get me one."

Phin took three steps and ripped the door open. "Are you still *drunk*?"

Yeah, I am.

No way he'd admit that. "Just get me the fucking Gatorade and give me ten to shower. Tell Zeke to keep his shorts on."

"Oh, *that'll* go over well."

"I heard that."

Just when Cruz thought he had a plan . . .

Zeke. Terrific. Not only was he their older brother, but he was now the guy in charge of Blackwell Asset and Recovery Services, aka BARS. The family business. Zeke had assumed the reins when Ash, the oldest of the Blackwell boys, decided his purpose in life meant wearing an FBI badge. That was a whole other thing Zeke had gotten his shorts in a wad over.

Holding the Gatorade, Phin swung his head sideways. Cruz didn't bother. He didn't need to see the derision in Zeke's eyes. Cruz simply rested his head back against the cabinets and focused on Zeke's jean-clad legs.

"What the hell's this?" Zeke asked.

"It's under control," Phin said, shifting slightly in a useless attempt to hide the empty Jack bottle. "We'll be down in ten."

Had to love Phin. Always ready to schmooze their way out of a situation. Still, Cruz wasn't gonna let him take the heat. Not when he'd screwed up so royally.

"I see the bottle," Zeke said.

Of course, he did. Finally, Cruz reclaimed the set of brass balls his father always said he'd inherited from him, peered up at Zeke and—yep, there it was—all his hollow-eyed disappointment.

"I fucked up," Cruz said. "Won't happen again."

Zeke cocked his head. "What's going on with you? We're running a goddamned business and you're hungover?"

Cruz wished it was only a hangover. He resisted sharing that factoid.

"It was one night," he offered in a lame defense.

"Was it?"

At this, Cruz found the strength to meet his brother's challenging gaze. He could deny it. Get all righteous about it, blathering on about how Zeke didn't know what he was talking about, but . . . really?

Big brother wasn't an idiot. The guy was a freaking mind reader sometimes and Cruz was in no condition to talk his way around being intoxicated from the night before.

All he could do was shift Zeke's attention. Nothing got big brother more excited than fresh business. "What's this recovery?"

"A painting. In Nashville. You're our pilot. Can you fly today?"

Well, the jig was up now because he could barely remain upright, never mind piloting a plane.

"Today?"

Phin sighed.

Zeke grunted.

A double disappointment. Excellent.

"I guess that answers my question." Zeke squatted in front of Cruz and poked a meaty finger at him. "I'm gonna see if I can cover your ass, but it'll only be this once. Be ready to fly tomorrow. In case you forgot, we're a team. You're costing us time and money."

He stood tall, staring down at Cruz, which was somehow worse than facing that poking finger. The poking finger he could swat at. Get all indignant and tell his brother where to shove it. Considering Cruz could barely move, *that* was fruitless.

Plus, big brother was right. Cruz had let the team down.

The weak link.

Dad had called that one, hadn't he?

Zeke turned and his booted feet squeaked against the wood, the sound shattering Cruz's battered skull.

"I'm sorry," Cruz said to his brother's back.

"You should be."

CILLA BOARDED HER FATHER'S GULFSTREAM AT 8:15 ON FRIDAY morning. This little impromptu Nashville trip, at Dad's urgent request, put a major kink in her prep time for an upcoming murder trial and none of it sat well.

Her client claimed innocence.

Cilla wasn't too sure.

It wasn't her business. *Her* job was to make sure the prosecution did *their* job. All while not violating her client's constitutional rights.

Thinking too hard about guilt or innocence was a rabbit hole she avoided. Otherwise, she'd get caught up in moral judgments that might sway her performance.

She'd learned to focus on the intellectual battle, something she'd craved since her prelaw classes. As for justice, if it didn't play out in court, the universe would balance the scales.

All she needed now was some extra prep time. None of which she had a lot of on a normal day. Throw in Dad and his never-ending requests and her career as a criminal defense attorney came second to all things Darren Randolph related.

So what that she'd just made the cover of *Charlotte Lawyer* magazine for the fourth time? Who cared that she was the local legal it-girl?

Despite her father constantly boasting of her success to anyone who would listen, if *he* needed legal advice, her paying clients didn't matter.

That was Dad. Always persistent. Never patient. And heaven forbid someone should say no.

As the CEO of the nation's largest manufacturer of firefighting gear, he'd earned power and influence and wielded both with expert precision.

In short, her father was a bastard.

And she loved him.

Go figure.

At least this trip had been postponed a day, giving her all day Thursday to grind through paperwork. Before Cilla landed in her seat, the one by the galley so she could quickly grab a beverage or snack during flights, her phone rang. She set her briefcase on the small table and eased into her favorite seat—she was nothing if not routine oriented—while she checked her phone.

Layla. Her assistant.

Not the expected call. She let it go. They had a wheels-up time of 8:30 and the prosecutor on one of her cases had promised to call beforehand about her professional football player client accused of insurance fraud. At least it wasn't rape or some other crime against women. Give her murders, robberies, and financial crimes all day long. Rape and assault against women? Not so much. Thankfully, after nearly ten years of hard work, she'd put herself in a position to be selective about which cases she took on.

Her phone rang again. Blair Overton. Bingo. She'd get this squared away before they took off and cross a task off her growing list. *Check, check.*

She picked up the call. "Hey, Blair."

"Cilla, hey."

They may have been opposing warriors in court, but Cilla respected the woman's work ethic and lack of tricks to win a case. Tricks led to appeals and Cilla, being the bulldog she was, never minded that process, but prosecutorial misconduct pissed her off. If they wanted to withhold evidence, maybe casually lose the DNA that would exonerate her client, Cilla thrived on busting them. When it came to the law, for Cilla, there were no gray areas.

Right versus wrong. Done.

Still, all this keeping the prosecution on their toes took

time and Cilla wouldn't mind having a life every once in a while.

"So," Blair said in her usual no-bullshit tone. "Tony Hadley We have a warrant in front of a judge. As soon as she signs it, we're picking him up."

Shoot. On a damned Friday. They'd probably wait until the end of the day so her client would have to sit in jail overnight.

"Thanks for the heads up. How about I bring him in? As much as I love the theatrics you guys create, I'll pass on you parading my handcuffed client in front of a bunch of reporters. Besides, it's football season and I know you're a fan. We're not talking about a violent crime here. He's not going anywhere. Let him play on Sunday, get a win for our home team, and I'll bring him in on Monday."

A noise sounded and Cilla glanced up, spotted Cruz Blackwell in all his long-legged, studly glory, standing in front of the cockpit door, a backpack slung over his shoulder and his mouth sliding into a cocky grin that only intensified his studliness. Add to the smile his crisp white button-down that hugged his clearly muscled chest and shoulders in all the right ways and a woman might be done for.

The truly shocking thing about her attraction to Cruz might be his hair. She'd never gone for a man with shoulder-length hair, but he had those curls that she'd love to wrap her fingers around while staring into his sultry blue-gray eyes. With her height and the added bonus of high-heels, it would be so easy to do. She'd snuggle up next to him, tip her head back and feast.

The guy was. . .a god.

They'd been circling each other off and on for months now. She'd met him when she'd been hired by Phin Black-well's girlfriend, Maddy, an art acquisitions manager who'd been suspected of stealing priceless jewels from the presidential center she'd been employed by.

Cruz had literally chased Cilla down an FBI hallway, asking for her number after she'd yelled at his oldest brother, the agent investigating Maddy's case. Cruz apparently had a thing for women who yelled at Cam, and it didn't matter that she'd been in the middle of saving Maddy's rear. The man knew what he wanted and went after it. No matter what.

That alone made her more than casually aware of him. Since that first meeting, she'd nicknamed him Mr. Delicioso.

And, oh, how she wanted to take a bite of him.

She tended to be surrounded by men who were intimidated by her success or her father. Either way? Boring.

But Cruz Blackwell? Trouble with a capital T. Too good looking and confident and those eyes were enough to distract her in ways she didn't need distracting.

Too busy, she'd regretfully told him when he'd texted her.

And she was. More and more cases piled up, all of them helping her get to a place of financial independence. Finally, she was there. A homeowner with retirement savings plus a wad more invested, she no longer relied on her father's vast wealth for support.

Somehow, she still had an office in her dad's building. Still there for him to barge in on whenever he needed free legal advice. Still there, being manipulated into telling him what he wanted to hear.

"Cilla," Blair said through the phone line. "Hello?"

Cilla kept her gaze on Cruz—why not?—but brought her attention back to the matter at hand. "I'm here."

"Give me your word. You bring him in on Monday and we'll hold off."

"Absolutely. We'll come in through the back door. The one in the gated lot, so we'll have privacy." Cilla smiled, simultaneously enjoying the chess game with Blair and the view of Cruz. "I know how you guys are. Nothing the DA's office loves more than a juicy leak."

Blair laughed. "I do love our chats, Cilla."

"Girl, I know you do. Do we have a deal?"

Still standing in front of the cockpit door, Cruz let out a soft laugh, clearly enjoying her machinations.

"Sure," Blair said. "What kind of football fan would I be if I said no?"

"Thank you. I'll have him there at nine on Monday. That work?"

"Yes. I'll let you know if something changes."

Cilla reluctantly pulled her gaze from Cruz, disconnected, and slid her phone next to her briefcase on the table before coming back to him.

"Good morning," Mr. Delicioso said. "I heard you'd be with us today. Nice to see you again, Cilla."

"Good morning, Mr. Blackwell. Nice to see you." *Very nice.* "Hope you don't mind my tagging along. My father's idea in case any legal issues popped up."

"Not at all. Whatever gets the job done. It's just me and Phin today. Should be quick."

Two months earlier, Dad had loaned a ten-million-dollar painting to a gallery. The written agreement stated a three-week loan, and the painting had yet to be returned. At her urging, Dad called in Blackwell Asset Recovery Services to get his painting back.

Cilla pointed to her briefcase. "I have the loan agreement. I believe you have a copy."

"We have it." He pointed out the door. "Phin is here. He's on a call."

"Excellent. I have some calls myself."

"Then I'll let you get to it."

He turned to enter the cockpit, his big shoulders filling the doorway, and regret assailed her. She'd never been alone with him and for whatever reason, she now didn't want it to end.

"I didn't realize you were a pilot," she said. "My dad told me. Handy that you're certified for a Gulfstream."

He set his backpack on one of the seats and faced her again.

"I am," he said. "I have my CPL."

"CPL?"

"Commercial pilot's license. Certified to fly any single or multi-engine aircraft." He hit her with another of those flashing killer smiles. "Don't worry, Cilla, you're safe with me."

She laughed. "No offense, Cruz, but I doubt any woman is safe with you."

Plus, there might not be a man alive who could handle *her* when she wanted to do battle that, in her twisted way, became foreplay. She couldn't help it. She loved the art of war. Something, she believed, which made her a formidable attorney.

Cruz? He sorta looked up to the task. Or maybe that was just wishful thinking because she really, really, wanted to explore his body. Run her hands along all those luscious muscles and dig her fingers into his long curls.

He might not be Mr. Right—*that* guy probably didn't exist—but he could definitely be Mr. Right Now.

2

CILLA SPENT THE HOUR-LONG FLIGHT CHATTING WITH PHIN, who sat in the seat across from her while he briefed her on their plan for the morning. The plan started with a soft approach by having her introduce herself to the gallery owner, Greg Adams, and informing him they wanted Dad's Banksy back.

Based on intel the BARS team had gathered, the painting was on display in the gallery. All in all, according to Phin, it should be an uneventful recovery.

Cilla hoped so. Despite her love of the area, she didn't have time for this. A shame because growing up, she'd enjoyed spending time with her parents in Nashville. After the divorce and her mother's subsequent move overseas, Cilla and her dad would spend long weekends here. Him golfing and her with her nanny visiting the Grand Ole Opry and various museums and touristy hot spots. In college, the fun began when she'd wander downtown with friends and barhop.

She hadn't been back in almost four years and the minute they cruised through downtown, she regretted it.

Once things settled down at work, she'd spend a few days. Maybe take an actual weeklong vacation and revisit all the places she loved.

For now? A painting to reclaim. They arrived fifteen minutes before the gallery opened and chose a parking space in front. Cilla sat in the passenger seat of their rented SUV with Cruz behind her and Phin at the wheel. Phin, usually decked out in a slick suit, had opted for the more casual vibe today of gray slacks and a light blue golf shirt.

The Blackwell DNA was something to behold. At one time or another, she'd seen each of the Blackwell men in person and every one of them, in their own way, could be a woman's sexual fantasy.

The one sitting behind her, though? His sexy, lady-killer vibe captured her attention in a way none of his brothers ever could.

It annoyed her.

Royally.

Who had time for distractions and disappointment when the relationship, if it got that far, failed? She'd been down this road. Understood the ramifications when her job and her father's constant presence and interfering smothered her.

It would take a self-assured and patient man to deal with that mess.

She checked her watch: 10:55. Five minutes until the gallery opened, and they'd take care of business and get back home.

Away from the mighty Cruz Blackwell.

Gleaming sunlight blazed through the windshield, so she rested her head back and closed her eyes, letting the heat seep into her. Thank goodness Phin and Cruz weren't the kind of people who had to fill silence because she needed a minute to calm her mind and get focused.

"We got activity," Cruz said, his resonant, deep voice immediately capturing her attention and pulling her from her subdued state.

The man *affected* her.

And that was *completely* annoying.

Cilla popped her eyes open and swung her head right. where a man unlocked the gallery's front door.

As galleries went, it wasn't the worst she'd seen. A storefront a few blocks west of Broadway, it sat nestled between a clothing boutique and a home interior design shop. Why her father had agreed to this loan, she had no idea and didn't care to ask since he'd more than likely take it as her questioning his judgment. *Heaven forbid!* She'd learned at a very young age some battles weren't worth fighting. Not with him, anyway.

Cilla peered back at Phin. "We ready?"

"Let's do it."

Wanting her hands free, Cilla tucked her purse behind the driver's seat so no one would see it through the darkened rear windows. She slid the loan agreement and one of her business cards from the outer pocket of her briefcase and stepped from the vehicle. She paused for a few seconds, stalling to adjust her blazer sleeves while she concentrated on the task ahead. Then she lifted her head to find Cruz, head cocked, lips slightly pursed, studying her with a sort of detached fascination.

She jerked her head once. "Watch me work."

"I look forward to it. We'll follow your lead."

He hustled ahead of her and swung the front door open. She strode by with Phin on her heels.

A guy, maybe late twenties, dressed in one of those

ankle-length suits she detested on men, gave her a once-over, taking in her Gucci shoes and black Valentino trousers. A low-key ensemble that screamed money and the ability to spend it on ridiculously expensive art.

This poor guy probably figured a sale might be in his not-so-distant future.

He offered a too-bright smile. "Welcome in! How may I help you?"

Cilla kept moving, her strides quick as she scanned the various art lining the walls. *Bingo*. She pointed at the Banksy. "That's it." She kept walking, her gaze on the kid. "Is Greg here?"

The loan agreement supplied by her father listed a Greg Adams as the soon-to-be-annihilated-by-Cilla owner.

The sales guy shifted his gaze to Phin, then to Cruz, who looked like King Kong compared to this kid.

"May I tell him who's asking?"

"Priscilla Randolph."

A scraping noise sounded and she swung back to Cruz, already moving the rope stands that kept patrons from getting too close to the art.

"Hey," the kid said. "You can't do that."

Cilla whipped back and shot a hand up. "My father owns that painting. We're here to collect it."

For a few seconds, the kid stood there, his face a mix of slack-jawed confusion and panic. "Greg!" he shouted. "Come quick!"

A man, likely Greg, stuck his head out of a doorway at the back half of the space. "What's wrong?"

Cilla flapped the folded agreement in the air. "Are you Greg?"

"Who are you?"

"Priscilla Randolph. I'm an attorney here to collect the

painting you were supposed to return to my father, Darren Randolph, three weeks ago."

Greg's focus wandered beyond her shoulder. "Don't touch that! The alarm will go off."

Cilla turned, found Cruz stepping toward the painting. "Ask me if I care?"

Hustling straight past her, Greg charged, knocking her sideways and sending her rocking on her spiked heels. Bastard.

"Whoa."

Feet from her, Cruz broke away from Phin and the painting and rushed toward her, grabbing hold of her arm before she face-planted. He shoved his free hand into Greg's chest.

"Easy there, guy," he said. "Don't do anything stupid. We're here for the painting. That's it." He swung his head to her. "You okay?"

Oh, she liked him.

"I'm good."

"Excellent." He let go of her and went back to Greg. "We're taking this painting whether or not you disarm the system."

"Touch it and the police will show up."

Cruz gave Phin a bored look. "You believe this?" He went back to Greg. "Dude. The cops showing up isn't our problem. *You're* the one violating the contract." He faced Cilla and held his out. "Give me that agreement?"

She smacked it into his hand. "This painting should have been returned three weeks ago. Mr. Randolph wants his shit back. *Today*. We're happy to show the cops the paperwork."

"Which," Cilla said, "I'm not sure you want to happen, considering you're currently illegally in possession of a ten-million-dollar piece of art."

"You know," Cruz mused, "I gotta wonder what other *borrowed* art is here. Maybe we should have the cops take a look."

Cilla tsk-tsked. "Art crime *is* quite prevalent these days."

"It is," Phin added helpfully. "Ask my girlfriend, the art expert. Or my brother, the FBI agent specializing in art crime."

Greg's face pinched tight, his skin flushing to a deep red bordering on purple. Rage. Cilla had seen it hundreds, if not thousands, of times on her dad and it ignited something in her. Something wild and primitive and . . . angry.

Wasn't this why she'd become an attorney? To fight back. To put bullies in their place?

She stepped closer to Greg. "Phin, pull that painting. Let the police come."

The blazing color faded from Greg's cheeks and he retreated. Literally taking two steps back and putting his hands up. "Y'all need to leave."

"Not without this painting, we don't." She slid her phone from her pocket. "In fact, I rather like the idea of bringing the police into it. I'll call and explain why the alarm is going off."

"Not a bad idea," Cruz agreed. "Just so we're on the up-and-up."

She made a show of tapping at her phone, but not actually calling. The last thing she wanted was to waste three hours while the cops investigated.

"Wait," Greg said. "Everyone, please, relax. I intended to call your father today."

"I'm sure." Sarcasm dripped like molasses. "Since he's called you twice a day for the last three weeks?"

"I've been busy."

"Apparently so. I'll say this, it takes a brave—or stupid—

soul to risk Darren Randolph's wrath. He'll ruin you." She went back to her phone pretending to search for the number. "Here we go."

She tapped the screen one final time and lifted the phone to her ear, the entire episode a charade she hoped he didn't call her bluff on.

"Wait!"

Folded like a house of cards.

Satisfaction flooded her. An absolute surge of energy shooting from her core and lighting her body up. She'd felt it before with every not-guilty verdict.

She loved—worshipped—that feeling.

This must be what her father felt, his drug of choice so to speak, each time he'd beaten someone into submission.

Ugh. Why, why, why did she draw *that* comparison? Did that mean . . . no.

Not like him.

"Hang up!"

Greg lunged at her. Whoa. An explosion of adrenaline poured from her brain. Everything flashed white and she blinked just as Cruz intercepted Greg, grabbing him by the shirt with both hands.

"Touch her and I'll bloody your floor." He shoved Greg against the wall, holding him there. "I'm done with this. We're taking that painting."

Pinned against the wall, a defenseless Greg jerked his chin at his employee. "Shut off the alarm. I want these animals out of here."

"Careful," Cilla said. "I might sue you for slander."

The kid ran behind the desk, did something they couldn't see. "Okay," he said.

"Go," Greg shouted. "Get out."

Phin removed a pair of cotton gloves from his trouser

pockets and slid them on before lifting the painting from the wall anchors. He peered at the sales guy. "Get me a box that we can transport this in."

"Yes," Cilla said. "We'd hate for it to get damaged."

With his boss still held in place by Cruz, the kid took off, running through the door Greg had just come from. A minute later, he returned with a large cardboard box.

"Thanks." Phin slid the painting inside. "Tape?"

"Please." Greg rolled his eyes. "I think we've done enough."

OUTSIDE, CRUZ LOADED THE BOXED PAINTING INTO THE CARGO area of the SUV while Phin and Cilla stood watch on the sidewalk in case old Greg called the cops.

A definite lack of sirens, however, indicated all was well in BARS land and they should toast to another successful recovery.

Too bad he had to fly; otherwise he'd suggest a pit stop.

Painting secured, Cruz hit the button on the tailgate and stepped back until it closed.

The three of them loaded up in the same seats as earlier and the beautiful Cilla spun back to face him.

"That was so much fun!"

Fun.

She had no idea.

"Yeah, it was. Welcome to our world, babe."

"It felt like winning a huge case. A total rush."

"We're adrenaline junkies," Phin said. "It never gets old."

"I can see why. Thank you both. Now my father can shut up about this painting. He was foolish to loan it out." She laughed. "Not that I'd be the one to tell him that."

Cruz let out a low whistle. "He doesn't strike me as the type to take that well."

"Um, no." She swung front again. "I'll text you the address so you can put it into your GPS."

"I've got it. Zeke gave it to us."

"Good. I'll call my father. Let him know we've got the painting and we'll take it to the Nashville house."

Phin nodded. "Once that's done, I'll drop you guys at the airport."

Baby brother had decided to make a long weekend of it with his girlfriend Maddy, who'd be flying down later that afternoon to meet Phin. Something Cruz didn't mind so much because it gave him time alone with Cilla to talk her into dinner.

He'd tried once already and got shot down. That had been nearly five months ago, but he hadn't forgotten about her. How any man could forget this woman was a mystery.

Smart, beautiful, and tough, Priscilla Randolph sparked something in him. He'd followed some of her cases, watching videos online and hearing for himself that acerbic tongue of hers.

In his mind, they might be a match made in heaven.

Particularly if her fire extended into the bedroom.

But she'd blown him off. Too busy, she'd said. Fine. He had patience and well, he wasn't stupid. He knew chemistry when he felt it and they had it in spades.

"I'll call the airport," Cruz said, "Let them know we're running a little early. How often does *that* happen?"

Twenty minutes later, Cilla entered a code into her phone and they pulled through the gate of Darren Randolph's Nashville home. Like the man, the home was full of flash. Lots of stone and floor-to-ceiling glass welcomed them as Cilla unlocked the front door and disabled the alarm. Inside, Cruz found more stone with wide planked wood floors and sharp iron lighting. Modern and plenty expensive. He somehow found the place . . . lacking.

Like no one lived there. Cold. That's what this place was. In all the meticulous decorating, they'd lost a homey feel.

Cruz had never met Darren Randolph, but this house said a lot about the man.

"It goes in here," Cilla said.

Behind Cruz, Phin carried the box in and set it on the floor in front of an open space on the two-story living room wall. He slid on a fresh pair of the cotton gloves that Maddy insisted they wear when touching art.

Cruz stood beside Cilla while Phin did his thing. "Let me know if you need help."

"I'm good," he said.

Keeping her eye on the placement, Cilla nodded. "Perfect, Phin. Thank you for hanging it. We so appreciate it."

Cruz shrugged. "We can't leave it sitting on the floor."

"My father won't be back here until next month. At least it'll be hung when he arrives. There's no food in the house, but can I buy you lunch on the way back to the airport? There's a great place near there. Best ribs in town."

"Not for me," Phin said. "I scheduled a meeting while I'm in town."

Cruz grinned. "I can always eat."

"Good. It's you and me then. We'll make it a to-go order and eat at the airport."

And that sounded just fine to Cruz.

A HALF SLAB OF RIBS LATER AND UNABLE TO CONSUME A BITE

of her remaining potato salad, Cilla rose from the picnic bench outside the airport lobby and stretched.

"You weren't kidding." Cruz tossed the last bone from his full slab onto his plate. "Outstanding ribs."

"They are. It's a good thing I don't live here. I'd gain fifty pounds in a month."

Lucky for her, she had a fast metabolism. A few weekly workouts plus the metabolism let her maintain her lean frame. Her mother's DNA, thankfully, since Dad had been forty pounds overweight for the last fifteen years. The man was a heart attack about to happen, but no amount of prodding from her or his doctors lightened his fast-food intake.

"I love a woman who eats," Cruz said. "My mother says I eat like a dinosaur, as if *that's* a crime, so it's good to have a healthy eater around. Takes the pressure off me."

She laughed. "Thank you. I think. You're funny, Cruz."

He dug into his coleslaw, shoving a forkful into his mouth and savoring it for a few seconds before swallowing. "My God, that's good."

Better than sex, she'd always said.

Then again, maybe it reflected a subpar sex life. Which brought back thoughts of Cruz.

Naked.

And her hands roaming all over him.

Oooh, bad girl, Cilla.

He gobbled up the last of his coleslaw, set the container down, and slid a wipe over his hands and mouth. "People tell me I'm funny all the time. Sometimes, it's not a compliment. Like when I forget to filter and just say shit people don't know how to respond to."

How she understood his plight. "That happens to me, too. Leaves you wondering if they're throwing shade."

"Yes! See, we're perfect for each other. I seriously hate that you won't go out with me. We'd have fun."

Cilla was starting to think the same thing. And when was the last time she'd actually been able to say that about a man? She'd dated plenty of nice, successful men any woman would be thrilled to have by their side. Yet . . . nah. Always something missing. That spark she couldn't quite define but knew she hadn't yet experienced.

Dating in the last couple of years had become routine.

Like window-shopping.

Something she did simply because she was hoping she'd discover someone special who gave her pleasure. So many of her friends and acquaintances had already settled into marriage and babies, something Cilla definitely saw herself experiencing, but at the age of thirty-five, it had eluded her.

She craved it. Not love, but . . . passion. A yearning that made her think about someone all day. That's what she wanted.

Her watch buzzed. A text from her assistant. She'd respond once she got on the plane.

"I have a murder case I'm prepping for," she told Cruz. "No time for a social life right now."

He studied her with those haunting blue-gray eyes. Add the curly hair blowing in the light wind and his close-cropped beard and all she wanted was to touch him. Experience him.

"Okay," he said. "Do you want me to give up? Or wait?"

Oh, this man. She let out a sigh. "That's not fair to you. You're an attractive, single guy."

He flashed a smile. "I'm also not stupid. If you're busy, I'll wait."

"Good. Because I like you." She picked up her plate and

tossed it in the bag their food came in. "And that, Cruz Blackwell, doesn't happen very often."

3

CILLA BOARDED THE PLANE AND DROPPED HER BRIEFCASE AND purse on her usual seat just as a flash of movement outside drifted into her peripheral vision. She leaned over, peering out the window of the opposite seat. Outside, Cruz stood in front of the wing and the bright white of his shirt accentuated his mane of dark, curly hair. Cilla let out a sigh.

Total stud, this guy.

And nice.

Smart, too.

She might have to sleep with him.

Enjoying the view, she slid into the seat for a second. Why not? Busy doing his preflight check, he paid no attention to her or her nose pushed against the glass.

Before he boarded the plane, she'd hop back to her usual seat across the aisle. Not that it made a difference, since the seats were the same, but she liked the other side. Her spot. And she was a creature of habit.

When Cruz moved out of sight, she faced front, ready to change seats, but spotted something in the seatback. A folder. Dad or one of the executives who typically used the plane must have left it.

She slid the plain manila folder out. Who knew what it contained and she didn't want to leave it. She'd take it with her and get it back to whomever it belonged to.

Flipping it open, she found a half-inch-thick stack of papers. No employee names were listed, but the subject line on the top sheet, the one that claimed it was a toxicology report, drew her attention. She didn't take part in the day-to-day legal wranglings of Dad's company, but he often sought her counsel on legal matters.

Ignoring the giant red "Confidential" stamp at the top—she probably knew more about Randolph Industries than ninety percent of its executives—Cilla perused the first page.

A memo regarding the attached toxicology report for a parcel of land in Morgan, North Carolina, the home of Dad's east coast manufacturing facility. According to the memo, the land sat two miles from the plant and Randolph Industries intended to purchase it. Dad's team had arranged for soil testing.

Cilla skimmed the report and flipped to page two. *Whoa.* She let out a hard breath. "Jesus."

If this report were right, the land held three times the limit of Perfluorooctanoic Acid, aka PFOA, a now-banned chemical compound that, for years dating back to the 1950s, had been used to create a variety of products including nonstick cookware, grease resistant goods and, yes, fireproof garments. PFOA, a forever chemical, stayed wherever it landed. It simply did not break down in the body or the environment.

Once the government had banned the chemical, manufacturers like Randolph Industries created new, similar compounds that did the same thing as PFOA, but were nontoxic.

Dad had assured her his company didn't use banned substances and that they complied with EPA guidelines.

She believed him. He might be a ruthless businessperson, but when it came to saving lives? Protecting firefighters? Dad was all-in. He had to be. It built his success. The company went as far as creating a nonprofit to aid the families of fallen firefighters. Sure, the PR didn't hurt, but the human element made her proud of her father's commitment to the firefighting community.

This report? Not good.

She flipped through page after page of details, all chemical-related lingo that reinforced her decision to study law instead of science.

Having seen enough, she flipped back to page one. No names anywhere in the report. All the cover page said was MEMO, stamped at the top. Totally generic.

Did Dad know about this?

He couldn't have. And they certainly wouldn't buy land contaminated with a forever chemical. Never mind excessive amounts of it.

When the EPA banned chemicals, Randolph Industries complied. Every time. Dad employed top scientists to create safer forms of the compounds used in their products.

Whoever this report belonged to, she couldn't leave it on the plane. As soon as they landed, she'd head to her office and bring the folder to her father.

Friday.

He'd told her he'd be out of town. Charleston. They'd be using the plane as soon as she and Cruz landed. Perhaps she'd see him at the airport.

She moved across the aisle and set the folder on the

small table. She snapped photos of each page of the report. If she didn't run into Dad, she'd email the images.

Just as she took the last photo, Cruz stepped onto the plane and glanced into the seating area.

Could he have seen this file? The thought slammed into her and she met his gaze while her mind kicked to warp speed.

She'd been first on the plane that morning. Hadn't she? Yes. But the door had been open. Maybe he and Phin had arrived earlier and went back into the office? If so, she could have missed them when she'd arrived. All she knew was she'd walked right up the steps and onto the plane.

NDA. Of course. As fast as her mind moved, it halted just that quickly, locking on to those three little letters. N. D. A.

BARS had made Dad sign a nondisclosure agreement that protected both parties. It included anything Cruz and Phin would hear or see regarding Dad's company or personal information while in Cilla's presence. Dad had asked her to review it and at the time, she considered it over-reaching. It amounted to a gag order for both parties. Dad didn't seem to mind and the document had been legally sound so she'd given her blessing for Dad to sign it.

Right now? Seriously happy she hadn't made a fuss over the document. If Cruz or Phin had seen the toxicology report, they were bound by the NDA.

And that might be an excellent thing. She'd know by the time they landed, because she intended to read this entire report while in the air.

Then she'd tell her father he couldn't buy that property.

. . .

AFTER LANDING IN CHARLOTTE, CRUZ, MIGHTY HAPPY WITH his piloting skills and the trip in general, stepped out of the cockpit, ducked into the cabin to check on Cilla and stopped short. She sat, head back, staring straight ahead.

He dropped his backpack and strode toward her, pausing in the aisle next to her seat. "You okay? Motion sickness?"

Three seconds. That's how long it took her to lift her chin, slap a fake smile on her face, and shake her head. "I'm fine. Just . . . tired. Some days it feels like there's never enough time."

In her lap sat a stack of papers marked confidential at the top. He averted his gaze. Being the curious type, he enjoyed snooping. Hell, BARS benefited from his research skills. But she was a lawyer, a good one, and he wasn't about to nose into one of her cases.

"No offense," he said, "but you look like someone stole your puppy."

She flipped the buckle on her seat belt and shook her head while gathering her purse and briefcase and shoving the folder inside. "Sorry. Guess the week caught up with me."

"Don't apologize. As long as you're good."

She hit him with another pasted-on smile. "I'm fine. Glad to be home."

More fake cheer. Excellent. It didn't take a genius——his 144 IQ put him close——to know talking would be a waste of energy.

When she fired up her phone, he took that as his cue to leave. He stepped back and nodded. "Okay. I'll get the door and the ladder. Let me know if you need something."

Before he could move, she grabbed his arm, her frigid fingers sending little shocks straight through his skin.

"Cruz, I'm sorry. I . . ."

"Hey, we're good. I'm guessing whatever is in that folder isn't good news and you can't talk about it. You're an attorney. I get it."

Phone in hand, she sat back. "Where have you been all my life?"

He snapped off what his brothers called his panty-dropper smile. "I'm here now. For whatever you might need."

Unfortunately, her phone let out a series of beeps and completely shattered whatever it was they had going there.

He patted her hand. "I'll let you get to that."

She released his arm and he headed toward the door to deal with the stairs.

"Cruz," she called, "I just got a text from my dad. He and his pilot are about to pull up. They're going to Charleston."

The old man. How *nice*. He'd never met the guy, but had seen enough online chatter to know Randolph didn't mind destroying people who got in his way. People like that, Cruz had no use for.

Cruz turned back and nodded. "It'll be good to meet the man who raised an amazing daughter."

At that, she rolled her eyes. Then she gifted him with that slow, wicked smile he'd seen in her online interviews. Sexy Cilla, back in the house.

"Easy there, Charm Boy," she said. "Don't stress yourself."

"Ha!"

Laughing, she stood, scooped up her briefcase, and slid the strap over her shoulder. "Still, compliments will get you everywhere."

Which was good because when it came to Cilla, everywhere was exactly where he wanted to be. His hands specifically.

On her.

Except, yeah, about to meet her father. He dragged his mind out of the gutter and focused on the door.

Two minutes later, he held his arm for her to disembark, grabbed his backpack from where he'd dropped it near the cockpit door, and followed her down the steps. A guy with short dark hair, black pants, and a golf shirt waited at the bottom, his gaze fixed on Cilla in a way Cruz wasn't exactly fond of.

Proprietary.

Hungry.

Or maybe that was just Cruz's impression because truth be told, he couldn't blame the guy. Cruz probably looked at her that way himself. Smart, beautiful women who took no shit?

Catnip.

"Hi, Doug," she said, breezing by.

Total strikeout there, pal.

Cruz paused, held out his hand to the guy. "Cruz Blackwell."

Doug shifted his backpack higher on his shoulder and shook Cruz's hand. "Doug Andrews. I'm Mr. Randolph's pilot. Thanks for handling the trip. I had a conflict." He jerked his chin at the Gulfstream. "How'd she do?"

"Good. She's a sweet ride."

"That she is. We're taking a run to Charleston. Any write-ups before we go?"

Cruz shook his head. "Nothing. Easy flight."

Doug held his hand out again and the two men shook. "I'll let you go. Mr. Randolph is ready. We still need fuel and I need to do my preflight."

The pilot climbed the stairs, probably intending on dropping his gear in the flight deck before doing his preflight check.

Cilla stood just outside the airport office, checking something on her phone. Cruz headed for her just as an older man, in a suit that fit too well not to be custom, stepped through the door. Tall with short dark hair that was graying at the temples, he had the stiff-backed posture of someone accustomed to entering a room and people noticing. Cruz had used that same posture—shoulders back, chin high——frequently to make sure people understood who the alpha dog was.

Based on photos Cruz had seen, this must be Cilla's father.

The two exchanged a peck on the cheek and a hug as Cruz approached. The man eyed him over Cilla's shoulder, which, yeah, maybe Cruz found odd since the man's attention was on Cruz rather than his daughter. But, hey, people were weird cats.

Cilla backed away from the hug and gestured to Cruz. "Dad, this is Cruz Blackwell. Cruz, my father, Darren Randolph."

"Sir, good to meet you. I love your plane."

And maybe your daughter. Doh! Totally not saying that. At least not yet.

But what a thought for a guy who hadn't yet fully experienced being in love. At least, he didn't think he'd experienced it and he kinda hoped he'd know when it happened.

"There's a lot to love," Randolph said.

Whoa. Had this dude read his freaking mind? He ticked back on the last thing he'd said. The plane. Randolph was talking about the plane.

Phew. Cruz nearly laughed over his own mental bedlam. Nothing new there.

"Thank you for taking care of the painting," Randolph

said. "First and last time I ever lend my art out." He turned to Cilla. "Did Greg give you any problems?"

She waved it off. "Cruz and Phin took care of it."

"I don't like the sound of that."

Randolph's gaze shifted to Cruz and stayed there. Clearly, he expected an explanation and since Cruz represented BARS, he jumped in. "Nothing to be concerned about, sir. Greg wasn't too happy about letting the painting go. Cilla convinced him he had no legal right to it and we were out of there."

Finally, Randolph gave Cilla a smile that could light Broadway. "That's my girl. Tough as nails."

"Cruz," Cilla said, "I need to speak with my dad. Would you excuse us?"

"Of course."

He held his hand to Randolph. "I'm sure you'll hear from my brother, Zeke, but thank you for trusting us. Glad we could recover your property."

"You did a great job, son. Great job."

Son?

That was . . . interesting. Never had a client refer to him as son. Cruz's own father had been dead for years and maybe Cruz was a tad sensitive to another man referring to him as son. And did Randolph just use a condescending tone with him?

Whether the tone or the phrase alone, it got Cruz's hackles up. However, straightening Randolph out on Blackwell lineage, and the use of the term "son," wouldn't help Cruz's current situation with a still-pissed-off Zeke.

Filter locked in place—bonus points for that—Cruz nodded. "Thank you, sir."

He glanced at Cilla. "Thank you for your help today. Take care."

"We'll talk," she said.

They sure would.

CILLA WANTED ANSWERS.

About the report, about whether her dad knew property he intended to buy was contaminated, and about who had left confidential information on the plane. At the very least, it was careless.

She waited for Mr. Delicioso to clear out, watching as he moved toward the airport office in all his long-legged, broad-shouldered confidence. Something about the way he moved drew her in. A sort of command presence she'd witnessed thousands of times in cops when they approached the witness stand. Sometimes, with cops, particularly those trying to intimidate her, she wasn't a fan. It screamed of condescension and arrogance and all Cilla wanted was to strip them of it.

With Cruz?

Big fan.

His don't-fuck-with-me-or-my-people attitude made her want to curl right into him and find shelter. And when the hell had that ever been the case for Ms. Independent?

She'd have to ponder that.

Right now, she had business with Dad. She shifted back to her father, who jerked his chin at Cruz. "Everything all right with him?"

"Absolutely. He's a rockstar. Total pro."

Dad's eyebrows lifted. "High praise coming from you."

Indeed it was. "It's deserved."

Not wanting to explore her feelings about one Cruz Blackwell, Cilla slid the folder with the toxicology report from her briefcase. "I found this on the plane. It's a toxicology report. Have you seen it?"

He held his hand up, shielding his eyes from the sun and squinting at her. "Sweetheart, I see hundreds of reports."

"This one is about a Morgan farm you're interested in purchasing."

Dad dropped his hand, letting the sun glare on him as he took the folder. He flipped it open and perused the first page. "This was on the plane?"

"Someone left it in the seatback."

"Paul used the plane last. I'll talk to him. He's on his way now. We have a dinner meeting tonight with the Charleston mayor."

"Why are you buying a farm?"

He closed the folder. "Paul is spearheading it. We need acreage to expand the landfill."

"For waste?"

"That's what you put in landfills, sweetheart." He checked his watch. "I have to go. Calls to return before we leave. I'll talk to Paul about being more careful."

He gave her arm a squeeze—the "you're dismissed" squeeze—and started walking.

Uh, not so fast. She loved her father enough to have studied his behavior. As a result, she recognized when he avoided situations and the whole walking away from her was a total giveaway.

"Dad, you can't buy that farm. It's contaminated."

His back to her, he halted, paused for a brief second and cocked his head before slowly shifting back to her. His dark eyes lasered into her and she steeled herself. Stiffened her limbs until pain shot from her heels while she waited for the blast of temper she'd witnessed hundreds—maybe thousands—of times.

Just not at her.

"Last I checked," he said, his voice low and rumbling. "I run my company. Not you."

Somehow, the quiet, controlled anger was worse than his normal yelling. Still, she breathed through her crackling nerves and pounding temples. Yes, she was pushing him. Risking his wrath, but it had to be done.

"Dad, you're always bouncing things off of me. This time, you don't need to. I read that report. PFOA levels are way above EPA limits. It's dangerous."

"I'll take it under advisement. Thank you."

That was his answer? Cilla stifled a huff. "I don't understand why you're so casual. According to this report, that farm is a toxic wasteland."

"How about because I haven't read the report?"

"I told you what it says."

He put his hand up. "Cilla, don't aggravate me. I'm done. Go home, get some rest. You said you had a long week. You must be tired."

With that he walked away. Just left her standing on the tarmac without a goodbye. Excellent.

And, hello? Tired? He had no idea how fucking tired she was. Before this impromptu trip he'd dumped on her, she'd spent half the week prepping for a murder trial and the other half in continuing negotiations on a plea deal for a banker who'd embezzled money from trust accounts at his family-owned bank. With the amount of evidence the prosecution had collected, she wouldn't find a jury within five states that would give her a not guilty. No. Her guy? He'd more than likely face conviction for various financial fraud charges and could spend a maximum of thirty years in prison. Which she wouldn't let happen. If it killed her, she'd get her client a bang-up deal of less than five years, restitution for the victims, and, assuming the judge agreed, call it a win.

To date, she'd never had a judge reject a deal. Never.

It helped that her father was, well, her father. His contacts ran far and wide. Congress members, media moguls, corporate CEOs. He had all sorts of friends in high places. She understood, all too well, that she benefited from the fear Dad inflicted on people.

In her mind, theirs was a partnership. All the legal advice she'd given him proved it. And now he walked away after she'd warned him about a potentially toxic site?

She watched him for a second. Waited for him to board his insanely expensive jet and knew that, for whatever reason, he'd just lied to her.

4

_____

IN THE PARKING LOT, CILLA SPOTTED CRUZ LEANING AGAINST the cab of a giant black Dodge Ram pickup while talking on his cell. The sight somehow propelled her in his direction.

Magnet to steel.

Oh. Boy.

She approached, pausing just out of earshot in case it was a private conversation, but then he waved her forward. She kept moving until she stood in front of him, looking into his mesmerizing not-quite-blue-not-quite-gray eyes.

Cruz Blackwell.

Super stud.

"Gotta go," he said into the phone. "I'll be home in a while."

He clicked off and held the phone up. "My brother, Zeke. I told him your father appeared happy."

With BARS, yes. "He has his property back. That makes him happy."

"I guess he loves that painting."

Debatable. Dad loved winning. The painting itself may not have mattered.

"Art is an investment and he's protective of his investments. And my father will *never* let someone take what's his."

"What about you?"

Her? Hmmm . . . "What about me?"

"You don't seem happy. Something rattled you on the way home."

Something rattled her all right. A farm in Morgan, North Carolina. The one contaminated with a now-banned forever chemical her Dad had told her they'd phased out years ago.

Dad, as much as he enjoyed healthy profits, refused to risk lives.

But PFOA? It didn't go away. It clung with brutal force.

"Cilla?"

She snapped out of her mind travel, but questions about a contaminated farm and the possibility of her father lying nagged her.

"Sorry," she said. "I'm distracted."

"I see that. Anything I can help with?"

Oh, she'd come up with a solid list of things he could do for her.

All pleasurable.

But right now, she had questions about a toxic farm. "Thank you, but I'm good."

He boosted off the truck and pointed to her car parked two spaces down.

"Is the Quattroporte yours?"

It sure was. She peered at the car and its custom cherry red paint gleaming under bright sunlight. She grinned. "It sure is. Got it last month. Treated myself after a big case. I love it."

"V-six or eight?"

"Pfft. Please. V-eight. You like cars?"

He brought his attention back to her and held her gaze. "I like anything that goes fast."

She'd bet he did. "Thus, the pilot's license?"

He shrugged. "Why not? If I want to go somewhere, I find a plane and go. It comes in handy with what we do. My goal is for us to have our own jet."

"That's a great goal."

"We'll get there."

Knowing Phin and his schmoozing talents, and now, after having spent time with Cruz, she had no doubt.

"Well," she said, "I should go."

He grinned at her. "Should you?"

At that she laughed and waggled a finger at him. "Oh, Cruz Blackwell, you are an evil man."

He raised his hands. "I know. I know. You're a busy woman." He walked to the driver's side door of his truck, then turned back to her. "Just remember, I'm here if you need anything."

CURIOSITY RAGING OVER WHY HER FATHER WOULD BUY A contaminated farm, Cilla entered her office suite and stopped at the reception desk where Layla, her assistant, swiveled from her computer. She wore a blue silk blouse and light gray slacks and her long, dark hair was swept into a low ponytail that accentuated her pretty round face and slight crow's-feet.

"Welcome back," Layla said. "I put a bunch of files on your desk."

At forty-six, Layla was Cilla's kinda gal. No bullshit, no touchy-feely small talk. It didn't lessen Cilla's appreciation for her hard-working assistant or the relationship between them. That was the joy of Layla. She knew Cilla loved her. Period.

Her ever-increasing paycheck and frequent bonuses helped.

"You're the best," Cilla said. "Seriously, you make my life easier."

She paddled her hands. "Blah, blah."

Cilla snorted. "Have you heard from Ed?"

Her full-time investigator, a retired Charlotte detective, tended to go dark for days. In the beginning, his lacking communication skills had irritated her. Three years later, she'd learned this was simply his way. When embroiled in a case, he didn't think about checking in. Then he'd show up, hand over a load of case-altering information, and her irritation vanished.

Cilla no longer bothered with anger. Why waste the energy when she knew her crack investigator always came through.

Plus, the man's contacts at the PD, the coroner, and DA's offices were outstanding.

"He was here yesterday," Layla said. "He's working on Kalper."

The murder case. Good. She'd need every morsel of dirt Ed could dig up on that sucker. Right now, they were woefully short of reasonable doubt.

Cilla nodded. "Okay. He'll update us when he has something."

That damned Kalper case had already worn her out and they were weeks from trial.

Cilla entered her office, sidestepped the three rows of bankers boxes stacked four high, and dumped her briefcase on the desk beside a bunch of folders. Everywhere she looked, neat piles of paper, folders, and boxes created an organized sense of chaos. More space. That's what she needed for her growing practice.

Maybe then it wouldn't feel so tight in here.

Shaking off thoughts of massive square footage, she pulled her laptop free. Layla's files could wait. She'd order dinner in—or maybe pick it up on the way home—and eat while reading.

Done.

Logging in, she retrieved from her cloud the toxicology report photos she'd taken. The farm's address was at the top of the report, so she plugged it into her browser and studied the street view.

Hold up here. She zoomed out, then clicked to aerial view. The property wasn't even next to the plant. *Click, click, click.*

Wait.

What the . . . ?

She tapped her mouse, zooming in on the one-story brick building beside the farm, where a jungle gym and various other playground equipment filled the fenced yard.

Back to street view she went and clicked a few times until viewing the front of the building.

Morgan Childcare.

"Oh no." A sick feeling ravaged her, eating away at her insides like acid.

A farm loaded with PFOA next to a daycare. Nightmare scenario. Did the homeowners—not to mention the daycare folks—know about this?

She had to assume not. Had to. The alternative would drive her to madness. All those kids . . .

Don't go there.

There had to be more. None of it made sense. Why would Dad want to expand a landfill using property that didn't neighbor the existing one?

Cilla opened another tab and logged into DOC, the software Randolph Industries used to share and house files, all of which she'd been given access to since her father constantly pressured her for legal advice.

What she was looking for, she wasn't sure. She'd simply plug the farm's address into the search field and see what popped.

At the login page, she entered her credentials and waited.

Access denied.

Being known to type too fast—how many times had she yelled to Layla that various passwords didn't work, only to find she'd rushed and missed a digit?—she tried again.

Denied.

Huh.

She checked her watch. Only 4:30. The Randolph IT guys worked until 5:00 and should still be in their offices three floors above. She scooped up her cell phone, found the number, and tapped the screen.

"This is Derek."

Derek. Great. Mr. Cocky. Mr. No-Help. Mr. You're-an-idiot-and-stop-calling-me.

No amount of sweet-talking had ever worked on *that* guy. The others on the IT staff? Fantastic. They didn't mind when she called for advice even when it pertained to her law practice and had zero to do with Randolph Industries.

"Hey, Derek. It's Cilla Randolph."

"Oh. Hi."

Mr. Excitement. Cilla stuck her tongue out, mildly satisfied with herself over the childish gesture. "Hi," she said. "I'm getting an access denied message for DOC."

"Hang on."

The tippety-tapping of a keyboard sounded and the theme from *Jeopardy* played in Cilla's mind. *Do-do-do-do.*

"Here it is," he said. "Your credentials were pulled."

At this, Cilla laughed. Couldn't help it. She wouldn't bother asking Derek if he knew who the hell she was and that her father, nearly on the daily, shared highly confidential company information with her.

"Huh," she said. "That's a problem. Who pulled them?"

More tippety-tapping. "Doesn't say specifically, but every quarter we review who has access to what and update it. You probably got mistakenly locked out."

"Can you get me back in?"

"Not without HR. I'll call Wilma. She's in charge of that. Hang on."

Once again, the *Jeopardy* theme streamed through Cilla's mind. While waiting, she peeked at the files Layla left her.

Kalper gunshot residue report, filed motions, a continuance on one of her cases.

Given her options, the GSR—gun shot residue—report took precedent because, according to the prosecution, her client was covered in GSR on the day of the murder. Something he had no explanation for and which she'd have to figure out how to resolve.

"Cilla?"

"I'm here."

"Wilma is gone for the day. We can't do anything until she comes back on Monday. I left her a voicemail."

Dang. Cilla grunted. No sense yelling at Derek. HR probably had to click a button somewhere that he had nothing to do with.

"There's nothing we can do tonight, then?"

"Nope. Gotta go."

He hung up and Cilla let out a sigh as she dropped her phone and sat back, studying her laptop screen.

Denied. Denied. Denied.

How she hated being stuck. Being unable to move forward when Dad's behavior puzzled her enough to make her want to dig deeper. The idea of him lying to her? Not trusting her?

Devastating.

But if he hadn't lied, she'd feel a lot better. She'd simply chalk his attitude up to fatigue.

Drumming her fingers against her thigh, she considered her options. *She* may have been locked out, but she might . . .

Nah.

She couldn't.

Could she?

Theoretically, Dad kept her, an attorney bound to confidentiality, in the loop on plenty of matters.

He trusted her. So maybe . . .

No.

Way out of bounds.

But there was that one time he gave her his password and had her log in as him to find a document she didn't have access to under her own login. If he'd allowed it then . . .

Too much thinking. That never served her. She sat up, tapped her father's e-mail address into the username field.

As savvy as her father was, he kept things simple with his passwords. His personal e-mail password was his birthday, for crying out loud. She'd often warned him about that, but his response was that if people cared about his country club dinner invitations, they were welcome to look.

She couldn't remember which password she'd used last time, but tried his birthday. *Denied.*

Now she needed to be careful because after three failed attempts, she'd lock her dad out of his own database.

She tried her birthday. Another one of his go-to passwords. Denied.

Hmmm . . . one more try. Rolling it over in her mind, she considered things he'd have a password for. Computer, phone, laptop.

Alarm system.

The Charlotte, Palm Beach, and Nashville houses all had the same security system passwords. Maybe . . .

Taking a deep breath, she went for it. Tapped in the digits and . . . voilà!

Dad, Dad, Dad.

Grabbing the farm's address from her browser, she typed it into the DOC search bar. A list of files popped up. Land surveys, images, and pdfs of varying reports. She clicked on one of the land surveys. Just the farm. She clicked another file and was gifted with a rendering of the manufacturing plant and the surrounding area. Two farms neighbored to the east on one side of the two-lane road leading to the plant. On the opposite side of the street, two miles down, according to the drawing, sat the daycare and then the farm.

Cilla shook her head. Not only was Dad buying a contaminated farm next to a childcare facility, it was two miles away and across the street from the existing landfill.

Clearly, her father wasn't up to speed on this purchase.

A knock sounded and Cilla looked up to find Layla in the doorway.

"Sorry to interrupt," she said. "Would you like me to order you dinner?"

Cilla checked her watch; 5:10. Wow. As usual, she'd

gotten sucked into the details and lost track of time. "Nah. It's too early for me. I'll take care of it. Go on home. Have a good weekend. And thank you for holding down the fort today."

"That's what you pay me for."

Layla disappeared and Cilla went back to her laptop where nothing made sense. When Dad got back, she'd have to press him on this. Owning toxic property would bring nothing but headaches with the EPA.

Before logging out, she printed the land surveys and a few other files she'd read later. One thing she didn't want to do was linger in Dad's files, just in case he tried to login remotely. *That'd* be awkward.

To say the least.

ON SATURDAY MORNING CRUZ ROLLED OUT OF BED AT 7:30, put his feet on the floor, and eyed the empty rock glass sitting on his bedside table.

While watching a movie in bed the night before, he'd gotten a hankering for a shot of whiskey, went as far as pouring a double, and wound up dumping it in the bathroom sink. First of all, it didn't seem normal to be drinking in bed. Second of all, the stuff had already gotten him in trouble with Zeke. He might as well try to lay off it.

Beside the empty rock glass sat a remote. He hit the button and the drapes swung open, revealing sunlight splashing over the mountains beyond.

He loved the view from this spot. On warmer days, he'd wander out to his patio with his morning coffee and sit quietly while the birds played in the wind and tweeted at each other.

Lately, he didn't bother. He wasn't sure why. Restlessness

and colder temps he supposed. Being still meant time to think and he didn't want that. Not when so many changes were happening and he wasn't sure how he felt about it.

Instead, his father's 1971 Stutz Blackhawk had been his therapy. Dad had rescued the frame from a junkyard, loaded it on a trailer, and hauled the mess home. Researching and tracking down parts had become an obsession for Dad, who'd refused to start until he'd had at least a fair percentage of the parts needed to rebuild his dream car.

Unfortunately, he'd died well before finishing the project. He'd never had the chance to drive it.

For Cruz, whose relationship with his father had more peaks and valleys than the mountains in their backyard, surviving grief meant finishing the project his father couldn't.

To this day, he wasn't sure why, but the Stutz had been his own special brand of therapy. Maybe it was the challenge of parts that sometimes fit and sometimes didn't and spending endless hours reading up on why that might be. Whatever it was, experiencing a rusted shell coming back to its extraordinary life brought him peace.

And God knew his rebellious soul hadn't had much of that in his lifetime.

Speaking of the Stutz and challenges . . . Cruz rose from the edge of the bed. An early Saturday morning might be a grand time to figure out where that fucking oil leak was.

Two weeks ago, he'd noticed the spot on the floor of the garage and had refused to drive the car until he found the source.

He got to his feet, padded to the bathroom to wash up and change before heading out to the old barn he'd converted into a workshop and garage. Living with his family didn't offer a ton of privacy. Cruz found the garage his haven when he needed alone time.

Away from people.

Even the ones he loved most.

Ten minutes later, dressed in his usual car-fixing attire of oil-stained jeans and a ratty long-sleeved T-shirt, he made his way to the kitchen to fill his thermos with whatever flavor-of-the-day Mom had brewing in the coffeepot. Typically, he'd brew his own, but Mom had started experimenting with flavors on the weekend and it had become a thing for him. Something to look forward to, which, yeah, was kinda pathetic. As if flavored coffee were the only thing he had to get excited about.

Whatever.

He entered the kitchen where light gray cabinets and slate countertops gleamed from his mother's usual attention to detail.

Whoopsie. Cruz stopped short, his work boots squeaking against the floor.

Shit.

Zeke sat at the giant island, mug in hand and reading something from a manila folder in front of him. Appearing freshly showered with still-damp hair, he wore his normal work attire of jeans and a blue golf shirt with the BARS logo on the chest.

After the I'm-too-fucked-up-to-fly incident, Cruz had done his best to avoid big brother. Being a failure—a *disappointment*—wasn't high on his list of priorities and looking at Zeke right now gave him a rash.

Before he could haul ass out of there, Zeke looked up, his face a full mask of nothingness. Which Cruz supposed wasn't a bad thing. He'd take nothing over disappointment any day.

"Morning," Zeke said.

"Morning." He held up the thermos. "Grabbing coffee."

His brother jerked his chin toward the pot. "It's still full. Get it before the other animals do."

Don't mind if I do. He made his way to the pot next to the sink, using the excuse of pouring to keep his back to Zeke.

"Working on the Stutz this morning?" his brother asked.

"Yeah. She's got a leak. Driving me batshit. Figured I'd jump on it."

"Where's the leak?"

"Question of the Month. It's oil."

"You need help?"

Um, no. Whatever peace Cruz might find in the garage would be shattered by Zeke's presence. Cruz had spent the better part of two days mentally whipping himself for almost blowing the Randolph gig. Adding Zeke to that chaos? Forget it. Terrible way to spend a morning.

Finished filling the thermos, Cruz tightened the lid and swung to face his brother. "Unless you can bring Dad back, I'm good."

Their father would find that leak in seconds. No doubt. Cruz? It took awhile. Dad always harped on him about that. About focusing and not getting distracted.

"You're spending a lot of time out there."

Where the hell was this going now? Suddenly his family was keeping tabs on him? "Just said there's a leak. Can't drive it until I figure it out."

Zeke cocked his head and narrowed his gaze. "Is that it? I mean, are you *ever* gonna finish messing with that car?"

Point there. The fam often teased him it was lucky he didn't have a girlfriend who had to compete with the Stutz for his attention. "Probably not," Cruz said. "It's an old car. Shit goes wrong with old."

He made a show of checking the time on his phone. "Gotta fly. I told Rohan I'd help him with research at ten o'clock."

Zeke nodded. "Everything else all right? Besides the leak?"

What the hell was with his brother today? Yes, Cruz had fucked up, but he'd also flown to Nashville, helped the fantastic Priscilla Randolph locate Daddy's precious painting, and he'd be helping Rohan in less than two hours. In Cruz's mind, he wasn't slacking off.

"Zeke, cut the shit. What's on your mind?"

"Your drinking."

And there it is. Suddenly, because he got wasted one time on a school night, he had a drinking problem. Totally not having this conversation.

Cruz tipped his thermos at Zeke. "Fuck. You."

He headed toward the back door, hoping his pain-in-the-ass brother would take the hint.

"I see the bottles," Zeke said, his voice quiet and so matter-of-fact Cruz almost shit himself.

What Cruz needed now was what Phin called spin control. He swung back and faced Zeke, who eyed him like a starving bear on the hunt.

Cruz's temples throbbed. He ignored the pounding and fought to focus his rioting mind. To stay in control and not kick the crap out of his brother. He held up a finger.

Not the middle one, which, yeah, in his mind would have been a better option. "What are you accusing me of?"

"I'm not accusing you of anything. I've made an observation that there are a fair number of empty whiskey bottles in the recycling bin."

"Last I checked, I'm not the only one who drinks whiskey."

"Not by a long shot. But it's the brand you favor."

"Dude, maybe you should quit going through the trash and concentrate on running our business."

"I am concentrating on our business. You're an employee of that business and my brother, who, for some fucked-up reason, I love. If there's something bugging you, you're not gonna find it at the bottom of a bottle."

Well, holy shit. Zeke actually thought Cruz was a goddamned drunk.

He snorted, adding an eye-roll kicker for that extra oomph that would clearly illustrate how ridiculous he found Zeke and his observations. "And what? Is this you doing an intervention? Next you're sending me to rehab?"

"Didn't say that. But if we need to . . ."

"Fuck *you*!" Cruz thundered, his head slamming so hard he might puke.

"No," Zeke said in his Mr. Rational voice that Cruz despised. "Fuck *you*. Do you think this is easy for me? I don't care if you tie one on occasionally, but when I find you passed out—"

"You didn't find me."

A piss-poor rebuttal, but whatever.

Zeke blew air through his lips. "You've gotta slow down. I've been checking the bin daily for two weeks."

"You're spying on me?"

"Damn straight. At first, I was dumping the kitchen recyclables and noticed a few empties in the bin. Next morning? Another one. Seeing a trend, I decided to have a conversation before our mother notices all those empties."

And here he'd thought he'd been careful, mixing the bottles in and taking some empties to town to dump them for just this reason. Living with his family, not much stayed secret.

So he liked a whiskey—or three—at night? It relaxed him. Took the edge off the amount of estrogen flooding their home since all the women had entered their lives. Then, with the Stutz crapping out, all Dad's warnings about staying focused and not screwing up bashed his skull in.

When Cruz was growing up, for whatever reason, Dad had hyper-focused on him. Always on him. Always correcting. Always, always lecturing.

If Dad were here? The whiskey would be considered a major screwup. And worse, Cruz knew it was happening. The occasional drink went to three times a week, then four, and then grew to nightly.

"When Phin finds you passed out on the floor," Zeke said, "and then does his best to cover for you, clearly I need to find out if we have a problem. Do we have a problem?"

Cruz locked his gaze on his brother, refusing to look away. Refusing to give in to the humiliation. No, he'd face this head-on and tell his brother just what the fuck his problem was. "Other than the women who seemed to have invaded our lives?"

Zeke's lips parted, then closed for a few seconds while he took that in. His eyebrows drifted together, squeezing the skin between them. "*Invaded* our lives? What the fuck, Cruz?"

Being the unfiltered one in the family, Cruz had never made friends with hindsight. Now was no different. Still, maybe he could have phrased that a *tad* softer.

Maybe?

Dang, he was pissy. He wasn't completely sure why. Other than the fact that the changes to his environment had been massive. And not by choice. He held up a hand. "That was out of line. Apologies."

"No apology necessary. Do you have a problem with Maddy, Liv, and/or Lena being here?"

Yes. "No."

"Are you lying?"

Goddammit. Cruz made a humming noise. "It's just . . ." He circled a hand. "A lot. I feel like I'm drowning in estrogen. Always watching my language. It was bad enough before with only Mom and Grams. Now I can't even drop a solid motherfucker when Mom and Grams aren't around. For me? A challenge on my best day. I'm constantly on edge trying not to offend someone. I'm . . . adjusting."

The heat in Zeke's eyes melted away. "Shit, Cruz. I didn't realize the effect their presence was having on you."

"If we didn't live and work on the same property, it'd be different. I live here, though, and I'm suddenly thinking twice about taking my shirt off after a workout because I might run into one of them on my way back to my suite."

There. Said it. Somehow, it didn't make him feel any better. Worse, he was a whiny asshole who should be happy for his brothers rather than complaining. Nope. Not an ounce of relief here.

Before this little suckfest of emotional vomit continued, Cruz whirled a finger. "Gotta go. Forget I said anything. It's not a big deal."

He beelined to the doorway.

"Cruz?"

Hand on the knob, he halted but didn't look back. "Zeke, I have shit to do."

"You're right. This is your home."

Gaze still straight ahead, Cruz stood stock-still. "Yeah. But it's your home, too. And Phin's and Ro's. One big happy family."

Along with all the women.

Before Zeke could answer, Cruz hauled ass out the door, shutting it behind him in case Zeke wanted to continue this tromp through hell.

He kept moving, cutting through the herb gardens Grams loved planting in the spring. All he needed was to get to the garage. Just forget the entire episode and slide under the Stutz where he could focus on something other than his life falling apart.

5

On Sunday evening, using the excuse of checking on his Charleston trip, Cilla swung by her father's house. As usual, she touched the doorbell, a useless endeavor since the guard at the gate had announced her, but this had been her habit since she'd moved out and she stuck to the ritual. She strode through the oversized door and stepped inside where her boot heel hit marble, the thunk reverberating through the two-story foyer and the grand curving staircase lined with gold railings.

"The mausoleum," she muttered, referring to her childhood home, "strikes again."

Closing the door, she set her purse and keys on the entry table. "Dad?"

"Kitchen!" he called.

She wandered the hall to the back of the house where Dad stood at the French doors peering out over the massive yard and the golf course beyond. He wore khaki pants, loafers, and a white collared shirt. Casual wear.

Hearing her clunking heels, he turned. "I've decided to put a putting green on the other side of the pool."

"Okay."

"Should have done it years ago. It's good for stress."

"I agree."

She moved closer and he opened his arms. Wrapping her arms around him, she pecked him on the cheek, took in the woodsy scent of his cologne and closed her eyes. There were moments with her father she'd always cherish. The smell of his cologne and that feeling of . . . home . . . were some of them.

No matter how he drove her bonkers infringing on her time, he loved her. Supported her. For that, she'd always be grateful.

She stepped back and squeezed his forearms. "How was Charleston?"

"Good. We're working on a new turnout gear design for their fire department. It might be huge. Huge."

"Sounds exciting."

"It is." He pointed to the sitting area beside the kitchen. "Let's sit. A drink?"

She shook her head. "Not for me."

He led her to the sitting area, where she took her normal spot in one of the wingback chairs.

Dad moved to the bar cart where he poured himself his usual scotch. "I'm glad you stopped by. I have some documents I need you to look at."

"Sure. If you have them, I'll take them home."

"I'll e-mail them to you. Listen, I want to talk to you about that property in Morgan."

"The one I found the report for?"

"Yes. I talked to Paul. He accidentally left the file on the plane. He reminded me we've had several toxicology reports done. For comparative purposes. Paul claims the one you read varies wildly from the other two we had done."

Interesting. Obviously, reports could be incorrect. She didn't question that. But given the levels of contamination, the findings would have to be enormously off. "Better or worse?"

"The one you read is worse. Significantly. We're having it retested."

"So, the other ones show lower levels of PFOA?"

"Yes." He pulled his phone. "I'll send them to you. I'd like your opinion. The other reports show levels within EPA range."

Could this be him playing cat and mouse with her? Testing *her*. He did that. A lot. Family, friends, employees. He'd admitted to her that he'd come up with questions he already knew the answers to in order to see if folks were lying.

Cilla found it annoying and manipulative and was always on the defensive, wondering if he'd do it to his own daughter.

"I'll be curious to read them," she said. "Something is definitely off if those reports show acceptable levels."

And what about the daycare right next door? She'd keep that to herself. For now. No sense tipping her father off that she'd been snooping.

Dad nodded so forcefully, the skin under his chin jiggled. "That's why we're having that test redone." He dug into his pants pocket and slid his phone free. He scrolled, tapped, and tucked the phone away again. "I just sent you the other reports. Do me a favor and read them when you have time."

Gladly. "I just don't understand how one report can be so skewed."

"Different labs, honey. Paul said our in-house lab did one

test. The other two were done by independent companies. One independent got it wrong."

Paul again. Could he be holding back info? Only giving Dad part of the story?

"Well," she said, "it sounds like you're doing everything you can. I'll read the reports. By the way, I realized the other day I hadn't logged into DOC in a while, so I tried it." She rolled one hand. "You know the system locks you out if you don't log in regularly."

At this, Dad laughed. "Tell me you, of all people, got bounced."

"I did! Derek in IT called Wilma. Hopefully, tomorrow it'll get squared away."

"It'll get fixed. If not, I'll take care of it. What's new on Kalper?"

She eyed him. She didn't talk about her cases, but with her client being a high-profile news anchor, GSR details had already been leaked. Probably by the prosecution, but it could have come from the PD. Or both. "GSR test is a problem. He somehow took a bath in gunshot residue."

"Could he have done it?"

"I think we're all capable of things, Dad."

"Can you get around the test?"

"Not unless we come up with a reasonable explanation. Outside of the GSR, it's mostly circumstantial evidence. I'm hoping a plea deal is coming our way."

"Will he do it?"

Again she shrugged. "I don't have the foggiest. Initially, he said no deals. The GSR could be a problem for the jury. If he tells me he wants to testify, I might have to run away to some tropical island and live the rest of my life in peace."

Dad's lips curved into a flashing, all-teeth smile that lit

up his face. This was the smile that had made him a billionaire. When he unleashed it, people fell in line.

"That'll be the day," he said. "You love it and you know it. You're like me that way. War excites you."

He had her there. Except, the difference between them was that Dad refused to lose. Always. He'd do whatever it took to win. Win, win, win.

Cilla? She despised losing, but if she didn't deserve a win and got one, she detested that more.

On Monday morning, a dripping wet Cruz stepped from the shower while the sports radio guys debated questionable calls by football refs the day before.

As if anyone could figure out that hot-ass mess? They'd blown more calls than there were stars in the sky.

Cruz might have to apply to be a ref. He'd be better than half those guys. Plus, Jayson Tucker, North Carolina's aging star quarterback, had spent the entire season getting his ass kicked because the offensive line couldn't seem to stop an ant, never mind three-hundred-pound defensive ends.

Madness. All of it.

Just as one host went into a fresh tirade, Cruz's phone rattled against the stone vanity top. He checked the screen.

Cilla.

Dripping wet and bare-assed naked and his fantasy woman calls. Had to be a sign. And, oh, oh, oh, didn't this add yet another layer to those fantasies. Say a good spin in the shower? Something told him they'd steam up the place.

With his luck, his mother would bang on his door.

His gut twisted enough to rip all thoughts of an orgasming Cilla right from his brain.

Shaking his head, he wrapped himself in a towel and punched the screen. "Good morning."

"Good morning, to you," she said, her voice streaming through the speaker. "How are you?"

"I'm freaking fantastic. What can I do for you, Ms. Randolph?"

He could come up with a few things. Assuming his mother didn't show up.

"I'm not sure if you've spoken to Zeke, but I thought I'd call you."

Cruz leaned in, checking his short beard in the mirror. Time for a trim. "I'm not in the office yet. Haven't seen anybody."

"I have another project that I'd like to speak to y'all about."

Interesting. "A recovery?"

"Mmmm, not exactly. Y'all signed the NDA."

Clearly missing something, Cruz shook his head while digging through the bottom drawer for his beard trimmer. "The BARS NDA your dad signed?"

"Yes."

That little factoid did zilch to clear anything up.

"At first," Cilla's voice filled the bathroom again. "I thought y'all were nuts because your NDA was so far-reaching. Now, it's helping me. Go figure."

Lawyers. Funny bunch. While in the bottom drawer, he grabbed his brush, dragging it through his hair. Before it dried, he'd put some of that frizz product in it that Maddy had given him. The stuff was aces with taming curls.

Most days, he liked his long hair. Others? He'd contemplated a head shave. The hair though? Total chick magnet.

"Honey," he said while working through a tangle. *Ow. That hurt.* "I don't have a clue what you're talking about.

Other than you have an additional project for us. Or is it your father's project?"

"Sorry," she said. "I'm still trying to work it out myself. I'm coming out this afternoon for a chat."

Today? Well, well, well, this day was sure starting off right. He might have to upgrade his normal jeans and T-shirt to something a little nicer. More client-visit appropriate. Which was also something since he rarely gave a rat's ass what people thought of his clothing choices. He did, however, try to keep Zeke happy by going with business casual when in the presence of clients.

"This new project," she continued, "involves my father's company. And based on the NDA, you can't discuss anything you heard or witnessed while in my presence."

This was true. They all knew and understood that. Not that they'd discuss jobs with anyone outside of BARS anyway, but the NDA covered all angles. Mom made sure of it. "You can thank my mother for that. She's fanatical about details. And protecting us."

"She's a smart woman."

Cruz set the brush back in the drawer and closed it. "You may meet her when you're here."

"I'd like that. I can tell her how impressed I am with her sons."

He peered at himself in the mirror and pumped a fist. "Now you're flirting."

She laughed. "Well, maybe I am. It's easy with you. *You're* easy."

"You have no idea how easy I am."

Silence filled the bathroom. *Got her.* Ha. When the seconds dragged on, he gritted his teeth. Had he gone too far? Six months ago, he wouldn't have wondered. Now? With all the changes in his surroundings, he questioned everything. Constantly second-guessed himself over who he offended and how.

Finally, Cilla snorted. "I enjoy this banter with you. Anyway, I'm busy with a client this morning, but I'll be there at three."

Phew! He blew out a breath and shook his head. Too much thinking.

"Three o'clock," he said. "Sounds good. Care to give me a preview of what we're talking about? Does it have anything to do with what upset you on the plane the other day?"

"It does. I've thought it through and found some additional information. But I'm slammed this week and I'd like to see if y'all can help me with research."

"We're good at research. What do you need?"

After setting the beard trimmer on the vanity–he'd get to that when off the phone–Cruz left the bathroom, moving into the bedroom where he dragged underwear from his dresser, then went to the closet to check out his clothing options.

He was a couple days behind on laundry, but he had more than enough to pick from. Running his hand over the hangers, he stopped at a blue button-down. Nah. A white BARS golf shirt was next.

Bingo.

He yanked it from the hanger and set it on the bed.

"Okay," Cilla said. "I'm about to tell you something you can't share with anyone outside of your company."

Phone to her ear, Cilla sat back in her desk chair and stared at the law books lining the shelves in her office.

Was she seriously doing this? Sharing details of her father's business that could prove damaging? Then again,

Dad seemed fairly convinced the report she'd seen contained erroneous data.

Maybe it did. Maybe all of this was a useless hunt for information when she didn't need it. All she knew was if that farm had toxic levels of PFOA, her father should not buy it. Under any circumstances.

His casual attitude toward PFOA contamination, despite an inaccurate report, bugged her. Why was he not running from this? If there was the slightest doubt about the toxicity levels of the property, he should be running.

"Uh," Cruz said, "sounds ominous."

"I'm hoping it's not. I'm *hoping* nothing comes of it. Remember the other day when you asked me if something was wrong?"

"I do. You were in a great mood when we left Nashville. By the time we landed, not so great."

"There's a farm down the road from my father's Morgan plant. He's trying to buy it."

"And the issue is?"

Giving up on the law books, Cilla swiveled and scooted her chair closer to her desk where she picked up a pen and twirled it through her fingers.

This was it. Her moment to turn back. To tell him to forget the whole thing.

But if that report was accurate? If the PFOA levels were that high? Disastrous for not only Randolph Industries, but the current owners. And who knew if any of that PFOA had leached into water wells?

Too many things to think about. Precisely why she needed help from the Blackwells. If nothing else, given they were bound by an iron-clad NDA, she could simply talk it through with them. Convince herself Dad wasn't up to something shady.

"The farm," she said, "has enormous levels of PFOA."

"The chemical?"

"You know about it?"

"I read, Cilla. It's used in nonstick products and food wrappers. There was something online about a lawsuit. Biggest class action in history."

"Exactly. It's a forever chemical, meaning it doesn't break down. Wherever it is, it stays there. At one point, Randolph Industries used it, but phased it out when Dad realized how toxic it was."

"The responsible thing to do," Cruz said. "How do you know this farm has it?"

"One of my father's executives left a file on the plane. I read it. It contained a toxicology report."

"Okay. Guessing that deal got eighty-sixed."

"You'd think. I mean, if I said you were about to buy a piece of land that contained massive amounts of a toxic chemical, you'd balk, right?"

"Oh, yeah."

"That's what's bugging me. After we landed the other day, I told my father about the report and the findings."

"What'd he say?"

Cilla stopped twirling her pen, shoved a stack of folders aside and tapped the pen on her desk pad. *Tap, tap, tap.*

Discussing her father with an outsider felt odd. Maybe because she simply didn't do it. Ever. According to Dad, outsiders couldn't be trusted. He had taught her from an early age not to share their business with anyone.

As if her thirteen-year-old friends were corporate spies.

She stopped tapping and dropped the pen. "He didn't know about the toxicology report and said he'd speak with Paul, the executive who left it on the plane. Last night, he told me that Paul said the report was wrong. They have two others that say the PFOA levels are within EPA guidelines."

"That's reasonable."

"For most people, yes. But my father is a micromanager. He knows everything that goes on in his company."

A squeaking noise sounded from Cruz's end. He'd said he hadn't made it to the office yet. Could he still be in his suite? Maybe getting ready for the workday.

Visions of beefcake Cruz wrapped in a towel filled her mind. Having never seen him without a shirt, all she could do was imagine it. Luckily for her, she had a healthy imagination.

"So," Cruz said, "you don't believe he didn't know about the report?"

"I don't know what I believe. He claims they need room to expand their landfill. Only problem is that the existing landfill is two miles away on the other side of the road. If he wanted to expand, why didn't he buy property closer? There's plenty there."

"How do you know he's not? Would he tell you?"

"If he needs legal advice, yes. He asks for that *a lot*."

Catching herself, Cilla lightly smacked her head. Too much information. She liked this guy. What she didn't want to do was scare him off before she figured out where those feelings might go.

"Cilla? You there?"

"I'm here. Just . . . thinking."

About you, Mr. Delicioso. A welcome distraction any day.

"I'm hoping," Cilla said, "y'all can help me with research, but I'm not exactly sure what I'm looking for. All I know is my father is about to buy toxic land and I have to stop him."

.   .   .

AT 3:00 ON THE NOSE—HE LOVED PUNCTUAL PEOPLE—CRUZ met Cilla at the Annex's vestibule and held the door for her. The woman came dressed to kill in a black, slim-cut pantsuit with a white tank top underneath.

The shoes, though? They were enough to drive a man to his knees. Sky-high with a sexy ankle strap he suddenly had fantasies of slow-oh-oh-ly inching off.

With his tongue.

Oh, man.

He held his hand to the pad at the inner door, holding it open for her. She paused in front of the stone wall—complete with BARS logo—that separated the entryway from what they jokingly referred to as the Theater. The place where all the drama happened.

As of two minutes ago, Rohan and Phin had been at the conference table, debating the logistics of an upcoming recovery. Now the room had fallen silent. Either the boys had reached an impasse or one of them had to take a piss.

Again, his gaze drifted to Cilla's shoes.

She peered down at her feet, then came back to him. "Are my shoes dirty or something?"

They're dirty all right. Shaking his head, he cracked up. "No. I like them."

"For what they cost, you should."

He waggled his eyebrows and leaned in, keeping his voice low in case any of the one million people inhabiting his home were in earshot. "Would it be inappropriate for me to say they give me naughty thoughts?"

For that, she offered an eye roll. "Men," she whispered. "You're all idiots. Yes, it would be inappropriate. However, I like you and I had similar naughty thoughts this morning."

Seriously? A bead of sweat dripped down the back of his neck.

"Do tell," he said, hoping to hell she'd share.

She leaned closer, getting right next to his ear. The subtle hint of vanilla charged his already taxed system and he inhaled, taking it in. Taking *her* in.

Lord, he wanted this woman. Not just sexually, although, yeah, there was that, but . . . so smart. And sassy.

"When we were on the phone this morning," she said, her warm breath easing over his skin, "I was wondering if you were in your suite. In a towel."

He closed his eyes, absorbing the downright giddiness taking over his nervous system.

"In fact," he said, "I was."

"Cilla!"

At the sound of Phin's voice, the two of them leaped backward like a couple of teenagers. Not so slick, that.

Being the consummate pro, Cilla recovered nicely, scooped her tote bag higher on her shoulder and held her arms out to Phin. "Hey, you. Good to see you."

His brother wrapped her in an affectionate hug that some guys might find intimidating, but these two were friends. Cruz knew it. Plus, Phin was crazy in love with his girlfriend, Maddy. Months back, he'd hooked Maddy up with Cilla when Maddy needed a top-notch defense attorney.

According to Phin and Maddy, Cilla walked on water. Lots of it.

Still hugging Cilla, baby brother shot a WTF look at Cruz. Probably over the whole leaping-backward thing. Phin wasn't stupid. He knew Cruz well enough to know beautiful, educated women didn't fall off his radar easily.

Having grown up the rebel of the bunch, Cruz didn't find it necessary to apologize. Or explain.

Cilla backed out of Phin's arms. "Thank you for seeing me so quickly."

"Not a problem. Come in. We're all ready for you."

At the conference table Rohan closed his laptop and stood to shake hands with Cilla. "I'm Rohan. It's nice to meet you. Heard a lot from Phin and Maddy."

Cilla eyed Phin and he shot his hands up. "All good. I promise."

Zeke also entered the fray, exiting his office with a coffee mug in hand.

He spotted Cilla, set his mug on the table and approached, offering a handshake. "Welcome. I'm Zeke. We spoke on the phone this morning."

"Yes. Thank you. I appreciate y'all squeezing me in."

Phin gestured to the table, then pulled a chair for Cilla. "Let's all sit."

She slid into the chair, conveniently next to Cruz's usual spot and Zeke took his seat at the head of the table. Once everyone sat and the whole can-we-get-you-anything routine was complete, they got down to it.

"Gentlemen," Cilla said, "I won't keep you. I'm hoping you can help me with research on property my father is trying to purchase in Morgan. Since we already have an NDA in place, it covers your conversations with me and saves time. Which, this week, I'm short on."

Before any of his brothers could respond, Cruz jumped in. "I shared our conversation this morning. I assumed it would speed things up. They know about the report you found on the plane."

"Excellent." She glanced at his brothers. "I found the file and spoke to my father. He wants to buy a farm to expand an existing landfill. He claims the report is one of three they had done on the property and is incorrect."

"You don't believe him."

"I believe he wants to expand. I could almost believe the report being incorrect. However, the property is nearly two miles from the existing landfill. And it's beside a daycare."

She hadn't mentioned that and it sure as hell got Cruz's attention. "A daycare? As in little kids?"

She bobbed her head, sending her silky straight hair swaying. "I had the same reaction. Why put a landfill next to a childcare facility? Particularly when there are two other farms in between."

Phin shrugged. "Could they be buying all of them?"

"Cruz and I discussed that. It's possible. I didn't get that far in my research. The problem is, based on the toxicology report I found, the farm is contaminated with PFOA."

"Cruz brought us up to speed on that," Zeke said.

"Good. Last night, my father shared two other toxicology reports with me. To say the reports are in conflict would be an understatement. According to last night's reports—one test was performed by Dad's internal lab, the other by an independent—the PFOA levels are within EPA guidelines. My father is having the property retested."

"Okay," Zeke said. "I'm still not sure how we can help you."

"I want to get to the truth about this property and why, if the levels are indeed that high, the reports are so varied. If the report I found is correct, the levels are toxic and my father has no business buying that property."

"But," Phin said, "he knows there's an issue. You said he's having the property retested."

Cilla nodded. "My concern is whether or not he's being misled by the executive handling the purchase. I can't say that without proof. That's where y'all come in. You have capabilities that far exceed what my investigator can do.

Plus, as I said, the NDA protects us. Can you help me figure out if this property is contaminated?"

Cruz swung to Zeke. This wasn't exactly what they did, but Cilla was right. With Rohan's hacking skills, there was no telling what they might find.

Although, Ro had that honor streak that wouldn't let him hack into anything unless he had a solid reason.

Polluting the environment should fit the bill.

"It's research," Phin mused. "Between Rohan and Cruz, we could knock it out pretty quick."

Cilla met each of their gazes and then landed on Zeke. "I'd appreciate whatever help you can give me. I took photos of the report before I gave it to my father and have copies of the other reports Dad gave me last night and some proprietary files I discovered. Full disclosure, I found those while snooping. My father doesn't know I have them. That's how I discovered the daycare. Children are playing beside what might be a toxic wasteland."

"Shit," Cruz said.

"Exactly," Cilla said. "This farm might be poisoning children."

6

After securing a commitment from BARS, Cilla had the pleasure of being escorted to her car by Cruz.

Outside, late afternoon sun dipped closer to the mountain's peak and Cilla stopped at her car door to take in her surroundings and . . . breathe. On an easy day, she worked twelve hours. "Relentlessly ambitious" was how a reporter had described her the second time she landed on the *Charlotte Lawyer* magazine cover.

At the time, she found the observation complimentary. What could be wrong with ambition? As time flew by and her biological clock continued to tick, she could list a handful of conflicts. The first being a total lack of personal life. Sure, there'd been men she'd dated, but—meh—the pull had never been strong enough to keep her from her professional goals.

Lately, with said clock ticking and the idea of having a family of her own bearing down hard, she'd thought maybe, just maybe, some work-life balance might be in order.

Perhaps spending time with the man beside her might

be a good start. She turned to Cruz. "It's stunning here. Just breathing gives clarity."

"For sure. Being surrounded by nature slows the brain." He shrugged. "At least for me."

"It's the perfect way to think of it." She gestured to the door leading to their offices. "So, what happens next?"

"My mom handles all the paperwork. It'll at least be a contract and—brace yourself—probably another NDA. You should have it tomorrow. Then we'll dig in. Do you honestly think your father is being duped by this executive?"

"I'm not sure what I think. All I know is my father would never knowingly buy a piece of property that might get him slapped with massive EPA fines. More importantly, I'm worried about those kids. I mean, a daycare?"

He reached for her, lightly touching her arm and sending an instant flow of calm breezing upward. Cruz Blackwell. He had an energy about him. Not Zen so much, but cool and self-possessed.

"I hear you," he said. "We'll figure it out. You heading back to Charlotte?"

"No. My trial is in Asheville. I'm staying in a hotel for a few days."

He cocked his head and smiled. "Lucky me. Since you don't have too long of a ride, there's a place in town the locals love. Triple B. They make a wicked burger. You interested?"

Typically, she'd beg off. Too much to do. Files and depositions to read. Payroll and expenses to approve. Never-ending e-mails.

The Cilla-doesn't-have-a-life routine. She peered back at the mountain and the dipping sun. More of this. That's what she needed.

Opening her car door, she tossed her tote on the passenger seat, shut the door, and came back to Cruz. "I love a good burger. Although—is there a conflict of interest since I'm a client?"

"Ha! *That's* funny. Two words for you. Phin. Maddy."

Having had a ringside seat to Phin falling—hard—for Maddy when she'd been one of their clients, Cilla laughed. "Who'd have ever thought those two would get together?"

Mr. Slick Phin paired with sweet-as-can-be Maddy? Pippi Longstocking meets *GQ* cover model. It shouldn't work. And yet . . . totally worked.

As kind and unassuming as Maddy could be, she had no problem calling Phin—or anyone else—out on inappropriate behavior. Smart and talented, she gave men and women alike someone to admire.

"Phin always went for the flashy type," Cruz said. "Not that Maddy isn't—" He shook his head. "Ignore me. I'm an idiot."

"No. I get what you're saying. Maddy is . . .different. Adorable and quirky and . . . nice. Phin is used to dealing with conniving politicians and she's the reverse."

"Exactly. Thank you."

"For what?"

He blew out a hard breath. "Understanding. Lately, all I'm doing is apologizing or overthinking everything. Fucking exhausting."

"Well, Mr. Blackwell, sounds like you need one of Triple B's famous burgers."

"Yeah? You have time?"

"Not at all. But sometimes, I suppose we make time. It must be the mountain air because I've suddenly decided I need a life."

He backed up a step and held his finger up. "Don't move.

Just . . . stay right here. I need to grab my keys. You want to come inside? I mean, you're not gonna run, are you?"

A vision of her car speeding down the long drive flashed in her mind. There'd been plenty of times she'd sneaked out on people. Her friend Aidan called it the Irish Goodbye.

Tonight? No Irish Goodbye.

Cilla held up three fingers. "I'll wait here. Scout's honor. I have a couple of calls to return while you're inside. And then, I suppose, we'll go on our first date."

Cruz disappeared inside and Cilla checked her missed calls. Ed had called her twice in the last two hours. Something must be popping. She tapped on his name and lifted the phone to her ear. One ring in, Ed picked up.

"Hey," he said. "We got a problem."

With Ed, a man who had a flare for drama, Cilla had learned to pace herself when buying into his claims.

"Okay," she said. "What's up?"

"My source at the PD went dark."

Cilla cocked her head. Problem indeed. Part of what made Ed so good at his job were his contacts in local law enforcement. "Went dark how?"

"As in totally ignoring me. I've been calling and texting him for a week. Usually he hits me back within a day."

"Did something happen?"

"Beats me. Known this guy ten years and suddenly nothing."

This she didn't need when prepping for a murder trial. Closing her eyes, she slowly inhaled, drawing in the fresh mountain air that did exactly as Cruz had said and calmed her mind. She wouldn't panic over this. Maybe the guy was on vacation or sick. Plus, Ed had other contacts to rely on.

It wouldn't be an issue. She hoped.

The sound of a door closing drew her attention to one

Cruz Blackwell exiting the Annex. "Ed, I have to go. Thank you for the update. Let me know if this continues."

"Will do."

"Thank you."

She clicked off, forcing her thoughts from MIA cops.

CRUZ HELD OPEN THE DOOR TO TRIPLE B, AN ADORABLE BAR and grill on Steele Ridge's Main Street. It sat nestled under a blue awning that stretched beyond the bar to the coffee shop next door.

For a Monday night, the place had a heck of a dinner crowd. The bar lined the length of the side wall with every barstool occupied. Some stood two deep in between the stools while the sound system and Tim McGraw battled crowd noise and the clinking of glassware.

"Hey, Cruz," a female bartender called.

"Hey, Randi. Got a table for two?"

The woman pointed. "Reid and Brynne just paid their check. Tell my future brother-in-law to get a move on."

"On it!" He turned back to Cilla, a shit-eating grin taking over his face. "*This* will be fun. That's Randi. She's the owner and engaged to my cousin—Reid's brother. Reid has the biggest mouth in the south. Plus, he's a former Green Beret who hates being told what to do. And I love telling him what to do."

Cilla rolled her eyes. "Toddlers."

"Yeah, but we're fun toddlers." He grabbed her hand, led her through the crowd toward a table with a seriously jacked guy who might rival Cruz in the muscles department. A pretty, fresh-faced brunette accompanied the man, the two of them making one heck of a striking couple.

The brunette spotted Cruz and waved, prompting the big guy to turn.

"Well, shit on a shingle," he said when Cruz and Cilla reached the table. "Look who's here. And the goddamned building didn't cave in."

An odd greeting, but whatever.

"No kidding, dude." Cruz extended his hand. "How are you?"

"Good. My mom is watching the rugrats. We're on a date night."

Cruz shook hands with the man, then moved to the woman, pecking her cheek. "Brynne, motherhood looks great on you."

"Duuuude," Reid said, "you're not making time with my girl are you?"

Cruz held his hands up. "Just complimenting a beautiful woman. Speaking of," he turned to Cilla. "Priscilla Randolph, meet Reid Steele, my pain-in-the-ass cousin, and his lovely wife, Brynne."

Reid stood and holy cow, the man was an absolute walking mountain. "Pleasure, ma'am. You look familiar. Are you new in town?"

"I live in Charlotte. I'm visiting the Blackwells."

Brynne smacked her hand on the table. "Got it! You're the attorney they always interview on the news."

All Cilla's efforts in working the media and getting her name out there apparently paid off if they had recognized her nearly three hours from home. "Yes," Cilla said. "That's me."

"Knew it," Brynne said. "You're amazing with the press. I love when women can show off how smart they are."

Considering she'd grown accustomed to being referred to as the ice bitch by her male counterparts, a spurt of pride warmed Cilla right to her heels. "Thank you. I appreciate that."

"You're welcome. Y'all want our table? We should get back anyway."

"You know it." Cruz pointed at Reid. "Randi told me to tell you to get out."

"Screw off. She didn't say that. But Brynne's right. We gotta fly or we'd hang out with you awhile."

Reid squeezed by them and with Brynne still seated, pulled his wife's chair out. A gesture that Cilla, who'd always considered it unnecessary, suddenly found endearing.

"Hey," Reid said, "how's the Stutz running?"

Cruz made a strangling noise. "It's not. Got an oil leak I can't find. Driving me batshit."

"Did you check the soft points?"

"Please. Every freaking hose."

"What about trace dye with a UV light?"

Whatever this meant, Cruz's shoulders drooped, his mouth right along with it.

"Trace dye. Dang. Should have thought of that." He clapped Reid on one of his massive biceps. "See, you're not useless after all."

Reid shot him a faux grin. "Yeah. Okay. Let me know if you need me, the expert, to take care of it."

"Don't start." Brynne gave her husband a shove. "I wanna see my babies before they go to sleep and you two might be here all night trading barbs."

Cruz and the big guy both cracked up, then exchanged a handshake. "Good night, guys." Cruz said. "Thanks for the tip, Reid."

After they said goodbyes, the couple made their way through the crowd just as a bus person wiped the table and gave them fresh silverware and napkins.

"Thanks, Jenny," Cruz told the young woman.

"Sure. Server will be right over."

When Cruz hit her with one of his panty-shredding smiles, Jenny's gaze locked on him. Cilla observed the exchange with a sort of detached fascination. The effect Cruz had on females?

Magical.

And for the first time in a very long time, she wanted to explore what the magic man could do.

She slid into her chair, not bothering to complain when Cruz stepped behind and pushed it in for her. Southern gentlemen. My, my, my.

Cilla perused the menu, found the burger Cruz had recommended. The description alone sent her stomach into a victory wail.

Done. She closed the menu. "Burger," she announced. "I'm trying it."

Eyes on the menu, Cruz nodded. "You won't be sorry. She's got a pot roast special, though, that I might have to try."

Closing the menu, he set it on the table and leaned in, giving her his full attention.

"So," she said. "What's a Stutz?"

"Oh, honey. Based on what you drive, you'd love it. It's a 1971 Stutz Blackhawk."

He slid his phone from his pocket, tapped the screen, and held it up. On-screen, an oh-so-sexy gleaming black sports car with spoked wheels and whitewall tires, held Cilla captive. She totally wanted that car. She took the phone, zoomed in. Red seats. Just wicked.

"Oh my gosh," she said. "Spectacular. It's yours?"

"Yeah. Well, I inherited it from my dad. The Stutz was his dream car. Elvis had one. Back in the day, if you had a Stutz, you were living large. We could never afford one, but my dad loved them."

She handed the phone back. "I can see why. It's so sleek and ... well ... seventies."

"Yeah. I think, for him, it represented a certain status he figured he'd never reach. The year before he died, he found a rusted-out frame somewhere in Georgia. He hitched a trailer to his truck, drove down there, bought it, and hauled it home."

"He wanted to rebuild it?"

"Yeah. He started but didn't get far before he got sick. I finished it."

Cruz lowered the phone, slipped it back into his pocket and focused on her again, his eyes a little sad. Here she was, moaning about her father when Cruz had lost his and clearly still felt the rawness of that loss.

"When did he die?"

"Almost twelve years ago."

"Did you work on the car with him?"

A guy who looked around thirty came by, smacking Cruz on the shoulder as he moved past.

"Hey, Jimmy," Cruz said. "Good to see you." He brought his attention back to her. "The Stutz? No. I didn't help. It was his project. He wouldn't let me near it."

Tragedy, that. She'd have thought any man would appreciate his son's interest in his hobbies. "Why?"

He shrugged. "He didn't trust me to not screw it up."

For a few seconds, Cilla sat, half stunned and not sure she'd heard him correctly over the crowd noise.

"Did you say ...?"

"Yeah." Cruz nodded. "He didn't trust me with it. It was rough back then. I suppose he had a point. I raced through everything. He'd always tell me that when I learned patience, I could work on the Stutz."

"Since the car is done, I guess you learned patience."

He blew out a long breath. "I sure did. Finding the parts alone can take months. But I finished it."

Cilla considered that. Her own father didn't have hobbies. Other than making money and golf, of course, but golf, in her mind, didn't count. He used a day at the club for business purposes more times than not.

"So, you're a pilot and you rebuild cars. What else do you do?"

"Random shit. If something has wheels, I probably know about it. You like cars?"

"I suppose. Not like you, but I appreciate exceptional vehicles." She leaned in. "And people. I like exceptional people." She met his gaze and held it. "I think you may be one."

OH, CILLA. DIDN'T SHE JUST MAKE HIS MIND GO STRAIGHT TO the sewer.

"Funny," Cruz said. "I was thinking the same about you."

"Lucky us."

She offered up a smug smile and leaned closer, propping her forearms on the table while Luke Bryan streamed through the speakers.

"I like it here." She scanned the room. "It reminds me of a barbecue place in Asheville. A friend of the family owns it. We grew up together."

"We should go one night."

She smiled at his casual mention of another dinner date. "I'd like that. I'll call the owner, make us a reservation. The place has a monthlong waiting list."

For barbecue? Come on. "No shit."

"Truth. It's eclectic. Interesting spins on everything. He'll get us in."

"He must like you."

"It's not about me. It's about me telling my dad he got us in and then fussed over me. It's a thing."

What the hell kind of thing could *that* be? Sometimes, Cruz just didn't understand people. "I'm not following."

She puckered her red-painted lips and—wow—the things he'd do with that mouth. Ooh-eee.

"My father," she said, "has certain expectations. People fussing over his daughter is one of them."

"Do you like that?"

She lifted one shoulder. "It has its perks, but in general? No. If someone befriends me, I want them to do it because they want to. Not because of who I am."

"I like that about you."

"What?"

"The intolerance for horseshit."

She burst out laughing. "That's one way of putting it, but you're right. I need to know the people around me are there for the right reasons."

Somehow, he considered that a message and moved close enough to get a whiff of her perfume. That subtle and sensual vanilla scent. Or maybe it was just his take on it because Priscilla Randolph fired his engines.

Big time.

The woman was a walking orgasm and he was just horny enough to forget his good sense over her being a client. Not ideal since he might still be in the doghouse with Zeke after the whole waking-up-drunk episode. Last thing he needed was to screw their very screwable client. But, hey .
. .

Phin.

Maddy.

End of story. He'd go slow. He liked her. Wanted to take some time and get to know her. Which didn't happen a lot. What that said about him, he wasn't sure, but it normally took minimal work to get women naked and horizontal.

Where Cilla was concerned, he wanted to work.

Hard.

"A woman," he said, "after my own heart. Most days, I can't deal with outsiders. I have my family and a few close friends. That's all I need."

"You don't date?"

"Wouldn't be here with you if there was someone special." He knocked on the table and smiled at her. "Hoping the woman in front of me can change that. And, let me tell you, there's a goddamned gold rush of girlfriends in Chez Blackwell. My brothers have taken the plunge on love these last months. I might be due."

Cilla laughed. "Does that seem weird? That they're all suddenly attached."

"Uh, yeah. BARS is like an estrogen pool. Everyone watching their language 24/7. Takes adjusting to."

"I get that. It's a change to your environment. Sometimes change is good though, right? I mean, you're adjusting?"

Where the hell was this going? He shrugged. "I have to. My brothers deserve to be happy. If having the women in their lives around makes them happy, I'm all for it. I love them. I'd jump in front of a bus for them." He narrowed his eyes. "Why do I feel like you're asking this for a reason?"

"I am. I'm considering a change. Office space in Asheville. Which takes me out of Charlotte and I have clients in Charlotte."

"Where's your office now?"

"In my dad's building. He doesn't charge me rent and I give him legal advice."

"Sounds like a good setup. Why do you want to leave?"

"He's . . . persistent."

"Meaning he's bugging you."

She clucked her tongue, pinched her nose tight, wrinkling her perfect face. "Bugging might be too strong. I feel like I need space. Room to breathe, if that makes sense."

"With the number of people in my house these days? Makes total sense."

"Let's hope my father feels that way."

"Why would he be upset over something that makes his daughter happy?"

"Simple. It's not about him. It'll disrupt his life. He's good to me. Always has been. He loves me, supports my decisions, watches my back. All of it."

"But?"

Cilla shrugged. "Every time he comes to my office, no matter what I'm doing, I drop everything. At first it was fine. Now, I have considerably more clients. Some accused of horrible crimes that could put them away for the rest of their lives. I owe them my full attention."

"And you think you'll be able to do that in Asheville?"

"I think it'll keep Dad from popping in whenever he feels like it."

"He'll call."

"I don't have to answer. It's hard to ignore someone standing in front of you."

Appreciating the rapid-fire exchange, Cruz nodded. "I get that. So, Asheville." He waggled his eyebrows. "It's close to Steele Ridge."

Playing along, she let a slow, wicked smile light up her

fantastic face. Jeez, he wanted to touch her. Run his hands over her skin, explore every curve and angle.

"I'm aware," she said. "I actually saw the office after meeting Phin for lunch one day."

"I knew I loved my baby brother."

"He's hard to resist."

What did that mean? Did she and Phin . . .

Nah. No way.

Or.

Cilla sat back and burst out laughing, completely breaking the spell. "Why is it that men always think sex has to be involved? Why can't a man and woman just be friends?"

"I never said that."

"You thought it, though. Didn't you?" She waved a hand. "Body language, Cruz. You stiffened, got a look about you."

Wow. She was good. He supposed, given what she did for a living, she'd have to be.

Now he had to talk his way around it. He went with the truth.

"I've made no secret of wanting to get to know you. From day one, when we met at the FBI field office. Agreed?"

"You've reached out a few times."

More than he'd ever done with any other woman. For him, if it took more than two calls or texts, he moved on. Why waste either of their time?

After the third time, she'd finally texted him back, saying she was busy. Fine. He'd left it there. Told her to call when she was ready.

"I'm interested in getting to know you and you've just told me my brother is irresistible."

"No. Didn't say irresistible. I said hard to resist. And how do you know I meant it in any way other than friendly? Someone can be hard to resist in a platonic way, Cruz. Maybe I enjoy his company because he's kind and smart and knows interesting things about interesting people? Why can't that be what I find hard to resist? It's intellectual with Phin. Not physical."

Whoa! What the hell? Why did this suddenly feel like a debate team event? Still, he wasn't sure he minded. Everything about her, it seemed, triggered something in him.

Something he wanted to experience.

He cocked his head, studying her for a minute, parsing out his thoughts. "I guess I've never had that experience with a woman."

"What about Maddy? Or your other brothers' girlfriends? Do you not like them?"

"Sure. What's not to like?"

"My point exactly."

"Okay," he said. "You win."

She pointed a finger at him. "Nuh-uh. It's not about winning or losing."

"Says the top-notch defense attorney who just had her picture on the cover of *Charlotte Lawyer* for what? The third time?"

"Fourth. But who's counting? I like to win. Professionally speaking. So do you or you wouldn't do your job. I don't measure relationships on wins and losses. Ever. And if you want to see me, that's a deal-breaker. When you keep score, I'm out. I won't live my life constantly feeling like I owe people."

"Dang, I like you. From that first day when you hollered at Ash – Cam. We call him Ash. It's short for Asher, his given name. Cameron is his middle name. Anyway, I knew I liked you because nobody talks to Cam that way."

"I thought he'd crossed a line with my client."

"I like that about you. You're fierce. No bullshit."

"A lot of men would run screaming."

"Yeah, they would. Guess what?" He leaned in on his elbows, his gaze fixed on her red lips for a few seconds before meeting her eye. "You don't scare me, Cilla. If I'm wrong, I'll own it. I'm okay with that. I'll learn from it and move on. No big deal. As long as you can do the same, I don't see where we have a problem."

She inched her head side to side. "I'm not easy. Most men like the challenge of me, but with the day-to-day stuff? My work schedule and tenacity? I fight hard, Cruz. In all aspects. It's a blessing and a curse. Throw my dad into the mix and my world gets complicated. Knowing what you do, he'll expect things. He'll recommend you to his friends and then feel you owe him. He'll put me in the middle."

"Wow. No wonder guys run screaming with that lead-in."

"Giving you the highlights. I like you. Must be something in that Blackwell DNA that makes the men so appealing— but if you're looking for a calm relationship that lacks drama, you won't find it with me. My phone rings at all hours and if a client needs me, I go. Now, if you're lying half dead in a hospital, that's different, but if we're watching a movie, having some quiet time? Rolling around in bed? You need to know, I'll leave. My career is important to me."

For once, Cruz did the smart thing and shut the fuck up while he mulled over the epic dump she'd just dropped on him. Finally, he sat back, rested one hand on the table and drummed his fingers. "Why do you do this?"

"What?"

"It's like you want me to walk away. Got news for you, the Blackwell boys are no cakewalk. Especially lately. Maybe I should ask *you* if you can deal with chaos? And for the record, my phone rings at inopportune times, too. Kinda like the job for your dad. Zeke told me I was flying to Nashville and we flew to Nashville. So, yeah, I might be the one leaving you for a job. Are *you* okay with that?"

Timing being everything, the server chose that second to appear. She made quick work of taking their order and disappeared again while Cilla rifled through her purse for something. She came away with her phone and punched the screen.

A second later, his phone vibrated and she grinned like a madwoman. Was she seriously calling him? From across the table? He slid the phone from his pocket. Her name lit up the screen.

Fine. He'd play. He picked up the call and brought the phone to his ear. "Hello?"

She kept her gaze on him. "Cruz? It's Priscilla Randolph. Sorry it took me so long to return your call. If you're still up for it, I'd love to have dinner with you."

"Well," he said, returning the smile. "I'm kinda busy these days."

"Oh, please," she said, half-laughing. "Now you're screwing with me?"

"I am, in fact, screwing with you. Yes, let's have dinner. Soon."

"Good."

She lowered the phone and disconnected. He did the same.

"Glad we got that cleared up," he said.

Still, his mind went batshit. He had to think about this. About taking it slow when all his body wanted was fast, fast, fast.

Despite his attraction to her, right now, she was his client and he wanted, needed to stay focused.

"This is fun," she said. "I enjoy talking to you. You make it easy. Thank you."

"You're welcome. It's fun for me, too."

She peered across the table at him, those sea-green eyes nearly paralyzing him. Dang, he could look at her for hours. Look at her, talk to her, banter with her. All of that wrapped into one? Damned near perfect night.

"Is it wrong," she said, "that I might want to sit here all night?"

"Not at all. Believe me, I'm thinking it, too. In fact, I'd like to take you somewhere and do naughty things to you. But I won't. We're doing this right, Cilla."

With that, she half rose from her chair, reached across the table, and gripped his shirt, dragging him closer. Then she did it. She smacked her mouth against his and kissed him. Hard. Right in the B.

Did she have a hearing problem with the whole going slow thing? Her sticking her tongue in his mouth made him assume so because . . . hello? He wanted to be a good guy here and this?

Too tempting.

So tempting that he gave in and lifted his hand, running it through her hair. Holding her head in place, he swept his tongue inside hers, then softened the kiss, easing into a gentle heated rhythm.

Damn, the woman.

Finally, she pulled back and returned to her seat, her eyes twinkling. Cruz glanced around, found the crowd more interested in whatever was going on in their world to pay attention to Cruz and Cilla devouring each other in the back corner.

"I repeat," he said, for his benefit, more than hers. "We need to wait, Cilla. Then we'll see what's what."

"I know."

"Then why are you torturing me?"

"Because I find something insanely hot about a man who knows what he wants and how to take charge. I'm in charge all day long. It's nice to have someone else do it. Sometimes."

"Ah. I see. And how do I know when 'sometimes' is?"

"You don't. That's what I warned you about. Welcome to my world, Cruz Blackwell. I think we're going to have fun together."

7

AT SIX A.M. CRUZ'S EYES POPPED OPEN AFTER A WICKED dream about one Cilla Randolph. After that scorching hot kiss that half of Steele Ridge was probably gossiping about, he couldn't get her out of his mind. Even in sleep she tortured him.

In the darkness, he smacked his hand around on the nightstand until landing on his phone. No messages. Should he text her? Say good morning?

Kinda early.

Although she struck him as someone who might be up and at it already. She *did* say she had a trial starting. Still, he just saw her last night. He should wait at least twenty-four hours. Hadn't that been his modus operandi?

Look where it got him. Thirty-one years old and alone.

Fuck it.

He shot off a text. A simple good morning.

Done.

Seconds later, a ding sounded. Heh, heh, heh. Yep. Early riser. Was it too soon to think she might be the woman of his dreams? He checked the message and found a photo of her with her silky, chin length dark hair combed to perfection, her green eyes sharp, and her tongue sticking out.

He cracked up. The killer attorney—Cilla Shark, the media had dubbed her—had a sense of humor. Everything about her made him smile.

He sent a photo in return. The one he'd snapped last week when he'd watched the sunrise while on a run.

That earned him a heart emoji and he called it a win. Perfect way to start the day.

Yes, indeed. He rolled out of bed, hit the button on the remote to open the drapes, and headed to the bathroom to shower. By the time he finished, it should be daylight. He could kill time and watch the sunrise from his suite, but . . . work to do.

He'd be able to get to the Theater early and get a jump on Cilla's project with no distractions from the five million people living in Chez Blackwell these days.

Cilla's paperwork might not be completed, but starting on the research would move them along faster. Plus, clearing Cilla off the books as a client meant getting busy with the personal aspects of their relationship.

And not giving a shit what Zeke had to say.

After showering and throwing on jeans and a T-shirt, he reached the Theater by 6:40, finding it blessedly quiet. Not a light on. Something he'd grown used to and found relaxing. He got more done before his brothers and their significant others showed up. No barrage of questions or talk about new shoes or who made the coffee, blah, blah. All of it a distraction that sent him running to his office behind closed doors when he preferred working at the conference table so he could make notes on the giant whiteboard. He performed better that way. Something about the visual of the board and handwriting things. Drawing connecting lines and graphs that he could stand back and get a wide view of.

Whatever it was, it worked for him.

He flipped on the lights, illuminating the space, then set his laptop on the table at his normal seat. Priority one? Coffee. The first to arrive started the pot. In his case, if history repeated itself, Maddy would complain he'd made it too strong.

Well, he liked strong and if she didn't, she could go to the Friary and get a not-so-potent cup of Mom's from the kitchen.

Sticking to his routine, he got the pot brewing, then made his way to the table where he logged into his laptop. He'd start with the basics. A real estate search for the property Cilla's dad intended to purchase.

Laptop and notepad situated, he went back to the kitchenette, snuck a cup of Joe—black no sugar—before the pot finished and returned to the table.

No sooner did he sit than Rohan appeared. There went the quiet. And the rare alone time he used to get and took for granted.

Across from him, Rohan set his computer bag on the table and pulled out his normal chair. His wavy hair was still damp from his shower and like Cruz, he wore his casual attire. Jeans, V-neck sweater with a T-shirt underneath. Probably sneakers on his feet.

Rohan and Cruz? They didn't get creative or fuss over their clothes like Phin.

"Hey," Ro said.

"Morning. You're up early."

"Figured I'd start on this Randolph thing. Should be quick, no?"

Cruz held his mug up in toast. "My thoughts exactly. We get it done and move on to the Hiller recovery."

Still standing, Ro eyed the mug. "How long have you been here?"

"Five minutes. Coffee is on. Good and strong."

At that, Rohan laughed. "You're such an asshole."

Truth be told, it wouldn't be the first time one of his brothers called him that. Still, this time, Cruz pondered it. "Because I like strong coffee?"

"Because," Rohan said, "you like strong coffee and have recently started strengthening it. I believe it was around the time Maddy complained it might put hair on her chest. Suddenly, we're drinking sludge."

Yikes. He took a sip and—wow—that extra scoop may have kicked it up one notch too many. He set the mug down, but would have to either drink it or dump it without Rohan noticing and roasting the shit out of him.

Cruz sat back, eyeing his brother while his mind whirled. Maybe Rohan was right. Maybe? Hell, yes, Rohan was right. Maddy *had* made that comment. She'd been joking and he knew it. For whatever reason it still triggered something in him.

Pissed him off. Royally. But, to his credit, he'd kept his mouth shut. Not one crack about her needing to toughen up because Maddy might be the kindest person Cruz had ever met. A total pleaser, that one. And the one time she comments on Cruz's coffee, he took revenge by adding an extra scoop—or two.

How incredibly petty.

"Oh, my God." He dragged his hand over his face. "I *am* an asshole."

Self-imposed flagellation in full swing, Cruz propped his feet on the table. "Jeez, I feel like a shit. And worse? I knew I was doing it. What am I? Three years old?"

Rohan waved it off. "You don't like change. We've had a lot of that around here."

"It's been fast. Suddenly we need to make room for Liv, Brodie, Maddy, and Lena. I mean, I love them all, but bro, it's getting crowded in here."

The minute the words left his mouth, Cruz regretted it. This was the problem. Everything was a minefield lately.

But Rohan, the brainiac thinker, did Cruz a favor by simply cocking his head and not reacting.

"Is it pissing you off?" Ro asked.

"Eh. I wouldn't say that. It's . . . weird. We're a family business. So, yeah, I kinda miss it just being us, but I get it. The women bring value. Immense value. They're helping us grow."

"True. But it *is* different. I feel it, too. We've doubled in number. Maybe it's too many people for you."

Yes! "God forbid someone burps," Cruz said.

"Or cuts one."

The two of them snorted and Cruz took the moment to conjure a burp that would earn him a head-smack from their mother and various comments of disgust from Liv, Maddy, or Lena. "For old time's sake," he said.

"Amen, brother. You good?"

Actually, yeah. He was. It felt . . . right. To be honest with his brother and not have said brother rip him one for it. Cruz set his feet back on the floor and nodded. "I'm fine. Just bitching."

"We all need that sometimes. I'm gonna get coffee."

A minute later, an interesting combination of swear

words came from the kitchenette. "Jesus, Cruz! This is undrinkable."

"I know!" Cruz hollered back, half laughing over the tension leaving his shoulders. Admitting it brought relief. Let him rid himself of the guilt over making such a childish move. "Throw it out and make another pot."

"Bet your ass."

Laughing, Cruz pulled up a browser.

When Ro returned, Cruz peered across the table at him. "How much do you know about PFOA?"

"Not a lot."

"All right. I'll jump on that. You take real estate history."

"Deal."

Cruz went to work plugging in various search terms for PFOA in North Carolina. *PFOA Morgan. Morgan Randolph plant. Forever chemicals, North Carolina.*

A variety of links popped up regarding water testing procedures. None of which helped him. He scrolled the list. Total bust. He tried another search. Farms and PFOA in North Carolina.

Another list of links for soil testing. *Jeez, with the testing.* He clicked on a couple, found them somewhat interesting and added them to his bookmarks to refer to.

Back at the original list of links, he clicked to page two. Often, the deeper he went, he'd hit on something. Sometimes he'd get ten pages in before something obscure popped.

He scrolled, clicking on a few of the options and then nixing them. What he was looking for, he wasn't sure. Working on instinct had served him well, though, so he continued scrolling. He'd know when he hit on something.

Page three.

Sludge.

Now that was fascinating. What the hell did sludge have to do with PFOA? Time to educate himself. He clicked the link and skimmed an article from a newspaper in South Carolina.

Water reclamation. Human waste. Sewage sludge given free to farmers as fertilizer.

Whoa. Hang on. "What the hell?"

He reread the last paragraph.

"You got something?"

He glanced over at Rohan eyeing him from the other side of the table.

"Speaking of sludge."

"What about it?"

Thinking, Cruz rocked back in his chair. Back and forth, back and forth, back and forth. "There's an article here. It's in South Carolina, but a water reclamation company treats the sewage, turns it to sludge, and gives it to farmers."

"Sounds like a win-win. They get rid of the muck and the farmer saves money."

"Except," Cruz got up, wandered to the whiteboard, uncapped a marker, and wrote PFOA. "Perfluorooctanoic acid. It's a chemical compound used to make heat and stain resistant coatings."

"Yeah. That much I know."

"It's now banned, along with PFOS. They're highly toxic. PFAS is the new version. It's not banned yet, but all are forever chemicals that don't break down in the environment. Or in people or animals. It literally stays in the body forever."

Rohan shrugged. "What does that have to do with sludge?"

Cruz walked back to his seat and spun the laptop.

"Think about it. Forever chemicals stay in the body. What happens when you take a shit?"

"*Uh*, human waste?"

"Human waste that has chemicals from your body in it. We take a dump, it gets flushed, and sewage systems pump it to a water reclamation facility that removes contaminants. Except, the treatment doesn't filter out forever chemicals." Cruz pointed at his laptop. "According to this article, it does the reverse. It concentrates the chemicals in the sludge."

Rohan considered that for a second, then narrowed his gaze. "You're saying this sludge is contaminated and the water reclamation company is giving it to farmers as *fertilizer*?"

"That's exactly what I'm saying. They spread the sludge, the crops grow and now the fucking plants are contaminated too." Cruz nudged the laptop. "One guy mentioned in this article was an organic farmer. He lost everything because the previous owners used sludge and he didn't know it. When he realized he had forever chemicals in his soil, he did the research. Sludge had been used years before on the property."

"Wow. He's an organic farmer selling contaminated vegetables."

Cruz grabbed the laptop, took his seat again, and started typing. "Let's find the water treatment plant for Morgan. We'll pretend to be farmers and ask if they give away sludge."

"And if they do?"

Cruz met his eye.

Rohan—Mr. Super-Ethical—understood exactly where this was going. He just didn't want to admit it.

"Come on, Ro. You know what I'm gonna say."

"You want me to hack into a water reclamation company?"

"It would save time. But I know how you are with stuff like this."

His brother's head snapped back as if Cruz, for the millionth time, had offended him with a comment.

Cruz threw up his hands. "Whoa. Don't get pissy. All I'm saying is you have a higher moral bar than me. You need to be convinced there's a solid reason to hack someone. Me?" Cruz grinned. "I'm not nearly that honest."

"There's a line," Ro shot back. "Boundaries we need to set."

Cruz shrugged. "Do we? I mean, if we don't get caught and it gets us where we need to be, what's the problem? It's not like we're leaking confidential docs. We're just looking."

"What if the Russians said that?"

Christ. Wouldn't be the first time they'd debated this. Wouldn't be the last. "Just trying to move us along. And maybe figure out if people are being poisoned by contaminated sludge."

That comment earned him a sigh and Cruz grinned again.

Ro flipped him the bird. "Fine," he said. "If they give away sludge, I'll see if I can confirm the farm we're looking at received it. If they have, what does that mean?"

As if Cruz knew? This was the fun of research. You never knew what you'd find. "How the hell do I know? It's a start, Ro. Let's see where it takes us."

"A plea offer," Cilla told Donovan Jenkins, her banker client accused of a variety of federal financial crimes that could earn him forty years, likely the rest of his life, in prison.

On the other end of the phone Donovan grunted. "A plea. Now? We're about to start jury selection."

They sure were. Plus, they had a sick judge who needed the day off, thus delaying the start of jury selection and leaving Cilla holed up in an Asheville hotel room. All of which apparently gave the prosecution time to consider a plea.

Cilla sat back in the desk chair and pondered a smudge on the wall. "Something must be spooking them. It's a good sign for us. However, you never know what a jury will do."

"I'm not guilty."

Cilla didn't respond. Didn't need to. The government had enough evidence to build a circumstantial case against her client. And when it came to mishandling the funds of hard-working people, jurists didn't play.

At all.

"Don, are you willing to entertain an offer?"

"I don't know. What would you do?"

No way, buddy. She'd learned this lesson the hard way early in her career. Confident in the defense they'd built, she'd answered honestly, telling the client she'd go to trial.

Unfortunately, the jury didn't buy it and the client railed on her about giving him crappy advice. That guy? Still in prison.

"I can't answer that," Cilla told Donovan. "It's a decent offer. I could probably sweeten it, but if you're not interested, let's not waste anyone's time."

"Send it to me. I'll look it over."

Cilla pumped a fist. As much as she loved battling it out in court, this case? Blech. At best, her client looked like a scumbag willing to siphon money from accident victims who trusted him to be their conservator.

He loaned himself, and his buddies, money from those funds at below market interest levels. And, hello? How about the private plane to the Super Bowl that cost the exact amount withdrawn from one account?

Callous idiot.

For that alone, he should be punished. However, his constitutional rights wouldn't be violated on her watch.

"I'll send it over," she said. "Call me with questions. Assuming Judge Nagle is well enough, we're due in court tomorrow. If you want to pursue a deal, let me know ASAP and I'll call the DA."

"Will do. Thank you."

"Of course."

She disconnected and checked the time on her phone: 3:00. Still time to review discovery on her murder case. Before she could pull up the notes on her laptop, her phone rang.

Cruz Blackwell.

"Rrowr," she said, because that man?

Hot.

Hot.

Hot.

She tapped the screen. "Good afternoon, Cruz Blackwell."

"Hey. You busy?"

Always. But something in his rushed tone gave her pause, sent her curiosity in all sorts of directions. "I have a minute. What's up?"

"We're working on your case."

Already? She'd just sent the paperwork back two hours earlier. "You got right to it."

"Truth is, we jumped on it first thing. We figured paper-work would get here today and wanted to get moving."

"I like the way you boys work."

"Yeah, well, it's a puzzle and we like those. Are you still in Asheville?"

"I am. My trial was postponed until tomorrow."

"Got some stuff to show you. We could do a video call, but a meeting might be better."

A video call. What fun was that when she had a trial postponed and might not have any downtime for a few weeks? "I need a couple of hours, but I could come out and meet with you. Besides, I wanna see that Stutz."

"Huh. So, this is how you are? You're weaseling a peek at my car."

Ohmygod, the man. Deadly charm. "Absolutely."

He laughed. "That works. Say five?"

"See you then."

AT 5:00 ON THE DOT CILLA PULLED THROUGH THE GATES AT Chez Blackwell, a name she'd originally heard from Phin, kinda liked, and now found implanted in her brain.

She cruised the long, tree-lined driveway as the waning sun washed over the roof of the Friary and the mountain behind. This place?

Stunning.

Cilla wasn't the religious sort, but at times like these she knew God existed. It gave her hope and with what she did for a living, that sometimes ran short.

Up ahead, one Cruz Blackwell and all his luscious muscles exited the Annex, apparently coming to meet her. She eased to a stop and did a quick, surreptitious check of her lipstick in the rearview. Minutes earlier, while stopped at a stop sign on the quiet mountain road, she'd slapped a fresh coat of her trademark red on and everything was still in order.

Outside, Cruz walked around the front of her car, his body moving with that confident purpose she'd witnessed in the professional athletes she'd represented. Certain people, without question, oozed it and Cruz was one of them.

He wore a loose white T-shirt that did nothing to hide rock solid shoulders and his jeans wrapped around his lean hips just right. Not too big, not too tight. And who knew *that* outfit could stir her up?

He opened her door, she slid one leg out, and smiled up at him. He dipped his head, did a visual sweep of her, paused at her high-heeled boots, then locked his gaze on her face. Studying. No. *Appreciating*. He had a way of looking at her, all heat and energy and . . . *want* that sent tingles shooting straight up her arms.

"Hey there," she said.

"Hey to you. Wow."

Before grabbing her purse from the passenger seat, she peered up at him. "Wow?"

"I've never seen you in jeans."

"Well, I ditched the lawyer clothes for the day."

"I see that. I like it." He jerked his chin to the building. "Guys are inside."

"I'm eager to hear what you have."

"Let's head in. If we get done early, will you join me for dinner again?"

Exactly her thoughts and the main reason she'd gone casual for this meeting. How convenient. "I'd like that."

"Good. Me too."

Two steps in, her heel caught on a pebble and she

wobbled sideways, catching herself before she tipped over. Cruz halted, clasping her arm. "You okay?"

"I'm good. My heel caught."

Then he did it. He flashed that smile, drew his hand down her sleeve and cocked his arm out for her to grab hold. "Well, since you're so unsteady on your feet, Ms. Randolph, allow me to help you inside."

"Ha! Nice try, pal. I can walk myself, if I so choose." That said, she slid her arm through his. "However, I wouldn't mind an escort."

They made their way up the path, their pace leisurely. When was the last time she'd strolled anywhere? If this could be considered a stroll. They may as well have been going backward and she didn't want it to end any time soon.

"This is nice," she said.

"Hell, yeah, it is. It feels . . . good." He stopped walking and faced her. "And the way things have been lately, that's saying something. Thank you."

"I swear, Cruz, if we weren't standing where everyone could see us, I'd suck face with you right here for the next hour."

He waggled his eyebrows in that playful way she mostly hated, but didn't mind at the moment.

"Lucky me," he said. "I'll take a raincheck."

"I'll anxiously await that moment."

"You're a wicked woman, Cilla."

If she had her way, he'd learn just how wicked she could be.

"Buddy, you haven't seen anything yet."

Minutes later, she stood across from Phin and Rohan at the conference table where Cruz rolled a chair out and then took the one beside her, all of them now occupying the same seats as the day before.

"No Zeke?"

"No," Cruz said. "He had another obligation tonight. It's been Rohan and I all day anyway. Phin's a bonus."

"Bet your ass," Phin said, and Cilla rolled her eyes.

"We spent the morning researching sludge."

What sludge had to do with this, she had no clue, but from what she knew of BARS, these people didn't do anything without a purpose.

Cruz must have sensed her hesitation because he held up a hand. "There's a method to our madness. We're trying to figure out how massive amounts of PFOA gets into soil. That doesn't just happen."

"Agreed," Cilla said. "It could be from the air or underground. Water from wells or streams."

"I'll spare you the boring details of our research, but we found info on water reclamation companies giving sludge to farmers for fertilizer. Problem is, most humans have forever chemicals in their system."

In her logical mind, sludge as fertilizer made sense. Except, from what she knew of forever chemicals, they didn't break down. They stuck.

Hard.

Could people be . . .

No. *Just . . . hang on.* Keeping her attention on Cruz, she opened her mouth, closed it a second while she forced her thoughts into alignment. "You're telling me, when people have bowel movements, the chemicals are in their *stool*?"

"That's exactly what he's telling you," Rohan said. "The water company treats the sewage, but the chemicals aren't filtered out. They stay in the sludge that's passed on to farmers."

Oh no. *No. No. No.* She knew where this was going. Felt it with every fiber—every nerve—inside her.

"What's worse," Rohan added, "is that the sludge contaminates whatever grows there."

Knew it. Dammit. Cilla stared at him for a solid ten seconds, trying to wrap her mind around the idea that, for years, she'd possibly been eating toxic food.

Being a criminal defense attorney, she'd seen the best and worst in people and thus, had built up a fairly strong shock meter.

This? Altogether different and her stomach revolted, tumbling enough that bile crawled up her throat.

She met Cruz's eye. "We're eating that shit? Literally?"

"If we eat produce from farms that use sludge, probably."

Blowing air through her lips, she went into lawyer mode, focusing on the facts and locking down emotional reactions. Part of her success meant compartmentalizing.

Lots of it.

"Okay," she said. "This farm my father wants to buy. Are they using sludge?"

"That's a puzzle," Cruz said. "Given the amount of PFOA shown on that toxicity report, we figured it had to be sludge. Except, the water reclamation facility for Morgan hasn't given sludge to that property."

"They told you that?"

"We pretended to be farmers looking for free sludge. They told us they could put us on the list. Once we confirmed they gave away sludge, Rohan did research."

Cilla glanced at Rohan. "You hacked their system?"

Ever the schmoozer, Phin cleared his throat. "We've confirmed they've delivered no sludge in the last ten years."

"What about before that? How long has this practice been happening?"

Cruz shrugged. "They could have spread sludge twenty, thirty years ago and the chemicals would still be there. According to what Ro found, no sludge has been delivered to that farm."

"Well, my father had those other reports that said the PFOA levels were lower. Maybe they were right and the one I saw was incorrect."

"Could be. You said they were retesting. Do you wanna wait? See what happens with that one?"

Did she? After hearing about toxic sludge, she'd like to call the local media and tell them to get on water companies giving away poison. She peered up at the whiteboard with handwritten notes regarding PFOA, PFOS, PFAS, and water treatment.

How many water companies gave away contaminated sludge? No wonder all humans had forever chemicals in them. They were literally consuming it.

She was consuming it.

"Cilla," Phin said, "can I ask you something?"

Shaking off her miserable thoughts, she turned to Phin. "Of course."

"It's . . ." he rolled one hand. "Personal."

"Phin, we've signed an NDA. More than that, we're friends and I trust you." She glanced at Rohan and Cruz. "All of you. Besides, I'm a big girl. If I don't want to answer, I won't."

He sat forward, resting his arms on the table. "You and I have talked about my work with Kayla Crowne. She's active with the environmental lobby."

Here it comes. That nagging question in the back of her mind. The one she didn't want to give oxygen to. The one she hoped hiring BARS would silence.

"Yes," Cilla said. "We've discussed it."

"We've also talked about how the EPA monitors Randolph Industries."

She swung a quick glance at Rohan, then landed on Cruz. "The firefighting foam made by my father's company contains certain chemicals. PFAS is one of them, but the company complies with EPA guidelines. Dad is steadfast about that."

"Has that always been the case?" Phin asked.

Heart slamming, she tore her gaze from Cruz and peered across the table. "Phin, are you asking me if my father is polluting our environment?"

8

When Cilla didn't answer, Cruz took it as their cue to take a break. Give her a second to regroup after they'd done a data dump on her.

"Fellas," Cruz said, "give us a minute."

After a few seconds, Phin and Rohan stood. "Sure," Phin said.

His brothers didn't simply go to their offices, they left the Annex completely, via the door that led to the Friary, giving Cruz and Cilla total privacy.

Once they were gone, he spun his chair to face Cilla. "Talk to me."

"About?"

Cruz waved a hand. "What the hell we're doing here. What specifically are you worried about?"

"Aside from my father buying a contaminated piece of property that could get him in trouble with a government agency?"

The corner of his mouth quirked. "Aside from that."

"Isn't that enough?"

"It's plenty. But you're an intelligent woman who, from

what I can see, doesn't suffer fools. You came to us with concerns over conflicting toxicology reports. You've done this, also from what I can tell, without your father's knowledge. I think you're wondering if your father is up to something with this farm."

Not a peep.

Which meant either she was about to blast him for the giant set of balls he carried or he was right about her suspecting her father. When the seconds dragged on, he narrowed his gaze, studying her for any body language.

Nothing.

Damn, she must be good in a courtroom. He'd like to see that. Just sit in the gallery and watch her work.

"What are you thinking?" he asked.

"I'm afraid to say it."

"Why?"

She shot out of her chair and headed to the whiteboard, staring at it for a few long seconds before turning back to him. "If I say it, it'll . . ."

She shook her head, clammed up on him. Whatever was working her over, she needed to get rid of it. Decompress a little.

He pushed back from the table and whirled a finger. "Let's go."

"What? Where?"

"The Stutz. You wanted to see it. We're gonna get out of here. Away from my family and Rohan's insane security. Just you and me. Then, if you wanna talk, I'll be happy to listen and it'll be between us." He met her eye, holding her gaze. "I promise you. It'll stay between us."

He walked around the table, met her at the whiteboard. "You got a jacket? We'll walk to the garage."

She nodded. "In the car."

"Good."

She picked up her purse and phone. "You can leave those. No one will bother them here."

"I need my phone. I'm waiting for a client to call."

"No problem."

Outside, a light breeze wrapped around him and he inhaled, taking in the fresh mountain air. He should have grabbed a jacket himself, but wasn't about to go inside to get one. With his luck, he'd run into Phin or Rohan, who'd pepper him with questions.

Besides, he kept a jacket in the garage just in case.

"How far of a walk is it?"

He peered down at her high heels that conjured all sorts of naughty thoughts his mother would smack him for. "About a quarter mile. Not far, but those might not be the right shoes. We can drive."

"Nah. I have sneakers in my trunk."

"I love a woman who's prepared."

She arched an eyebrow. "Cruz Blackwell, I'm always prepared."

And, oh my goodness, she might be the love of his life. "Then, honey, we'll get along just fine."

After retrieving her jacket and sneakers, they marched down the drive as the sun dipped lower in the sky giving the mountain an eerie, yet spectacular orange glow.

"Wow," she breathed. "That's gorgeous."

"It is. I've tried a thousand times to capture it with a camera. Never does it justice."

He led her toward the garage that had formerly been an old barn. After they'd bought this property almost three years earlier, he'd called dibs on the barn and made it his dream workspace. Hell, he didn't pay rent, so might as well break the bank on a restoration his pops would have drooled over. He'd spent a fortune adding every tool and toy he could think of that Dad could never afford.

"My father," Cilla said as they walked. "He's told me they're EPA compliant."

Clearly, she wanted to talk about this. Right? Already cursing himself for his lack of skill interpreting cues, his mind spun. He tended to just say shit when it entered his mind. A habit that got him into trouble, but seriously? No one should be afraid of the truth.

Still, he enjoyed Cilla and based on their discussion at dinner the night before, she definitely had some sort of twisted push-pull relationship with her father. Nuances he couldn't yet grasp, given they were still getting to know each other.

He halted, doing a half turn to face her when she did the same.

"I've mentioned," he said, "I have a filter issue. As in, barely having one. I prefer to be open with people. Not constantly stress over what might fly out of my mouth. Can we talk openly? Are you okay with that?"

"We're alone and you've promised me confidentiality. So, yes, I'm okay with that."

"Good. Thank you. Here's my question. If your father's company was polluting the environment and he knew it, would he tell you?"

"Honestly? I'm not sure. Nothing is adding up. I want to believe he's being duped by Paul, his number two at the company. Dad is incredibly—almost stubbornly—loyal to people he believes are loyal to him, and that definitely includes Paul. If Paul is misleading him about the farm for some reason, it's possible that Dad wouldn't see it. However, not a lot goes on there that Dad doesn't know about."

"Does he play fast and loose with what he tells you?"

"Typically, he comes to me when something has potential legal issues. The EPA falls under that purview. I'm bothered by that toxicology report and his belief that it's wrong. Can it be that far off?"

"I'm no scientist, but it happens. Phin just worked with Kayla on a project for an environmental group trying to sue a town over contaminated water and . . ."

Whoa. *Wait a second.*

"And what?"

He let out a half laugh. "I'm an idiot. Cilla, the plant is only ninety miles from here. If you want to know what's up with this farm, let's test the soil."

"We can do that?"

"Sure. On that case Phin worked, Kayla didn't believe the town's reports and paid for their own testing. Phin can tell us how she did it."

Cilla started walking again, moving at a decent clip so Cruz fell in step, his longer strides catching up.

"I'm thinking," she said. "Trying to decide if I'm crossing a line."

"If you weren't Darren Randolph's daughter, would it be crossing a line?"

She halted. Swung back to him, her green eyes wider than dinner plates. "You do have a gift for cutting right to the bone, don't you?"

"Sorry. But yeah. It's how I fly."

"Don't apologize. I prefer honesty." She jerked her head. "Let's do the testing."

Yes, indeed, a woman on a mission. He slid his phone from his front pocket and punched up Phin, who answered on the second ring.

"Hey," Cruz said. "I'm putting you on speaker so Cilla can hear."

"Yep."

Cruz hit the button and held the phone between he and Cilla. "You're doing some environmental stuff with Kayla, right?"

"A little. Not much. She's trying to grow that arm of the business. I basically have training wheels on."

"That might be enough," Cilla said. "This property my father wants to buy. Can we test the soil ourselves?"

"Without the owner's permission?"

Cilla considered that. She couldn't knock on the door and say, "Hey, you don't know me, but do you mind if I test your soil for toxic chemicals?"

"Yes. What's to stop us from sneaking a sample if it's for our own purposes? I just want to know for sure."

"Seriously," Cruz said, "I think I love you."

On the other end of the phone Phin laughed. "Ignore my idiot brother. Anyway, unless you get caught trespassing, I don't see why you couldn't grab a sample and send it to a lab. I've got a bunch of containers in my suite from Kayla's project. They're from the lab she uses."

Cilla met Cruz's eye. "If we're careful, no one will know."

"I'm in," he said. "Phin, how do we do it?"

"Easy. You take three or four samples from different sections of the property. Gotta use a stainless steel trowel. Get at least six inches deep and fill the container. Label them and we send them off."

Cilla smacked her hands together. "Piece of cake."

How fun was she? No fear and all in.

"Thanks, Phin," he said. "I'll get those containers in a while."

"I'm meeting Maddy for dinner. They'll be on the table in my suite. Just grab them."

"Will do. Tell Maddy hi."

Cruz tapped the screen and jumped right in. "We can run up to Morgan and take care of this quick. As you said, we're not using the results for anything other than our own knowledge, so nobody would have to know. At least then, you'd have the answers."

"Exactly. At least I'll know."

"If the PFOA is high, you have decisions to make on how to handle your dad."

She peeled her lips back, making that same face as earlier when he'd told her about people shitting forever chemicals.

"Hey," he said. "It'll suck, but you'll have answers."

"I suppose." She waved a hand toward the barn. "I don't want to talk about it anymore. Distract me with this car."

Once again, they fell in step, side by side. Cruz peered up at the darkening sky over the barn. He'd have to grab a flashlight for the walk back.

They approached the giant, glossy, black doors and he slid them open. Inside, he flipped on the overhead track lights illuminating the spotless interior. Not an easy feat in a garage.

Toward the back sat the Stutz where he'd yet to find that frickin' leak. He had, however, ordered the dye and UV light Reid had suggested. Now all he needed was the stuff delivered so he could get this baby on the road again.

Cilla peered up at the muted gray side walls lined with cabinets and hooks. Workbenches stuffed with tools and organized down to the smallest wrench.

"Wow," she said. "Not your run-of-the-mill garage."

"Yeah. Barn on the outside, state-of-the-art inside."

He walked to the front of the Stutz and held his hands out. "This is it."

Cilla let out a low whistle and immediately went to the driver's side, bending to peer inside. "Oh my. She's sexy."

She sure is.

The car, too.

"I love the red interior." She stood tall, meeting his gaze over the hood. "Can I buy her from you?"

Ha. Wouldn't be the first offer he'd gotten. Probably not the last. He smiled. "No."

"I'm serious. How much do you want for it? I'll buy it right now."

Sassy woman right here. Good for her. He shook his head. "Sorry, babe. Not for sale."

Ever. He'd had a dozen offers in the last few months. Two of them above six figures. No amount of money would do it. Not only did he love this car, his father would haunt him forever if he let it go.

And that scared the hell out of Cruz.

Cilla puckered her perfectly lipsticked red lips. The red, he'd decided, must be her favorite color because she wore it constantly. He liked it. Loved it in fact.

"My father," she said, "claims everything has a price."

"He'd be wrong. I don't mind telling him either."

"Oh, Cruz Blackwell, where have you been all my life."

"Honey, I could ask you the same thing."

His response drew a half-crooked smile out of her and a finger wag. She ran that finger along the door frame, then bent over again to look inside.

"The wood trim is amazing."

"Yeah. That was a bitch."

She stood tall again, her eyebrows hitching slightly. "You did that yourself?"

"I did. When my dad died, he'd only gotten to starting the engine. None of the body work." He pointed to the wall behind Cilla and made his way to where he'd framed photos from the various rebuild stages. Cilla joined him and he tapped the photo of his dad standing in front of a flatbed carrying the car's rusted frame. "This is my dad the day he brought it home. The damned thing didn't have tires."

She leaned in, craning over his workbench to study the photo. "Look at his smile. You look like him."

Yeah, he did. Out of all of them, Cruz was damned near the spitting image. "This was his dream car."

"You mentioned that last night." She faced him, crossing her arms casually. "It's a shame he didn't let you help him with it."

"I was a teenager then," he said. "Running wild. He was afraid I'd do something stupid and hurt myself. Like I said, I had no focus. Or patience."

"Considering you now fly airplanes, I'm guessing you learned to focus."

Resting one hip against the workbench, he nodded. "Thanks to wrestling. I had that wild streak. Getting into fights a lot. Drove my parents nuts. I couldn't help it. Plus, I'm competitive." He gave her a wolfish grin. "Like your dad, I like to win. My mom used to say I got an overload of testosterone. Pretty much, I enjoyed putting hands on people. It was an outlet."

"Fascinating."

"Nah. I was a kid with too much energy. Anyway, one year I got suspended three times. Dad sat me down and told me I could straighten up and make something of myself or continue doing what I was doing and get locked up. Then they made me sign up for wrestling. Dad figured since I liked to fight so much, it might be a fit. He was right."

"Phin told me you were a state champion."

Look at Phinny, helping his cause. Go, little brother, go. "I was. Worked my ass off."

All to please his father. Which, hello, never happened. It still stuck in his craw. As much as he idolized his father and admired his toughness, Cruz could never quite live up. He was the fuckup. If he put his fork an inch too far from his plate, he'd get popped on the head. If he left his backpack by the door? Popped in the head. Meanwhile, his brothers might do the same and them?

Told to move it.

The pops to the head were solely for Cruz.

And yet. He'd adored the man. Total hero worship. When Dad died, Cruz grieved so hard he thought he might die himself from the pain. From the all-out shattering of his chest.

Cilla reached for him, wrapping her warm hand around his wrist and sending heat storming his system. "We're alike in that way. Both of us wanting to please our fathers."

"Yeah, but . . ." He shook it off, looked back at the photo of his father.

"But what?"

He'd never admitted what kept him up at night. Sometimes, he wasn't sure he could identify it himself. Never mind talking to Mom or his brothers or Grams. Voicing it, whatever it was, he imagined, made him soft.

"Cruz?"

He looked back at her with her sharp green eyes and perfect red lips and . . . *yes.*

"Sometimes," he said, "I feel like I'm chasing a ghost."

And, whoa. What the hell, man. *Shut the fuck up.* He shook his head. "I don't know why I said that. I'm an idiot."

"Uh, no. You're not. There's nothing wrong with still trying to please him. You were barely an adult when you lost him. I'm lucky. I still have both my parents, but spent my formative years separated from my mother. There's a piece of me that understands being without a parent. Not that I'm comparing the two. Totally different. For you, it's a wound that probably won't fully heal."

She got it. Holy, holy shit. A rush of air escaped and a surge of ugly, absolute filthy, emotion gripped his chest, squeezing so dang tight it might asphyxiate him.

Look away. He had to. Those devastating eyes of hers had him all churned up. If this kept up, he'd be on the floor bawling like a whiny toddler.

He faced the wall, tapped the picture of his father, and cleared the mess that caught in his throat. "I know he's looking down on us. I feel him. Every time I touch this car, I feel him."

"I think he'd be proud of what you've done."

Looking back at her, he smiled. "Thank you for saying that. It means . . . a lot. He was tough. But I think he'd be happy I finished his project."

"Of course, he would."

She peered back at the photos and pointed to the very last one on the far right. "What's this one?"

Ah. *That* one. "The first day I drove it. I finished at four in the morning, but wanted to wait until the sun came up to drive it. I got into the passenger seat and took a nap until seven o'clock. Then I woke everybody up. Ash took that pic right before my mom hopped in and we went for a drive through town."

Dang, his dad would have loved that. The defiance. The up-yours of driving this exceptional car through a town full of gossips who constantly snickered and looked down on "those Blackwells."

It was the ultimate fuck you. Cruz may not have been

Dad's favorite of the bunch, but that day? His father would have enjoyed that.

"Amazing. You're a talented man."

"Not particularly. Hardheaded. When I put my mind to something, I do it."

He gave her some hard eye contact. Let her know without saying a word where his current focus was.

She stepped closer, gave his shirt a gentle tug. "Another thing we have in common."

"Hardheaded?"

"Determined."

He dipped his head lower, brushed his lips over hers, let the warmth of her creamy lipstick ease over him and settle his always chaotic mind.

Just as she did the night before when they'd shared that whopper of a kiss in the B, she arched into him, cocooning herself against his body.

Why she did that, he had no clue, but he'd never complain.

He backed away. "You sure do tempt me."

"Right. I forgot. We're taking this slow."

"We sure are. But look out, Cilla. I'm coming for you."

"Yay, me," she said.

He waved one hand. "We done looking at the Stutz?"

"Have you found the leak yet?"

"No. Parts aren't here yet. As soon as its fixed, I'll take you for a ride."

"Then, I guess we're done. For now."

"All right. Let's go make a soil-testing plan."

9

By noon Wednesday, after spending the morning volleying with the DA's office over Donovan Jenkins's plea deal, Cilla negotiated a twenty-two-month sentence plus community service where her client helped struggling families manage their finances. All of course monitored, given his history of theft.

Done.

Trial avoided. Good news since Cilla had no desire to try that mess. She, in fact, couldn't stomach the man and his greed. Still, she'd set her personal issues aside and had done her job, getting him what she believed was a fair sentence.

Now she sat beside Cruz in his truck as they cruised the rural road leading to her father's manufacturing facility. In the distance, the plant's giant smokestacks loomed high in the air. On either side of her sat acre after acre after acre of sun-dappled farmland.

In the heat of summer, it'd be an explosion of green crops. She'd like to see it. Revel in Mother Nature's fantastic work.

For now, all evidence of that beauty had been mowed down, leaving a flat, drab landscape.

Cruz pulled to the side of the road and pointed. "This is the address."

Just yards ahead sat a charming and obviously freshly painted farmhouse.

Her intention had been to do this field trip on her own, but he'd insisted on taking the drive with her. Something she rather enjoyed since he didn't mind her pounding away on her keyboard—and asking him to pull over twice so she could take calls in private—while finalizing the plea deal.

Men Cilla had dated in the past would have resented her work distractions. No wonder they hadn't lasted.

Shaking off thoughts of failed relationships, she took in the vast property her father intended on buying. Beyond the farm, she locked on to the daycare.

That made no sense. If he intended this to be a landfill, why wouldn't he purchase the two parcels across the street that butted up against plant property?

Cilla dug in her briefcase for the land survey she'd printed and held it between them. "Here's what I don't get. My father wants this property." She circled the property with her finger. "However, the Randolph Industries landfill is not only across the street, there are two other farms and a daycare in between. How does that make sense?"

Cruz shrugged. "Maybe the plan is to buy up all the property. He's starting with the farthest one and working in?"

"It'd make more sense to start with the closest ones. What if he buys this one and the other two aren't interested? Then he's stuck."

"Good point. Whoopsie." Cruz jerked his head. "We got company."

Cilla peered out the windshield, found a dark-haired woman in workout tights and a light jacket eyeing them from the front porch of the farmhouse.

Shoot. They'd been here sixty seconds and already called attention to themselves. A second later, a big guy joined the woman.

"And," Cruz said, "guessing that's the husband."

"Shoot."

What now? Driving off would only create suspicion and more than likely a call to the local police. All while this was supposed to be a clandestine mission to collect soil samples.

Cilla lifted her door handle. "Wait here."

"What are you doing?"

"Talking to them. Obviously, they're wondering who's sitting in the giant black pickup and I don't want them calling the cops."

Wouldn't that be fun? Dad probably had a mole in the PD and she'd have to explain herself. She'd rather poke out her own eye.

Dad's motto rang in her ear. *Never apologize. Never explain.*

"Want me to come with you?" Cruz asked.

"No. It might spook them."

He considered that a moment and must have agreed because he jerked his head. "Fine. But I'm watching. If you need me, wave."

Once again, many men would simply impose their will and follow her. *Cruz, Cruz, Cruz.* The man might be her downfall. "Will do."

She hopped out of the truck, her hiking boots helping her to stick the landing in the dirt alongside the road. Jeans and boots were definitely the way to go for this trip.

Striding toward the home, she held up a hand. "Hello."

The couple stepped off the porch, marching toward Cilla. The woman's ponytail bobbed as she struggled to keep pace with the man's much longer strides.

A few feet from Cilla, the woman came to a stop "Can we help you?"

Thinking quick—she wasn't Charlotte's top defense attorney for nothing—Cilla dug her phone from her jacket pocket and held it up. "We were in a dead zone and I got a signal here."

The woman cocked her head and continued to stare at Cilla. Questioning. Probably because, why, if she'd found a signal, wouldn't she be on said phone?

"I got distracted." Cilla made a show of looking at the surrounding land. "It's so peaceful here."

"It is. You lost or something?"

"No." She turned, pointed at Cruz still in the truck. "We're looking at the area."

The woman continued to give her the hard stare. This, for Cilla, wasn't uncommon. When it came to their husbands, married women often gave her the stink eye. As if it was her fault she been blessed with her mother's looks and her father's brains, and men found that killer combo intriguing.

Newsflash, DNA isn't my fault.

Finally, the woman cocked her head. "Wait. You're Priscilla Randolph! I recognize you from your pictures online."

In the words of the immortal SpongeBob, *"What the ...?"*

Gobsmacked, Cilla remained still, lining up her thoughts. She'd wanted this trip to be on the QT and off—way off—Dad's radar. She hadn't anticipated being recognized.

Behind her, Cruz's spidey sense must have gone on alert

because she heard the truck door open. She glanced back, spotted him coming toward them.

She turned to the couple. The only thing to do would be to admit it. Cut the tension immediately and then come up with a reason they were here.

"Yes," she said. "I'm Priscilla."

"Knew it!" The woman laughed. She looked up at her husband. "She's Darren Randolph's daughter. Remember, I told you about her a couple of weeks ago."

"The bigshot lawyer out of Charlotte?"

Gosh, how Cilla loved when people spoke about her as if she weren't witnessing the entire exchange.

"Yes! That's her."

Um, right here, folks.

Cruz stepped up, nodding at the couple.

"This is my friend, Cruz." Cilla swung to him. "These fine folks recognized me."

Hellos and handshakes were exchanged and the woman —Sherry Tate—met Cilla's gaze. "I'm not a stalker. I promise."

"Well," the husband cracked. "Not totally."

She laughed and waved him off. "Hush, you." She came back to Cilla. "Your daddy called us."

Her father *called* them? Beside her, Cilla felt Cruz's gaze on her. She couldn't look. Couldn't let these people, these strangers know they'd just shocked the hell out of her.

"We know the name, of course," Sherry continued. "Everyone in this town does. But imagine my surprise when Randolph Industries came up on my caller ID. Well, it was the man himself. He's so kind to check on us."

What in the hell was this woman was going on about? And why would Dad be checking on them?

Hoping she'd continue her prattling, Cilla nodded. "He's good that way."

"And so kind! He wanted to tell us about the Randolph Community Resource fund. I can't tell you how much that'll help with bills."

Community Resource Fund? This rabbit hole got weirder and weirder. Attempting to stay focused on the conversation, Cilla filed that away to research later.

"Sherry," Jake said, "too much information."

"Oh, I'm sorry. I do that sometimes. Anyhoo, we got to chatting about our kids and your daddy was going on and on about you. You know, he's awfully proud."

She did know. Absolutely. Everywhere she went, people told her. What she wasn't altogether sure of was if Dad's pride revolved around her or himself, since he'd raised her and could therefore take complete credit for her success.

Dad, she'd learned, didn't do a lot of things that wouldn't somehow benefit him.

Still, Cilla played along, nodding at Sherry. "Thank you for saying that. He's been good to me. Makes me happy he's proud."

"Oh, he is. When I got off the phone, I told Jake I needed to see who you were because you were some kind of legal Wonder Woman."

Smiling, Cilla held up a hand. "Okay. *That's* overkill."

"I showed my daughter all the magazine covers you'd been on. She's ten and still dreaming about what she wants to be when she grows up. I keep telling her, go to school. Get an *education*. Be a businessperson or doctor or lawyer, like you."

Jake snorted. "Whoa, girl. Take it easy."

She peered up at her husband, then let out a laugh.

"Right?! Listen to me carrying on." She faced Cilla again. "I get a little excited when it comes to my baby."

In that moment, Cilla loved this woman. Her openness and her ability to poke fun at herself. To own it.

"I envy you," Cilla said. "With what I do, it's sometimes hard to get excited."

Behind the woman, the screen door came open and a girl—at least Cilla thought it was a girl given her pink jacket—about half the height of the woman stepped onto the porch. She appeared young, barely a teenager and Cilla's gaze locked onto the scarf covering the child's head.

Ohmygod.

"Speak of the devil," Sherry said. "This is our Brittney." She paddled her hand at her daughter. "Come on out. I want you to meet someone."

The girl hopped off the porch, her steps quick, her smile wide as a blast of wind blew Cilla's hair in her eyes. She tucked the wayward strands behind both ears as this apparently bald child charged toward them.

As she came closer, Cilla noted the lack of hair sticking out from beneath the scarf. Focusing on the girl's large brown eyes, Cilla held out her hand. "Hello. I'm Priscilla."

"Hi. You're pretty."

Clearly, the girl inherited her mother's talent for openness.

"In case y'all were wondering," Jake laughed. "She's my wife's mini-me."

"She sure is!" Sherry said.

Cilla grinned, enjoying the banter between them. "Thank you," she told Brittney. "So are you."

The child beamed up at her mother and something inside Cilla's chest caved. Just imploded.

"Thanks," she said. "I like your hair. I have cancer and all my hair fell out, but when it grows back, I'm gonna cut it just like yours."

Cancer.

Oh, no. No. No. No. And Cilla had just told this woman she envied her. Terrible thing to say.

"Britt," Sherry said while Cilla's intestines went loose, "this is the lady I was telling you about. Mr. Randolph's daughter? The lawyer in Charlotte. This is her friend, Cruz."

Brittney's jaw flopped open. "Wow. Cool. What are you doing here?"

Her youthful energy knocked Cilla's thoughts back to focus and she glanced at Cruz who flashed that killer smile that somehow buoyed her.

"Oh, we're just looking around."

"If this is about buying the farm," Jake asked, "I'm sorry we're taking so long to get back to y'all."

"Yes," Sherry said. "You know, we've lived here so long and farming is all we know. We can't decide if we should sell or not. We'd just have to buy another farm and . . ."

Jake touched her arm, silencing her.

"Oh," Cilla said. "That's not . . ." She stopped talking, remembering Dad's motto. *Never apologize. Never explain.* "Take your time. We're just looking at the properties surrounding the plant. It's been so long since I'd been out here, I wanted to see for myself what the layout was."

"We talked to the neighbors," Jake said. "They haven't heard from your father yet. But I gotta believe he's looking at that property, too."

She'd have to be careful here. "I'm not sure. I don't work for the company, so I only know what Dad tells me."

Beside her, Cruz made a show of checking his watch. "I'm sorry to be rude, but we should probably get going."

Bless him. "You're right." Cilla nodded at Sherry. "I'm sorry to have bothered you. We'll be on our way."

"Not a bother at all. We don't meet celebrities around here."

"Well, thank you. But I'm hardly a celebrity." She peered down at Brittney. "Your mom said you're trying to decide what to be when you get older. I enjoy being an attorney. It's hard sometimes, but I love the law."

"Maybe I'll be a lawyer. Or a judge!"

"That would be terrific." Cilla turned to Sherry, her internal warning system raging. *Too bad.*

"If you're ever in Charlotte and want to come by, I could show Brittney my office. Or maybe you could come to court one day and watch."

Brittney gasped. "No way."

"Wow," Jake said. "That's some offer. Thank you."

"Can we do it, Daddy? Please?"

Jake looked down at Sherry, the two of them exchanging a look that Cilla, not having kids, didn't exactly understand, but reminded her of her childhood, right before her parents told her they'd be splitting up and mom moving overseas. That look? It screamed of pain.

Sadness and doubt.

"We'll talk about it," Sherry said. "Maybe after this round of chemo. Thank you. That's a wonderful offer."

They said their goodbyes and Cilla and Cruz headed back to the truck, buckling in while Brittney, Sherry, and Jake made their way back inside.

"Too bad about the kid," he said.

But Cilla had nothing. Not one word. Her frantic brain couldn't contain them long enough to conjure a sentence.

PFOA in the ground. Daughter with cancer.

They had to know. Didn't they? That their property was

contaminated? According to her father, who called this family out of the blue to check on them, the PFOA levels were fine. Which in itself was a load of crap because when would PFOA ever be fine?

Dad *had* to know. The man wasn't stupid. That one test, false-positive or not, had to have given him pause.

But he'd explained it away. Whether for his own benefit or hers, he'd minimized it. Someone on his staff might be shielding him. Paul probably, since he handled real estate transactions.

In which case, did they also know Brittney had cancer? Real estate transactions didn't exactly contain health histories of the occupants.

Mind reeling, she peered back at the house. "Cancer," she said. "How is that fair to a kid?"

"It's not."

Dragging her gaze from the now-empty porch, she met Cruz's eye. "This is a farm. They probably grow their own vegetables."

"Probably an accurate assumption."

"Are you thinking what I'm thinking?"

"Well, sugar, if you're thinking these people eat food they grow in soil saturated with toxic chemicals and now their daughter has cancer, yes."

She braced her hands against the doorframe and dipped her head. She'd offered her father legal advice plenty of times. More times than she'd preferred. And wasn't that part of the problem? The reason she was shopping for an office in Asheville? She needed space. Needed Dad to stop constantly strolling in, disrupting her day, when he felt like it.

Yes, she'd always be grateful that he'd paid for her

education and given her a suite of offices in his company's Charlotte headquarters. But lately, who truly benefited from that generosity? With the number of times he called on her for legal advice, she might as well be his in-house counsel.

That irritated her. Made her feel . . .

Used.

And now this farm and a little girl with cancer. Him calling to check on them. He had to know about her.

Sickness rolled in her stomach, the nastiness crawling into her throat. She bent forward and breathed through it. *Just breathe.* That's all she needed to do.

Cruz's hand rested on her back. "Hey, hey, hey. What's going on? You okay?"

She shook her head. "I don't know. This is . . ."

She needed to get herself together. Put on her attorney hat and think. She bolted upright, sat back and Cruz slid his hand to her shoulder, leaving it there and giving her a gentle squeeze.

"You're okay," he said. "Take a breath."

Following his advice, she inhaled, drawing in fresh oxygen and the scent of his truck. That woodsy, soapy smell of Cruz. She exhaled and repeated the process, over and over, until her system settled down.

Yes. That felt better. She turned sideways in her seat, peered into his eyes that somehow offered comfort, not pity. Strong, steady comfort.

Goodness, he affected her in ways she'd never experienced. Ways that made her feel open and . . . vulnerable.

And not in a bad way.

"What are you thinking?" Cruz asked.

"I'm worried."

"About?"

"Make a list. At the top would be my father's company wanting to buy property where a little girl has cancer. Worse, I'm worried that he lied to me about what he knows."

"Only one way to find out."

"Yes. Let's get those soil samples."

BY 2:00, AFTER TROMPING THROUGH DIRT AND GRABBING A dozen samples from three farms—no way to sneak onto the daycare property—without getting caught, Cilla and Cruz sat at a table at a roadside joint on the edge of town. Remnants of the Mighty Joe, a pulled pork sandwich big enough to feed King Kong, were splayed across Cruz's plate.

In short, the man could eat.

She pointed at the half piece of cornbread waiting for his attention. "Seriously? You're going to leave that little bit?"

"Yep. Totally stuffed. I love this place. Food is tremendous."

"I bet a lot of the people at the plant come here."

Cilla glanced around at the mostly empty twenty tables. Not a surprise given the post-lunch hour. Maybe some folks in here right now worked for her father. None of them seemed to recognize Cilla, but that didn't mean a thing, considering the number of people the plant employed.

When she turned back, she found Cruz eying the last bit of cornbread, but . . . alas . . . he pushed the plate away, throwing his napkin on top as if it were his final thought on the matter. Then he leaned in on his elbows and eyed her.

"Let me ask you something," he said.

"Ask away,"

In the time she'd spent with Cruz, she'd come to be fairly certain of one thing: Cruz Blackwell spoke his mind. He also didn't shy away from asking tough questions. For someone who spent the better part of her professional life around liars, she found his honesty wildly intoxicating.

Cruz nodded. "We have samples Phin said he'd send to Kayla's lab. Then what?"

Unsure of how to answer, Cilla shrugged. "Um, we wait for results?"

He rolled a hand. "After the results. What if they're the same as the report you saw. What then?"

Ah. No-brainer. "Easy. I'll tell my father he can't buy the property."

"You'll say you hired us and we ran our own tests?"

For this, she paused. She'd been thinking about this all day. About having to admit she'd meddled in her father's business and about raising his ire. In truth, anticipating Dad's wrath gave her a sick feeling.

Still, it had to be done. They needed answers. "I'll have to. I believe someone on his staff might be keeping him in the dark about the PFOA levels."

"Why do you need to tell him?"

"Aside from the EPA fines that rack up to millions? Not to mention possible class action lawsuits. If he intends to buy contaminated property, he needs the entire picture, even if it pisses him off that I'm questioning the inner workings of his company. He doesn't like to be questioned."

"Even when you're helping him?"

"He might see it as interference. Or me judging the performance of his handpicked executives."

He took a second, apparently running her comments through that whip-smart brain of his. "Why do I feel like there's more?"

"More?"

"Yeah. Your father wants to buy property he may know is contaminated. Obviously, since your dad called the Tates, someone on his staff knows their daughter is sick. Why else would he tell them about a Community Resource Fund?"

So intuitive. What had she said that led him to nail exactly—exactly—what she'd been worried about? As if he'd crawled around in her brain, rooted through all the nonsense, and drilled down to the one thing she didn't want to believe.

That her father would try to avoid a lawsuit by buying the property before the Tates thought to have the soil or water tested.

"Speaking of which," she pulled her phone from her jacket pocket. "I've never heard of a Community Resource Fund. Let's check on that."

"How?"

"I can remotely log into the company's system. I'll do a search and see what I find."

Using Dad's login again, she got to the knowledge database and searched for Community Resource Fund. Nothing.

Hmmm . . .

She narrowed her search. Service fund. Nothing.

Next she tried the word community and received dozens of hits. *Here we go.* She scrolled the list of topics, clicking on a couple that looked promising yet fell flat.

Terrific. She'd have to dive in later. She logged out and set the phone down.

"I found a bunch of links," she said. "Too much to mess with now."

He narrowed his gaze, and then ripped off a tantalizing smile. How she wanted those lips on hers again.

"Nice job deflecting," Cruz said.

Busted. "Deflecting?"

"I think you're worried about how much your father knows. I hit a nerve and you distracted yourself with a search for some Community Resource Fund that may or may not exist."

Damn. The. Man.

If he expected her to slice open a vein and bleed out all her emotional rubble, he'd be waiting awhile. A long while. What was the point of sharing her worries? Worrying did no good.

She rested her forearms on the table and loosely clasped her hands. "What do you want me to say?"

He shrugged. "Nothing. And everything."

All righty then. "What does that mean?"

"I'm trying to help you. We're on this goose chase with soil samples—"

"*Goose* chase?"

He held up a hand. "My bad. Poor choice of words. We're collecting samples and I'm not sure, once we have answers, what the outcome is supposed to be. If we find PFOA, what then?"

As if she knew? The idea that her father knew about the PFOA levels terrified her. She simply couldn't imagine he'd hide it from residents and risk their health.

Cilla let out a soft sigh. "I wish I knew. And that's as honest as I can be. The thought of my father knowing that property is toxic is killing me. Throw in him knowing that little girl has cancer and I'm not sure how to process that."

She sat back. "Happy now?"

"Nothing about what you said makes me happy. But at least I know what and why we're doing this. You're trying to figure out how much of an asshole your father is."

Cilla may have gawked. She wasn't exactly sure. All she knew was Cruz said whatever came to mind. Somehow, it didn't feel like a bad thing. At least she'd always know where she stood. No games. No testing her loyalty. No shenanigans.

"Oh, hey," he continued. "I've spent the last ten years trying to figure out how much of an asshole *my* father was. Why he was constantly on me." He offered an all-teeth smile. "I call it self-reflection."

Intrigued by his admission, she propped her elbow on the table and tucked her chin into her hand. "What has your self-reflection garnered? Why do you think he was so hard on you?"

Something outside caught his attention and he pulled his gaze away, narrowing his eyes. Stalling? She didn't know him well enough, yet, to understand his tells. No matter. She'd learned patience over the years. Questioning witnesses had taught her plenty.

Silently, she counted to ten. A little trick one of her professors had taught her about giving people time to think.

Seven, eight...

Cruz finally peered back at her, but sat silently, simply staring at her. Waiting for her to speak. Maybe change the subject. Little did he know, she'd sit here all day until he answered her. They'd see who gave in first.

Nine...

"Out of all of us, I was probably most like him." He pointed to his face. "I look like him. My eyes are his. I think when I look in the mirror, he didn't want me to see him."

Holy cow. Cruz's lack of filter definitely had an upside if he allowed himself to be that open. *Wow, wow, wow.*

"That," Cilla said, "might be the most profound thing anyone has ever said to me."

"Doubtful. But it is what it is. My dad wanted better for us. He was a repo guy who had bigger dreams for his sons."

"What dreams?"

"I'm not sure. I never got the chance to know him like that. Which, hello? That sucks. Part of it was probably some mash-up of BARS. I don't think he could visualize that far out of his box, though. Taking BARS to this level with art recovery was Zeke's doing. Before that, we were doing automotive and planes."

Cilla sat taller, releasing her chin from her hand. She reached across, touched his forearm and a zip of heat shot clear through her fingers. Enjoying that brief surge of . . . something . . . she made no rush to move.

His gaze dropped to her hand, then back up to her eyes and everything beyond their little table seemed to blur, to float away while they sat quietly lost in whatever was happening between them.

He set his free hand over hers and squeezed. "This is nice. Sitting here with you."

"I agree." She smiled. "If this keeps up, I may never leave. But who's deflecting now? No changing the subject. Back to your dad. He'd be proud of what y'all have done, right? That he gave you the tools to build the company."

"He'd definitely be proud. Mom tells us that all the time."

"So, why wouldn't he want you to see him when you look in a mirror?"

"I don't know."

"Did you ask your mom?"

Now it was his turn to gawk. "*Hell* no. *Not* doing *that*."

Men. So complicated. He'd just revealed all this self-reflection, yet he wouldn't ask his mother a simple question. "Why?"

He snorted. "Uh, it's weird."

Oh, please. "It's not *weird*."

"Yeah, it is. Anyway, and yes, I'm changing the subject. Me going at you about your dad? I'm not being an ass. I'm trying to help you."

This, she didn't doubt. For whatever reason, Cruz had

wormed his way inside her. She trusted him. And that was saying something, since she'd been taught from an early age to always question motives.

"I believe that," she said. "Thank you. I need to figure out what's going on with him. Why he'd buy contaminated property."

"Okay."

He nodded and then in one smooth motion, grabbed the check, stood, slid his wallet from his front pocket, and threw bills on the table.

"Let's go," he said. "We have a few extra containers. I think we should get water samples. Maybe from that stream we saw while driving into town. We're checking soil, we may as well check the water, too."

Still seated, Cilla shook her head. "I don't think the water is the issue. The plant has their own water reclamation facility."

That stopped him cold. *"Really?"*

"When they proposed building the plant, the town had concerns about such a large facility taxing their infrastructure. Water specifically, because the town's system was already old. Rather than stress the town's water system, Dad agreed to build their own. They're self-sufficient with water. They recycle water for flushing toilets."

"Huh. Do they give sludge away?"

Oh, no. No, no, no. They'd just discussed this. How water treatment plants gave away contaminated sludge.

"I don't know," she said. "I'd never heard of it until you told me."

"Can you find out? Is there someone at the company you can ask? If not, I'll see if Rohan can research it."

Cilla stood, pushed her chair in and leaned closer to Cruz. The place was nearly empty, but keeping her voice low wouldn't hurt. "Meaning hacking into my father's company?"

"It's a thought."

"One that's unnecessary." She scooped her purse from the back of her chair. "I can get us in."

10

A LITTLE AFTER FIVE, CRUZ AND CILLA ARRIVED AT THE Annex, where Cruz set his gym bag with the soil and water samples on the conference table. A few months ago, at this hour, he'd have found at least one of his brothers sitting at the table busying himself with . . . whatever.

Now? It seemed everyone cleared out between five and five-thirty, off to have dinner with their significant others.

Another change to adjust to.

Voices sounded from Phin's office. Cruz cocked his head, waited a beat for the talking to stop and whistled.

"Seriously?" Phin hollered from behind the half-closed door. "Are we dogs?"

On Cruz's left, Rohan emerged from his office, shaking his head. "Hey, Cilla."

"Hi, Rohan."

He poked a finger at Cruz. "If Cilla wasn't here, I'd tell you where to shove that whistle."

"Oh," she said. "Don't let me stop you. I'd sure as hell tell him."

"Hey!" Cruz said, laughing. "Whose side are you on?"

"Right now?" She jerked her thumb at Rohan. "His. Deal with it."

"Man, oh, man." Rohan smiled like a freaking madman while peering at Cruz. "I *like* her. You can shove that whistle so far up your ass it'll come out your ear."

Cruz raised his hands and waggled them. "Now I'm scared."

Phin, wearing one of his slick suits, joined the party. He nodded at Cilla and then pinned his brothers with a hard look. "You two, shut up. It's been a long day, I'm tired and I have a fundraiser tonight. I need to conserve energy." He pointed at the duffel. "What's this?"

"Soil," Cilla said. "We took water samples from a stream while we were at it. Just in case."

"Speaking of water." Cruz pointed at Rohan. "Remember our convo about free sludge? Randolph Industries has its own water reclamation facility."

"Huh."

His brother. A man of many words.

Rohan shifted his gaze to Cilla. "Why their own facility?"

"The community had concerns about Randolph taxing the town's water facility. My father agreed to build their own. Everything is self-contained."

"And," Cruz said, "they recycle the toilet water for flushing."

"Are they giving away sludge?" Rohan asked.

Cruz pulled the chair next to his out for Cilla. "Have a seat."

He waited for her to sit, then dropped into his chair. "We don't know about the sludge. On the drive back, Cilla tried searching the company database. It's a lot of files."

Cilla nodded. "I didn't want to be in there long."

Phin took his normal seat and unzipped the duffel. "Why?"

She glanced at Cruz, her green eyes holding a question Cruz couldn't decipher. But nothing they discussed in this room would be shared outside of BARS.

Cruz did the only thing he could and jerked his head, letting her know it was safe to talk and they had her back.

Cilla turned back to Phin. "I logged in using my father's credentials."

"Nice," Phin said. "Go, you."

"I found out the other night that my own credentials expired. I was locked out. HR is supposed to be working on giving me access again, but so far, no luck. I'm not exactly a priority unless Dad tells them I am. I figured out my father's password and logged in. Today, I searched for sludge, but there were too many files to look through."

Rohan met Cruz's gaze, sending him a WTF look.

"I know what you're going to say," Cruz said. "You need a good reason, blah, blah. I get it. Earlier, we met a little girl, maybe ten-eleven years old. Bald as a cue ball."

That got Rohan's attention. He sat back, drummed his fingers on the arm of his chair. "Don't tell me."

"Cancer," Cruz said.

"Shit," Phin said.

"Dammit," Rohan said. "I told you not to tell me."

Cilla cleared her throat, drawing all eyes to her. "Brittney is her name. She's the daughter of the people who own the farm my father is trying to buy."

"Does your father know she's sick?"

"I think he might."

More drumming of Rohan's fingers. "Which," he said, "would be why you want to know if these folks are getting sludge from the plant?"

Cilla's only response was to touch her nose.

Rohan stood. "I hate when kids are sick. Give me a while. I'll do some phishing."

With that, he left the table, striding into his office and closing the door. More than likely, he'd be in there for hours.

Sorry, bro.

"It would certainly suck," Phin said, "if these people are getting toxic sludge."

Cilla nodded her agreement. "Agreed. How fast will we get the samples back?"

"I'll see if we can rush it." He checked his watch. "I gotta go. I'll talk with y'all tomorrow."

Phin grabbed the duffel before heading out the door.

Alone at the table, Cruz spun his chair to face Cilla. "Here we go," he said.

"Here we go."

"You scared of what we might find?"

"Terrified. But I'd rather know the truth. Even if it changes everything."

THE FOLLOWING MORNING, CILLA PUSHED THROUGH HER office suite's entrance a little after 8:00, her mind gloriously busy with all things Cruz Blackwell. His refreshing honesty and bluntness, she had to admit, offered an odd sort of comfort that relaxed her. Parsing her words drained her. With Cruz, she didn't have to check herself every time she wanted to voice an opinion.

Then there was the body.

The.

Body.

He wasn't one who opted for second-skin shirts that put

cut muscles on display. Hiding those muscles under loose clothing didn't exactly seem his style either. Cruz had found the perfect middle ground of fitted clothing that let the world see broad shoulders and sinewy forearms. All of which sent her hotness radar pinging and her imagination running wild.

And her without a fan.

Oooh-eeee.

Entering the suite, Cilla found Layla, as usual already at her desk pounding away on her keyboard.

"Morning," Cilla said.

"Hiya." Layla swiveled from the keyboard, grabbed a couple of folders, and handed them over. "Ed's notes on Kalper. He said you'd be happy."

Excellent. By now, her investigator knew her well enough to gauge her reactions to certain information.

And she liked happy. Particularly when it involved a murder case that, right now, looked like it would wind up with her client spending the rest of his life in prison.

She held up the folders. "Thank you. I'll look."

"You need anything?"

"Not unless you can get me an extra twelve hours in a day."

"Sorry. Still wouldn't be enough."

True that. Would any amount of time be enough?

She entered her office, unloaded her laptop and phone, and set the tote and her purse on the sofa before moving to her desk.

Lowering herself into her chair, she paused for a few seconds, taking in the light gray walls, bookshelves stuffed with law books and her leather sofa and chairs. If she went ahead with her plan for a new office, she'd need something big enough to fit everything. Maybe she'd set up appointments for the weekend to look at the few spaces she'd seen online.

Add it to the to-do list.

Ignoring her laptop, she flipped open the first file Layla had handed her. Before she'd started reading, her intercom buzzed.

"Cilla? Paul Benzman is here for you."

Paul? What was this about? It wasn't unusual, per se, for her father's second-in-command to show up, particularly if he had a legal question because, sure, why not ask Cilla when they had in-house lawyers?

Curiosity hounding her, she mulled it over. She should tell him to come back later. That she was in the middle of dealing with the problems of her paying clients.

Then he'd complain to Dad and she'd have to see him anyway. Who had time for this nonsense?

"Thanks," she told Layla. "Send him in."

She flipped the file closed and stood. Seconds later Paul appeared at her door. As usual, he gelled his mousy brown hair into place and his navy suit, white shirt, and paisley tie were pressed to perfection. Cilla wasn't a fan of paisley, but Paul's wardrobe wasn't her problem.

"Good morning," she said.

"Morning. Thanks for seeing me."

"Of course."

She waved to her guest chairs in front of the desk. "Have a seat."

He chose the chair on the left, straightening his tie as he sat. Paul had that way about him. All slick polish and pristine suits. When he started picking at invisible lint on his slacks, it was time to move him along.

"What's up, Paul?"

Abandoning the lint, he peered across the desk at her.

His mouth dipped into a frown and he squinted. "What are you doing?"

Huh? If she was supposed to know what he was talking about, she didn't. She rolled her hand. "About?"

"You were in Morgan yesterday. Why?"

Cilla's limbs simultaneously turned to steel, paralyzing her in place. *He knows.* How the hell . . .? And did he know Cruz was with her?

She could easily explain two single people on an outing together, but anyone within five miles of her father knew Cilla had little time for dating.

Despite her raging panic, she forced her body to a relaxed state and eased back in her chair, folding her hands in her lap. "Last I checked, I don't report to you. And you have no right to question me on my whereabouts."

"You're denying it?"

"Not at all. I am, however, a tad curious how you know I was in Morgan."

"Easy. I checked in with the Tates this morning. They've had an offer—an extremely generous offer—for over two weeks. I'd like an answer. Imagine my shock when she rattled on about meeting you. She's a talker, that one."

Oh, Sherry. The woman had inadvertently outed Cilla. *Dang it.* "She is," Cilla said. "I experienced that when I met her."

Paul stared with cold, dead eyes that sent a fresh bout of panic swarming her. She'd have to be careful here.

"So," he said, "again, I ask, why were you in Morgan?"

She could fabricate something. Spin a tale that he might —or might not—believe. Either way, he'd inform her father and then she'd have to deal with him, too.

Might as well admit it. Cilla leaned in, resting her

elbows on her desk. "I'm sure by now you realize I saw that toxicology report on the plane."

"Yes. I was irresponsible about leaving it."

"Thankfully, it was only me who saw it."

"I believe your father told you we're having that test redone."

"I'm aware. However, to answer your question about why I was in Morgan, I was curious. I'm an attorney and my father's daughter. I see it as my responsibility to protect him. That's all I want."

"And you don't think I do?"

Cilla shrugged. "I don't know you well enough to guess what you want. I saw a report claiming extraordinary amounts of PFOA on a property Dad intends on buying. I owe it to him to voice my concerns. Plus, if you want to expand the landfill, why not buy property next to the existing one? None of this makes sense. That's why I went to Morgan."

Paul's mouth slid into a greasy, almost caustic how-dare-you smile that sent equal parts infuriation and fear snaking inside her.

Paul could create havoc between her and her father. Havoc with Dad? Not fun.

"Look, Cilla, I know your father confides in you. This isn't your business."

"I respectfully disagree. Anything regarding my father and potential legal exposure is my business."

"You don't think I'm worried about legal exposure?"

"Frankly, Paul, your concerns don't matter to me. You may be an executive of the company, but you don't own it. It's not your legacy. You realize, I'm sure, Brittney Tate has cancer."

He let out a frustrated huff. "Wow. Sherry was chatty yesterday. How the hell long were you there?"

"Long enough to have concerns about a so-called incorrect toxicology report and a little girl with cancer. Brittney came outside while I was trying to make sense of buying property, supposedly for use as a landfill, beside a daycare. I can't imagine the town will allow a landfill to go in next to a daycare."

"For your information, we're interested in all the surrounding property. I need you to stay out of this, Cilla."

Having had enough of Paul, Cilla stood. "I will not. At least until I see a toxicology report that clears that property. My father seems convinced it's safe."

"It is."

"Since you're so confident, my involvement shouldn't worry you."

Finally taking the hint, Paul stood, adjusting his suit sleeves before meeting her eye. "I don't want you screwing up this deal. Please don't talk to the Tates again."

Whether he was asking or telling her, she wasn't sure. Either way? No promises.

"Thanks for the talk. I have work to do."

"I'm sure. Just so we're clear, you need to back off. Understood?"

Wait one second . . . Was Paul *threatening* her? And did Dad know? At the very least, Dad probably knew she'd gone to Morgan and that Paul intended to speak with her. Beyond that? No way to know.

However, she'd learned early in her career to never give her power to a man. *Ever.* Feeling intimidated was one thing, showing it another.

She tilted her head, offered her own sleazy smile. "I don't take orders from you. Now, get out of my office."

. . .

THE SECOND PAUL LEFT THE SUITE, CILLA DROPPED INTO HER chair, blew out a hard breath, and shook off the chill that landed on her.

What the hell had just happened?

She and Paul? They'd had hundreds of conversations. All of them friendly. In short, nothing like what just happened.

What now? Call Dad? Give him an earful?

Or wait. See if Dad reached out. Rethinking her earlier assumptions that Dad was in the loop on Paul talking to her, she walked it back. Paul could be up to something and hiding it from Dad. Which might be why he'd taken such an offensive tone with her.

In which case, if Dad didn't know, should she beat Paul to it and tell him?

That would most definitely create a scenario where she'd have to explain herself and she'd rather wait for the toxicology reports on her samples before doing that.

What to do?

She scooped up her cell phone and dialed Cruz. And, yes, she hated the fact that her finger trembled ever so slightly as she tapped the screen. The entire episode had rattled her.

Never had Paul come at her like that. Never.

"Well, good morning," he said in that deep, confident voice that instantly set her at ease.

"Hi. Are you busy?"

"Heading to the Annex. You okay?"

No. This from Ms. Independence. Admitting it to herself was painful. "I had a visit from Paul Benzman. My father's second-in-command."

"Is that normal?"

"Mmmm, it's not abnormal. He doesn't make a habit of coming to my office. He knows we, well, I'm not sure if he knows you were with me, but he knows I was in Morgan yesterday. And, before you ask, he called the Tates to check on the status of the offer to buy the farm. Chatterbox Sherry told him I was there. He mentioned nothing about you. I'm thinking he doesn't know. Surely he'd have asked, right?"

"Maybe not. Depends. I hold back intel when I'm digging. I like to see what people will tell me. Was that all he wanted? To ask you about Morgan?"

"Heck no. He made it *exceedingly* clear I should back off. Actually said that to me. To *me*."

Cruz let out a whistle. "Ballsy. I'd like to pound the shit out of him for thinking he could talk to you that way."

Yada, yada. Cilla rolled her eyes. Men. "Well, thanks, but I took care of it and threw him out of my office. He's antsy. Definitely not happy with our field trip yesterday. Which makes me more curious than ever. He's hiding something. I feel it. Any update from Rohan on the sludge?"

"I'm walking in now. If he's not in the office yet, I'll call him. Phin texted me this morning. He had a meeting with Kayla at nine and would drop the samples at the lab on the way."

"So, we're in a holding pattern."

"For now. The day is young, Cilla. Don't let this guy screw with you. Let me find Rohan and I'll hit you back."

"Thank you."

"You're the client. It's my job."

"Not for that. For answering. For making me feel . . . not alone."

"Honey, if I have my way, you'll never be alone again."

And didn't that soothe her embattled nerves? Something

warm and silky washed over her and that vision of a naked Cruz sent her girly parts swooning.

Cilla, being Cilla, didn't swoon.

Overconfident men typically found themselves on the receiving end of her let's-be-friends speech. Cruz? He had a way. A way that didn't sound like a load of insincere charm meant to make her clothes fall off.

And, yes, she definitely wanted her clothes, not to mention his, off.

"Careful what you wish for, Cruz Blackwell."

"Why? You think it'll scare me if I get it?"

"You don't strike me as the fearful type."

"I'm afraid of a lot. Any man who says he isn't is a liar. However, you don't scare me. Just the opposite, in fact. I want more of whatever you're giving. You okay with that?"

Yes.

If he gave as good as he got, they'd be a solid match. Hell, they might make each other happy. And when had she ever thought that way about a relationship?

"You'll never have everything, Cruz. No one will. You might get more than most though. Especially if you tell me Rohan found something on that sludge."

"Remember you said that." A beep sounded from his end. "I'm walking in now. I'll call you back. And Cilla? Get ready. I'm coming for you."

11

FEELING WAY TOO HORNY FOR A GUY ABOUT TO SPEND THE DAY with his brothers, Cruz strode into the Theater and found Rohan already at the conference table with his nose in his laptop. His ugly orange tumbler sat in front of him along with another refillable bottle he used solely for water. Add the manila folder and legal pad and little brother was settled in for the long haul.

"Morning," Cruz said. "You must have gotten here early."

"Shit to do."

Rohan finally peered up at him, eyeing him like he had toothpaste on his cheek. Which, he knew he didn't since he brushed his teeth before showering.

"Why are you looking at me like that?"

"I don't know. Something's different."

Cruz snorted. "What the fuck are you talking about?"

"You look . . . rested . . . I guess. Brighter or something. I don't know. Just different."

The booze.

Or lack thereof.

He'd been so tired the night before, after he'd walked Cilla to her car, he'd gone up to his suite, fought the craving to pour himself a whiskey, and dropped into bed.

"I slept good," he said.

Rohan sat back and spun his chair a quarter turn to face Cruz. "It shows. Anything you want to talk about?"

"Like?"

Rohan shrugged. "Why you slept good."

Holy hell. This was the problem with communal living. A guy couldn't get a decent night's sleep without it being analyzed.

"Maybe I was tired, Ro."

Maybe I didn't drink half a bottle of booze. Dammit. Zeke was right. His occasional two fingers of whiskey had turned into an every-day habit. And sometimes, it wasn't just one or two.

Cruz shook his head, then glanced at the closed doors of Zeke's and Phin's offices. "Zeke came at me about drinking too much."

"Uh-*huh*. He didn't mention it."

Well, that was good at least. That Cruz wasn't the target of some twisted family intervention.

"I'm glad he said something," Rohan continued. "I noticed it."

"What?"

"You were off. Not as sharp these last couple months. At first, I thought you were distracted. But there were a few mornings you looked . . . puffy. And tired. Then I saw a half-full bottle in your kitchen one day. Next day? The bottle was in the trash."

Jesus. Was his entire family rummaging through the trash?

"It's not a problem," Cruz said. "Believe me. After the shit show with Zeke last week, I haven't touched it."

"Does Cilla have anything to do with it?"

Maybe. "No."

Rohan laughed. "Okay. Sure. Whatever, asshole."

At that Cruz smiled. Had to love his brothers. "I like her. She's wicked smart."

Unlike other aspects of his life, she made him feel things he didn't want to numb with booze. Dang, what a thought. That he'd let himself slip that far into the habit just to numb himself.

Numbing himself.

As if there weren't better ways to deal with his emotional rubble.

"She'd be good for you," Rohan said. "She won't take your shit or get insulted when you say Cruz-like things."

"Right? I thought the same thing."

Rohan waved it off. "Whatever the reason, I'm glad you're cutting back. I was going to talk to you about it, but hadn't figured out how to start the conversation."

"Zeke sure as shit figured it out. *That* was humiliating."

"It got you thinking, though."

Sure did. Having had enough of this little analysis of his drinking habits, Cruz pointed at Rohan's laptop. "What are you working on?"

"I had an idea on getting into Randolph's files."

"And?"

He flipped the folder open and handed Cruz a sheet of paper. "E-mails. It was painfully easy. Someone should speak to Cilla's father about cybersecurity."

Cruz perused the e-mail dated two weeks ago and let out a soft whistle. "According to this, the current owners have taken no sludge."

"Correct. But the previous owners did. This Paul guy had someone go back and look."

"Which means they suspect there's PFOA."

"Fair assumption. Why would they go back and look otherwise?"

Cruz handed the document back to Ro. "Abundance of caution?"

"If you say so."

Cruz didn't believe it. Two days ago, before meeting a little girl with cancer, maybe he'd have bought that, but now? The child with cancer combined with that toxicology report? Too much.

"I'm laying odds," Cruz said, "those samples come back positive for PFOA."

"Wouldn't shock me."

"That shit has been sitting in that soil for years. It's a wonder they're all not sick."

Not wanting to lose his chain of thought, Cruz ignored the aroma of fresh-brewed coffee and walked to his seat across from Rohan. He dropped into his chair and rocked back, setting his feet on the table. Mom would scream, but given she wasn't in yet, what she didn't know wouldn't hurt her.

"So," he said, "Darren Randolph knows sludge was delivered twenty years ago. Back then it would have been PFOA. They didn't ban PFOA until 2015. From what I read, before that, the EPA asked companies to reduce emissions of all perfluorooctanoic acids. They wanted them eliminated by 2015."

"But the chemical companies aren't risking profit margins by not using these chemicals. They tweak until the EPA catches up with the new formula and bans that one, too."

Unfortunately, Rohan was right. Happened all the time. "Or they suck up the fines because they're less than what they'd lose in profits and the public doesn't know."

Cruz ran his hands over his face. "Looks like we answered the all-important question of Randolph knowing that property is contaminated."

Ro held up a finger. "Not necessarily. He knows the Tate farm received sludge. He could be in serious denial and, like Cilla said, waiting on the retest. Aside from the one she found, she said Randolph's internal lab and another outside one performed the other two tests."

"Yeah. I'm not giving much weight to the internal report. They could doctor that."

"What do we know about the other lab?"

Cruz shook his head. "Nothing. Cilla didn't give us a name."

"Let me see if I can find anything in Randolph's files. Give me a couple hours."

"Go for it. I'm in no hurry to tell Cilla her father knows exactly what he's doing."

Phin, in his usual finery of suit and tie, entered the Theater with the leather briefcase Mom gave him slung over one shoulder and his BARS travel mug in hand.

"Hey," Cruz said. "You leaving?"

"Yeah. Kayla needs me for a meeting. Got an e-mail from the lab. We should have results around noon. I'll send them. Watch your e-mail."

Cruz checked his watch. Noon was still hours off and he was sufficiently in limbo waiting on Rohan's research. He had more than enough time to hop in his truck and head into Charlotte.

For what reason?

To meet with Cilla, of course. By the time they had the lab reports, he could deliver the news personally. Win-win.

"Once we have the results," Cruz said. "I'll talk to Cilla. Rohan found some e-mails."

"Anything good?"

"Enough to prove Daddy Randolph knows sludge was delivered to the previous owners of the Tate property."

"Do the Tates know?"

Both Cruz and Rohan shrugged and Phin met Cruz's eye. "Are we thinking that sludge was contaminated?"

"I'm betting on it," Cruz said.

Phinny groaned. "Shit. Cilla won't be happy."

"Ya think?"

"Her father is allowing people to be poisoned. We can't deliver that news over the phone."

"Way ahead of you, little brother. I'm in standby mode here. If Cilla is available this afternoon, I'll drive into Charlotte and meet with her."

"Good. I'd do it, but . . ."

Cruz waved him off. "I got it. Trust me. It's not a hardship."

"Oh, come on." Phin laughed. "Are you *still* chasing her? Usually, by now you've moved on."

Yikes. What did that say about him? Nothing good, that's for sure. Still, little brother needed to wise up. Cruz would be a fool to *not* be chasing Cilla. "Easy there, pal. I think the chasing part is done. We're moving to phase two."

"Phase two," Ro said. "Can't wait to hear this one."

Cruz shot him a look, then went back to Phin. "You're smart enough to figure out phase two. And don't have the balls to lecture me about getting involved with a client." He wagged a finger between Rohan and Phin. "None of you fuckers have room to talk. *All* of you got hooked up with people involved in cases."

Rohan put his hands up. "Did I say anything?"

"He's right," Phin said. "What crawled up your ass? I like Cilla. She's smart and loyal and easy to talk to. Hell, there was a time . . ."

Totally baiting him. That's what Phin was doing. "Ha!" Cruz said. "Nice try, asshole. I know what you're doing. Don't make me mess up your pretty-boy suit by kicking your ass."

It wouldn't be the first time one of them got bloody throwing hands. Mom would be pissed, but sometimes it just felt good to beat up on each other. Total stress buster. For all of them.

Phin snorted. "I'm fucking with you."

"I'm aware."

Little brother cocked his head. "Huh."

"What?"

He shrugged. "It's finally happened. Ro, can you believe it? The mighty Cruz may actually be falling for a woman."

Ro went back to his laptop, his fingers flying across the keyboard. "About time. She's perfect for him."

Phin held up his coffee in a toast. "True. She won't overthink his inappropriate comments."

"Hey," Cruz shot. "Honesty shouldn't be a crime."

His brothers exchanged a look and cracked up, the two of them clearly enjoying themselves.

Feet still on the table, Cruz stacked his hands on top of his head. If he wasn't mistaken, his brothers might be (A) Gloating and (B) Happy for him.

Both A and B were okay.

They were, in fact, exceptional.

· · ·

AFTER A MORNING OF BACK-AND-FORTH WITH THE PROSECUTOR regarding the Jenkins plea deal, Cilla dug in her desk drawer for a mirror.

Ooofff.

Flyaway hair, lipstick gone, and mascara smudged under her eyes. How the hell does that happen sitting at a desk?

Not that it mattered. This overhaul required a trip to the ladies' room.

An altogether fun distraction, considering one Cruz Blackwell had called her earlier requesting a meeting—she checked her wall clock—in thirty minutes.

One o'clock he'd said, and Cruz, from what she knew so far, liked to run on time.

Moving to the bottom desk drawer, she retrieved her spare makeup case that held duplicates of her favorites. Her emergency kit saved her a trip home if she had a dinner or function to attend after work.

On her way to the ladies' room, she passed Layla, seated at her desk and organizing a stack of folders that would no doubt come Cilla's way.

"I forgot to tell you," Cilla said, "I have a meeting at one o'clock. Cruz Blackwell from BARS."

"Ooh. I like his name. Sounds hot."

Cilla rolled her eyes, but Layla wasn't wrong. "Well, brace yourself. He *is* hot."

"Nice. Are you calling dibs?"

Cilla cracked up. Considering Layla's twenty-four-year marriage and two grown sons, Cilla didn't suspect Layla was asking on her own behalf. No. She was simply nosy.

Extremely.

A fact that prompted Cilla to keep her loyal assistant in suspense over her dating life.

Cilla walked to the office door and swung it open before turning back to Layla.

Maybe she could give her a tad of gossip. "You know," she said, "I might call dibs. He lives in Steele Ridge, though. Not sure how I feel about a three-hour commute."

Layla scoffed. "Please. You're so busy, it could be what you need. He won't be on you all the time."

True. But what if she *wanted* him on her all the time?

Literally and figuratively. What a thought. Finally, a man possibly capturing her interest enough for her to actually miss him.

"I suppose," Cilla said, "you have a point. Something to consider."

With that, she left her assistant stewing in her chair.

Ten minutes later, hair and makeup far from perfect, but as good as it would get without a complete do-over, Cilla returned and found Cruz sitting in reception scrolling on his phone. At his feet sat a leather Cole Haan backpack. Cruz didn't strike her as the designer label type, but Phin? Totally. The backpack, Cilla supposed, could have been a gift from Phin.

At her desk, Layla peered over, a smug smile lighting her face. After setting eyes on Cruz, the woman would more than likely prattle on for hours about Cilla and Cruz and a love match.

Too early to tell. But Cruz? So freaking hot.

"Well, hello." Cilla tucked her makeup case under her arm. A piss-poor hiding place, but whatever. "You're early."

He stood to his full over-six-foot height and Layla cleared her throat, drawing a glance from Cruz and a hairy eyeball from Cilla.

Cruz drew his eyebrows together in a puzzled frown that Cilla ignored.

"Sorry," he said. "If you're not ready, I can wait. No problem."

From her seat, Layla eyed them, her big brown eyes pinging back and forth.

"Not at all." Cilla waved him toward her office. "Follow me."

She led the way, glancing back at Layla, who fanned herself behind Cruz's back.

"Layla, would you hold my calls please?"

"Of course," she chirped, still fanning.

Cilla let out a laugh and Cruz turned, taking in the spectacle of Cilla's oversexed assistant.

"Layla," Cilla said, "is apparently having a hot flash."

"Layla sure is," Layla said.

"Oh my God," Cilla muttered.

"Eh," Cruz said, completely unfazed. "I have that effect."

"In your humble opinion?"

"Nothing humble about it. It is what it is."

She paused at her doorway. He did the same, their eyes locking on each other. "I believe you," she said. "Nothing about you strikes me as arrogant. Cocky maybe, but not arrogant. I like that."

"Excellent." He strode by, stepping into her office. "Something else we agree on."

Mmm, mmm, *mmm.* "Have a seat."

"Couch?"

"Sure."

They each took a seat. Cruz on the sofa and she in the lone side chair. "You didn't mention you'd be in Charlotte today."

"I wasn't planning on it."

Uh-oh. Had this meeting been the reason? If so, it probably meant bad news. Why drive nearly three hours to deliver good news when video conferencing would do it?

Definitely bad news.

She sat back, squared her shoulders, and crossed her legs. "Why do I feel like I won't be happy at the end of this meeting."

"Because you're a smart woman." He pulled a folder from the backpack he'd placed beside him. "Got a few things to show you."

"Did the sample results come back?"

"They did." He passed the report over and she perused it, searching for the magic PFOA amount on the Tate property. Her heart, along with every other organ, sunk. "Three times the limit."

"Same as the first report."

Still scanning, she shook her head. "I was hoping for a different outcome."

"I know. Sorry."

"Me too. The stream samples tested positive for PFAS." Yet another forever chemical. Cilla set the report on the table in front of her and sat back again. "I'll meet with my father this afternoon about this."

"You're gonna show him the report?"

"After meeting Brittney yesterday and knowing she's sick, I have to."

"And if he asks why you have it?"

She hadn't quite thought it all the way through, but lying wasn't an option. Not for her, anyway. She'd share her concerns over Dad not having the full picture, particularly after Paul's threat this morning, and add that she'd hired BARS to look into it since they were already limited by an NDA.

Still, the conversation wouldn't be an easy one. He'd

most likely rail on her, something that didn't happen often, but definitely had happened.

She'd survived his wrath in the past. She'd survive it again.

"I'll tell him I had concerns and hired y'all. I'll make sure there's no blowback on BARS."

"I'm not worried about that," he said. "We're big boys. It's you dealing with this that worries me."

"Thank you. But I'm a pro when it comes to Darren Randolph." She let out a sarcastic chuckle. "Years of practice."

It sounded good. Too bad she didn't feel the confidence she'd just proclaimed.

"Anyway," she brightened. "Is that it?"

He handed over a few more sheets. "These are e-mails Rohan found. Between your Dad and Paul. The second one is from someone else."

Cruz held her gaze and something in those blue-gray depths made this little impromptu meeting painfully clear. Whatever was in these e-mails, it wouldn't be good. Not for her. And probably not for Dad.

"This is why you came here, isn't it? To deliver these in person."

Which, hello? She was a criminal defense attorney. Did he think she'd fold to the floor in a heap of tears over whatever these documents contained?

Hang on. This was Cruz being a decent human being. Not like some men she'd worked with in the past who'd assumed her father's influence got her a law degree.

She took a quiet breath, got her mind right. "Don't answer that," she said.

He lifted one shoulder. "Why? I'll admit it. But if you're

thinking I came here out of some sense of playing hero, you're wrong."

"Add mind-reader to your list of talents."

"You had a look about you. A pissy one." He sat forward, propped his elbows on his knees, and clasped his hands together. "Coming here meant seeing you. Letting you read the report and if you wanted to talk it through in private, we could do that. That's it."

He wanted to see her. He'd slipped that right in there. A burst of sunshine through gray clouds.

"Thank you."

He sat back. "You're welcome. Now read that shit and tell me what you think."

She skimmed the first e-mail. Sludge. Twenty years ago. Former owner.

Twenty . . . No way. She went back to the beginning, read it word for word, absorbing every syllable. Before moving on to the next page, she peered over at Cruz who sat quietly, watching with narrowed eyes and slightly puckered lips. Attempting to decipher her reaction, no doubt.

"If I'm reading this right, my father learned weeks ago that the Tate property received free sludge from the plant prior to the Tates owning the property."

"That's correct."

"Back then, the EPA hadn't banned PFOA yet and Dad's company was using it. So, if the prior owner took sludge and used it as fertilizer, it's still in the ground after all these years."

She tossed the e-mails on the coffee table and stood. "So," she walked to her desk, grabbed a legal pad, and came back to Cruz. "What do we know? PFOA numbers on the Tate farm are triple what they should be. The PFOA is probably from the sludge."

"From our research," Cruz said, "it could be from the air as well. Smokestacks release chemicals and when it rains, the water pushes the pollution to the ground. Sometimes it leaches into waterways or wells. Which could explain the stream's results."

He'd nailed it. Everything she knew to be true about forever chemicals. "Dad says they've been compliant. Every time I ask him, he says it. I believed him."

"You think he's lying?"

"I think he's not a stupid man. I *think* he knows enough that he's aware something is going on that shouldn't be. Add these e-mails and a little girl with cancer and it doesn't take a rocket scientist to figure out Randolph Industries might have something to do with it. I mean, hey, they're the nation's largest supplier of firefighting gear and foam. Before some of these chemicals were banned, they used them to manufacture their products."

She dropped into the chair, pressed her palms against her forehead. *Calm.* She had to think. To stay rational. Not get ahead of herself. Her father might be ruthless in business, but he cared for people.

For human life.

He'd never intentionally let people, little girls, succumb to life-threatening illnesses.

She straightened up and peered across at Cruz. "I have to talk to him."

"Now?"

She shot from her chair, grabbed the e-mails and the toxicology report. "Right now. And don't bother asking if it's a good idea. It's not. I know it's not, but I'm so flipping mad, I need answers. If he—they—are knowingly risking lives to save profits, I'll lose my mind."

Cruz stood, stepped around the table, and stopped

barely a foot in front of her. "You're a big girl. You make your own decisions. Do what you need to. Want me to wait?"

Yes. "You don't have to."

"But if I want to?"

She lifted her free hand, set it on his thick forearm and let every ounce of his skin's heat soak into her. Calm, steady, Cruz. Just what she needed.

"I'd love that," she said. "I may need a sounding board when this is over."

12

AFTER COOLING HER JETS FOR FIFTEEN MINUTES IN DAD'S office while he finished a meeting in the conference room, Cilla pasted on her best fake smile as her father entered the office. Between her research, the trip to Morgan, Paul's visit, and this, she'd lost a good chunk of precious time on Dad's PFOA issues.

Hopefully, it would all end here. "Hi, Dad."

He paused where she sat in one of his guest chairs and bent low for their customary cheek peck. "Hi, sweetheart. This is a pleasant surprise. I thought you were in court today."

"I was supposed to be. Judge Nagle has been sick."

"That's too bad. I'd heard he wasn't at the club over the weekend."

Her father's list of contacts ran far and wide. Including judges he golfed with.

"I think he's better. In his absence we worked out a plea deal."

"That's my girl. Never wasting time."

She watched as he cornered his desk, slid his suit coat

off and hung it on the stand in the corner. Then he went to work unbuttoning his shirt sleeves and rolling them. His comfort mode when settling in for hours behind the desk. Sometimes he'd ditch the tie. Today, he left it and Cilla assumed more meetings required the full suit-and-tie look.

Finally, he claimed his seat, quickly checked a stack of notes in front of him and gave Cilla his attention. "What brings you by?"

"I won't keep you." She held up the documents Cruz had given her. "I have something for you."

"My girl looks so serious." He held out a hand. "What have you got there?"

During her fifteen minutes of waiting, she'd read through the pages again and opted to hold back the e-mails. Sharing those meant answering questions on how she got them. Not going there. Hacking would take Dad to DEFCON 1.

Prior to Dad entering, she'd folded the e-mails and tucked them under her thigh. Now, bracing herself by pinning her shoulders back, she handed over the toxicology report. *Here we go.* "This is a toxicology report on the Tate property."

Dad's eyebrows drew together, the dark hairs forming almost a straight line across his forehead while he stared at her, completely ignoring the report. "Why do you have it?"

"After seeing that initial report and discussing it with you, I had concerns."

Finally, he glanced down at the pages. "What concerns?"

"Legal concerns. You've always told me you consider me part of your legal team. I take pride in you trusting me. After reading the report Paul left on the plane and then our subsequent conversation, I'm worried you might not have the entire picture."

Dad dropped the report, the pages floating to the desktop while he nearly singed her with a fiery glare that sent her pulse slamming.

"Paul has been my right hand for years."

Easing out a breath, Cilla lifted her chin. Just a conversation. That's all this was. But heaven help her if Dad lost his shit on her. She'd have to absorb his wrath until he worked through the anger. His temper had a pattern. An instant spark that burned hot and fast and then extinguished itself.

She simply had to ride it out.

"I know you trust him," Cilla said. "However, he's not family. As protective as you are of me, I'm equally protective of you. So, when my legal radar pings, I do something. Did Paul tell you he visited me this morning?"

"He mentioned it."

Dad knew.

It hit her like a runaway bus. He knew she'd been in Morgan and hadn't bothered to call her? To give her a heads-up, a minute to prepare herself for Paul's questions. And threats. Furthermore, why hadn't Dad been the one to speak to her?

None of it made sense.

She shook it off. Time later to mull it all over. Now, she focused on her next words. "I went to Morgan yesterday and collected soil samples from the Tate farm and the other two properties beside the plant."

Dad's gaze narrowed, his cheeks flushing slightly, the soon-to-be explosion simmering. "Who told you to do that?"

"No one. I wanted answers on the amount of PFOA in the soil and the only way to ensure the test's chain of custody was to take the samples myself."

"It's not your business."

"*You're* my business, Dad."

For a few seconds, he simply stared at her, the pink in his cheeks retreated as his lips quirked. Cilla's pulse knocked back and she let out a breath. Maybe this wouldn't be the shitshow she'd expected.

"Let me ask you something," Dad said.

"Of course."

He nodded, then sat forward. "Do you think I'm an idiot?"

"What? No! Of course not."

"Well, you must since you think I don't know what's going on in my own goddamned company."

His cheeks hardened and the heat returned to his eyes, lighting them up like lasers pointed straight at her.

"Dad, that's not it at all. It's a big company. You can't keep your eye on everything."

He picked up the report, balled it and whipped it at her. *Whoa!* She swatted it down and let it hit the floor.

"Dad! What the hell?"

A mix of heartbreak and . . . yes . . . anger pelted her. She fought back a rush of tears and locked her jaw against the attack of emotions.

He stood and jabbed—*jab, jab, jab*—his finger at her.

"If I need your help," Dad fumed, "I'll ask for it. Stay the fuck out of this, Cilla. Whatever you're doing, stop. Paul is on it."

Cilla stiffened. It wouldn't be the first time Dad had dropped an f-bomb in her presence, but it sure as hell was the first time he'd directed it at her.

And the door was wide open. Anyone in the executive suite, including Paul, could hear them.

However, she might capitalize on Dad's inappropriate behavior. When his temper flashed, he got loose lips. She'd witnessed it hundreds of times.

She gripped the e-mails under her thigh and stood, kicking the balled report out of her path. "You said Paul is on it. How?"

The color in his cheeks fired again, his fury whipping back around. "What did I just say?"

Oh boy. Never had she pushed his buttons like this. Never. But Brittney Tate and her parents deserved answers.

Locking her gaze on his, Cilla readied herself for the next round. "Dad, are you poisoning people in Morgan?"

His eyes bulged and a muscle in his jaw jumped. "Get out of my office," he said, his voice carrying the rough edge of shattered concrete. "Right now."

His hand sliced through the air, the move so violent and fast, Cilla flinched. Dammit. He'd never once put a hand on her. That flinch? No idea where it had come from, but she'd broken her cardinal battle rule.

She'd shown weakness. Dad? He exploited weakness. Carved it into tiny pieces. And she'd just handed it to him.

Stepping sideways, away from the chair blocking her path to the door, she waited for another blast of temper. For his denial that would surely come.

Something inside Cilla, hope maybe, disintegrated. Dropped like a brick from seventeen stories.

No denial. He knew.

At some point, she'd have to process this. Force herself to accept that he'd obliterated the boundaries she thought he'd never cross.

He knew about the PFOA. What else did he know? Was Randolph Industries knowingly polluting the environment?

All that fear and sickness tearing her apart morphed into swarming anger that fired her own temper. She'd come this far. Might as well push a little more. "Dad, what are you hiding?"

A guttural roar sounded. His eyes blazed, the look so evil, it should have burned the building down. He picked up the brass football paperweight sitting on his desk and hurled it. Not at her, sideways and into the wall, just inches from the framed painting of the flagship Randolph factory. The paperweight dropped, leaving a gouge in the wall, and hit the floor with an echoing clunk.

"Dad!"

Fuming, he pointed to the door. "Get out." Then he jabbed his finger again. "When I'm ready to talk to you, I'll call you. In the meantime, keep your ass in your office and out of my business."

Her *ass*? She let out a huff. "Are you hearing yourself?" Before he could holler, she slapped up a hand. "No. You know what? I'm finally seeing it. After all these years, I *see* why Mom left you."

"You shut up!"

She'd come this far. Might as well keep going. It wouldn't hurt to inform him she knew all about the PFOA and little girls with cancer.

"No. I've done your bidding for years and this is how you treat me? I'm done."

She glanced down at the e-mails, folded in her hand. No sense tipping her hand that she'd used his login to access the system.

"By the way," she said, "while I was in Morgan. I met Brittney Tate. How convenient that you offered to help with their medical bills since your company probably gave that child cancer."

"*Get out!*"

Final blow leveled, Cilla spun and headed for the door. "Gladly!"

· · ·

HURRICANE CILLA CAME STORMING INTO HER OFFICE, slamming the door behind her. From his spot on the couch, Cruz looked up from scrolling through his e-mails.

Call him a shithead because *obviously,* with the way she barreled in, hands balled and those green eyes the color of a Caribbean sea during a thunderstorm, her meeting with daddy-o hadn't gone well.

Obviously. Yet, in this moment, everything about her screamed power and rage and passion that made him immediately think of a bed and bare skin and . . .

What in the hell was wrong with him?

He cleared his throat, tried to ignore the start of an erection. *Jeez.* "Didn't go well, I take it."

She stalked the room, her blazer flapping open while long legs effortlessly ate up the space. Day-am, those wicked spiked heels didn't slow her down a bit.

Cilla threw her hands up. "He threw me out."

That was unexpected. At least *he* didn't expect it. Cruz stood, tucked his phone into his front pants pocket and stepped around the coffee table. Giving her a wide berth, he paused beside her desk. "No shit?"

"No. *Shit!*" She stopped pacing, flapped her arms again and huffed so hard it should have blown him back a step.

"At the risk of sounding condescending," he said, "you need to breathe."

Fire shot from her eyes. "*Totally* condescending!"

But she bent at the waist, bracing her hands against her thighs and . . . breathed. Her silky hair fell against her cheeks and he focused on the top of her head. Wrong. *Wrong, wrong, wrong* thing to focus on because that got him pondering different angles he'd see the top of her head from.

"Holy cow." Still bent over, she inhaled again and blew it

out. "I've never seen him like that. Not with me. He has a brass paperweight on his desk. I gave it to him for his birthday when I was in high school. All these years, he's kept it."

"And?"

"He threw it."

A nasty throb banged against Cruz's temples. Made him want to put hands on someone. Someone like Darren Randolph.

"He threw it," Cruz said. "At *you*?"

Finally, Cilla stood tall. "No! If I'd gotten hit with that thing, I'd be dead. It hit the wall."

"Oh." Cruz nodded and flexed his fingers a few times, ridding them of the urge to pound the shit out of Darren Randolph. Even if the guy was thirty years his senior.

Cilla propped her hands on her hips. "It took a chunk out of the wall. That's how hard he threw it."

"You pissed him off."

"I sure did."

They stood in her fancy office with the stuffed oak bookshelves and lawyerly furniture that must have cost a small fortune while Cruz pictured a man hurling a brass paperweight anywhere near his child.

Any man who would do that? Asshole.

He didn't like Darren Randolph.

At all.

He held his hands wide. "Are you okay?"

"I'm fine. Stunned."

"Rightly so. He had an interesting reaction, no?"

"What do you mean?"

Risking his life, Cruz moved closer, stopping two feet in front of her. "He could have played dumb. Gone for the I-have-no-idea-what-you're-talking-about defense. Instead, he went apeshit."

She inched closer, lifting her hands, then letting them drop, the whole effort seeming to take the last of her energy.

Family drama sucked.

"I caught him," she said, her voice sharp. "I caught him lying and he must have panicked. He's so used to me being an ally, he probably didn't know what to do."

She swung away, wandering to the window and staring out at the building across the street.

"He lied to me," she said, her voice barely a whisper. "About the reports and being EPA compliant. All along, he knew." She peered back at Cruz. "I can only imagine what else he's lied about."

Yeah. That would be interesting to know. "Maybe he just found out."

To Cruz, it sounded like a hustle. A total snow job that earned him a bored look from feisty Cilla Randolph.

"It's too late to give him the benefit of the doubt," she said. "I don't care how long he's known. The e-mails Rohan found prove it's been at least a couple of weeks. He lied to me, Cruz. I've repeatedly asked him about the EPA. Long before this, I've been asking. And he's lied to me. All this time. There's just no way around it."

"Now what?"

"I haven't the slightest idea. All I know is Brittney Tate has cancer and her parents may not know why. Those people are living on a toxic wasteland. I have to do something."

What she needed to do was slow the fuck down. Take a minute and think this through. He'd have to be careful delivering that message. Otherwise, she'd knock his head off.

And nothing about that should have been appealing. However, he did enjoy a sassy woman.

He moved toward her, close enough to draw her a quarter turn and face him. "I think," he said, "you might want to take a second here. You're churned up."

"Of course, I'm churned up. I just found out my father's company is poisoning people. I can't do nothing."

"Fine. But you don't have to fix everything right now. Just —" He shook his head.

What the hell kind of advice could he offer?

Cilla poked him in the chest. "You're right. I need to make a plan. Calm down and get my head together. I know one thing for sure. I'm tired of being under my father's thumb. I'm due in court in Asheville at eleven tomorrow. I've had my eye on a small office there. It was once a home that was rezoned. I'm calling the realtor. See if I can look at it first thing tomorrow. If I like it, I'm buying it."

Whoa. Buying an office? "Wow. Big step. Don't you want to lease first?"

"No. I want my own space where I have control. Wanna come along and help me decide?"

"Honey," he said, "there's no place I'd rather be."

13

HAVING HAD ENOUGH OF RANDOLPH INDUSTRIES—JUST BEING in the building infuriated her—Cilla packed up files to take home, where she'd work for the rest of the day and evening.

After a quick meeting with Layla to discuss the schedule for the following week, Cilla stepped off the elevator and into the glass-enclosed lobby, accompanied by Cruz, who'd dutifully dragged her giant rolling briefcase along.

They walked out of the building, standing still for a moment while small clusters of pedestrians navigated the sidewalk.

Late afternoon sunshine beamed down. Needing the respite after the draining interlude with her father, she took a second to tip her head back, take in the heat, and breathe.

Immediately, some of the tension left her neck and shoulders. Amazing what fresh oxygen and sunshine could do.

She pointed to the corner. "I'm in the garage across the street." She reached for the briefcase. "I can take that."

He waved her off. "Nah. I'm parked there, too. I'll walk you."

Never one to pass up an excellent offer, Cilla nodded. A few minutes with Mr. Delicioso would settle her nerves. And how pathetic was she, considering a brief walk to her car companionship?

Need a life, Cilla.

At the corner, a car took the turn too sharply and Cruz reached his arm in front of her, backing her up a step. "Slow down, asshole," he muttered to the driver.

While waiting for the light to change, he faced her. "Are you sure I can't buy you an early dinner?"

"I would, in fact, love that. But this PFOA project has me backed up and I have a murder case to prep for."

The plea deal she'd managed helped. At least she wouldn't lose days or a week on a trial. However, the murder trial loomed and she needed to get cooking on that. She'd yet to fully study her investigator's notes that Layla had given her days ago.

A clone.

That's what she needed.

But how long would a man like Cruz Blackwell wait around for her to become un-busy? The way he looked? He probably had women lined up for a chance to screw his lights out.

And, ugh. A vision of Cruz and some sexy blonde banging each other filled her mind, sent heat straight to her cheeks because she did *not* like that.

At all.

Still waiting for the light, she gripped his arm. "Ask me again, though. Okay? I enjoy your company."

A horn sounded, drawing their attention to the light that had just turned green and a seriously impatient driver honking at the car in front of him.

People angled around them, hustling across the street,

but they stood there, gazes locked and Cruz flashing his killer smile.

"Honey," he said, "I'll ask you every day if you want."

No. She didn't want that. Some women might get an ego boost out of Cruz Blackwell chasing after them. Her? Out of simple respect, she wouldn't allow it.

Which meant making the time. Tomorrow was Friday, she'd have the entire weekend to hunker down and work. Not exactly a fun-sounding time, but it might give her wiggle room for a date with Cruz.

"Tomorrow night," she said. "How's that? You available?"

He tipped his head one way, then the other. "A Friday night date? I like it."

"Perfect. I'll be in Asheville."

"Good. But, hey, since you're not available tonight, maybe I'll call Ash. See if he's around." He pointed to the red don't-walk sign. "Missed the light."

She bumped him with her shoulder. "It was worth it."

Five minutes later, dinner plan for tomorrow secure, they approached her car in the garage. For ease, she paid for a reserved space on level one because she didn't want to be lugging files to the roof when she couldn't find a parking space after hearings.

"It's not an awful walk," Cruz said.

"Not at all. That's why I like the reserved spot. If I'm in a hurry, I can be here in four minutes. Yes, I've timed it."

Cruz laughed, then gestured to the briefcase. "Where do you want this?"

"Back seat is fine."

She clicked the unlock button on her key fob and opened the driver's side door, tossing her purse on the passenger seat.

Out of the corner of her eye, something yellow registered and she glanced at the windshield. Envelope. Tucked under her wiper blade.

She backed out of the car and reached around the frame just as Cruz shut the back door.

"What is it?"

Slipping the envelope from under the blade, she held it up. "I don't know."

The edge of her finger caught something hard and she ran her thumb over it. "It feels weird."

"Cilla, the whole thing is weird, unless people randomly leaving envelopes on your car is normal."

"Not normal, per se. But, with what I do, people send tips in many ways."

Threats, too, but she wouldn't mention that.

Maybe whatever was in the envelope might help with one of her cases. She tore the top off the envelope and peeked inside.

Was that?

She tipped the envelope over, dumping the contents into her free hand.

One lone bullet shell.

"What the fuck?" Cruz breathed.

"This," Cilla said, forcing air through her nose as pressure built in her chest. "Not normal."

"I fucking hope not. Is there a note?"

Still holding the bullet, she peered inside the envelope. "Nothing."

Her mind reeled. Over the years, she'd received a handful of threats that turned out to be just that. Hateful e-mails and packages from desperate folks hoping to scare her into throwing a case. Which did nothing but piss her off.

And now, a bullet. Just as she was about to start another murder trial.

Terrific.

"Nine-millimeter," Cruz said. "Why would someone put this on your car? And please don't tell me it's what I think it is."

"I believe," she said, "it might be a scare tactic. It happens."

He gawked. "It happens? What the fuck does that mean?"

"I practice criminal law. Some people don't like that. I occasionally receive threatening mail." She gestured to the bullet with her free hand. "And apparently bullets."

In an instant, Cruz was in motion, grabbing her briefcase and reaching for her purse on the front seat.

"Whoa," she said. "What . . . what are you doing?"

"Put that bullet in the envelope."

Yes. Good idea. Dammit. She, of all people, should have known better than to touch it. They might have gotten fingerprints or DNA from it. She eased the casing into the envelope being careful to only touch the edges, before placing the envelope in the outer zipper pocket of the briefcase. Her prints would be on it, but hopefully they'd find others too.

Cruz grabbed her hand, tugging her behind him.

"Get away from the car," he said. "You're coming with me."

Wait. What? "I am?"

"Yes. We're calling Ash. I want someone to check this car. Make sure nobody fucked with it."

Cilla nearly laughed. "Cruz, there are security cameras. No one is that dumb."

"They were dumb enough to leave this envelope in full view of those cameras. In fact, where *is* the security office?"

This, she wasn't sure of. For a woman who walked to her

car alone, sometimes late at night, it was something she should know. "I have an office number to call."

"You do that while I track down Ash. Tell them we need to see footage of this area. We're gonna find this fucker."

"Hey, you're moving way too fast here."

"Okay," he said. "Without looking at security video, how sure are you that someone hasn't messed with your car?"

Huh. Had her there. She supposed it wouldn't hurt to at least look. She dug out her phone, checked her contact list for the office that charged her credit card every month.

Could someone have seriously sabotaged her car? In broad daylight? No. That'd be ridiculous. Completely.

They were being paranoid. *Thanks, Cruz.*

"It's me," Cruz said into his phone. "Call me. ASAP."

Cilla, too, wound up in voice mail. She left a message, then disconnected.

"Holding pattern," she said.

"Me too. Ash is good, though. He'll call back fast. We'll get the car checked out, have him run prints on the bullet, and then you'll come home with me."

"Pardon?"

"Until we figure this out, you shouldn't be alone."

Now, she full-on laughed. "One second, here. When did I put you in charge of my life?"

He gave her a bored, are-you-nuts? look. "You didn't. I'm suggesting you not be alone. In fact, you have court in Asheville tomorrow. Steele Ridge is much closer." He rolled his hand. "Follow my logic. We get the feds over here to check your car, we drive to Steele Ridge, and you stay in one of our guest suites. Much shorter drive to court in the morning. By then, you should hopefully have security video and we find this fucker. Solid plan right there."

Bastard.

He'd totally cornered her. She hated him for that. Hated that she couldn't come up with one argument.

Shoot.

"Tell me," he said, "it doesn't make sense. I dare you."

At that, she bared her teeth. And growled. "You're a pain in the ass sometimes."

"Ha! You know it, babe. Let's go. My truck is up on five."

BY THE TIME CRUZ ARRIVED HOME AND PARKED IN FRONT OF the Annex with Cilla right behind him in her sexy as hell— and tamper-free—Quattroporte, it was nearly seven.

At the Annex entrance, he pressed his hand against the security pad and held the door for Cilla before escorting her into the Theater where Zeke and Rohan sat at the conference table.

"Hey, guys," Cruz said, trying and more than likely failing to not sound pissy.

Spotting Cilla, the two of them shot up from their chairs —good Southern boys, right there—and Zeke gave Cruz a little extended eye contact, more than likely telling him you-could-have-warned-me-sooner-than-thirty-minutes-ago about their client visiting.

After the ultra-awkward conversation in the kitchen about Cruz drowning in estrogen, he'd avoided being alone with Zeke and continuing the convo regarding empty whiskey bottles.

Fucking nightmare, that.

Now, the silence in the room lingered and Cilla took control by clearing her throat. "I'm sorry to barge in."

Ro flashed a welcoming smile. "Not at all. Sit. We're sorry about the . . . you know."

"Thank you. Hopefully, it was just a scare tactic. I have a

couple of big cases coming up. Your brother was terrific in getting guys over there. They took prints and such."

Cruz gestured to the other side of the table and she reclaimed the chair she'd occupied for their last meeting.

"Hope you don't mind," Rohan said, "Cruz gave me the garage info and I was able to look at the security video."

Little brother worked quick. Although Cruz knew this. "What you'd find?"

"Nothing that'll be of help, unfortunately. Someone in a hoodie, looks like a man by the gait, but he was smart. Kept his head down, hood pulled forward. Unless Ash can grab other video from businesses on the street and see where the guy went, I'm not sure it'll amount to much."

Cilla nodded. "Rohan, thank you for doing that. I appreciate you trying."

"Sure thing. This pissed me off. Nobody should pull stunts like this."

"I agree, but unfortunately, it happens. When I was a prosecutor, it happened more often, but even now, people resort to things like this. Particularly if it's a high-profile case, which I currently have two of. People don't want celebrities getting off easy and they take their frustrations out on me. Threats aside," Cilla said, "my father isn't happy with me."

Zeke winced. "Sorry about that."

"Why? You did your job. Now I have to figure out how to proceed. Based on our collective research, my father is aware there's a contamination issue."

"Well," Ro said, "we don't have proof of *that*. We only know of these isolated properties."

Cilla, bless her beautiful heart, gave his brother a you-poor-misled-child look, and that? Hilarious.

Cruz snorted, drawing the attention of both his brothers.

He jerked his thumb at Cilla. "This woman? I might love her. Just so you know."

This actually got a laugh out of Zeke—score one for Cruz. Cilla shook her head, clearly questioning his said love. Who could blame her? The fact that he'd even said it shocked the shit out of him.

Gaze still on Rohan, Cilla cocked her head. "How do we find out if other properties in town are contaminated? Or, heaven help me, the water system. We know the streams we took samples from contain PFOA and PFAS. It could have seeped through the ground into wells."

Cilla was right. Rohan and Cruz had come across case after case where runoff from chemical plants leached into a town's water supply via the ground.

"EPA, maybe," Zeke said.

Cilla made a humming noise. "That would mean reporting Randolph Industries. I'm not ready for that yet. I know how that must sound. That I don't want to turn in my father. It's not that. Well, yes, partially it is. I don't want to rush this, though. The impact could be devastating to not only the company but its employees. I want to be sure of what we have."

"Plus," Cruz added, "we can't. We signed an NDA."

"I'm not worried about that," Cilla said. She shifted back to Zeke and Rohan. "There are whistleblower laws. I need to brush up on them, but I think that if I'm the one talking, it'll leave BARS out of it. Before I do anything, I'd like to know how bad it is."

Cruz snapped his fingers. "I remember reading something. If a water supply is tainted, the town has to alert the residents."

"Right," Cilla said. "It's typically a letter worded in a way that won't create mass panic. The ones I've seen are generic enough to assure residents that the town is cleaning it up and there's no cause for concern. Then the town council sits back and hopes a class action suit doesn't come their way."

Cruz and Zeke, apparently sharing a wavelength, eyed Rohan.

"Great," Ro said. "There goes the rest of my night."

Ouch. Guilt slammed Cruz. Rohan, thanks in large part to falling in love with Lena, had finally decompressed. To not be so freaking obsessed with keeping them all safe, doing the right thing, blah, blah, blah and generally making himself nuts. Now they were demanding all his newly-found free time.

"Wait," Cilla said. "What did I miss?"

Cruz met her eye. "Ro will do research on the town's water reclamation company."

"I see."

That task being dispensed with, Cruz stood. "Cilla has business in Asheville tomorrow. I invited her to spend the night. I'll put her in the guest suite by mine. Did y'all eat?"

"Not yet. We got caught up. Mom and Grams went out. Liv and Brodie are visiting her parents. Phin is working with Kayla."

"I'll buy," Cilla offered. "Whatever y'all want."

"Absolutely not," Zeke said. "You're our guest."

"An unannounced guest whose fault it is Rohan has to spend his evening doing . . . *research.* The least I can do is supply dinner. I'm not taking no for an answer."

Having spent some time with Cilla, Cruz got the idea that a bloody battle they'd lose might ensue. "She's a freaking lawyer," Cruz said. "It's not worth arguing over. Let her buy us dinner."

"The B," Rohan said, "has that fried chicken family meal

deal tonight. I was thinking about that anyway. Lena is holed up trying to finish a painting."

"Randi's fried chicken works for me," Zeke said.

"Excellent," Cilla said. "Family meal deal it is then. And thank you for not debating with me. I owe y'all for what you've done."

Zeke stood. "You don't owe us anything. We appreciate you treating us to dinner. Cruz, you order. I'll pick it up. I could use some air."

Rohan stood, folded his laptop. "I'll be in my office. Maybe I'll find something quick."

By 8:30, everyone had eaten and Cruz sent Zeke and Rohan out of the kitchen, offering to clean up since Zeke had played delivery boy, and Rohan busied himself hacking into the Morgan Water Treatment Facility. So far, no luck, but knowing Ro, that wouldn't last long.

Cruz loaded the last dish into the washer while Cilla carried leftover potato salad and chicken to the fridge. Door open, she stood back and twisted her lips. No doubt in awe of Mom's organizational skills.

"Just shove it anywhere," Cruz said. "When my mother gets back, she'll move it anyway."

She always did. Her military habits clung like stink on a hog. Everything had a rightful place. He'd put something in the drawer and the next morning? Moved. He'd grown used to it. Came with the territory when living with people.

Cilla placed the items inside, closed the door and came to stand by him at the sink. "Does it bother you?"

Drying his hands, he hung the damp towel on the dishwasher handle and lined up the edges the way Mom liked.

He studied his handiwork, considered it a done deal, and faced Cilla again. "Does what bother me?"

"That she moves things?"

At times, yes. He considered it a difference of opinion since he couldn't think that hard about organizing a fridge.

"Eh," he said. "I'm used to it. She likes order. Plus, if anything is lost, she knows where it is."

He glanced around the kitchen, found it in acceptable condition, and then looked out the window at the darkening sky. According to his weather app, it should be clear skies. Which meant a bazillion stars.

Lucky me.

He faced Cilla again and propped one hip against the counter. "I know you have work, but I'd like to show you something."

Her gaze narrowed, her lush lips coming to a pucker that damn near begged for him to lean in and . . .

"I'm a criminal defense attorney," she said. "In my experience, surprises aren't fun."

Considering she probably dealt with murderers and lowlifes on the daily, he saw her point, but she needed to lighten up. Cut loose a little and enjoy spontaneity.

He reached up and gently tugged on her poker-straight hair. "Trust me. This'll be fun. I promise. You'll need a jacket."

For a few seconds, they stood in the quiet kitchen, gazes locked while Cilla decided. If she'd insisted on knowing, he'd tell her. No problem there. In his mind, respecting people meant not pushing his own agenda on them. If she didn't like surprises, he'd deal with it.

"Okay." She nodded. "I could use some fun. But seriously, I have work to do after. Let me get my jacket."

"Might want to change your shoes, too. Something you can walk in."

She saluted. "Sir, yes, sir."

At that, he laughed. Cilla the smart-ass.

Ten minutes later, after grabbing her jacket and tote and doing who knew what else women did that took ten minutes and left Cruz leaning against his truck while waiting, Cilla walked out the Friary's front door. She strode toward him, her long, jean-encased legs and running shoes drawing every bit of his attention.

He enjoyed seeing her in her high-powered suits, but tight jeans? They made his heart—and other things—go pitter-patter.

As she approached, the path lights illuminated her and he noted the fresh layer of creamy red lipstick that made her eyes pop. Total vixen, this one.

He opened the passenger door and then pointed at the tote strung over her shoulder. "You won't need that. We're not leaving the property."

She paused before climbing in, her green eyes a little snappy because—oh, right—she didn't like surprises.

"Sorry," he said. "Guess I could have told you that."

She settled herself into the truck and buckled her seat belt like they'd be in traffic or something.

City girls.

He hopped in the driver's side, ignored the seat belt, and fired up the truck for the drive down the dirt road that would lead them to their destination.

On the way, he cruised by the tiny chapel they'd left intact when they bought the property. Moonlight threw shadows across stained glass, but otherwise, the building sat almost invisible in the darkness.

Cruz pointed. "That's the chapel. This property was an

abandoned church camp when we bought it. The Friary and chapel were here, along with some cabins and barns. Mom liked the chapel and wanted to keep it. The marble floors, stained glass and pews are original, but they were in rough shape. She had those refinished."

Cilla leaned forward, staring out his window as they cruised by. "I'd like to see it in the daylight."

"Sure. Just need to make sure it's empty. We have an unwritten rule that if one of us is in there, nobody goes in. Unless it's an emergency."

"I love that rule. It must be peaceful inside."

Oh, hell, yes. "It is. It's tough sometimes. Living with so many people. Someone's always up your ass."

The rustling sound of fabric, drew his gaze to where she shifted to face him. "This property is amazing. Would you ever leave all this?"

He'd been asking himself that very question for months. He peered over at her. The dashboard lights illuminated the cab and he met her gaze. "I'd be foolish. Right?"

And why the hell was he asking her? She hadn't lived here. Hadn't roamed these grounds and sat staring up at stars on clear nights, like tonight, listening to wildlife.

God's country, his mother said.

He didn't disagree.

"Not at all," Cilla said. "It's beautiful, for sure. You have everything you need. No city sounds. No sirens waking you up at all hours. The view from the guest suite is stunning."

Yeah. He'd be a fool to leave. She hadn't said it. Probably wouldn't.

"There are other considerations, though."

He blew out a breath. Relief maybe. He wasn't sure. "Like what?"

"Well, there's the part about your mother rearranging

and your brothers always being around with their girl-friends. I see how that might be hard sometimes. I haven't had roommates since college and coming home after a tough day to a quiet house isn't awful. Most of the time."

Most of the time. Was there a hidden message there? Something she didn't want to admit. Maybe like how insanely lonely and boring it was?

Because, yeah, that too scared him. What it would be like, sitting by himself with no one to harass or mouth off to. No door to knock on when he wanted to talk sports or bitch about a client.

He'd never—including college—lived alone and he couldn't wrap his mind around that kind of change.

Still driving, Cruz tapped a finger against the steering wheel and kept his eyes on the pitch blackness in front of him. Sometimes, it was weird. Like driving into a black hole, but most of the time? Pretty cool. "You don't get lonely?"

There. Said it. Put it right out there.

And she hadn't laughed at him. Or called him soft.

"Everyone gets lonely, Cruz. It's life. I manage it. I call a friend or meet someone for drinks."

Didn't that get his mind motoring. He imagined there was no shortage of men, him included, willing to meet her somewhere.

The thought made his stomach pitch. He'd never been a jealous sort. Never cared all that much.

Until now.

He stole a quick glance at her. "Can I ask you a question?"

"Absolutely."

"Do you date a lot?"

"No. When I told you I was busy, I wasn't lying. I don't have the time or patience for dating. Throw my father into the mix and it's a . . . chore. Half the men want access to Darren Randolph, the other half are intimidated. There's no middle ground. Not that I've found, anyway."

He got that. Understood how power-hungry hustlers might use Cilla as a steppingstone to meet one of the country's most powerful business executives.

"Just so you know," he said. "I don't give a shit about access and I'm sure as hell not intimidated by him."

He pulled to a stop in the middle of the grass. Behind them, off in the distance, barely visible lights from the Friary glowed.

Cilla glanced out the windshield, then her window. "Um, why are we stopping?"

"We're here."

"Where?"

He shrugged. "Nowhere. That's the point."

When she rolled her bottom lip out and stared at him like he'd lost his mind, he laughed. City girls.

After killing the engine, he slid from the truck and hustled to open her door. "Come on, city girl. It'll be worth it. I promise."

Grabbing his hand, she hopped down and walked with him to the back of the truck where he lowered the tailgate and climbed into the bed. He unrolled a rubber pad and comforter he kept stowed in the bed's storage trunk.

"Welcome to the Chez Blackwell light show."

Clearly confused, she didn't move. "Come again."

He pointed to the sky. "It's a clear night. You won't get this view in Charlotte. If we get lucky, we'll see a shooting star."

She peered up for a few seconds and he waited, counted off the seconds until—bam—he saw it. That moment when she finally noticed what kept him sane. When she allowed herself to be present and stop thinking. Just take in the wash of stars thrown across the sky like tiny multicolored lanterns.

Until they'd moved here, further up the mountain, he'd never appreciated how the higher elevation took them above denser air. Dense air meant haze and fog and smoke that masked the full beauty of stargazing.

"Holy cow," she said, swinging her head all around. "How did I not notice this?"

"Easy. Your mind was occupied. Coming out here relaxes me. Zeke thinks I work in the middle of the night. Sometimes I do. Sometimes," he gestured to the sky, "I come out here. Hell, I've slept out here. The fresh air, the stars, there's purity here. Goodness."

"I need some of that."

He smiled. "No! Not you?"

"Oh, ha, ha."

"Slide on in here," he said. "We're gonna lie down, throw a comforter over us, and hang out awhile."

She helped him spread the blanket and they both crawled under, staring straight up at a starlit sky.

"Wow," she said. "I already feel less stressed. Who knew a night sky was all it took? Or." She turned her head, met his gaze and held it. "Maybe it's the company. Or both. I needed this. Thank you."

The woman tempted him. Made him want things, houses and privacy and quiet nights together, he'd never craved before.

"You're welcome," he said. "It's good to shut everything down. Quiet the madness in our brains."

"I don't do that enough. I'm always moving, reading notes, prepping for trial."

"You're successful because of it. Nothing to be ashamed of. There's something to be said for balance, though."

She rolled sideways, propped herself on one elbow. "Balance. What a concept."

She inched closer—a go-sign if he'd ever seen one—and he lifted his arm, sliding it around her shoulder and giving her a pillow for her head.

This? Never a bad thing.

"Guessing you can see why I like it here. I love walking to the barn to work on cars and sitting out here by myself at night."

"All solitary things."

She had a point there. "I guess I never thought about that, but yeah. I like my alone time."

"You mentioned the recent addition of girlfriends to the house."

He did mention that. To her, to Zeke, to Rohan. As if down deep, some unacknowledged part of him wanted everyone to know of his displeasure.

An unintended shot across their bow. "I feel . . . trapped," he blurted.

Ach. That sounded bad. Like he, a grown-ass man, was being held against his will.

"No," he said. "That's not it. I'm not a hostage, for Christ's sake."

"I didn't think that's what you meant. I get how it can feel like the walls are closing in. I feel that way about my current office. Everything is tight."

Yes.

Finally.

He could say it out loud without feeling like a selfish prick who paid not a dime's worth of rent, mostly had meals at the ready and yet, felt stuck.

"Every time I turn around," he said, "there's someone there. Before, it was just Mom and Grams and my brothers. We were used to each other. Now? We keep adding personalities. Female personalities who don't appreciate how a bunch of guys talk to each other. I'm constantly on alert, always watching what I say."

"Ugh," Cilla groaned. "Exhausting. It's like prepping for trial. I have to craft my openings, my questions, my closings, just so. I go over and over and over it. It can be maddening."

He peered down at her, meeting her gaze under a moonlit sky. "Where the hell have *you* been all my life?"

At that, she grinned. "You stole my line." She snuggled closer, brought her hand up, resting it on his chest.

That was kinda nice. Just . . . casual. Relaxed.

"Would your family be upset if you moved out?"

Thinking about that made his dinner tumble inside his belly. "Probably. Ash did it. Hell, he left BARS altogether. I love working for BARS, so I'm not going anywhere on that front."

Opening her hand, she drummed her fingers against his chest, lighting something up inside him and sending the little brain below his waist thinking things he shouldn't be thinking.

Things like ditching their clothes, rolling her to her back and . . .

"So," she said, "you're going with the argument that it's not as bad as Ash?"

"Bet your sweet ass. Wouldn't be the first time one of us has thrown the other under a bus."

She cracked up. Just let out a belly laugh that warmed him right to his goddamned soul.

"You've got a great laugh," he said.

"Thanks. Haven't used it a lot lately. Feels good."

She snuggled closer. Leaned her cheek against his chest and ran her hand over his stomach. And, uh-oh, if she kept that up...

He cleared his throat and gently set his hand on top of hers, stopping her exploration.

"I like you," she said. "A lot. I like kissing you and talking to you and lying in an open field together on a cold night while staring at stars."

"All good things."

"They are. And something I'm not used to. But you have to know what you're getting into with me. My father can be aggressive. I can figure out how to limit his access, how to find some balance, but he's part of the package. And now, with him being so mad at me, we may be at war with each other. Who knows how he'll behave. Are you up for that?"

CILLA WAITED FOR THE ANSWER SHE DESPERATELY WANTED, but probably wouldn't hear. Cruz Blackwell was a total catch. A stud among studs.

Why would he subject himself to the drama that came with Darren Randolph?

Maybe for me.

Barely knowing each other, did she have the right to ask that?

Moonlight shined down, spraying silvery highlights across his dark curly hair that hung nearly to his shoulders and gave him an almost angelic quality.

Cruz might not be an angel in the traditional sense, but he might be *hers.*

The thought alone was a minor miracle, since the implosion of her parents' relationship had destroyed any chance of Cilla being a romantic. The whole dating thing irritated her. Too much thinking. Too much questioning. None of it natural the way she wanted to believe falling in love should be.

Right now, looking at Cruz gave her . . . what? Peace? Hope?

No.

Faith.

Dammit, she might be a romantic after all.

"You know," he said, "I mentioned to you that when I was younger, I got in trouble. A lot."

Cilla's chest collapsed. She'd allowed herself to be vulnerable, to take a chance that maybe, just maybe, having a man in her life, a good, solid man unafraid to take on Darren Randolph, might make her happy, and Cruz wanted to reminisce?

When Cruz didn't continue, Cilla helped him along. "Yes. Too much energy, you said."

"Yeah. But it was more than that. Ask me why I got in trouble?"

Where the hell was this going? All she needed was a straight answer. Yes, he could deal with Randolph drama or no, not happening. Fairly simple.

However, Cruz, so far, didn't strike her as a guy who avoided conflict. He ran straight toward it.

Clearly, he was trying to make a point.

"All right," she said, "I'll play. Why did you get in trouble?"

"I loved fighting. Twisted as it may sound, it released stress. I was good at it. I don't know why, but I always knew how to win."

"Some people have that instinct."

"Like your dad?"

Whoa. She'd never say that. Two completely different

men, and yet, maybe that side of Cruz reminded her of Dad. How they never backed away from conflict. She closed her eyes. *Please don't tell me I'm one of those women wanting a man like my father.*

That would put her over the edge.

She opened her eyes. "I'm not comparing you to my father. Totally different. You're kind. You don't manipulate situations, at least not that I can see. I'm just saying, some people have that warrior instinct."

Overhead, clouds shifted, blocking the moonlight and plunging them into blackness. He locked his gaze on her and even in the darkness she saw it. That spark of heat.

He held his hand out and, working on instinct, she grabbed hold and he wrapped his fingers around hers.

"I'm one of those people, Cilla. I love battle. And winning. It's why my folks got me into wrestling. They figured if I needed to put hands on people, maybe I could find a constructive way to do it. They were right. It helped me tunnel that desire. Instead of wanting to pummel someone for no reason, I could do it legitimately and become a state champion. Wrestling changed my life. Anyway, back to you asking me if I'm up for dealing with your father. Darren and me? We share that love of battle and winning." He squeezed her hand. "I understand what drives him, Cilla. I'm not afraid of it. I embrace that shit. And if he does something I don't like, I'll throw his sorry ass on the pile with the rest of the guys I've kicked the crap out of. So, when you ask if I'm up for dealing with your father, the answer is yes. No problem there. Ever."

Oh.

My.

Cilla suspected that her hormonal function had just

gone bonkers, because on a chilly fall night, a furnace blast erupted inside her and sweat beaded on her neck.

And she was way too young for hot flashes.

Cruz Blackwell might be too good to be true. For years, Cilla had dated and experienced Mr. Right Now. Slick-suited men willing to use Darren Randolph's daughter to further their careers. Then there were the others who wouldn't go near Dad. Too afraid to piss him off and make an enemy.

Powerful men. Intimidating.

Enter Cruz Blackwell. A guy completely throwing her off her game.

She slid her hand from his and scooted even closer. He brought his arm up, pulling her into him. Curling into his warmth, she rested her head on his shoulder and ran her hand over his chest, her fingers exploring the rock-hard planes of his torso. Oh, she needed to see him naked.

She looked up, taking in his short beard and fantastic curls. Never, ever, would she have expected him. Rough-edged Cruz might be just what she needed.

Once again, she moved her hand over his chest, inching it down and feeling his tight abs through the soft cotton of his shirt. "I like being with you."

"That's good. I enjoy it, too." He set his hand over hers, stopping its movement. "But, honey, you've got to stop touching me like that. Totally killing me."

Didn't that give her a rush? She straightened up, met his eye, and bit her lip to smother a smile.

She slipped her hand free. "What exactly is killing you?" She stroked down his torso again. "Is it this?"

His eyes fluttered closed, and he tipped his head back. She'd love to know what he might be thinking. What little fantasy rolled in his brain.

Whatever it was, he let out a low groan and Cilla's body

responded. Every nerve ending exploded, sending tingles rocketing from her crotch straight to her nipples.

She had to have him.

They'd be perfection together. She knew it. A couple of feral animals going at it. Hard, fast, and completely unhinged.

The release would be amazing.

She dragged her fingers over him, getting dangerously close to the button on his jeans and then stroking back up as she leaned in, getting close to his ear, her breast brushing against his arm. "Tell me, Cruz," she whispered. "Do you like this? Is it what's *killing* you?"

"Oh, boy. Playing with fire, Cilla. Just sayin'."

She licked his ear. A fast strike that made him flinch. "What if I like fire?"

He turned his head, met her gaze, his focus laser sharp. "Then I'd roll you on your back and make you come in no less than ten different ways that would make us both extremely happy. *If* that's what you wanted."

She considered that. What woman could spend time with a man like Cruz—kind and honorable and . . . protective . . . and not want him inside her?

Not her. That's for sure. She wanted everything he'd give. "Go for it," she said.

14

CRUZ HAD TO BE OUT OF HIS MIND.

Jesus, he was like a horny teenager about to humiliate himself.

But she'd just green-lighted him and in the state he was in, his very hard state, his body had drop-kicked any rational thought about taking this slow and her being a client, blah, blah, blah.

All he knew was he'd never had a client put her hands on him like this.

Madness. Fucking fantastic madness.

Lifting his free hand, he dug his fingers into her hair, gripping the strands lightly. "You sure? Tell me to stop and I'll stop."

"I wouldn't have told you to go if I wanted you to stop. I say what I mean, Cruz. Always."

Go time.

In an instant, she was on her back, the two of them frantically tugging at each other's clothes, working zippers on jeans and trying like hell to maneuver out of them. Damn, he was about to explode.

Condom. Fucking condom.

Shit. Wallet. He had an emergency one there. But, *shit, shit, shit!* Where was it? Probably in his suite.

No. Wait.

Glove box. He'd thrown the wallet in there after lunch in Asheville. Had he taken it out? He shook his head. Couldn't remember.

"Wait." He hopped to his feet. "Don't move, Cilla. Don't fucking move!"

"What?" She gawked at him. "Where are you *going*?"

Zipping his jeans, he jumped off the tailgate and threw his hands up. "I wasn't prepared for this! We were supposed to be stargazing and you turned into a horny wench. I need a condom. My wallet better be in my glove box or I'm going back to the house tent-poled."

Behind him, Cilla cracked up, the full belly laugh that split his face into a smile he couldn't help. What a freaking fiasco.

He hustled to the passenger side, ripped open the door, and popped the button on the glove box.

Wallet.

"Bing-o!" he sang, his voice way too hap-hap-happy.

"Hallelujah!" she shouted back, her voice equally hap-hap-happy.

He ran to the back of the truck, boosted himself up, and found Cilla already shoeless and wiggling out of her skintight jeans.

He grabbed the comforter, tossing it to her while he unzipped, kicked off his shoes and socks, and dropped trou.

"Shirt too," Cilla said. "I know it's cold, but . . ." She held up the comforter. "We'll throw this over us. All I know is I've been thinking about you with your shirt off and I want it off."

"Jesus," he laughed. "No pressure or anything."

Still, he ripped his shirt over his head. No problem there. He knew his body. And his ten percent body fat.

Naked as a newborn, he stood over Cilla, still in her underwear and shirt. He pointed. "I'm freezing my ass off and you're still half dressed. Get going."

She let out a whoop, tugged her shirt off and then her bra while he did his thing with the condom.

Creamy white skin flashed against the darkness. Later, when they got inside, he'd leave every light on so he could look at her. Every inch. Every curve.

All for him.

He grabbed the blanket, flipped it over him, and hit his knees. "My God," he said, "I'm about to freaking explode. I'm like a teenager getting laid for the first time."

"Good," she said. "We can take our time later."

She gripped his shoulders, digging her nails in and yanked him down on top of her. "I want you inside me. Right. *Now*."

Day-am. Talk about fantasies.

"Well, honey, I aim to please."

He hooked his hands under her knees, shoved her legs up and—boom—drove into her. The two of them cried out and she pumped her hips, urging him on.

"Harder," she said.

Doing as he was told, he pushed into her again, easing out and then back in, each time, a little harder.

She cried out and he pulled free of her. "Sorry!"

She groaned, dug her fingers into his hair and tugged. "Harder," she said. "Pull out again and I might have to kill you."

Being the obliging sort, he slammed himself into her, then lowered himself on top, rocking his hips slowly, in and out, in and out. He nuzzled into her hair, moving his lips over her ear. "You know," he said, "I don't respond well to threats. I've always been rebellious that way."

Slowly, he moved his hips, torturing her with the pace.

"Look at me," she said.

Angling back, he met her gaze and she brought her hands to his cheeks. "Have I mentioned I love rebellious men?"

Then she clamped her hands over his ass and pumped her hips, driving him closer and closer to that edge he didn't want to reach. Not yet.

"Honey," he said, "keep that up and this'll be over quick."

"Harder," she said. "Please. I'm right there with you. Dammit, Cruz! Don't. Stop!" She brought her hands back up to his face. "I love this. This is . . . perfection."

That did it. He reared back, changing the angle and once again shoving her knees up. "I want to hear you scream, Cilla. It's just us out here. No one will hear you."

He pumped and pumped and pumped. In his hands, her legs stiffened. Close. So close.

"Come on, sweetheart," he whispered. "I've got you."

He sure did. Hopefully forever.

But, jeez, if she didn't come soon, he'd leave her in the dust. He changed the angle again, hoping beyond hope they'd explode together.

She lifted her head, stared right at him. "Don't stop. Don't, don't, don't!"

"Oh." Her body froze and she shoved at his shoulders, angling her head back.

Her cry shattered the quiet night air and the sound drove Cruz wild, sent his own tight body spiraling. He pumped his hips, faster, so close to that edge.

"You're amazing," Cilla said, her gaze on him.

Back in the game after her own orgasm, she lifted her hips, rotating them, banging against him, the whole thing rougher than he'd have wanted for their first time, but . . .

His eyes nearly exploded and his body bucked. Hard. He rode it out, focused on the release and that massive high he knew would leave him in seconds.

So good.

He let go of Cilla's legs and collapsed on top of her, catching himself before he crushed her.

"Holy shit," he said, trying to catch his breath. "You might be the love of my life."

"Oh, Cruz Blackwell." She reached up, set her hand on the back of his head and stroked his hair. "Ditto."

ONE THING ABOUT PRISCILLA RANDOLPH, ESQUIRE. SHE didn't screw around. No bullshit, no waffling back and forth. About anything.

Including buying an office.

Cruz loved it.

The morning after a truly stupendous night of love-making Cruz definitely wanted a repeat of and would remember until his dying day, he and Cilla left the Friary, each in their own vehicles. They'd met thirty minutes ago at a one-story, brick office that had once been a residential bungalow in downtown Asheville. She'd apparently seen the space online a week ago and liked what she called the cottagey feel. He couldn't disagree. The minute he stepped inside it felt . . . good. In a fixer-upper sort of way.

Now, after they'd done two passes through, she stood in what would be the reception area and did a slow circle, eyeing the marred paint and holes along the wall. How many pictures did the previous tenants hang?

"It needs work," Cruz offered.

"It does. All cosmetic, though. And look at the tin ceilings? I'd bet those are original. A fresh coat of paint and it'd be stunning."

Cruz shrugged. "I'm not a decorator, but yeah, they're pretty cool."

She pointed at the bay window along the front of the building. "Plenty of sun probably comes in here. We make this the seating area." She swung around, gesturing with one hand. "Receptionist would be here in one of those U-shaped desks."

Before he'd visualized it, Cilla was off, hustling down the hallway where she stopped in front of an open door. "I don't need five rooms so maybe we can knock out this wall, connect the two rooms and make it a conference room. I wonder if that's a load-bearing wall."

Stepping behind her in the doorway, Cruz peered inside. "If it is, you put a beam in. It'll be four or five grand, but if it's what you want, it could probably be done."

She nodded. "It's what I want."

On the move again, she strode by the next office, this one on the right. "Layla will be here. She'll love her own office. And not having to answer phones."

Like he said, no bullshit. No waffling. The woman knew what she wanted.

At the end of the hallway sat a bathroom on the left, a set of French doors and another office on the right.

Cilla ducked her head in the bathroom. "I'll rip this out and put in new."

While she was in the bathroom, Cruz glanced out the French doors to a courtyard surrounded by other single structure offices.

Just outside the doors, a cement patio with broken edges and deep cracks begged for a redo. "Patio is rough."

"I saw that. Ripping that up too. I'll put in a stamped patio and some nice outdoor furniture."

Behind him, she darted across the hall into the last room. He followed and found her dead center, her gaze darting all around. "This would be my office."

She did a slow 360 turn, taking in the windows lining two of the four walls.

"Oh my!" she squealed.

Cilla squealing? Total pisser, that and Cruz couldn't help smiling. She made him smile. Particularly when naked and on top of him.

"The natural light," she said, "is amazing. All I'll need here is fresh paint. I'll leave the windows bare. Maybe some shades, but no curtains. That way I can look out at the trees in the courtyard."

"It sounds like you love this place."

She raised her arms in victory. "I love this place!"

Then she marched over to him and laid a monster smacking kiss on his lips.

He stood, half-stunned for a second and then—why not? —slid his arms around her, his hands running along the soft fabric of her suit jacket and settling at the base of her spine.

She made a move to pull back—not so fast, sweetheart —but he held her there, softening the kiss, letting his lips brush hers and taking in the minty taste of her breath.

Kissing Cilla? Making love to Cilla? Nice.

Forget nice. Superb. And not in a slam-bam, let-me-get-laid-and-move-on way. This?

Different.

A fine-ass different that he was in no rush to see end.

"Mmmm," she murmured, easing back from the kiss. She

held up her wrist and poked at her watch. "I love this, however, I'm on a schedule so we'll have to pick it up later."

The lady lawyer had shit to do. She'd warned him about her schedule and times she'd be forced to walk out on him.

Somehow, knowing he'd have to do the same at some point, he didn't mind.

Mutual understanding might be a beautiful thing.

He nodded. "I'll look forward to it."

"Oh, me too, fella. Me too. Now, I'm calling the realtor and getting this train moving. I want to be in here in three weeks."

AFTER CILLA FINISHED WITH THE REALTOR, MAKING AN OFFER thirty grand below asking, Cruz followed her to the court-house, ensuring her safe arrival. Something she hadn't argued with him over, considering the whole bullet-on-her-car episode. At the courthouse, she bid him a joyful and rushed goodbye.

The woman had fantastic energy. All fast-moving, get-shit-done energy that Cruz enjoyed.

He watched her go, waiting until she entered the court-house before hopping back in his truck to make his way home.

Too bad Cilla had to work or he'd have treated her to a late breakfast at one of the cafés. Asheville had always been a tourist hot spot, but Cruz, as somewhat of a local, never minded the constant activity. The restaurants and culture inspired him. Settled his soul in a way wrestling and bar fights used to.

To avoid a mini-traffic jam, he made a left down a tree-lined street occupied by a mix of single and two-story homes. Great location right here. Walking distance to bars and restaurants. Suddenly, he envisioned strolling through Asheville with Cilla after picking her up at her new office.

What the hell was wrong with him, daydreaming about couple shit? Too many women around the Friary, that was the problem.

On his right, a glossy white realtor sign caught his eye and being nosey, he lifted his foot off the gas. House for sale. A blue Craftsman with white columns and trim. Not too big. Not too small. Damned fine house.

Enough so that he hooked a U-turn, swung back for another look, and found his foot on the brake, slowing the truck to a crawl.

He might paint it a lighter blue like the one in his suite at the Friary. His mom called it cornflower blue and he liked the soothing warmth to it.

Out of curiosity, he pulled to the curb and shifted to park. The realtor sign had a QR code. Maybe he'd look. Just to see the asking price.

He had a place to live. One most would kill for. Except there were a whole lot of people in that home now. Each with their own quirks and habits and needs and—Jesus—he could never relax. In his own suite he'd hear people talking or in the hallway and it reminded him. Reminded him that things had changed. And they'd never go back to what it was before.

Maybe that was his problem. He wanted it back the way it was. Without all the people. Something that, in the grand scheme, didn't have a lick to do with Maddy, Liv, and Lena, specifically. Cilla was right. It might just be too many people.

He sat back, let that sink in. These last few months, he'd beat up on himself. What kind of guy hates his brothers' girlfriends for existing? That made him a class-A jerk. No wonder his father had been so hard on him growing up. Over and over, his brain railed on him. Warned him to be nice to the women. To everybody. To be happy for them.

Happy. Happy. Happy.

And he was. Down deep. He loved his brothers. He'd waste no time stepping in front of a train to save them. Every one of them.

He just didn't want to live with all these people.

Resting his head back, he closed his eyes and smiled as relief took hold. "I'm not an asshole."

Well, sometimes he was, but not about the women. He simply needed space.

He opened his eyes, turned, and peered at the house. Not that he was in the market, but . . . investment property. He'd make it a vacation rental to cover expenses and then, when it wasn't booked, he'd have an escape. A place to go for a break from cohabitating.

Yeah. Why not?

He scanned the code and pulled up the listing. Three bedroom, two bath, eighteen hundred square feet.

And a detached garage.

"Ooh-wee," he said. "You just want me to love you, don't you?"

He took another gander at the house, put the truck in drive until he reached the driveway. At the end, all the way at the rear of the property sat the garage. A *two*-car garage where he could park the Stutz on one side and have a workshop on the other.

Working on nothing but pure adrenaline, Cruz dialed the realtor.

15

DELIGHTED OVER THE IDEA OF OWNING HER OWN OFFICE, Cilla breezed into the courtroom, inhaling the stale, closed-in air that she never minded because everything about this place charged her. Her soon-to-be-pled-out client, Donovan Jenkins, trailed behind.

There was something about a hundred-year-old building, the rich history, oiled benches, and towering ceiling that made her pulse thrum.

In front of her, the empty judge's bench loomed. Large and imposing, its glossy finish caught the glare of the overhead light.

One day, maybe she'd sit there, presiding over her own courtroom.

Maybe.

Someday . . .

Making her way down the aisle, her heels clickety-clacked against marble, drawing the attention of Rick Bandy, who perused his notes at the prosecution table. Cilla pointed her client in the direction of the defense table and offered a cheery good morning to Rick.

Cilla had worked with him on several cases and had found him to be more than competent. Sure, there'd been the usual tricks—she'd busted him on all of them—but for the most part? Stand-up guy.

He stood, shook her hand, and they exchanged small talk about the long security line to get in the building.

Chitchat complete, Cilla swung her briefcase on top of the defense table, unloading her portfolio while waiting for the judge to come in and settle this matter. Then she'd be on her way. Done.

A familiar voice sounded behind her. Was that . . .?

No way.

Cilla turned, spotted her father—what was he doing here?—talking with a reporter she recognized from the NBC affiliate. The man could spot media people a mile away.

She stood with her gaze pinned to him and his Baroni suit, while she shuffled through reasons he might be in an Asheville courtroom this morning.

Had something happened to Mom? Some emergency he might know of? Her chest tightened, the thump of her heart echoing in her ears.

She'd checked her phone before coming into the courtroom and there'd been nothing.

Finally, Dad broke from the reporter and met her gaze, holding it for a long few seconds that sent tension curling down her arms. No emergency. She knew this for sure. If there had been, since court hadn't started yet, Dad would have marched straight for her.

"All rise," the bailiff said.

Time to go to work.

Cilla faced front, gave her suit jacket a light tug and adjusted her cuffs. All neat and tidy and ready for action.

The clerk, a woman in her mid-forties with a scowl

carved into her face, called the hearing to order. Judge Nagle entered and took his seat on the bench. He wore a dark robe with a red tie peeking from underneath. His thinning gray hair was combed back away from his face, accentuating his heavy jowls and large nose.

Nagle.

He and Dad were golfing buddies. Maybe *that's* what brought her father to court this morning. Could be lunch afterward.

"Court is now in session," Judge Nagle said. "Please have a seat. Counsel, please state your appearances again?"

Both Cilla and Rick stood.

"Good morning, Your Honor," Rick said. "Rick Bandy for the government."

"Priscilla Randolph for the defendant, Your Honor. And Mr. Donovan Jenkins is here as well."

Rick and Cilla reclaimed their seats and the judge peered at Cilla. "Ms. Randolph, visiting from Charlotte today, I see."

She smiled. "I go where my clients need me, Your Honor."

"Good to know. Okay. I understand the parties have finally reached a plea agreement."

"Yes, Your Honor," Cilla and Rick said.

"All right then." He cut a glance at her, then to Rick. "I've read through the most recent signed version, and although I generally honor plea agreements, in this case, I find the sentencing options completely inadequate." His gaze came back to Cilla, giving each of them equal parts of his attention. "After much consideration, I can't find one justifiable reason to accept this agreement. The charges here allege greed and selfishness that caused financial ruin for victims. Therefore, I'm rejecting this agreement."

Wait. What? Cilla cocked her head. Did he just say . . .?

Beside her, Donovan leaned closer, bumping her arm. "What's going on?"

Good question. In ten years of criminal work, she'd never had a judge reject a deal.

Until now. Until her father unexpectedly showed up to watch a proceeding that he had zero connection to other than his friendship with the judge.

Cilla lifted her hand, silencing her client while her mind went warp speed, her thoughts banging around like bumper cars. "I'm sorry, Your Honor. You're rejecting the agreement?"

"Good to know your hearing is intact, Ms. Randolph. Yes. I'm rejecting the agreement. How would you like to proceed?"

Um, no idea.

Pushing her shoulders back, she took a second to organize her zipping thoughts. *No guilty plea.* Donovan wouldn't be pleading to anything until she and Rick figured this mess out.

"Your Honor," Cilla said, "my client would like to withdraw his guilty plea. We also request a continuance so we may confer with the government."

Nagle peered down at her over the rim of his black-framed reading glasses. "As long as the government has no objection, you can file a written motion and I'll grant the continuance." Nagle swung his head to Rick. "Mr. Bandy?"

Rick paused for a few seconds, clearly as stunned as Cilla. "No objection, Your Honor. I'll be in touch with Ms. Randolph on this."

"Fine," Nagle said. "Does the government agree to the continuation of current bail conditions?"

"The government does, Your Honor."

"I order continuation of bail." Nagle brought his attention back to Cilla. "Anything else, Ms. Randolph?"

Cilla shook her head. "No, Your Honor. Thank you."

"Then we are in recess. Back to the drawing board, counselors."

BLOOD ROARING, CILLA MARCHED TO THE COURTROOM DOOR, her heels once again clickety-clacking, but this time the sound didn't take her back to the decadence of marble floors and well-oiled woods.

Now? Pissed. Royally.

This was a solid deal that had taken hours and hours of negotiating, and the judge had simply tossed it.

On her way to the door, she met Dad's eye and . . .

The smirk. That triumphant tilt of his lips she'd seen repeatedly when his machinations came to fruition.

Nothing about this situation should make him happy. He'd spent half his time touting his brilliant daughter's success. This? Humiliating.

If she wanted to be truthful, the origin of his dismay wouldn't be for Cilla and her loss. He'd have to face his cronies after years of relentless bragging.

As much as she'd like to stop and question his presence, Cilla had a furious client storming ahead of her. She'd have to talk him down. Keep him from tweeting or making statements or doing just about anything that would aggravate Nagle.

After pushing through the heavy oak courtroom door, Donovan angled back, and she pointed to an empty bench where she set her briefcase down and faced him. The blast of rage should have blown her back a week.

"What," he said through gritted teeth, "the fuck happened? I thought we were done."

That made two of them. She'd be lucky if he didn't fire her. Still, she didn't appreciate his tone. She folded her arms, lifted her chin. "Occasionally, judges reject deals. Go home. Keep your phone close while I speak to the prosecutor."

Donovan gawked. "That's what you have to say? You've *completely* fucked this up."

Oh, please. *She* fucked it up? Perhaps her client should question his total lack of moral compass that had allowed him to break more than a dozen finance laws.

"I understand this is frustrating. But there's a process. I'll fix it."

Behind him, the courtroom door swung open. "There's the prosecutor," she said. "I'll call you."

Before Bandy got away, she grabbed her briefcase, side-stepped her raging client, and charged.

"Rick," she called, squeezing between a few people in the hallway and catching up. "Hold up."

He kept walking, but glanced back at her, his cheeks as saggy as she felt. "Hey, Cilla. Before you start in, I don't know what that was. I'm just as pissed. I've got cases stacked to my ass and Nagle goes rogue?"

"What could have spooked him?"

"I don't know. Let me see what I can find out."

Cilla nodded. "Okay. Let me know if I can do anything."

"Will do."

Bandy strode off, probably to track down Judge Nagle and ask him WTF?

"Hello."

Dad's voice. From behind her. In the middle of the

towering hallway, she spun back, spotted him walking toward her among a handful of other folks.

She stood still, briefcase in hand until he reached her. He leaned in, gave her their customary cheek peck. "Morning."

Yesterday, he'd hurled a paperweight and thrown her out of his office. Today? Like nothing ever happened.

Life with Dad.

The entire thing exhausted her. Made her feel . . . small. And she despised that. This must have been how her mother felt. Always on alert. Waiting for the next eruption from her moody and volatile husband.

Cilla took a tiny step back, putting just enough distance between them to look straight into his eyes. "I'm surprised to see you here after our argument yesterday."

He shrugged his beefy shoulders in that "eh" way he used when either stalling or screwing people. Here, she hadn't figured out which. Could be both.

"You know me," he said, keeping his voice light. "I support you. Thought I'd see you in action." He held his hand to the courtroom doors. "Rough day for the defense. What's your plan?"

"Aside from figuring out how a done deal went off the rails?"

The corner of Dad's mouth quirked. "Aside from that."

Not wanting bystanders overhearing the conversation, Cilla pulled Dad off to a nook of useless space at the end of the corridor.

"I'm confused," she said. "Nagle is always so reasonable. And that was a fair deal."

"He must not have liked something."

Ya think? She'd mentioned to Dad the day before that Nagle, his golfing buddy, had been sick.

"You and Judge Nagle are friends," Cilla said. "Have you talked to him?"

"Huh," Dad said.

That was his response? No useful information that might help her. Just "huh." Could he have ...

No way. Screwing with people was one thing. This was her client's freedom in jeopardy.

Still, Nagle's rejection was so completely out of character. Someone had to have influenced him. Someone like Darren Randolph, who made it a mission to know juicy details about anyone who might, at some point, prove helpful.

Plus, her father enjoyed vengeance. If he felt he'd been wronged, look out. He took fantastic pleasure in showing folks just how much power and influence he wielded. She'd known this for years, witnessed it with her own mother.

Sweat pooled in her palms, the slick surface making her briefcase slip. She squeezed the handle tighter. "Dad?"

"Yes?"

She focused on his eyes, on holding his gaze and forcing him to look at her. "Are you messing with my cases to get back at me for yesterday?"

He cocked one eyebrow. "Now, Cilla, is that a nice thing to say? After all I've done for you?"

No denial. No outrage over her accusation.

The hot stab of pain shot through her ribcage. *Stab, stab, stab.* She breathed through it, concentrated on her father's eyes and not on the betrayal.

Not on the fact that a man she'd loved forever, despite his flaws, and who supposedly adored her, could do this.

She shook her head, let out a soft huff. "Dad, I've done nothing but try to help and protect you."

"As have I."

She squeezed the briefcase tighter. Tension ripped through her knuckles. "Dad, if you did this, you've just cost my client years in prison. It's not me you're punishing. It's my client, who has nothing to do with this."

"Well, Priscilla, based on what he's done, maybe it's what should have happened. Maybe Nagle thought the deal wasn't punishment enough."

And, oh, there it was.

The admission without the admission.

She blinked and blinked again, trying to absorb it. Her father, who'd supported her career in every way possible, had just dismantled her case.

After taking all the free legal advice and disrupting her days whenever he pleased, he'd sabotaged her.

His own daughter.

Her world crumbled. The one man she'd actually trusted and he'd let her down.

What a mess. Blowing out a hard breath, she sighed. "What'd you do? Call in a favor or promise one?"

Now his gaze heated, his pupils shrinking to a pinhole. "Careful, Cilla. That's a strong accusation."

"Oh, Dad." She caught her breath, squeezed her eyes closed because never—ever—had she been on the receiving end of his venom.

She'd learned a few things growing up. Witnessed his ruthlessness firsthand when he'd used Cilla for leverage during his and Mom's divorce. He'd put Cilla smack in the middle, making sure she knew her mother would pay, somehow, she'd pay, if Cilla moved with her overseas.

The worst of it? The absolute horror that Cilla had never fully allowed herself to consider until this very second? None of it was about what was best for her.

Now, standing in front of her father with that gleaming

spark in his eye, she finally understood. Finally experienced how far Dad would go to get his way.

"Should have known then," Cilla said.

"Pardon?"

"I *said*, I should have known then. Meaning when I was twelve and you and Mom were at war, and you gave her an ultimatum. I'd have to stay with you or you'd make her suffer."

"I never said that."

"Come on, Dad. You knew what you were doing. Manipulating a woman who had no power."

Rage fueling her, Cilla stepped closer, got right into his personal space. "I'm not twelve anymore. I support myself. Keep sabotaging my cases and you'll see what I'm capable of. After all, I am my father's daughter."

Then she turned. Walking away from someone she'd never imagined would betray her. That alone devastated her.

"Cilla! You come back here," Dad thundered, his words echoing against the ancient marble.

People in the corridor turned, looking at her as she hustled to the staircase and then behind her to the unhinged man screaming at her.

"Are you okay?" a man asked.

No. After this, she'd never be okay.

"I'm fine," she said. "Thank you."

Then she marched down the steps, leaving her father behind.

16

Cilla pushed through the courthouse's door and glanced back. No Dad.

Good.

At least he wouldn't make a scene by following her.

I'm okay.

I'm okay.

She thought she was, anyway. Time would tell. Still, someone to talk to wouldn't be a bad thing.

She made her way down the stairs, walking to the park across the street where she plopped on a stone bench. She dragged her phone from her briefcase and spotted a text.

Cruz. Wishing her good luck.

She checked the time stamp. He'd sent it just before she'd walked into the courtroom, but she'd already silenced her phone and stowed it.

She tapped on his contact and hit the phone icon because he might be exactly what she needed right now.

Strong, calm Cruz who seemed to bring order and reason when there was none.

"Hey," his deep voice came through the phone line. "You done already?"

"Oh, I'm done alright."

"Yikes," he said. "That doesn't sound good. Didn't go well?"

"The judge rejected the deal."

"No way. That's a thing?"

"It doesn't happen often, but it just did."

"Jeez, Cilla. I'm sorry. You worked so hard on that."

Yes. Yes, she had and it took a man she was just getting to know to recognize that when her own father hadn't. If Dad had noticed, it obviously didn't matter to him.

"Thank you," she said. "You have no idea how much that means to me right now."

"Good and, hey, I'm still in town. Can you meet me?"

She perked up. Given what just happened, the last thing she should do is play hooky with Mr. Delicioso.

But maybe a quick visit might help her decompress. "Want to grab lunch? I'd planned on heading back to Charlotte, but . . . I could use the break."

"Would love to. In fact, since I helped you this morning, maybe you can help me."

"Of course. What do you need?"

"You inspired me. I'm about to look at a house. Wanna come with me? We'll make it a two-fer. You look at the house and then at lunch you can tell me about your shitty hearing. Deal?"

She shouldn't. She *should* figure out how to salvage her mess of a case and keep her client from doing time he didn't necessarily deserve. All because of her father's petty revenge.

Not to mention that she had an upcoming murder trial to prep for. Work, work, work. All the time.

A couple of hours with Cruz would be nice. Very nice. Plus, she always enjoyed house hunting. And, hello? He's looking for a house?

In Asheville.

He'd failed to mention that.

"Deal," she said. "Where are you?"

"I'll text you the address. It's about five miles from the office we looked at this morning."

She stood. "Okey-dokey. I'll be there in fifteen."

"No problem. The realtor can't get here. He's gonna let me in remotely."

After touring an adorable Craftsman-style cottage, Cilla and Cruz stood on the curb while he took one last look. Then he turned to her, leveling those amazing eyes on her.

"What happened in court?"

Funny guy. "I have a million questions about this house, and you want to know about my day?"

"Yeah." He gestured to the house. "I don't know. I mean, it's a great house, but am I being hasty?"

Interesting. "I see. Who knew you were looking?"

He laughed. "I wasn't. I was trying to avoid traffic and drove by it. Something drew me to it. That sounds weird, doesn't it?"

"Not in the least."

Nodding, he peered back at the house. "I was thinking an investment property. I could rent it as a vacation home and then come and stay here when I want."

"Sounds like a solid investment."

Waving it off, he turned back to her. "We'll talk about it later. What happened in court?"

She let out a soft groan. "I don't know. Like I said, the judge rejected the deal and told us to try again. Did I mention the judge is my father's golfing buddy? Never had an issue in his court before now."

She waited a beat, let that sink in. For both of them. *Dammit, Dad.* Another bout of soul-crushing agony stabbed at her.

Later. She'd deal with the emotional fallout later. For now, she'd focus on how to help her client.

"Is it a coincidence," Cruz said, "that we were poking around Morgan and now your father's buddy screwed you?"

She reached up, pressed her finger against his nose. "Precisely. Technically, he screwed my client, but yes, I suspect my father called the judge. Worse, he showed up in court this morning to watch."

Cruz gawked, his mouth dropping open like something out of an old cartoon. Any other time, she'd find it funny.

"He all but admitted it," she said. "He's punishing me for nosing around in his business."

"Wow. He is ruthless. His own daughter."

Yes. His own daughter. She shook her head, pulled her gaze from his because those eyes? Too beautiful. Too stormy. Too . . . everything. Cruz's eyes made her want to curl into him, take comfort from a man when she'd always prided herself on not needing that.

But it would be so nice to just . . . have someone.

Her throat clogged. Ignoring it, she stared at the pretty cottage with its blazing white trim and blinked back tears. Crying? When's the last time that happened?

Shoving that nastiness away, she looked back at Cruz. "My failing would be continually letting my father get away with his stunts and manipulations. I still do it. Like my office. Before I moved into his building, I knew he'd be barging in asking for legal advice. As if I'm his corporate in-house counsel, which by the way, he has. The guy's office is right down the hall. But the people around him, me included, have been conditioned to give him what he wants. He *knows* I'll eventually tell him what he wants to hear. That I'll offer a way to bend, not break the law. And I despise that. I despise that he puts me in that position. It's not right."

"Thus, the new office."

"It's far enough where I'll have distance. I think that's what I need. Distance to figure out how to have my dad just be my dad and not drive me mad all the time."

"And if you can't?"

"After he made my client collateral damage?" She shrugged. "I guess I can't have him in my life."

Then he was on her, pulling her into his arms and kissing the top of her head. "You're not the asshole here," he said, "he is. You know that, right? I mean, Brittney Tate has cancer. Probably from toxic sludge the former owner got from your father's company. You're not the asshole. You're a strong, caring woman who thought you were helping him."

I'm not the asshole.

She snuggled into him. Cradling her face into the crook of his neck and inhaling the clean scent of his soap while the hairs of his short beard tickled her forehead.

"If he keeps this up," she murmured, "he'll wreck my career."

"We won't let him."

We. That sounded so good. We.

She drew a hard breath and nodded like he could see her. "He's a bully," she said. "I know this."

Regrettably, he stepped back, taking all that glorious comfort with him.

He held her at arm's length and squeezed. "And the best way to get rid of a bully is?"

This she knew. Had learned from the best.

She knew what she had to do.

"Fight back," she said.

He jerked his head. "Damn straight. Come out to our place. We'll dig into more files, see what we can find that might back him off."

Yes. She liked that idea. He'd help her. His brothers would help her. It might be the only thing she was sure of right now, but it was something.

"Stay at our place tonight," he continued. "I'll show you around the property and you can decompress."

She *did* have extra clothes since she'd intended on being in Asheville for a few days. "Your family won't mind?"

"Given what just happened? No way. One thing I can promise is that we'll plan out how to fight a bully together."

Together. Oh, this man. Not only would he help her, but he also had the balls to take on Darren Randolph.

For that alone, she could love him.

AFTER A QUIET DINNER IN CRUZ'S SUITE—SHE WASN'T READY for dinner with the fam after her own father had sabotaged her—Cilla caught up on some e-mails and they added an insane romp, besides the ones the night before, to Cilla's sexual hall of fame.

Magic man, Cruz Blackwell.

He'd been gentle yet edgy. Not rough, but . . . something. Intense, maybe. Whatever it was, she liked it.

A lot.

Mired in a sleepy fog, she rolled sideways and smashed into what felt like a brick wall. She opened her eyes. A shaft of light from the living room squeaked under the closed door. Cruz's bedroom. Obviously, she'd fallen asleep after the romp. He must have done the same.

The sound of deep breathing whipped her mind to attention.

Beside her, Cruz, flat on his back, one hand thrown above his head, snoozed away, his ripped chest rising and falling with each breath. Even now, completely worn out and her body sore in places where she hadn't been sore in a very long time, she wanted more of whatever he might offer.

Passion, hugs, conversation, companionship. All of it.

How fascinating that this particular man, one unafraid of conflict, should come into her life just as Dad turned on her.

A bully. That's what Cruz had called her father. He wasn't wrong. She'd always known it, but hadn't experienced Dad's wrath firsthand. Then again, she'd never given him reason to turn on her. Maybe that was part of the problem. For years, she'd toed the line. Offering legal advice when he came dangerously close to breaking laws. In her own way, she'd managed him. Balanced keeping him satisfied while staying on the right side of the law.

All that changed when she'd run headlong into a ten-year-old with cancer.

She'd known the dangers of forever chemicals, and Dad's insistence over the years that his company followed EPA guidelines had eased her concerns. Each time the government banned a substance, Dad assured her they'd stopped using it.

Instead, it appeared he'd been lying. Brittany Tate became the catalyst Cilla needed to recognize the line she wouldn't cross. For anyone.

Now she needed to do something. But what?

Lying in bed with Cruz-the-hottie in the middle of the night and fantasizing about him inside her wouldn't solve her problems.

She didn't know *what* would solve her problems. And when that happened, when mental paralysis set in, she got moving.

Data.

That's what she needed.

She eased from under the covers, slipped into the T-shirt Cruz had thrown on the chair next to the bed, and tiptoed from the room, gently closing the door behind her. Earlier, she'd brought her tote with her laptop from the guest suite and had set it by the door.

Now, guided by the lit lamps, she grabbed the tote and settled onto the man-sized sectional. Unless her father had changed his password, she still had access to his files and could hunt around. For what, she wasn't sure, but she might find something that would confirm whether Randolph Industries was unleashing toxic levels of forever chemicals on the environment.

Firing up the laptop, she logged in and opened an incognito browser window. Who knew if that would keep her from getting caught, but couldn't hurt, right?

Once there, using Dad's credentials, she remotely logged into the server and found his files. Tons of them.

Literally years of work, right there in front of her.

She'd have to be methodical. Start at the root folders and work her way through.

First, she searched for PFAS and PFOA . . . wow . . . a lot of folders there. Her heart slammed and moisture flooded her palms. Whether it was guilt or fear or both she couldn't think too hard about it.

She skimmed the folders. Contract, financials, OSHA, legal.

Legal. Right up her alley. She clicked on it and another row of sub-folders popped up. All with what looked like surnames. Another click opened the one named Cartwright.

"Cilla?"

She lurched backward, the sound of Cruz's voice startling her and sending her pulse slamming.

Curly hair a raging and adorable mess of frizz, he stood in the bedroom doorway wearing only boxer briefs and the sight of him—all broad shoulders and cut muscles with that smattering of chest hair right down the middle—might be enough to lure her back to bed.

"Ooff." She forced out a breath. "You scared me."

"Sorry. It's three in the morning. What are you doing?"

"I couldn't sleep." She whirled a finger around her ear. "It happens sometimes. I wake up and my brain starts going."

"I get it. That happens to me. Zeke gets on me about it. What am I supposed to do? Lie in bed frustrated that I can't sleep?"

"Exactly."

He lowered himself into the spot next to her and pointed at the laptop. "If Rohan were here, he'd be in full security mode."

"Why?"

"He has software that blocks our IP address. He's a freak about it."

Cilla glanced back at the laptop. "Oh no. I'm so sorry. I didn't think about it."

"It's okay. You didn't know. But if you're good with it, we'll have him install the software."

"Of course. That's fine. Whatever you need."

"What are you working on?"

"Research. I used my father's login again. I thought if I could find files that mention PFAS or PFOA, I could determine how much he knows about Morgan contamination."

Cruz sat back and stacked his hands on top of his head, the position revealing that glorious chest she might never tire of.

Magic man.

He eyed her for a few seconds. She had been a trial lawyer long enough to recognize when someone had something to say.

She held her hand out. "What?"

He shrugged. "Are you ready for what you'll find?"

"You mean if my father is aware his company caused a ten-year-old to get cancer? No. I'll never be ready for that. But I'm a big girl and if they're poisoning people, they need to be stopped."

"I agree. Just making sure you'd considered all the angles. What can I help with?"

She went back to her laptop. "Nothing. One-person job. Go back to bed."

"Eh," he said. "I'm up. There's no way I can sleep knowing you're out here."

Understanding that all too well, she glanced around. "Got a printer? You can help read through some documents."

"Sure." He pointed at the laptop. "May I?"

She handed it over and stood. "Of course. Do you mind if I get a glass of water?"

"Help yourself. Glasses are in the cabinet by the sink."

While Cruz connected her laptop to the printer, she made her way to the kitchen, opening the cabinet to the right of the sink where—one, two, three—five bottles of whiskey stood like soldiers in perfect formation.

Wrong cabinet.

But, hello? How much whiskey did he drink that he needed five bottles on hand? Might this be the crack in his armor?

"Not there," Cruz said. "Next one."

Closing the cabinet, she found the correct one and filled a glass from the fridge dispenser.

Glass filled, she padded back to the living room where Cruz had apparently successfully connected her to the printer and now sat staring at her after her discovery of his stash.

"You can ask," he said. "About the bottles."

"All right. I'm assuming you're a whiskey drinker. Beyond that, is there anything I need to know?"

"I'm not . . ." He shook his head. "I don't think it's a problem. I'm stopping. Full disclosure. The last couple of months, I've fallen into the habit of a drink every night."

Every night. *Oh-kay.*

"Some nights," he continued, "more than others. Zeke called me out on it. The day before we flew to Nashville, Phin woke me up that morning. I didn't know I was supposed to fly that day and the night before I . . ."

He stopped. Dragged his hands through his hair and stared down at his feet for a few seconds before looking back at her.

Cilla rolled her hand. "Overindulged?"

"Yeah. I swear, I didn't know I had to fly." He shook it off. "Well, I shouldn't have let it happen and Zeke was as pissed at me as I'd ever seen. *That* scared me. After we got back from Nashville, he called me out on it. Said he'd seen the bottles in the trash."

"Ew. That had to be awkward."

"Uh, yeah." He met her gaze again. "I promise you, I haven't touched it since. Not one drop."

Double phew. "That's good. How's it been?"

"The first few days I felt off. Tired."

"You were probably detoxing."

He shrugged. "I guess. Then, my energy came back and we've been busy, so I haven't thought about it. I just . . . dang. I fucked up and I don't want my family disappointed in me."

First crack in the armor, indeed. She sat back, bumping his shoulder. "I kinda love that you're mature enough to own your mistakes."

"Hell, yes. It'll never happen again. Ever."

"Did you tell Zeke that?"

He shrugged. "Yes and no. At the time, I was pissed at him."

She snorted. "Men. You're all so stubborn. You need to talk to him. Assure him you've got it under control."

For a few seconds, he simply sat, taking that in. Now she'd see how determined he was to stay off the booze.

"Yeah," he finally said. "You're right. I'll do that in the morning."

Cilla jerked her head. "Excellent. And thank you for being honest. After seeing the bottles, I'd have wondered."

"Anyone would. I wanted you to know I'm not hiding it. I'll always be honest with you, Cilla. Being unfiltered is my fatal flaw."

"I prefer that. I don't enjoy deciphering messages." She patted his knee again and sat up. "As for the whiskey, you let me know if I can do anything. Otherwise, I'll assume you have it under control."

"I do. I'm done with the nightly stuff. Maybe even altogether. We'll see. Thank you."

"For what?"

"Hell, where do I start? Understanding. Being smart and kind."

She bumped his knee with hers. "You're human and deserve a little grace. We all do."

Maybe even her Dad. Maybe.

Taking a deep breath, she pointed to the laptop. "Now, let's get back to work since I want another round of hall-of-fame sex before I have to leave for work."

Cruz let out a low whistle. "Wicked woman."

She laughed, then sat forward to resume her hunt for information. Ten minutes later, after printing documents for Cruz, she landed on another folder entitled *Cases*. She clicked and the screen filled with a list of documents that had to be at least fifty deep. All PDFs. She clicked the first one.

Oh no. *No. No. No.*

A settlement agreement.

She perused the document, her gaze darting along, picking up certain words that made her *so* unhappy.

Closing that document, she went to the next agreement. Same language, different case.

Dammit, Dad.

Sickness swirled inside her and a weird thrumming bashed her ears and made her head pound.

Ignoring her rebelling body, she clicked on the next file. Then the next. Over and over again, all settlement agreements.

Cilla sat back and threw her hands over her face.

"Cilla?"

Pull it together. She had to. She'd simply compartmentalize. Treat it like a grisly case that required emotional control.

Total lawyer mode.

After a second, she brought her hands from her face and pointed at the laptop. "These are all settlement agreements over PFOA and PFAS contamination. Randolph Industries is quietly paying people off."

17

CRUZ SWUNG HIS HEAD TO THE LAPTOP SCREEN, SAW A LOAD of legalese that it was way too early to tackle, and went back to Cilla. "Settlement agreements for what?"

"I was skimming, but they all involved chemicals and the environment. The more we dig, the more I'm discovering things I don't want to know. Things that could cost Randolph tens of millions if they weren't buying people off."

Cruz scoffed. "We have a ten-year-old with cancer, who cares about money?"

Whoopsie. Too bad he hadn't employed the filter his family always begged for. *Shit.*

However, Cilla took it in stride.

"Gah!" she said. "I can't stop thinking about her. But if I do something, I'd be risking ruining my father's company and putting thousands out of work. Could you do it? If one of your brothers—your *mother*—did something like this? And please, don't tell me they wouldn't. I thought the same thing about my dad and look where I am."

He thought about that. About their family motto. *Family*

first. Through blood, through hate, through fear, through joy. No exceptions.

No exceptions.

He ran a hand over his face. Freaking three in the morning. Too tired for this. "Okay," he said. "I get it. I'm honestly not sure what I'd do. Let's think it through. Kick around some ideas."

She stood, walked the length of the room, then spun back, holding up a finger. "We should talk to Phin or Kayla."

"About?"

"Their EPA contacts. If EPA opens an investigation, I'd be out of it. There has to be a way to get them to do that."

Excellent idea. He boosted off the couch and headed for the bedroom thinking about all the ways his brother might kill him for waking him up in the middle of the night. And if Maddy had stayed over? Who the hell knew what he might be interrupting.

Certain things were more important than getting laid.

Or sleep.

He grabbed his phone from the nightstand and punched up Phin. Two rings in, a groan that sounded packed with broken concrete came through the phone line.

"This better be good."

Cruz winced. "It is. We'll come to you."

"Who's we?"

"Me and Cilla."

His brother let out a long sigh. "Christ. I don't want to know why she's with you in the middle of the night."

A rustling noise sounded. Probably little brother throwing the sheets back and getting out of bed.

"Maddy is here," Phin said. "I'll come to you."

"Fine." Cruz hung up and strode back to the living room,

waving his phone. "He's lecturing me about having you here when Maddy's in his suite."

Cilla laughed. "Y'all are practically running a brothel."

Cruz cracked up. God bless her, for making him laugh again. "Holy hell, sugar. I'm straight-up crazy about you. Just, you know, don't let my mother hear you call her house a brothel."

Five minutes later, Cruz held his suite door open. Phin stood there in basketball shorts and a T-shirt that looked straight off the hanger. Even in the middle of the night, his brother looked neat.

By the look of it, he'd wet his normally stylishly shaggy hair and now had it slicked back, a look Cruz wasn't used to, but couldn't think too hard about.

Phin was the fashion junkie. Constantly worried about his clothes and appearance. Cruz? Give him a good pair of boots, some jeans and T-shirts and a haircut every couple of months and he was good to go.

"Hey," Phin said, striding by Cruz.

Once inside, he glanced at Cilla, now standing in front of the couch dressed in the jeans and sweater she'd worn earlier.

"Morning," Phin said.

"Good morning to you. Sorry we woke you."

Cilla did her best to act like it was completely fucking normal for her to be in Cruz's suite. She'd changed into her own clothes and did her best to fix her hair, but it didn't take a rocket scientist to know they'd just thrashed each other.

A few times.

And what a thrashing it was. *Eh-hem.* But this was . . . weird.

Cruz hated weird. Hated it more that she should feel awkward.

The whole thing only reinforced the idea of having his own place—and privacy.

Phin swung an accusing gaze at Cruz, the message clear. Cilla was his friend and Cruz better not be doing a fly-by.

Which, yeah, despite his reputation for being a womanizer, kind of insulted him. He could be serious about a woman. He could. He just hadn't found the right woman.

Until now.

Until smart, sexy Cilla Randolph almost broke him in two.

"Uh," Phin said, hands on hips, "does anyone want to tell me what I'm doing here?"

Cruz hopped to it. "Yeah. We were researching Randolph Industries."

"This is the forever chemicals issue?"

Cilla nodded. "Yes. I found some documents."

She broke eye contact and moved from behind the coffee table to the French doors leading to the patio where she peeked out.

Stalling.

Had to be.

Behind her back, Phin shot Cruz a WTF face and Cruz shook him off while he stepped closer to Cilla.

"You okay?"

She spun back to him, gave him a forced smile. "I'm good. Just getting my thoughts together."

Then, like the warrior she was, she patted his arm, stepped around him to face Phin,

and Cruz knew he had to have this woman.

Forever.

"The files I found," Cilla said, "are settlement agreements

with residents of Morgan. From what I read, the settlements don't reveal that Randolph Industries has contaminated their property. In exchange they get cash, free medical and remediation attempts."

"Well," Phin said, sarcasm dripping like molasses, "I guess that answers your question about what your father knows."

"It sure does."

"How many cases?"

Cilla shrugged. "From what I could tell, at least fifty. Those are the settled ones. Who knows how many are in the works."

"All righty then." Phin let out a huff and dropped into the overstuffed side chair. "What can I do?"

"I don't know. I wanted so badly to believe my father didn't know about the contamination. I can't walk that back now. He knows. Plus, he sabotaged one of my cases today. Probably reminding me how much power he has."

"No way. He admitted that?"

"First thing to know about my father? He's a narcissist. He will admit nothing. He says enough to get the message across. And he got the message across. Loud and clear. Now, I face blowing the whistle on the man who's given me everything."

"That's not true," Cruz said. "He gave you a start, but you've built your own life."

Phin pointed at Cruz. "He's right. Besides, the way your dad talks about you, you've given him bragging rights. You don't owe him anything, Cilla."

She gave them a piss-poor attempt at a smile. "Thank you. I appreciate that, but what kind of daughter does it make me if I squeal on him?"

"Um," Cruz said, "how about one who cares about saving lives?"

"Wait." Phin blew right by Cruz's statement, "Maybe it doesn't have to come from you."

Cilla nodded. "That's why we called you. Randolph Industries is on the EPA's radar. I asked Dad about them the other day and he told me the company is compliant. Which, based on those settlement agreements, appears to be a lie."

Cruz wagged a finger at Phin. "Maybe we get Ro to see if he can hack into Randolph and find anything on pending cases."

Phin shrugged. "How does that help us?"

"If the agreement isn't signed, the people involved aren't bound by a confidentiality clause. They could talk."

Cilla narrowed her gaze. "They sure could. Dad is settling these individual cases to avoid a class action suit. That could cost billions."

Cruz put up his hands again. "Maybe we can leak one of these documents?"

Phin gawked. "And give Zeke a coronary? We signed an NDA."

Again with the NDA? Come on! His brother did not just fucking say that. "People could be dying. Fuck the NDA."

"Whoa." Cilla walked to him and gripped his hands. "Phin is right. If you violate the NDA, my father will destroy you. There's another way." She turned back to Phin. "Kayla knows someone at the EPA, right?"

"Yeah. At the federal level."

"Doesn't matter. They'll probably know someone at state. Can you put me in touch with Kayla?"

"Absolutely. I'll do it first thing. But, seriously, are you sure about this?"

When Cilla went silent, Cruz turned to Phin. "Sorry we dragged you down here. Go back to Maddy. I'll call you in a couple hours."

"Not a problem. Keep me posted." He headed for the door, but turned back. "By the way, it's gonna be warm the next couple days. Mom told me last night she wants a family cookout. Be ready for her to mention it. You got plans tonight or tomorrow?"

Uh, yeah. After last night, he intended to spend every ounce of spare time naked and in bed with Cilla. He wouldn't tell his brother that, though. At least not in front of Cilla.

Phin, being Phin, sensed hesitation. His eyebrows hiked up half an inch and then he swung to Cilla. "You wanna come to a cookout? Best ribs you'll find in four counties."

When she didn't answer and walked back to the doors to stare out, Cruz swung around. "I love that idea. You can help me make sure I say nothing that'll piss off the women."

"Terrific," Phin said. "Again with this? I don't know why you think our girlfriends are offended by you."

"I didn't say that. What I said is that I have to watch what I say."

"You're the only one who thinks that."

"Yeah, until I call one of you a fucker in front of them."

That shut his brother up.

"My point exactly." Cruz didn't have time for this. Way too early. He waved him from the room. "Go back to bed."

Phin exited and Cruz stepped behind Cilla at the doors, gently placing his hands on her shoulders and kissing the back of her head. "How can I help?"

She shook her head. "If I do this, there's no telling the impact it'll have on Randolph Industries. I know my father, he'll never forgive me." She turned to face Cruz. "I can live with that. If it saves one life, I'll live with it."

"You're worried about what he'll do?"

She nodded. "Is that selfish? That I'm worried about my career?"

"Honey, it's not just your career. It's about making a living. Your Dad has a long reach. He could impede your ability to support yourself. If you *weren't* worried about that, I'd think something was seriously wrong with you."

"I could go back to the DA's office. Not here, but another state maybe."

Another state?

Oh, hell no. They'd just started whatever the hell it was they had going and she's talking about leaving?

No way he'd let that happen.

"Whoa. You're getting too far ahead. Phin trusts Kayla. Talk to her. See what she says."

Cilla nodded. "Will you go with me? Just as . . . I don't know . . . a neutral party? I'm too close to this, Cruz, and I hate working on emotion. I need facts."

Zeke would love that. He'd wave his precious Randolph Industries NDA under Cruz's nose and lecture him about the risks.

Too bad.

People could die.

"I'll do whatever you want," he gave her a wolfish grin. "As long as you come to our cookout."

CILLA LEFT STEELE RIDGE AT SIX A.M. AWAKE ANYWAY, AND not needing the distraction of Mr. Delicioso, she showered in the guest suite, slid into a suit and her favorite Gucci shoes, and found relief that it was Saturday and there'd be no morning traffic.

Arriving at the office just before 9:00, she found Layla already at her desk. Cilla had texted the night before saying she'd be coming into the office in the morning to catch up and Layla, being Layla, had offered to come in.

Today's ensemble included a white cotton button-down, blue blazer, and her long dark hair loose over her shoulders. If Cilla were to guess, the lower part of the outfit would be fitted slacks and flats.

"Morning, boss." Layla spun from her keyboard and faced Cilla. "Sorry about Nagle screwing you."

"Morning. I could live with him screwing me. Our client? Not so much. Rick Bandy is as shocked as I am. We're back to working out a deal."

Layla peered at Cilla over the top of her reading glasses. "Wow."

"What?"

"You're so calm. I expected you'd be steaming mad."

"Oh, I was."

At least until one Cruz Blackwell fulfilled his promise and gave her all sorts of life-altering orgasms. "I'm better today. Ready to get back at it. I'm locking myself in my office. Unless it's Rick Bandy, would you please hold any calls?"

"You got it. How'd the Asheville office tour go?"

"Great. They accepted my offer."

"Whoa! That was fast."

That brought her up short, and she realized that in all the drama of the day, she'd neglected to let Layla know about the offer on a new office. She'd cleared the move with Layla months ago, posing it as a hypothetical, and when Layla had mentioned the easier reverse commute to Asheville, Cilla's worry over losing her melted away.

But now, her assistant's big brown eyes were on her and Cilla needed to make sure everything was fine between them. "The move is okay, right? We talked about it."

"No." Layla bopped herself on the head. "I mean, yes. It's all right. It'll be easier for me. I just didn't expect it so quick."

Cilla let out a laugh. "Phew. You scared me. I'm sorry, Layla. I should have kept you in the loop. Yesterday was . . . a day and I was full steam ahead."

"Please," she said. "You've got so much going on. No apology necessary. Tell me what you need."

Layla. Godsend. "Truly," Cilla said. "I'm lost without you. Would you please call moving companies for quotes? Find three and we'll go from there. My goal is to be in the new place within a month."

"Yes, ma'am." She picked up a stack of messages along with a few folders. "Your mom called."

"This early?"

And on a Saturday?

Layla shrugged. "She said she tried your cell, but it went straight to voice mail."

After living overseas until Cilla graduated from law school, Mom had finally moved back to the States. She'd invested in a small winery in Napa, wound up falling in love with the owner, Daniel, whose wife had died eight years earlier, and he and Mom were now living and running the winery together.

Mom also still worked as a sommelier part time and since she worked a lot of late-night events, she slept later in the day. Calling this early meant Mom had something on her mind.

"I'll call her before I go into lockdown. Anything else?"
"Nope."

"Good. If my father calls, tell him I'm not here." She

turned, peered at the office entry door. "In fact, if Ed isn't coming in today, lock the door."

"Really?"

"Yep. No interruptions."

She hopped up from her desk. "I like it!"

"And I'm leaving at two-thirty." She smiled brightly. "I've been invited to a barbecue in Steele Ridge."

"Steele Ridge?" After a second, Layla's jaw flopped open. "The hottie? Cruz Blackwell? See, I remembered his name. That's how hot he is."

"So hot!" Cilla laughed and gave her assistant a backward wave as she walked to her office, taking in all the artwork lining the walls that would need to be packed. She'd have to get organized. Set aside time each day to box things. Or splurge and let the movers do it.

A plan, and the excitement that went with it, took shape. Confidential files and the contents of their desks, she and Layla would handle. Everything else? The movers.

Between Layla's regular workload and the move, she'd be inundated. Cilla swung into her office, set her tote and purse on the couch before grabbing her cell and moving to the desk. Still standing, she jotted notes in her planner about a spa day for Layla at that fancy place in Asheville she'd discovered a few months back. The whole works. Facial, massage, whatever she wanted. Maybe they had a full-day package and Layla could pick what services she wanted.

She tapped the screen of her cell and found the missed call from her mom. How did she not get that on the drive? Must have been a dead zone somewhere.

She tapped Mom's name and seconds later, her mother picked up. "Darling, good morning."

"Hey, Mom. You're up early. Is everything all right? Daniel okay?"

A few months back, Daniel's cholesterol had spiked, and Mom went into full Nurse Ratched mode, methodically carving out rich foods and saturated fats from his diet.

"He's good. Cholesterol dropped ten points." She laughed. "I'm letting him eat cheese again."

"Well, thank goodness. He owns a winery. It's downright cruel."

"Tell me about it? I caught him sneaking from the trays in the cooler."

Cilla snorted. "Poor guy."

"Anyway, darling. I'm hearing things."

Oh boy. "Things" was code for gossip and Cilla didn't have time today. Between her father and the forever chemicals, Nagle flipping on them, and needing to prep for the upcoming murder case, Cilla was. . .busy.

But Mom calling this early? Had to be something juicy.

Or personal.

And that was never good.

Cilla dropped into her desk chair, rocking back. "What things?"

"Your father, apparently, is on one of his rampages again."

As if this were news? "Mom, he's always on a rampage. We know this."

"Yes, my darling, but what's this about him meddling in your cases?"

"Wow. Your pipeline is no joke."

"Sweet girl, I still know people. Rosemary Nagle called me last night."

The judge's wife. Cilla sat straighter, focusing on her mother's words.

"That woman," Mom said, "is such a pill. She loves giving bad news. Particularly concerning my daughter."

"What'd she say?"

"She told me about her husband rejecting your plea deal."

For a second, Cilla's throat clogged. "She *knew* about that?"

"Of course. It irritated Judge Nagle that your father put him in such a position."

Ohmygod. Dad *had* done it. She'd known, but having it confirmed?

Entirely different matter.

Who the hell did this to their child? A narcissistic animal, that's who.

Cilla squeezed her eyes closed, fought the heartbreak—the rage—that nearly stole her breath.

She wouldn't let Dad win. Not this way. She opened her eyes, focused on the abstract painting she'd picked up at a street fair after she'd passed the bar exam.

Back then, she believed in a fair system. Now? She wasn't so sure.

"Dad threatened him," Cilla said.

"She wouldn't get into details. But whatever your father has on him, it must be big. He's always been a womanizer. I chose not to remind Rosemary of that. I was focused on getting as much information as I could."

Her mother, the spy. She should put her on the payroll. "Dad came to court yesterday. At first, I wasn't sure why. When Nagle flipped on us, I figured it out and confronted him."

"Oh, Cilla, I'm so sorry."

"I finally get it, Mom. How horrible he was to you. I

never truly understood what could be so bad that you moved halfway around the world to get away."

"He loves you, Cilla. Probably more than anything or anyone. I don't understand why he's turning on you."

I do. Should she confide in Mom? Her parents had been civil over the years, but it wasn't as if they spent time together or spoke. Cilla, this conversation aside, didn't discuss either parent with the other.

"Mom, I don't want to involve you. All I'll say is I have information about his company."

"Something he's hiding? Is it illegal?"

"Let it go."

Her mother huffed. "Leave it to him to put his daughter in the crossfire. Darling, I'm your mother. I appreciate you wanting to protect me, but please, if you need anything, tell me. I've been through this with him. He won't stop until he gets his way."

"I'd hoped he wouldn't use my career as leverage."

"He'll use whatever means necessary. How do you think I wound up in Europe alone? My intention all along was to take you. To prevent it, he didn't care who he destroyed."

What did that mean? She'd known her father had threatened to cut her mother off financially, but was there more? "Who besides you was there to destroy?"

The line went silent for a few seconds and Cilla pulled the phone from her ear, checking the screen. Still connected. She brought the phone back. "Mom?"

"You, Cilla," she finally said. "He threatened me with minimal child support. And he'd turn your friends against you so when you went back to Charlotte, you'd have no one. But if I went quietly and let you stay in Charlotte, he'd leave you alone. He was willing to sacrifice you to get his way."

Another knifing pain ripped at Cilla. She slouched back

in her chair, breathing through the mental chaos and anger over her parents' fighting. Over being stuck at home with a nanny during her formative years when she so needed her mother.

All that time resenting her mother for leaving when it should have been Dad she aimed her anger at.

Her father, knowing Mom had big dreams for Cilla, had threatened to ruin his own child's life. Her poor mother. No one should be tormented that way.

"I'm so sorry, Mom."

"Before this, I'd have never told you. However, I believe you should know how far he's willing to go. You're an adult. You can make your own decisions."

"Thank you. Let me know if you hear anything else. But, Mom, please, don't initiate anything. I don't want him coming after you."

"Honey, I've taken on the beast before. I have my own money now. I don't need his. He can't hurt me, Cilla."

"Still, let's not have you poking the bear."

Cilla would do enough for both of them.

JUST AFTER 5:00, CILLA PULLED THROUGH THE GATES OF WHAT Phin called Chez Blackwell. Cruising along the winding drive, she took in the mountain backdrop and its forested hills. Nature, in all its forms, held its own stunning beauty that somehow settled her.

This place, along with one Cruz Blackwell, offered . . . peace. Respite she hadn't realized she needed.

Just as she pulled into the parking area in front of the Annex, Mr. Delicioso came through the doors, his long strides eating up the path between them and Cilla's midsection caught fire. His curly hair hung loose around his face, and he wore jeans, rubber-soled boots, and a long-sleeved navy T-shirt that hugged his big shoulders in all the right ways.

At least in Cilla's opinion.

The sight of the man did things to her. Really good things.

She pulled next to a Mercedes that cost over a hundred grand—she'd looked at that model herself—and shut the engine. Then she sat, simply watching Cruz move toward her, his gaze connecting with hers through the windshield.

Yes, she'd screw his lights out tonight. No doubt about that.

Apparently reading her mind, a slick smile eased across his face. *Naughty boy.* How she loved it.

Reaching the car, he swung the door open. "Welcome back."

"Thank you." She grabbed her purse and tote from the passenger seat and slid out of the car. "Are you thinking dirty thoughts?"

"When it comes to you? Always."

"Excellent. Me too."

The two of them burst out laughing and that? After the last few days? A gift.

If he broke her heart, she'd have to kill him. That's all there was to it.

Apparently not caring who might watch, Cruz leaned in, brushing his lips against hers, back and forth, back and forth, in what might be the softest kiss she'd ever experienced. And, yet, raging heat shot from her core. It'd be a miracle if her clothes didn't burn clear off.

She reached up and touched his cheek, her fingers caressing the short hair of his beard. Her mind went back to the last two nights and all the places he'd explored with his mouth and the sensation of that prickly yet enticing beard on her skin.

A low moan came from her throat, and she pulled back. "We have to stop," she said. "Or I'm taking you to your room and having my way with you. Right now."

"And the problem is?"

"Aside from your entire family being here for a barbecue?"

He winced. "Good point."

"Don't I know it?" She pointed to the Mercedes. "Who does this baby belong to?"

"Kayla Crowne."

Phin's boss.

"She's here?"

"She is. Phin invited her."

These Blackwells. They knew how to get things done. Phin had promised her he'd set up a meeting and he'd done it in expeditious fashion.

"She's inside," Cruz said. "We figured we could talk before dinner."

"Sounds like a plan."

Cruz escorted her into the building where, for the first time, no one sat at the conference table. "It's quiet."

"Yeah. Zeke and Ro are out back with Liv, Maddy and Lena. Phin is in his office with Kayla."

"I hope Maddy isn't upset with me for stealing Phin away."

"Nah. She loves you. She's excited to see you, though. No dawdling. Her words. Not mine."

The feeling was mutual. Months earlier, Maddy had been wrongly accused of stealing priceless jewels. The two of them had gone to war and cleared her name and Cilla considered Maddy a friend.

Cruz led her around the conference table to an office wedged between two others with closed doors. Voices drifted into the hallway.

"Knock-knock," Cruz called, alerting Phin and Kayla of their presence.

"Come in," Phin called.

Cruz stood aside, waving Cilla into the roughly twelve-by-twelve office where Phin sat behind a glass desk. Between the desk, the chrome guest chairs, and ornate steel sculpture by the window, the room absolutely screamed Phin and his stellar taste. A woman—Kayla presumably—with long, sun-kissed blond hair sat in one of the chairs across from Phin.

When Cilla entered, Phin came around the desk, holding his arms open for their normal, friendly hug.

After a few seconds—nothing smarmy about Phin Blackwell—he stepped back, gesturing to the blonde.

"Priscilla Randolph, meet Kayla Crowne."

Kayla stood, extending her hand and giving a solid shake. Her bright green eyes crinkled at the edges and her smile came fast and easy, lighting up her face in a way that showed confidence times twelve.

Describing Kayla as beautiful might be a travesty. An understatement if ever there was one.

Phin gestured to the empty chair beside Kayla's. "Sit."

Given the lack of seating, Cruz leaned against the wall.

Cilla angled sideways and faced Kayla. "Thank you for meeting with me."

"Absolutely. After Phin called me, I thought a few days at my Asheville home would do me some good. Phin updated me on the situation in Morgan and the toxicology report. How can I help?"

Could Cilla out her father to the EPA? After he had sabotaged her case, and might continue to do so?

Yes. If nothing else, she refused to cower to his intimidation tactics.

"My father's company is producing toxic chemicals that are contaminating the environment. And making people sick."

Kayla nodded. "Phin told me about the little girl. Horrendous."

"It is. My problem is I'm mentioned in an NDA that BARS signed with my father's company. I believe I can get around that with whistleblower laws, but I don't want BARS to suffer any blowback."

"Understood. Would you like me to leak something?"

Boom. That fast. She just laid it out there like it was no big deal to wreck a billion-dollar company.

Before Cilla could respond, Kayla put her hand up, her elegant French manicure catching the overhead light. "Gentlemen, could you give us the room?"

Cilla met Cruz's eye and she nudged her chin.

"Sure," he said. "We'll wait outside."

The men cleared out and Kayla shifted her chair to face Cilla. "We're both successful women playing in a man's world. I asked Cruz and Phin to leave so we could talk openly. No bullshit. No measuring our words. We don't have time for nonsense and if what you believe is happening in Morgan, people's lives are at risk."

"It's not what I believe. The reports are proof."

"Then let's do something."

Cilla nodded. "I've been thinking about a friend from law school. He's tort law."

Kayla rolled her lips into a pucker. "A class action suit?"

"Maybe. It's a ton of work. The other option, which could be in addition to a class action suit, is the state leveling fines on Randolph Industries for polluting the environment. My father has been working—supposedly—with the state's EPA. Just last week, he told me they've continually cooperated. Investigators show up, Randolph turns over requested data, and nothing happens."

Kayla cocked her head, considered that. "Nothing? Sorry, but hard to believe. If the toxicology reports are correct, there are forever chemicals in all the areas you tested. Including a stream. And that's probably not all of it. The town's water could be compromised."

"Exactly why we're having this meeting. I've spoken to my father. Showed him the reports."

"Let me guess, he played dumb."

Cilla didn't bother responding. This entire episode was sickening enough. Not only was she betraying her father, she'd lived life on the spoils of Randolph Industries' success. While she'd led her privileged life, people might have died from Randolph's pollution.

She shook it off. *Can't go back.* Only forward. If Dad won't get out of his way, she'd do it for him.

"I have a contact at the EPA." Kayla slid her phone from her purse and started typing. "Let's have her look into past investigations. See if they found any violations. I'm fighting these battles on behalf of environmental groups. Fines don't scare large companies. Compared to the profits they make, it's pennies on the dollar. They can afford the fines easier than losing their profits."

"Well, that's a sad situation."

Kayla set her phone down. "I made a note to call my friend. If she can't help, she'll find someone at the state level who can. They're probably the ones who investigated anyway."

"Thank you."

"Protecting society from men like Darren Randolph is

sort of my thing." Kayla tilted her head, assessing Cilla. "You're a brave woman. Many people in your position would look the other way."

Cilla met Kayla's eye. "I'm about to wreck my personal life." Not to mention make an enemy of her father, who'd already shown his willingness to blow up her career. "But there's a ten-year-old in Morgan with cancer. There may be more. For me, that's worse than my discomfort."

"Amen to that. My concern with the EPA is that if investigations show Randolph Industries' improper handling of chemicals contaminated Morgan and the EPA did nothing, they'll look like idiots."

In the Doomsday thinking Cilla had done, in all the scenarios she'd conjured, she hadn't considered that little fact. "And no one wants to look like an idiot."

Cilla sat back, thought about their options. Maybe she could log in again as Dad and search for EPA reports. Rohan had found those e-mails about the sludge. Maybe . . .

"Oh!" Cilla said.

"What?"

"Stay here. You may not want to hear this."

"Terrific."

Cilla pushed out of her chair and hustled to the door, swinging it open and then closing it again. Cruz and Phin sat at the conference table, both with their feet up while debating some football trade. She charged straight for them.

Cruz met her gaze, his eyebrows hitching.

"You okay?"

"I'm fine. I have an idea, but can't say it in front of Kayla. Not without an NDA."

"Ho-kay," Phin said. "This should be interesting."

Cilla gave them the summary of her conversation with

Kayla. "So," she said, "suppose Kayla's contact can help us, what if the EPA closes ranks? What then?"

Phin shrugged. "We pressure them. Get the environmental lobby on it. Kayla can whip up a good protest in minutes."

"Forget that," Cruz said. "It'll take too long."

Cilla snapped her fingers. "Exactly. How would Rohan feel about hacking into the EPA?"

18

CRUZ SWUNG TO PHIN, GIVING SOME HARD EYE CONTACT. "I'LL say this, the lady has guts."

Phin snorted. "She sure does."

Cilla scrunched her nose. "Too aggressive?"

"Depends," Cruz said casually. "If he gets caught, will you represent him for the litany of charges housed under the Computer Fraud and Abuse Act? He'll rattle them off."

"Yes," Phin said. "He'll start with unauthorized access into a protected computer."

"Obtaining confidential national information," Cruz added.

"Knowingly causing the transmission of a program or information or code."

During their volley, Cilla put up her hands. "Enough. I get it. I can't ask him to do that."

Cruz shrugged one massive shoulder. "Sure, you can. We do it all the time. If he thinks it supports the greater good, he'll do it. He'll moan about it, but he always comes through."

"It's a federal offense," Cilla said. "It could cost him ten years."

"We know," Phin said. "He'll tell you that, too."

On cue, Cruz's phone rang. Rohan. "Speaking of." He answered the call and brought the phone to his ear. "We were just talking about you."

"Where are you? Mom wanted a family cookout and y'all are AWOL."

Cruz winced. They'd get a tongue-lashing for being late, no doubt. "We're in the Theater. Gotta talk to you about something after dinner."

"What is it?"

"Hacking into EPA files."

"I see," Ro said, his voice so level they could build a house with it. "Is that all?"

Cruz couldn't help it, he smiled. Had to love Rohan. "That's all, bro. You up for it?"

In the background, Mom's voice sounded. Something about getting their butts outside. Yikes.

"Mom, they're coming," Ro said, then came back to Cruz. "Is this about the PFAS? The little girl with cancer?"

"It is."

"Let me think on it. In the meantime, y'all had better double-time it over here."

Cruz disconnected and set his phone on his lap. "That went better than expected." He pointed at Phin. "Mom's losing her shit because we're not outside."

Phin stood and straightened the sleeves on his pullover. Sufficiently groomed, he looked over at Cruz. "Will he do it?"

"He's thinking about it." Cruz stood. "Now, we need to go."

Cilla's gaze darted between Phin and Cruz. "I'll get Kayla. What should I tell her about the EPA?"

Cruz shrugged. "If she has a contact, it wouldn't hurt to see if they can give us something."

"Hang on," Phin said. "Let's talk to her."

"Make it quick. Otherwise, I'm telling Mom it's your fault."

At this, Cilla shook her head. "Brotherly love. How nice."

Cruz flashed a smile. She did that to him. Made him happy.

And damned if he didn't mind.

The trio walked back to Phin's office, where he knocked once, pushed the door open and stepped inside. Cruz and Cilla huddled into the doorway.

If Cruz had his way, the way that meant not getting his ass reamed by Mom, they wouldn't be here that long.

"Sorry," Phin told Kayla. "We were discussing illegal things you don't need to be implicated in."

"Fantastic." She smiled. "I appreciate your consideration."

"Your contact at the EPA," Phin said. "How much of a stickler is she?"

"A company knowingly polluting? She doesn't play. But outing the EPA as incompetent? I doubt she'd agree to that."

"There might be another way," Cilla said. "We have toxicology reports from the soil samples we took. Depending on what Rohan can . . ." she peered at Kayla, clearly thought twice, and turned back to Cruz. "Whatever *we* come up with, we can leak it to the press."

Cruz cocked his head, considering it. "Not a bad idea."

"If it gets enough traction," Cilla said, "the EPA will have to cover their rears."

"And do what?"

"If they do what I think they should," Cilla said, "they'd turn everything over to the North Carolina attorney general, who could sue Randolph Industries."

The room went silent, all of them staring at the dark-haired woman Cruz might be in love with.

"Whoa," he said. "That's. . .big."

Cilla met his gaze, her sea-green eyes clear and direct. "Believe me, I know. But Kayla just told me companies aren't afraid of the fines. A lawsuit from the attorney general? That'll terrify my father. We've discussed this very thing because other states have done it. The highest settlement so far was a few years ago: $850 million. The threat of that? It'll force my father to clean up his mess."

UPON DECIDING TO TABLE THE CONVERSATION UNTIL ROHAN could do some digging, Cruz and Phin led the ladies out the back door to the patio where Mom and Grams had the outdoor kitchen in full work mode.

Someone had gotten the fire pit going and Zeke, Liv, Maddy, and Brodie, Liv's son, stood around it while Rohan and Lena shared the bench across from them.

These people were his family. All here to spend time together and laugh over stupid shit only they might find funny. Something Cruz had always loved. Now, with the setting sun dropping behind the mountain, he breathed it all in, absorbing the scent of burnt wood and fresh air.

The Craftsman cottage flashed in his mind. Could he leave here? All this open space and peace?

Leave his family?

"Finally!" Mom called. "Y'all just about ruined these ribs."

She closed the cover on the grill, wiped her hands on a towel and marched toward them. "Hello, Kayla."

Mom stepped to Kayla, bringing her into her arms. Between giving Phin a job that made him happy, helping

Zeke locate a priceless family heirloom and assisting Rohan in finding a cyberstalker, Kayla had rescued a Blackwell more than once.

"Thank you for having me," Kayla said. "I always love spending time with your family."

"There's always plenty for friends."

Releasing Kayla, Mom set her sights on Cilla. "And this must be the famous Priscilla I've heard so much about."

"Oh, boy." Cilla laughed. "I'm not sure if that's a good thing or not."

Mom grinned. "It is." She peered at Cruz, then Phin. "I like to think my sons, although late to my cookout, are excellent judges of character and they've spoken highly of you."

Cilla and Mom shook hands and watching them, seeing his mother touch Cilla for the first time, made Cruz's chest do a weird bumpety-bump. What that was about, he wasn't sure, but it definitely had something to do with the first woman he ever loved meeting Cilla.

"Cilla!"

Maddy's voice. Thank God for that distraction because Cruz was somehow turning soft.

Mom let go of Cilla's hand and spun to Maddy, who moved toward them like a freight train. Her curly hair bounced, her smile took over her adorable face and Cruz once again saw how his brother had fallen so hard for this woman.

Maddy, in short, brought joy.

"Hey, you." Cilla opened her arms and the two women hugged. "How are you?"

Maddy gave her a squeeze and stepped back. "I'm good. These boys are keeping me busy. It's been fun."

"Good. You deserve fun."

"Hey."

At the sound of Ash's voice, Cruz and Phin turned to where their brother walked through the back door.

"Well, shit," Cruz said. "Look what the cat dragged in."

"You're late," Mom said.

Ash, being Ash, rolled right over that and kissed Mom on the cheek.

"Suck-up," Cruz joked.

"Oh, hush!" Mom shot.

Backing away, she peered up at Ash, her eyes a little misty and glowing. All her boys under one roof. That's what his mother wanted. Always. Ash had destroyed her by leaving and now Cruz was contemplating the same move.

Dang. He'd fight any man, all day long, but hurting his mother? Did he have that much fight in him?

"Sorry," Ash said. "But I'm here now and it smells great."

Mom waved everyone over to the giant outdoor table. "All right, y'all. Let's eat!"

STUFFED WITH RIBS, CORNBREAD. AND CHEESY TWICE-BAKED potatoes that would give the healthiest of men a coronary, Cruz sat back and patted his stomach.

"Good stuff, Mom."

"There's leftovers."

Mom peered at Cilla. "He'll come down looking for food in about two hours. I swear, he's just like his father. No idea where they put all this food."

At the end of the table, Zeke cleared his throat. "I, uh, didn't intend to do this tonight, but since we're all here, I've got something for you."

What the hell was this now?

Zeke pushed his chair back and stood. "We need to head to the garage."

"Why?" Ash wanted to know.

Pausing for a second, Zeke eased out a breath. "I just said, I have something for you." He gave Ash a forced smile. "A surprise."

"Well then," Mom said, waving everyone from their seats. "Let's see what your brother is up to."

All of them schlepped down the road to the garage—not Cruz's renovated barn, but the one that housed their personal and BARS vehicles.

Once there, Zeke opened one of the bay doors, made them all step into the pitch-black space.

"Okay," he said. "Before I turn the lights on, close your eyes. Everybody."

"What are you up to?" Phin wanted to know.

"Close 'em! Keep 'em closed. Another second. Okay. Open!"

Cruz did as he was told, blinking against the flash of light when Zeke flipped them on. Never one to be overly joyful at any one moment, Zeke wore an all-teeth smile that could have lit the room without the lights.

Cruz's gaze landed on one, two . . . six ATVs. All, it appeared, custom painted and sending Cruz's happy meter off the charts.

Toys, toys, toys. How he loved them. "What the hell's this?"

"*This,* boys," Zeke said, "is our reward for busting our asses this year. Sorry, Grams, no ATV for you. If you behave, we'll get you a new gator."

"Smart mouth," Grams said. "And don't think you'll be destroying all my plants with these things."

"Cruz, yours is the black one."

Cruz hustled over, nearly gawking at the shiny chrome rims and jet-black paint. "Wait," he said, looking closer at the faint flecks of metal. "Is this the same paint as the Stutz?"

"Yep. You can thank me later because that was a total pain in the ass to figure out without asking you."

Nearly fucking bursting, Cruz threw his leg over the ATV and ran his hand over the chassis. So flipping cool. Then he met Zeke's eye. "Thank you," he said, his voice catching.

He cleared his throat. "This is amazing. Dad would love it."

Zeke jerked his head and turned away, facing the rest of the crew. "Ro, yours is the blue one. Phin the red one. Brodie, you're the camo. It's a little smaller, but you'll be more comfortable on it."

Brodie, gasped. "I got one, too?"

"Yeah. But your mom doesn't want you riding alone. One of us has to go with you. Understood?"

The little guy bobbed his head and ran to the ATV.

Then Zeke turned to Ash, who stood behind him, laughing at all his brothers acting like toddlers. "And that leaves the last two. Mine is the one with the four-headed wolf. Yours has the FBI crest. I thought you'd like that."

For a few seconds, Ash stood, apparently paralyzed and Cruz's stuffed stomach rebelled. Shit on a shingle, they'd better not be about to argue and ruin this perfectly fantastic family moment.

"I don't understand," Ash said. "Why'd I get one?"

And, oh, shit.

"Hey!" Ro pointed to his ATV. "Check this out. There's code imbedded in the paint. Very cool."

Zeke, however, blew right past that. He slid his shoulders back and focused on Ash. "Last I heard, you *are* part of this family."

"I don't work for BARS anymore."

"Jesus Christ." Zeke let out a frustrated huff and held his arms wide. "I'm trying to do something nice and you're giving me crap? If you don't want it, fine. I'll sell the fucker."

"Language!" Mom said.

Ho-kay. Time for an intervention because clearly old wounds over Ash leaving BARS were about to be torn open. Cruz hopped off the ATV and hustled to his brothers, clapping Zeke on the shoulder. "Nobody is selling anything. I don't think he's giving you crap. He's surprised. We all are."

"Yeah, well, he could say thank you and be happy about it."

"Boys," Mom said, "knock it off. We've had a pleasant night and I don't want you two spoiling it."

Tell 'em, Ma.

But Zeke? His cheeks hardened into that stubborn mask this family knew all too well. "I'm not spoiling it, Mom." He kept his gaze on Ash. "*I'm* trying to give my brothers—*all* of them—a gift. I'd appreciate it if we didn't have to dissect it."

Phin being Phin, smacked his hands together. "I say we all get dessert. Then tomorrow, we'll take these babies for a ride."

"I have to leave tonight," Ash said. "Meeting in Asheville tomorrow."

He turned, headed for the open bay door, but turned back. "Zeke, I appreciate the gift. Thank you."

With that, Ash left the garage, leaving Cruz to wonder how things between his brothers got so fucked up.

Perfect excuse for chasing down Ash and picking his brain about moving out. Cruz peered at his mother and hustled toward the door. "I'm on it," he said.

Once outside, the unusually warm evening air tickled his cheeks. He glanced up at the cloudless sky where a bazillion stars winked. Tonight would be a great night for stargazing.

Time for that later. Now, he had to catch up with his brother, illuminated by moonlight as he marched up the road like a thief running from the law.

"Ash," he called. "Hold up. Gotta talk to you."

His brother halted and swung back, giving Cruz a chance to catch up.

"If it's about Zeke," Ash said, "forget it. I've tried—several times. All he wants is to be pissed at me. Now, I'm done. I'm here if he wants to talk, but he doesn't get to buy me an ATV and think that fixes things."

"For what it matters, I agree. He's being his usual stubborn self. But that's our brother. We still love him, right?"

Cruz reached him and stopped, the two of them faced off smack in the middle of the dirt road.

"Of course, I love him. I can seriously dislike him at times, though."

"Hell, yeah. We all hate each other at some point. No big deal. Just, you know, have patience. He's a work in progress."

At that, Ash shook his head. And laughed. "Fucking Cruz. Always worried about everybody."

Cruz shrugged. "I hate when we fight. Actually, Mom hates when we fight, and I hate that. So, yeah. I'd like you and Zeke to kiss and make up, but you're grown-ass men and I'm not gonna hassle you about it."

Enough with this nonsense. In a rare moment alone with Ash, Cruz had other things to discuss.

He gestured toward the house and started walking. "I got something else to talk to you about."

"Great," Ash said, sarcasm dripping like tree sap. "First, we didn't get any hits on the prints from Cilla's car. Whoever left that bullet isn't in the system."

"Well, that sucks."

"Sorry. Have there been any other incidents?"

"No."

"Good. Now, what do you need from me?"

Typically, talking to Ash meant either a job that could somehow involve the FBI or something else that might piss him off.

Which, in Cruz's mind, was kinda sad. Since Ash had moved out, they didn't talk much about stupid, mundane things—like football or debating the merits of filet versus sirloin. The best whiskey, which, yeah, he wouldn't mind two fingers of right now, but he hadn't touched the stuff since getting busted by Phin and Zeke, and although he missed the routine of it, of settling down with a drink at night, he felt . . . better. Not as sluggish.

Still, part of him missed that smooth heat moving down his throat.

"Cruz? Are you going to tell me what it is and put me out of my misery?"

At the sound of Ash's voice, Cruz snapped out of his little mind travel. "Yeah. Sorry. When you moved out—"

"Oh, Christ. Here we go."

Halting in the road, Cruz reached for his brother's arm and the two of them faced off again.

"I need advice," Cruz said. "I want to . . ." Dang it. Just saying it sucked. "I'm thinking about . . ."

"Spit it out, Cruz."

That's what he needed to do. Say it aloud. Let the words fly. Cruz jerked his head. "I wanna buy a place of my own."

"Like a vacation home or moving out?"

"Moving out. Maybe split my time between here and Asheville."

"Well, holy shit. Another defector."

Oh, hey now. "*Not* defecting. I love working for BARS. Some of us don't have dreams like you had. Nothing I have an itch for. Not yet anyway. I'm satisfied with the work."

"So, what's the problem?"

Cruz glanced back at the Friary. At all the cars in the drive. "It's kinda tight lately."

"Ah," Ash said. "The inn is full."

Yes. His brother might be a pain in the ass sometimes, but he'd always been the one who knew what to do. Especially after Dad died. Somehow, Ash had become their de facto father figure.

At least until he left for the FBI and he and Zeke had been at each other ever since.

Cruz shrugged. "Maybe a little."

Ash took that in, considering it. "Anyone in particular?"

"What? No! Not at all. Honestly, if I had to pick women for you fuckers, I'd have picked those women. They're fantastic. It's just . . . different. The vibe has changed and I'm afraid to open my mouth. I mean, you know me. If I'm thinking it, I say it. Now, if I utter something that might offend someone, I need to apologize. In my own house!"

"Take it easy. What did you have to apologize for?"

"I didn't. *That's* the problem."

Still lit by moonlight, Ash cocked his head and stared at Cruz like his brain had just spilled out of his skull.

"Hang on," Ash said. "I'm not following."

"I'm on eggshells. All the time. It's fucking exhausting. You have no idea."

"Actually, I do. Not so much the eggshells, but after I moved out, I realized I liked being on my own. No comments from the peanut gallery. No one offering their opinions. The lack of pressure trying to live up to expectations."

Come fucking again? What was he talking about? Expectations. "Dude! What the hell does that mean?"

"Come on, Cruz. You know I didn't have choices after Dad died. Someone had to run the business and I'm the oldest."

"Is that how you felt? Like you had to prove something?"

Now it was Ash's turn to shrug. "I don't know. It just felt like . . . pressure. I didn't have the passion—or vision—for BARS that Zeke does. So, yeah, for me, when I left, it was total freedom."

"Wow. I'm sorry. I hope I never—"

"You didn't. It was self-imposed. Once I got over disappointing Mom, I gotta tell you, Cruz, it's nice. I can walk around my apartment bare-assed naked if I want and it doesn't matter."

That's what Cruz wanted. Not so much the bare-assed part, but the freedom. The alone time where he could relax. Shut his brain off and not worry constantly.

"I looked at a house yesterday," he blurted.

"No shit? You're serious."

"I drove by it and before I knew it, I was looking in windows and calling the realtor."

A flash of white teeth lit Ash's face. "Good for you. Did you like it?"

"Yeah. Maybe too much. It's in Asheville."

"You love Asheville."

"I do. And it's three bedrooms, so people can stay over. Eighteen hundred square feet. Two-car garage in back for the Stutz and a workshop. Everything I need."

"Then buy it. You, out of all of us, have never been indecisive. You know what you need. And, trust me, this family? Everyone in it wants you happy. You're the one always taking the underdog's side. No matter who it is, you always make sure there's peace. That's what I thought you were doing when you came after me. Trying to talk me into working things out with Zeke."

"Hell, we're way past that stage. Y'all gotta figure that shit out on your own."

Voices sounded and Ash peered back toward the garage, where their family came through the open doors. He came back to Cruz and met his eye. "I know. But it won't come from me. Ball is in his court. Anyway, if you want this house, buy it. Life is too short. Sometimes I feel like we're all chasing a ghost. You especially. Dad was downright shitty to you."

Chasing a ghost. Hadn't Cruz said the same damned thing to Cilla? Maybe he and Ash had more in common than Cruz thought. And suddenly, Cruz didn't feel quite so alone in a house full of people.

He blew out a quick breath. Got his head together. "I was a handful."

"We all were. He was hardest on you. His intentions were good, but he was tough. He couldn't see you wanted to please him. But he's gone, you've grown up, and if he were standing here, he'd tell you to buy that house if it'll make you happy. If you want my opinion, you're done earning his approval. Go get what you want. The fam will get behind you. I promise."

AT 4:00 A.M., WIDE AWAKE AND THINKING ABOUT NOTHING but Rohan hacking into a government database, Cruz left Cilla snoozing in his bed and headed down to his workshop to deal with the Stutz's oil leak.

The trace dye kit had finally been delivered and he

needed the mental break that working on cars allowed. His own form of therapy, he supposed.

Walking in the chilly darkness that a sixty-degree morning offered, he shoved his hands into the pockets of his hoodie and took in the fresh mountain air. Already, his mind quieted and his neck loosened.

He pushed the barn doors open, entered the garage, and slapped the switch to his left. Artificial light assailed him and he closed his eyes for a few seconds before slowly opening them. Eyes sufficiently adjusted, he made his way to the worktable where Mom had left the trace dye kit. Apparently, she didn't want it cluttering things up in the Friary so she'd walked it all the way down here.

Jeez, could she give a guy a second to pick up a package?

That was his mother, though. Neat Nelly.

Grabbing his top-up bottle, he poured half an ounce of dye into it, combining it with the bit of oil inside before popping the hood on the Stutz. After pouring the mixture into the engine, he closed the hood, hopped behind the wheel, and fired up the car, taking pride in the low rumble. It soothed him, brought him back to the first time he'd driven this baby. Dang, he loved this car.

He let the engine run for a minute, flipped on the headlights, and eased out of the garage into darkness. He'd drive around long enough for the oil to leak and then put his handy-dandy UV light to work.

Three miles later, he cruised up the driveway and spotted a light on in the Theater.

Rohan no doubt.

Guilt slammed him. He'd saddled his brother with Cilla's case and here he was screwing around with the Stutz.

Just a little longer.

That's all he needed to find the leak. Then he'd get cleaned up and join Rohan.

He backed the Stutz into its normal spot, shut her down and slid old newspapers he kept on hand under the car to catch the leaking oil.

After killing a few minutes, he spotted a few fresh drops —*beautiful*—and grabbed the yellow glasses out of the box the kit came in. Glasses on and UV light in hand, he raised the hood again.

Aiming the light at the engine, he hunted around. Nothing glowing. He kept at it, bending and twisting, checking seals and tubes and . . . *nada*.

Time to look from underneath. He raised the car up on the hydraulic lift—worth every penny, that sucker—and repeated the same routine with the light.

Bingo.

Oil drain plug.

Green glow.

Seriously?

He'd checked that thing. Maybe ten times. Might as well have been a hundred. He'd *checked* it.

But there it was, glowing like a Times Square marquis. Could be worn. Or misaligned. After all this nonsense, he'd change it out completely. See if that did the trick.

Too tired to be pissed off, he laughed. Had to.

At least now he knew and could swap it out, since he had backups of just about every part needed to keep this baby running. Relief took hold, easing the tension out of his shoulders and chest.

He'd done it. Got Dad's car on the road again.

He'd have to call Reid and tell him the dye worked. And maybe make up some complicated issue that sounded a whole lot better than a leaking plug.

Something that would have been hard to identify because God help him if Reid knew the actual story. That guy would never let him live it down.

All Cruz knew was, for the first time in a few months, he was . . . dare he say it, content. It wasn't lost on him that the mighty and brilliant Cilla might have a lot to do with it. She'd churned him up in some freaking phenomenal ways. Including itching to get back to his suite where she slept in his bed and he could steal glances of her silky hair against his pillows. Or the way her tall, lean body curved into his while they slept.

Good stuff right there.

Now, he knew how his brothers felt, wanting the women in their lives close.

It wouldn't change his mind about needing his space, but maybe he could be less of a brat about it. Less resentful and more grateful that the people he loved most were happy.

Yeah, that sounded good. Great, in fact.

Patience. A novel idea.

After swapping out the oil plug, Cruz made his way back to his suite where Cilla still snoozed. Remembering the guilt of Rohan being up so early, he resisted the urge to crawl back into bed and grabbed a quick shower, kissed Cilla good morning, and headed to the Theater.

If Rohan didn't need his help, he'd get prepped for the 9:00 meeting to discuss the recovery of a three-million-dollar violin. An e-mail containing background on said violin had gone out, but Cruz hadn't yet cracked that sucker open. He and Ro would most likely be doing the research, so Cruz needed to get his ass up to speed and not disappoint his brothers again.

Still, leaving Cilla sucked.

She'd be on the road by six to get back to Charlotte at a decent time. Between the two of them, they were both working on a Sunday and who knew when he'd see her again? Soon. He'd make sure of it.

Dressed in only a long-sleeved T-shirt and jeans, he hustled along the path to the Annex.

Inside, lights blazed. As expected, his brother sat at the conference table, fingers flying on his keyboard. The faint scent of fresh coffee caught Cruz's attention and he glanced at the giant travel mug on the table beside Rohan's laptop.

"Hey," Cruz said, setting his laptop on the table and logging in before making his way to the kitchenette for some of that fresh coffee.

Rohan didn't bother to look up or stop typing. "Hey."

"You're early."

"Could say the same for you."

"I wanted to look at the intel on the Caldwell case."

"It doesn't appear complicated. Divorce situation. The husband is holding the violin hostage. It's in a temperature-controlled storage facility."

Cruz shook his head. "People."

Storage facilities, however, could be tricky. Busting into one meant dealing with pain-in-the-ass security guards or cameras and gates.

Rohan sat back and stared at his screen. "Coffee is on."

"Good. I need it."

"Cilla still here?"

Cruz flashed a grin. "She sure is. Dude, she might break me in two. I think I'm in love."

Rohan gave him a pained look. "Dude, I didn't need to hear that."

What? Why? Was that bad? All he'd said was . . . wait.

Pondering it, he rolled his bottom lip out. Maybe the "breaking him in two" crossed a line. "TMI?"

"Not the being in love part. That might be the best thing you've said in years. The rest? Not so much." Ro pumped a fist. "But good for you."

Cruz mirrored the gesture. "She's amazing. Smart. Driven. Takes no shit. And I'm not terrified I'll offend her every time I speak."

"A fortunate thing for you."

Oh, hey now. Was that nice? Cruz flipped him the bird and laughed. "Fuck. *You*."

Ro snorted.

"*Anyway*." Cruz gestured to the laptop. "What are you working on?"

"The EPA thing."

Cruz hated that his brother was losing sleep over this. Cilla, of course, was a client, but even so, Rohan didn't need to be down here at all hours. "Sorry it dragged you out of bed."

"Don't worry about it. Have to say, I'm impressed with the EPA."

Nothing his brother loved more than a challenge. "It giving you trouble?"

He shook his head. "The process is taking longer than expected. I'm close, though. Go get coffee. By the time you're back, I might be in."

Doing as he was told, Cruz walked to the kitchenette, found the pot half full—how the hell long had Ro been down here?—and grabbed a mug from the dish drain just as his phone chirped.

He checked the screen. Text from Cilla. Wondering where he'd gone. He typed out a quick response apologizing but telling her to go back to sleep and he'd be up to see her before she left.

Her response was to love his message.

Not a generic thumbs-up.

The heart? An altogether different message. One that perhaps indicated she too enjoyed having him around.

And, yes, he'd gone totally soft. Not that he'd admit it to anyone.

He poured his coffee, left the kitchenette, and joined Ro at the conference table.

"Bam," Ro said.

"You're in?"

"Bet your ass."

Cruz walked around to look over Ro's shoulder at a screen filled with code that made Cruz's vision blur.

Ro sat back, held his hands wide. "What am I looking for?"

"Beats the shit out of me."

"Great. Thanks, genius."

Sipping his coffee, Cruz pondered it. "Start with Randolph Industries. Let's see what's there."

Rohan's fingers flew and he sat back as a list of files filled the screen.

"Whoa," Cruz said. "Guess they're familiar."

"Looks like."

Thinking they'd be there a while, Cruz slid into the seat next to Ro, set his coffee down, and perused the list.

One file caught his eye and he pointed. "Drinking water."

"Didn't you tell me Randolph built their own water reclamation facility?"

"Yeah. The town didn't want them stressing theirs. Let's look at that file."

Rohan clicked and they both leaned in, reading the file —dated eight years earlier—the second it appeared.

"This is bad, bro," Ro said. "Real fucking bad."

According to the report, Randolph Industries, as part of an EPA stewardship program that required committing to eliminating PFOA from emissions and their products, had hired outside contractors to test the soil and water in Morgan. The results showed Morgan's drinking water contained PFOA, as well as PFAS concentrations six thousand times higher than the EPA's latest health advisory.

Six *thousand*. No way. Cruz read it again.

"Unbelievable." Cruz said. "That was eight freaking years ago. Scroll down."

Cruz continued reading.

"This gets crappier and crappier," Ro said. "According to this, over the years, emissions from the Randolph facility polluted the air and most likely settled in Morgan's water wells."

Cruz pictured poison drifting from the air into the ground. If this air pollution theory stuck, who knew how many properties they had loaded with toxic chemicals.

Cruz sat back, stuck his hands on top of his head and sorted his thoughts. "It's not just the soil on the Tate farm that made their daughter sick. If they're drinking the town's water, they're fucked. The whole town is fucked."

19

At 5:30, Cilla had just stepped from the shower after hitting the snooze button on her phone one too many times and setting herself back a solid thirty minutes. Today would have to be an express primping day.

Not one to wear a ton of makeup, she still liked to take her time with it. Make sure the eyeliner matched on both eyes. She'd long ago realized her eyes—her mother's crystal green— caught attention. For that reason, she played them up. Used them to her benefit. Particularly during media interviews.

Now she found herself cutting corners. Not a big deal since it was only on her morning routine, but she'd already experienced falling behind at work because of this PFOA issue and time spent with Cruz.

Being self-employed had its perks. She'd built her reputation on hard work and top-notch legal advice. All of which would suffer if she kept commuting from Charlotte and losing sleep.

"Cilla?"

Cruz's voice. Wrapping a towel around herself, she slipped her fingers through her hair.

"Bathroom," she called. "Be right out."

Her slacks and blouse hung on a hanger on the door. She dressed quickly in case Cruz had any ideas of luring her back to bed. Which could not, would not, happen. As it was, she'd probably not get to the office until 9:30.

Swinging open the bathroom door, she found him in the living room. He sat on the sofa with a stack of documents in front of him and if his hardened cheeks were any indication, he wasn't happy.

What could have happened in the hour since he'd left her? She cocked her head and pinned her gaze to him. "You okay?"

He peered up at her with those soulful eyes she'd never forget. "Yeah," He patted the cushion beside him. "Sit. Got something for you."

Oh no. There went her already taxed schedule. She pointed to her still-wet hair. "Cruz, I'm running late. Is this about the bullet again?"

Although, considering the prints the crime scene guys had lifted netted zero results, she wasn't sure what more there could be.

All she knew was the incident sat in the back of her mind like an annoying gnat.

"It's important," Cruz said. "Trust me, you'll want to see it."

Meaning it more than likely involved Randolph Industries. She moved to the sofa, claiming the space next to him. He pointed to the documents.

"Rohan was in the Theater when I got there. He got into the EPA files."

Oooh. "He's fast."

"He's *good*."

"Why do I feel like I won't be happy when I read these?"

"Because you're smart and have great instincts."

Had to love Cruz and his direct approach. "All righty then. Guess I'll dive in."

She started at the top, skimming each paragraph.

Water contamination.

PFOA. PFAS.

Six thousand times higher than EPA recommendations.

Whoa. Panic roared, burning through her shoulders into her neck. She needed to stay focused. Keep her neutral, lawyer brain in charge.

Treat this like any other client file. And not her father. Who'd apparently been poisoning an entire town for *years*.

How could he do this? After all the conversations they'd had. All the assurances he'd given her, he'd been lying. Straight to her face.

She shook it off and went back to the documents. Fifteen minutes later, she'd skimmed every page, flipping the last one on top of the others and lining up the corners before turning the stack over.

She sat back and peered at Cruz. "This is all from state EPA?"

"Yes. It's all we've found so far."

"So, in summary, Randolph Industries has polluted the air, which, in turn contaminated the town's drinking water. The EPA knew this, told Randolph to fix it, and left it up to them to handle. And then," she pointed at the stack, "Randolph executives told the EPA there were no effective techniques to clean up their mess and EPA said, 'Gee, that's too bad, but okay. We'll allow you to poison an entire town.'"

Cruz winced. "Well, *that's* an exaggeration. From what we can tell, Randolph slipped through the cracks."

"They allowed my father's company to self-police." She smacked at the documents on the table. "Did y'all download these?"

"We did."

"Good." Cilla stood, smoothed her slacks and adjusted her shirt sleeves. "I have to finish getting dressed. Before I leave, would you be able to put everything on a thumb drive for me? I don't want them e-mailed."

Cruz lifted one hip, shoved a hand in his pocket and tossed a thumb drive on the table. "Already done. What are you thinking?"

"A couple of things. I have a contact at the *Charlotte Times*. I think she'll be interested in this."

"Ballsy. You sure you want to do that? Considering it's your dad."

"Oh, believe me. I'm aware. But I've been talking to him about the environment for years and he's been lying." She smacked her hand against her chest. "To *me*."

She paused, squeezed her eyes closed and swallowed, fighting the mix of rage and heartbreak building in her throat. She opened her eyes and met Cruz's gaze. "It rips me clear open. I mean, what kind of man lies to his own daughter and knowingly poisons land and the people on it?"

At that, Cruz shook his head. "I'm sorry, Cilla."

"Me too. Something needs to be done. I'm over talking to him. It's a waste of time I don't have. I'll call my contact at the *Times* and *then* I'll send Kayla copies of everything for her EPA friend to see. I'm going to create as much chaos as I can."

ON MONDAY AFTERNOON, CILLA SAT AT A BISTRO TABLE IN THE quaint coffee shop half a block from the massive *Charlotte*

Times building. She'd been here before when meeting with Allison Caplin, the *Times*'s bulldog investigative reporter. Over the years, Allison had been equal parts foe and savior when public opinion might sway a case.

Glancing around, she saw that the place was barely half full. Cilla supposed peak hours came in the morning, not 3:45 in the afternoon. All evidenced by the shift change that took place fifteen minutes earlier when three employees left and only two came in.

For Cilla's purposes, the quiet helped, but she wouldn't have minded a busier location where she'd get lost in the crowd. This, however, was across town from her office and chances were that no one from Randolph Industries would spot her during what Allison called a dead drop. Meaning, Cilla would get up from her table, exit the shop and leave behind a tote with the various e-mails and toxicity reports she'd collected. Allison would then take over said table and pick up the tote on her way out.

No conversation.

No acknowledgment.

No interaction.

The only part of this operation to give any sort of comfort would be Cruz insisting on playing driver. He'd parked four doors down, a spot that gave him a view of the door for when she exited. In the meantime, she had strict orders to text him a 9-1-1 if she needed him.

Her hero.

For a second, her own sarcasm stopped her short. She'd never *needed* a man before. Still didn't. But the companionship, the having-someone-to-lean-on, gave her hope that perhaps she could have it all. Career. Family.

Love.

Maybe he *was* her hero.

Blech. The entire thing sounded way too sappy for a girl whose idea of happily-ever-after meant avoiding everything she'd witnessed in her parents' relationship. Up to this point, marriage had seemed a formality.

A piece of paper that legally bound two people and risked financial war when it all fell apart.

Wow. She nearly winced at how cynical she'd become.

Allison, a woman in her mid-forties with long platinum blond hair that was too white not to be dyed, strode by the plate glass window, not bothering to look inside. Acknowledgment or not, they both knew what they were here for. From the corner of her eye, Cilla watched Allison make her way along the sidewalk and enter the shop.

She wore a buttoned navy blazer over a white blouse and tan slacks. The heels of her flat shoes clacked against the scarred wood floor, reminding Cilla of the lack of a crowd.

Don't think about it.

That's all she had to do.

A vision of Brittney Tate popped into her mind. Yes, Cilla was about to blow the whistle on her father, a man powerful enough to wreck not only her career but her personal life. She'd tried, several times, to talk to him and, based on the evidence she'd found, ten-year-olds with cancer didn't seem to bother him.

That alone devastated her and she let the heartbreak roll over her. Being her father's daughter—he'd been good for certain things—she'd use it. Allow it to motivate her.

At the counter, a customer ordered some complicated triple espresso concoction Cilla had no desire to taste. A whole lot of caffeine and sugar she didn't need in an already fried nervous system.

Seconds later, the whirring of a machine sounded,

scraping against Cilla's last functioning nerve. Her temples pounded, her stomach flipped and what little food she'd eaten threatened to evacuate itself.

Vomiting in the middle of the shop hadn't been part of the plan so she inhaled and fought for focus, zeroing in on the next two minutes.

Get up and walk out.

But, man, her stomach twisted. She had to move. Get fresh air.

Panic brewing, she checked on Allison, now stepping up to the counter. Bile filled Cilla's throat and her stomach clenched hard enough that she gasped. Saliva poured into her mouth and—*oh no, oh no, oh no.*

Air.

Get out.

She needed to go. Now. Before she vomited and completely blew the plan for a casual exchange of information.

Cilla rose from her seat, scraping the chair against the floor as she stood. She stunk at subterfuge. The woman who'd ordered the sugary coffee glanced over, meeting her eye. Her eyebrows hitched up and . . . uh-oh . . . Cilla's frequent media spots suddenly didn't seem like such a great idea.

Had this woman recognized her?

Don't think.

Allison glanced over at her. So much for zero interaction. Cilla considered it close enough, grabbed her purse from the table and headed for the door.

"Wait!" The young woman waiting for her order said. "You forgot your bag."

Panic raging, Cilla met Allison's eye. *What now?*

Clearly understanding Cilla's unspoken message,

Allison halted, letting out an exaggerated sigh. "Oh! Thank goodness!"

Bypassing Cilla, she strode to the chair. "That's actually mine. I forgot it. I was hoping someone gave it to the barista."

Okay. Good one. Cilla rolled with it. "I've been sitting there for a little while. I didn't notice it." She thunked herself on the head. "So distracted today."

"Wow," the young woman said. "That's lucky."

And a load of crap.

Allison lifted the bag to her shoulder, gave Cilla a wide-eyed you-almost-blew-it stare. "It sure is."

THE SECOND CRUZ SPOTTED THAT FLASH OF POKER-STRAIGHT dark hair, he fired up the truck. He'd stick to the plan and let Cilla walk around the block where he'd scoop her up on the far corner. Not that they'd done anything illegal, but she'd wanted to maintain as much privacy as possible and chances were this busy street contained more security cameras than the side street.

His phone rang. Cilla. He picked up the call. "You okay?"

"I may vomit. I'll try to do it before I get in the truck."

Poor thing. "Walk around the corner and I'll grab you. If you puke, you puke. The truck can be cleaned."

"I hate this," she said.

"I don't blame you."

"Cruz, who does this to their own father?"

Guilt. A bastard he'd given in to many times. Loving people, he supposed, brought a mass of conflicting emotions and decisions.

"Someone," he said, "doing the right thing. The question

you should ask is why aren't more people doing it? Honey, you're my fucking hero."

And he wasn't blowing smoke up her ass. Even he, a guy who thrived in battle, wasn't sure he'd have the stones to out his own father.

Then again, his father hadn't poisoned an entire town.

Finally, he pulled from the spot, cruising down the street and hooking a right at the corner where Cilla's trim frame came into view. A few other pedestrians strolled along, some window shopping, others hustling by on their way to wherever they were going.

Cilla's long legs moved at a clip. The commuter walk, Phin called it. Not rushed, but not exactly slow either.

Easing his foot off the gas, Cruz drove by and pulled into a loading zone at the corner. He checked his passenger mirror and three seconds later, the door came open. Cilla tossed her purse on the floor, hopped in, shut the door behind her, opened the window, and stuck her head out, sucking in air.

Was she seriously going to blow chunks? Out his window? *That* might draw attention.

"Cilla, if you're going to puke, please don't do it out the window. People will notice."

Clearly seeing his logic, she took one last deep breath and leaned back inside. She rested her head against the seat and squeezed her eyes closed tight enough to scrunch her face.

Checking traffic, he pulled from the curb, then reached over, grabbing her hand. "I've got you," he said. "Just breathe."

Silence filled the truck and not knowing what else to do, Cruz let it drag out, giving her a minute to think.

That's what he would want. No platitudes. No talking him off a ledge.

Just silence.

An agonizing three minutes later, movement in his peripheral vision caught his attention. He peered over at her, found her staring at him with those sharp green lasers that had enthralled him since day one.

No tears. *Thank you, sweet baby Jesus.*

"I'm good," she said.

He laughed. "No, you're not, but I am, as usual, wildly impressed with your determination."

She snorted, drove her fist into the air. "That's me. Never let 'em see you sweat."

"How'd the exchange go?"

"Horrible. I suck at this."

She gave him a quick rundown of the drop and having experienced many jobs that went sideways, he sympathized.

The difference for him? He always had his brothers backing him up. A team figuring things out on the fly.

Cilla, at her insistence, had gone in alone to protect him from violating Zeke's precious NDA. If he got caught being the driver, plausible deniability sat on his side. *What documents? I thought she wanted coffee.*

This woman? Total rockstar. And he had to have her.

"The good news," he said, "is that you salvaged the drop and got out of there fast." He flashed her an all-teeth smile. "Gold stars for the rookie."

"I don't feel triumphant. I feel shitty."

"How about I take you home? If you're hungry later, we'll get some food."

He waited half a beat for her to, as usual, protest any suggestion of time off or relaxing. But, hey now, was she actually pondering this?

Priscilla Randolph, work-a-holic?

The sun glinted off her face in a way that accentuated the slight puffiness under her amazing green eyes.

His girl needed some rest, and he might have to push her on it.

"That sounds great," she said. "I have some work to do, though. Are you okay with that?"

Relief over not having to argue—or point out she looked like hell—settled on him. Progress. Always a good thing.

The light on the corner flipped to amber and he pressed the brake, easing to a stop behind the two cars in front of them. He swung his head, meeting her gaze. "If you can focus on work," he said, "I'm good with it. Gotta do what you gotta do."

"It'll only be about ninety minutes. Frankly, it's probably all I could stand tonight. You don't have to stay with me. I don't need a babysitter."

"Hell, no you don't. Trust me, this is a completely selfish gesture. I like being with you." He grinned. "It has nothing to do with you and everything to do with me."

That earned him a laugh. *Go, me.*

"Excellent." Gaze locked on him, she let out a breath. "I need a shower and clean clothes, then I'll feel better. If you want to help me, you'll take that shower with me."

And, hello. Jackpot. He made a show of rolling his eyes, letting out a long sigh to emphasize the point. "Now, you're asking a lot."

"Oh, please. Somehow, I think you'll rise to the occasion."

"Honey, I sure will."

. . .

THE FOLLOWING MORNING, AFTER WAKING UP WITH MR. Delicioso, Cilla regretfully left him naked as a jaybird in her shower when she hustled off to work. Distractions had put her behind and now with the added pressure of an office move, she needed to log some serious work hours.

But...Cruz.

Thank goodness he wasn't high-maintenance. Who had time for nonsense and men who needed constant stroking? If he were to survive in her world, particularly with her father involved, Cruz would quickly learn she moved fast and sometimes selfishly. All of which she tried to make up for along the way by not expecting too much.

All she needed was good company, good sex—something Cruz Blackwell had definitely cornered the market on —and good laughs.

Done.

Cilla strode into her office suite just after 8:00 and found Layla at her desk, grabbing something off the printer beside her.

"Morning," Cilla said.

Layla handed her the documents. "Morning, boss. Moving quote estimates. All three companies are coming over in the next two days to see the furniture. We'll have final numbers then, but this is a start."

As usual, her assistant doubled as a rockstar.

Cilla glanced at the quotes. All similar and way more than she'd expected. Yikes.

There went the emergency fund she kept in case every one of her clients suddenly fired her and she couldn't make payroll.

Next career? Moving company owner.

She held up the document. "Thank you. Have I told you lately that I love you?"

No-fuss Layla jerked her head. "You have. And thank you. Once you decide on a company, they'll supply us with boxes."

"Perfect."

The suite door opened and in stepped Paul Benzman. He wore a navy suit with a bright white shirt and a paisley tie that Cilla instantly hated. The matching pocket square was a nice touch, however.

But two visits in less than a week from someone who rarely came down here? Something told her this wouldn't be fun.

"Ladies," he said. "Good morning."

"Good morning," Layla chirped, then swiftly turned to her keyboard, smacking at the space bar to fire up the computer.

Layla, being an excellent judge of character, had never warmed to Paul. She found him, in her words, to be a pompous egomaniac who gave her the willies.

Cilla couldn't disagree. But she swung back, fully facing him and offering what she hoped was a pleasant smile. "Morning. What do we owe the pleasure?"

He shifted his gaze to Layla, then came back to Cilla, his message a no-doubter that he didn't want an audience. "Got a second?"

In actuality, no. She didn't have one second to spare for Randolph Industries. Not after the time she'd given them over the last weeks.

Some battles? Not worth fighting.

"I have a few minutes."

She led the way, her mind lit with zooming thoughts. The first visit from Paul resulted in him warning her about nosing around Morgan. Not only had she not backed off, she'd leaked confidential documents.

He just didn't know it. Yet.

Or did he?

No. He couldn't know. Could he? She'd anticipated at least having a day to come up with a decent denial in case Dad—or one of his executives—traced the betrayal to her.

Then again, Allison Caplin didn't win a Pulitzer for investigative reporting by sitting around daydreaming.

Cilla swung a right into her office, tossed her tote and purse on the sofa, and grabbed her phone, before moving to her desk and setting down the moving estimates.

She gestured to one of the guest chairs. "Have a seat."

"I'll stand. Won't be here that long."

"All right."

Not one to let people assume a position of power over her, Cilla remained on her feet behind her desk. "What can I do for you?"

"I got a call this morning. A reporter from the *Charlotte Times.*"

Should have pondered that cover story. Dammit. "*Oh-kay,*" Cilla said, laying on a why-should-I-care? tone she'd perfected over her years as a trial lawyer. Part of what she loved about presenting a case was the drama. The theatrics she practiced and employed while rolling out her client's version of events. Sometimes the difference between winning and losing came down to the best storyteller.

Cilla?

Solid storyteller.

Paul cocked his head. "Come on, Priscilla. We talked about you backing off our Morgan real estate deals. And now, suddenly, I'm getting calls from reporters about toxic levels of PFOA and PFAS in"—he threw his hands in the air —"what do you know, *Morgan.*"

Talk about good acting. Broadway at its finest, right here.

Ignoring his sarcasm, Cilla gave him her best bland look. No raised eyebrows or puckered lips or squinty stare. The nothing face. "I haven't spoken to any reporters about PFOA or PFAS."

Technically, that was true. She hadn't. Documents of interest is what she'd told Allison. No mention of forever chemicals.

Was her defense a stretch? Sure. But Paul didn't know that and she wasn't about to admit it.

"So," he said, "this is a coincidence?"

"Paul, I don't know what it is." She gestured to her office. "I'm busy managing a law practice. Now, I have work to do."

She picked up the estimates again and perused them. Still in front of her, Paul stayed put. So much for her not-so-subtle dismissal.

"Cilla," he said, "you're fucking up. Trust me on this."

A flash of white-hot anger burned right through the back of her neck. Already exhausted, not to mention stressed over her father's deceptions, she didn't need his lackey coming into *her* office and treating her poorly.

She dropped the document, then casually rested her fingertips on the edge of the desk. "Guess what, Paul? You don't get to come into my space and speak to me that way. Don't do it again. Ever. In fact, I'm getting tired of kicking you out of my office. Please leave. If my father has concerns, he can speak to me himself." She offered a sarcastic grin. "You have a lovely day."

Apparently unfazed, he lifted one shoulder. "I'll go. There's one more thing."

Great. "What's that?"

"Every week, IT gives me a report of when management-level employees remotely log in to our system."

He knows.

Or at least suspects she'd logged in as Dad.

Shit, shit, shit.

A thrumming at her temples nagged and her fingers tingled. Panicking wouldn't help. Still working for that Academy Award nomination, she gave him nothing. Zero body language. "So, you spy on your employees to see if they're working hard enough? Excellent."

"Actually, it's the reverse. We don't want them burning out. If they're putting in too many hours, we address it. Part of HR's work-life balance initiative. Frankly, it's a pain in the ass."

Heaven forbid he should care about his employees' well-being. "Well, since I lost my access, I know you're not about to tell me I'm logging in too much."

"Not you." He met her gaze, the hardness enough to split her skull. "Your father."

She forced out a laugh. "Now that's funny. I suppose you want me to tell him to slow down? Good luck."

"Not at all. Your father has a pattern. Once he leaves the office, he doesn't log in unless there's an emergency. He delegates. He's rarely in the system after hours."

"Good for him."

She picked up the quotes again, started reading while her mind zonked. Totally busted. He'd have to provide proof before she'd admit to it.

"Imagine my surprise," he said, "when the IP address came up as Steele Ridge. Wasn't that company your father hired to recover his painting in Steele Ridge?"

The IP address.

Dammit.

No wonder Rohan was a freak about IP address blocking

software. But how was she to know Randolph Industries pulled reports on their employees? Dad had never mentioned *that*.

She lifted her gaze to Paul's. "I'll give you some advice. My father doesn't like people disparaging me. Be careful who you're accusing."

"So," Paul said, "when I ask him about why he logged in at three in the morning from Steele Ridge, will he be surprised?"

"I have no idea when my father logs in and out of DOC. Nor can I tell you how he'll react to that question, other than to be offended that he's your boss and you're attempting to manage him. That doesn't work with Dad. But, hey, if you enjoy sacrificing yourself, go for it."

Having had enough of this trip through hell, she eased around the side of her desk and strode to the door, waving him out. "If you'll excuse me, I have work to do."

Finally, he turned, headed for the door and then . . . dammit . . . stopped right in front of her, invading her personal space. Refusing to cower, she cocked her head and the two of them locked eyes like a couple of stubborn rams.

Paul smiled an oily smile, then dragged his gaze over her body as if *that* would back her off. *Moron.*

"Take my advice, Cilla. Be careful. I've worked for your father a long time. He doesn't play nice when it comes to his company's profits."

Once again, threatening her. This was becoming a pattern. She ticked back to finding the bullet on her car. She'd chalked it up to her upcoming murder trial.

Could Paul have . . .?

Nah. Too much of a weasel. Then again, his annual bonus depended on profitability and pissing off the environmental lobby wouldn't bode well financially.

Cilla let out a sigh. "Again with the veiled threats?"

He shrugged. "I know what he's capable of. Family or not, we'll wreck you."

20

Eleven hours later, Cilla unlocked her condo, pushed the door open, and reached inside to flip on the entryway light. For a full thirty seconds, she waited to step in and peered around as if she could miraculously see through the wall that made up her entry hallway.

What the hell was she looking for?

A masked intruder? A bloody message scrawled across her meticulously painted soft-gray walls?

The run-in with Paul had rattled her. That alone pissed her off.

"High-security building, dingbat," she muttered.

Shaking her head, she stepped inside, closing and locking the door behind her. Not only did she have a door-man, they needed a code to enter the building from any entrance. Including the lobby. And the garage had an entry gate. If someone sneaked through, they'd still need the code to access the building.

No boogeyman here.

Besides, Cruz was ten minutes behind her. He'd spent the day doing research—whatever that meant—in Charlotte for a new assignment BARS had taken on. When she'd spoken to him after her impromptu meeting with Paul, he'd insisted on coming by the office to check on her. A gesture she found sweet and oh-so-welcome, but she had work to do. Important work that she'd sorely neglected.

Save it, she'd told him. That led to their first mini argument, which wound up with them compromising. She'd lock herself in the office all day, leave with Layla, and then Cruz could meet her at her condo for dinner.

At no point during the day was she to be alone. Blah, blah. Still, part of her found his concern sweet.

Blech!

She'd stuck to her word and now, every ounce of her wanted to see the big man walking through her door.

Maybe he'd stay again tonight. Was that too much to ask? Or maybe too needy for someone who scoffed at neediness?

Leaving the small entryway, she walked the few feet to the giant kitchen island and set her tote and purse on the end barstool. She still marveled at the green velvet cushions. Having gone with mostly soft whites and beige everywhere, the owner of the home decor store she'd purchased some of her furniture from had recommended a pop of color to warm things up. Cilla nearly gagged when the woman showed her the velvet stools, but she'd taken one home to test and gave it a solid ten on the I-love-it scale. Baffling as it was, it worked.

She adjusted her tote, making sure it didn't tumble off and noticed a scuff marring the edge of the deep green, velvet cushion. When did that happen?

Lurching bolt upright, she stood still, listening while a ball of tension lodged between her shoulder blades.

After a few seconds of once again convincing herself

there could be no boogeyman, she relaxed, let the silence draw her tight shoulders down.

Her cell phone buzzed. Doorman. She hit the speaker button. "Hi, Tom."

"Hello, Ms. Randolph. Cruz Blackwell to see you."

"Thank you. Send him up, please."

Two minutes later, the soft knock came. Checking the peephole first, she opened the door and found her own not-so-little piece of heaven standing there.

Grabbing his T-shirt, she hauled him close and kissed him, throwing every bit of herself into it, angling her body into his while their tongues did a lovely little dance that made every sexual fantasy she'd had about him come alive. Instantly, her nipples hardened, the sheer lace of her bra only intensifying her body's response.

At least until Cruz pulled himself away. "Well," he said. "Hello to you, too."

Still gripping his shirt, she dragged him inside, shut the door behind him, and locked it. "I've had a shitty day," she said. "You can make it better."

She kissed him again, sealing her mouth over his and working her hands down to the button on his jeans.

Again, he pulled back. "Whoa," he said. "Hang on."

What? Leave it to her to find the one highly sexual man who'd actually hit the pause button when she wanted to strip him naked.

No. No hanging on. She needed something she couldn't quite put into words, and she needed it now.

"Where's the fire?" he asked.

Oh, she'd tell him where it was. She headed toward the bedroom, stripping off her blouse and tossing it over her shoulder. "Listen," she said. "I'll be naked by the time I hit my room. You can join me or you can stand out here and I'll gratify myself. Either way, I'll have had an orgasm by the time I come back out here."

"Holy shit," he said.

Her bra went next. Before tossing it, she turned back, let him get a full view of her extremely hard nipples. His gaze drifted south, then back to her face and something in her softened. Went way too mushy for her own liking.

Him.

That's what she wanted. All of him.

"Cruz, I'm throwing myself at you. I need . . ."

Ugh. She broke eye contact, stared up at the ceiling for a few seconds to get her head together.

"What?" he asked. "Tell me what you need."

Frustration raked up her arms. Whether it was his refusal to screw her blind or her own neediness, she wasn't sure, but none of it sat well. A chill smothered her. So many feelings all at once. She gave up on the ceiling and met his gaze.

"I need you. That's all. You make everything better. There. Said it. Happy now?"

"Actually, I am."

"Excellent." She jerked her thumb toward the bedroom. "Then what's the problem because you're not moving?"

"Uh, no problem with that. Ever." He kept his gaze pinned to her face. "But let's talk a second. Tell me more about this situation with Paul."

Sigh. She stood literally half naked in front of him and he wanted to *talk*? A man. Wanted to talk?

This would only happen to her.

She let out a laugh, walked back to where she'd tossed her blouse and slipped it on again, not bothering with the buttons. If she had her way, it wouldn't be on long. "Paul suspects I've been logging in as Dad. I have to figure out a way out of it. Fairly simple." She reached for him again. "Now. Fuck me blind."

He laughed. "Talk about a one-track mind. Did he talk to your father about this?"

"You want to talk about my father? *Now?*"

"No. Trust me on that. I'm worried about you."

"You don't need to be. I'm a big girl and I know you'll help me." She lifted the hem of his shirt. "Now, let's get this off and you can give me what I need. I will, of course, reciprocate. How's that sound, fella?"

"That sounds freaking spectacular."

He let her pull the shirt off—*Yay, Cruz*—and she immediately went to work, dragging her fingertips over the rock-hard planes of his chest, down his cut abs to the button on his jeans.

"How much time," she asked, "do you spend in the gym?"

"Five days a week. Two, three hours a day. This week? Not so much. Been a little busy."

Her phone rang. *Dammit.*

Cruz stepped back. "Go ahead," he said. "Might be important."

She slipped the phone from her pants pocket. Tom again. "Hi, Tom," she said, her tone a tad too sharp.

"Sorry to disturb you. I have your father down here."

Cilla glanced back at a shirtless Cruz Blackwell and nearly cracked up over the smattering of her lipstick smeared across his mouth. He'd have to wipe that clean if her father were coming up.

Gah. She pondered her options. A.) Ditch Dad and screw Cruz's lights out. B.) Talk to her father and then screw Cruz's lights out.

She'd spent most of her life putting her own wishes and schedules aside in service to her father's whims and lately, all it got her was aggravation. And it was her own fault for not setting boundaries.

Time to take control and put herself first.

She'd tell her father to go away. That she had company and she'd speak to him tomorrow.

Cruz frowned. "What is it?"

"Tom, would you please hold a second?" She pulled the phone from her ear and tapped mute. "My father is downstairs."

"Awkward," he said.

"Should I tell him to leave?"

Putting his hands up, he snorted. "Hey, now. That's *your* call."

"Cruz!"

He laughed. "If it were up to me," he pointed to his crotch "and my extremely hard dick, yeah, I'd tell him we're about to fuck each other stupid and he should come back later. You? Not so sure that's the way to go."

Horrified, Cilla gasped. "You wouldn't say that to my father!"

"You sure you want to test that theory?"

She bared her teeth at him and he snorted. "Don't get pissy with me. Not my fault he's got rotten timing."

"I'll talk to him and get him out quick." Bending to pick up his shirt, she tossed it to him. "You'll need this back on. You might want to wipe my lipstick off." She tapped the mute button again and lifted the phone to her ear. "Tom? Sorry about that. You can send him up."

Minutes later, after Cruz scrubbed lipstick off and Cilla situated her clothing and fixed her hair and makeup, a knock sounded. She glanced at Cruz, propped on the edge of one of her island stools.

"Here we go," she said. "Other than my little meeting with his lackey this morning, I don't know why he's here."

"I guess we'll find out."

She marched to the door, paused a second to center herself and take a breath. Maybe paste on a smile and rid herself of the tension plaguing her a lot more lately when it came to Dad.

Too close. That's all it was. She needed distance. Something she'd have in a few weeks when she moved into her new office. Now wouldn't be the time to tell Dad about that. Too personal of a conversation to have in front of Cruz.

She swung open the door. "Hi, Dad."

He was still in his buttoned-up suit, and his stiff posture told her everything she needed to know. Pinched lips creased the skin around his mouth, his telltale that whatever he had going on—she could take a guess—wasn't good.

Dad nodded and without being invited in, stepped through the door. "We need to talk."

No peck on the cheek, no smile, no how-was-your-day.

Yep. Cilla was in the doghouse. Either Allison had called Dad for a comment or Paul filled him in.

Dad marched right past her into the open living room and halted.

"By the way," Cilla quipped, "I have company."

"I see that."

"Sir," Cruz said from behind her as she closed the door. "Nice to see you."

Walking the few feet to the living room, she found Cruz on his feet, shaking her father's hand.

"Cruz," Dad said, "didn't realize you were here. Apologies for the interruption."

Cilla joined them just as Cruz reclaimed his seat on the stool. "What's up, Dad?"

He swung his head to Cruz, then back to Cilla. "We need to talk. Privately."

Meaning, Cruz should get lost.

But guess what? This was her house and her father had shown up unannounced, probably to ambush her because that's the way he operated.

Right now, she wasn't inclined to allow him to control the situation.

"Cruz and I were about to grab dinner. Can you and I talk in the morning?"

"No."

Cilla turned back to Cruz. For what reason, she had no clue. All she knew was she was stuck and she thought . . . what? That he'd help her? Rescue her from the big bad wolf.

Piss on that.

Since when did she need anyone to fight her battles?

"Uh," Cruz said before she could spin back to Dad. "I can give you a minute."

"That'd be fine," Dad said. "Thank you."

All right. She could live with that compromise. However, she wouldn't have him cooling his jets in there for an hour simply to please her father. No. This meeting had a time limit.

A short one.

"Thank you, Cruz. It'll only be a couple of minutes. There's a television in my office."

She watched him walk down the long hallway to the second door on the right and turn into her office. The soft click of the door latch sounded and Cilla, already short on patience, turned back to Dad.

"What's so important?"

"I got a call from Allison Caplin an hour ago. Apparently, she called Paul this morning, as well. I avoided her call but tracked down Paul. He claims Allison has internal documents. He also shared his conversations with you regarding minding your own goddamn business."

And wow. Over the years, they'd disagreed plenty of times. He'd hollered occasionally, but this tone? The disgusted I-loathe-you tone she'd heard him use with her mother was new to Cilla.

She cocked her head, studied his pinched lips and the resulting deep lines around his mouth. "Dad, I don't appreciate your tone."

"I don't care what you appreciate. What did you do?"

A lot. That's what she did. And, although it felt dirty, slime on her skin, she didn't regret it. She'd tried to discuss it with him and he'd lied.

In Cilla's mind, he'd brought this on himself and she wouldn't be his punching bag.

"I'm not discussing this with you now. I've had a long day and you've barged in on my evening. We can talk tomorrow, but tonight? I'm out."

Dad, in his slick suit, perfectly groomed hair, and broad-shouldered posture, remained in his spot looking like the king he considered himself to be.

"We'll be done when I say we're done."

"Dad, you don't own this condo. I say what happens in here and what doesn't. Now, I don't want to argue with you. I'm tired and I've offered to talk tomorrow. That's all there is. Take it or leave it."

She angled around him and marched to the door, setting her hand on the lever before turning back to check on him, still rooted in his spot.

Even with the distance between them, his eyes bore into her, a look so fierce her knees nearly buckled. No way. She'd come this far, she wouldn't cave now.

He took two steps toward her and jabbed a meaty finger. "Who the hell do you think you are?"

She let go of the lever and marched back to him, leaving an arm's distance between them. Her father had never, not once, struck her, but based on the reddish tinge to his cheeks, his temper was about to flare.

Something she, never wanting to have that ire aimed at her, typically found a way to diffuse.

Today? Too tired. Too sick of navigating the minefield known as her father. She'd spent her life pleasing him. Trying to keep him happy and stay in his good graces.

Tired.

Really tired.

"I'm my father's daughter," she said. "*And* my mother's daughter."

"What the hell does that mean?"

"It means, Dad, I learned the hard-nosed stuff from you and doing what's right from Mom."

Dad's head snapped, the shock clearly hitting him. Good. Someone, finally, standing up to him.

"You did it!" he thundered. "You signed in as me and leaked those fucking documents! Goddamn you, Cilla!"

The words knocked her back a full step. After everything she'd done, all the legal advice and time lost trying to keep him and his company out of trouble, he dared to swear at her.

I'm so done.

"Goddamn *me*!" she roared. "All I've done for years, years, Dad, is save you from yourself. Try to keep you from making potentially devastating—and illegal—mistakes. Now, I won't help you. Knowing your company is polluting Morgan—and probably other communities if the chemicals have leaked into ground—and doing nothing while ten-year-olds get sick? Disgusting, Dad!"

Now it was Dad's turn to step back. She'd done it. She'd stunned him. Fired back at the bully and silenced him.

Satisfaction filled her.

As was typical, he recovered quickly, stabbing that finger at her again while his face morphed into an ugly purplish hue. "Have you lost your mind? I *gave* you your *life*," he thundered. "I *handed* you a career. *My* contacts put you on the map. Without *me*, you'd still be stacking cases in the prosecutor's office. You spoiled, ungrateful little bitch!"

Cilla gasped. Couldn't help it. Horror smothered her. He may not have physically struck her, but he didn't need to. His words did more than enough damage.

Once again, she steadied herself, digging her heels into the floor and stiffening her spine. "You may have sent clients my way, but I did the grinding. Staying up all night prepping for trials. I won't let you take credit for that."

Movement in the hallway caught her attention. Cruz. Striding toward them, his big body moving fast, his features like granite.

"Getting loud in here," he said, looking straight at her. "You okay?"

"She's fine," Dad said. "Go back to the office."

At that, Cruz halted. His arms hung loose at his sides, but the rest of him? The stiff shoulders and focused gaze were tight, tight, *tight*.

And that terrified her.

He'd told her about his past. His love of fighting and his parents' desperate move of getting him into wrestling.

She took a few steps, positioning herself midway between Cruz and Dad. Just in case.

Slowly, Cruz cocked his head. "Mr. Randolph, I don't take orders from you. I also wasn't talking to you."

Go.

Cruz.

Dismissing her father, he faced Cilla. "Are you all right?"

Oh, Cruz Blackwell, I might love you. Finally, a man not intimidated by the mighty Darren Randolph.

"I'm fine. My father was just leaving."

Dad's face twisted. Nostrils flaring, he gritted his teeth. "We're not done. And as soon as I find out what you leaked to Allison Caplin, I'll be back. You better not have done something we'll both regret."

"Whatever I've done, Dad, I'll never regret. And by the way, I bought office space. I'll be moving out of your head-quarters by the end of the month."

"Well," he said, "you have been busy." He flung a hand in Cruz's direction. "Funny how this guy comes into your life, and you've suddenly gone rogue. Trust me, Cilla, a good lay won't get you anywhere. Ask your mother."

Horror and a hefty dose of humiliation sent heat to her cheeks. Who the hell was he? Not the father she thought she knew.

"That's it," Cruz said, "this is done."

Wait. Her *mother*? What did that mean?

"My God," she said, "you truly are disgusting."

Cruz headed straight for Dad and no, no, no. She would not have the two of them screaming—or whatever else Cruz had on his mind—at each other in her home.

She stepped between Dad and Cruz, placing one hand on Cruz's chest and pushing him back. "Arguing won't help. Dad, I think we've said enough. Please leave."

He spun from her, stomping his way to the door, the rage flying off him like machine-gun fire.

At the door, he stopped and turned back. "Get your things out of my building by the end of the month. Otherwise, you'll pay me rent. You've gone too far. You betrayed me. And that's not a place anyone has ever found pleasant."

21

"So," Cruz said when Randolph slammed the door. "That went well."

Cilla stood in front of her massive kitchen island, her face pale. Still staring at the door her father had just stormed through, she shook her head. When she opened her mouth, the only sound was a strangled scoff.

She faced him, her green eyes flat and blown out like she'd been hit with a bomb.

"I'm . . ." She pushed her palm up her forehead leaving a slight red mark. "I don't know what I am."

"Has that ever happened before? A fight like that?"

"Um . . . *no*. I've witnessed it, but never directed at me."

Dang. He stepped closer, slid his arms around her and drew her close. "I'm sorry."

Snuggling into his neck, she nodded. "Me too. Thank you, though, for trying to intervene."

He backed up and gently gripped her forearms. "I promise you, I was attempting to stay out of it. When I heard him say bitch, I was cooked."

"He said that to me. Can you believe it? Who calls their own child a spoiled bitch?"

That one, he couldn't speak to. His own father had been rough on him, telling him not to be a dummy when he put hands on people and got tossed out of school for a few days.

Back then, Cruz was too stubborn to let it bug him. Plus, in Dad's defense, he hadn't actually called him those names. It was more his twisted way of offering advice, warning him to not make choices that would land him in a cell one day.

As a grown man? Cruz wasn't sure how he'd have handled his father speaking to him the way Cilla's had. He replayed the exchange in his mind and his fingers curled into fists. *Again.* When he'd first heard it, he stood in that office, behind the closed door, blood pressure in the red, ready to throw hands. He may have been sweating.

No one would ever—ever—again talk to this amazing woman that way.

He'd make sure of it.

"You'll never go through that again. I promise you that."

Being Cilla, she rolled her eyes. "Relax. It's done now. I don't need you playing hero. If you'd put a hand on him, he'd have had you arrested." She shook her head. "Wouldn't that be fun?"

Ew. He hadn't thought that far ahead, but yeah. Not good.

He dropped his arms to his sides and flexed his fingers—in, out, in, out—releasing some of the rotten energy. "Are you okay? I mean, relatively speaking?"

She moved to the island, rested her elbows on it and dipped her head to the surface, holding it against the cool marble.

"I don't know what I'm doing," she said. "It's like, the life I thought I had two weeks ago is gone."

"Hang on. That's not true. You're still you. You've got a successful law practice, you just bought real estate for a new office. Yeah, you're making changes, but you're still you."

"My father has been a huge part of my life. I see him nearly every day. Now? I don't know if he'll ever speak to me again."

"Cilla, no offense, if that's how he interacts with you, you might be better off."

As soon as the words left him, he shut his mouth. About now would have been a great time to engage some sort of self-control. Something. Anything. Speaking of fathers, his own would smack him upside the head.

He held up a hand. "I'm sorry. Shouldn't have said that."

Finally, she lifted her head. "Why? Because it's the truth? Because it's hard to hear?"

"It wasn't . . . nice."

"Please, Cruz. Screw nice." She stood tall and gestured to the door. "I've spent the better part of my *fucking* life trying to please that man. Literally saving him from himself while keeping him happy. Do you know how exhausting that is? It never stops. Every day, every week, every month, walking the tightrope. And he just called me a spoiled bitch."

Spinning around, she marched to the fridge, grabbed a bottle of wine—uh-oh— from the fridge and held it up.

"Want a glass?"

"No. Thanks. I'm good."

As dedicated as he'd been, after this shitshow, if she'd offered him a shot of whiskey, he'd have gone all in. What that said about him wasn't anything good.

He shook it off, gave himself at least some credit for not drinking in almost two weeks.

She smacked open a cabinet, sending the door slamming into the side of the fridge.

Yikes. "Stop." He strode around the island, gently shoved her aside and took the glass and bottle. "Keep it up and you'll wreck your house. It's not worth it. *He's* not worth it."

Cruz yanked the cork free, poured, and recorked the bottle.

She eyed the half-filled glass. "After what I just went through? Half a glass?"

He lifted one shoulder. "Drink that and see where you are. Trust me, satisfaction isn't found inside this bottle."

She took the glass, downed a healthy gulp, swallowed and peeled her lips back. "Ugh, I just remembered why I've had that in there so long. The stuff is terrible."

For some reason, Cruz laughed. Maybe it was relief. He didn't know. All he knew was he didn't want her drowning her senses in alcohol.

Uncorking the bottle again, he dumped it in the sink, rinsed the bottle, and set it beside the sink before facing her again.

"It's been a rough day," he said. "Why don't we order some food up, watch a movie, and chill."

She glanced at her tote sitting on the stool. "I brought work home."

"Can it wait?"

"That's the problem, Cruz, it's *been* waiting. It's a murder case. My investigator sent me his notes and I need to go through them."

"All right. Let's have dinner, I'll kill time while you catch up on work and then we'll watch a movie. How's that?"

"You're not mad?"

He blew raspberries. "Why would I be mad?"

"I've had relationships stall because of my job."

"Then those guys were idiots. I've told you, Cilla, there will be nights when I'm gone. Nights when one of my brothers will call me at two a.m. and I get up and leave. No question. It's what we do. I have a responsibility to my family. What kind of asshole would I be if I got pissed at you for meeting *your* responsibilities?"

She lifted her hands, covering her face. "I can't believe this," she said, her voice muffled.

Not knowing what the hell he was supposed to do and too terrified he'd say something stupid, Cruz stood there, waiting for her to finish rolling through whatever mind melt she currently had going.

When she dropped her hands, she let out a snort. "I can't believe I have met a man ornery enough to deal with the insanity known as my father."

"That's where you're wrong. I'm *not* dealing with your father. You are. Unless he comes at you the way he did tonight, I'm a bystander. Personally, I know he's your dad, but you don't need him. You can take care of yourself. Why do you need someone who makes you feel shitty?"

"In my mother's absence, he was all I had." She dipped her head. "He's my family."

He stepped closer, tucked his index finger under her chin and gently tilted her head up. "If I have my way, maybe my family can be that for you. One thing I can promise, no one will call you a spoiled bitch. We don't play that way."

Those amazing green eyes pooled with tears. Wow. His hard-nosed defense attorney who'd seen probably all sorts of atrocities, got sappy over the idea of having a family who'd be nice to her.

"That," she croaked, "would be great."

Then she kissed him. Full on, tongues and all, absolutely swallowed him. Not that he minded. Never.

He hoped they'd spend every night this way. Talking, eating, screwing.

Then doing it all again the next day.

Yep, yep, yep.

That would be a fantastic life.

WELL BEFORE DAWN, CILLA'S EYES POPPED OPEN, HER MIND A beehive of activity over her growing to-do list. Not just clients, but an office move and a war with her father. In the last two weeks, her world had gone completely sideways.

She'd roll with it. No other choice. Dad wanted her out. Fine. She'd get out faster than he could sign his name to another one of those lawsuits that hid the poison Randolph Industries pumped into the environment.

How could he have done this? Just sat by while his company risked people's lives?

Was he that much of a monster?

Apparently so.

She couldn't spend too much time dwelling on it. What's done was done and she needed to move on. Figure out where her relationship with her father could go. If anywhere.

Beside her, in the darkness, Cruz snored softly.

Slowly, she reached for her phone on the bedside table. As soon as she picked it up, the screen illuminated: 5:36. At least the daily barrage of texts hadn't started yet.

Concerned over waking Cruz, she glanced back at him. He'd thrown one hand over his chest and it rose and fell with each breath. She shifted her gaze to his relaxed cheeks and lips and smooth forehead that clearly, in sleep, found peace. Gone was that tough-guy hardness she'd seen the night before when he'd basically told Dad to fuck off.

She liked the tough guy, but she might love this relaxed, peaceful Cruz. Or maybe she loved both sides of him. His ability to be gentle while taking control when the occasion warranted.

A lovely reprieve since she didn't have to be in charge all the time. Particularly with managing her father.

She was simply . . . worn out. Exhausted from the mental bedlam Dad constantly created.

Throw in heartbreak to complete the emotional gutting.

Forget him. She had to. Had to put his harsh words, aimed at his own daughter, out of her mind.

Setting her phone down again, she lay back and peered at Cruz, lost in unconsciousness that she wished for.

When was the last good night's sleep she'd had? A while. Months. Maybe years.

Afraid to move, she studied him, the one who'd been dropped into her life at the exact time she needed him.

The universe at work? She'd never bought into all that mumbo jumbo, preferring to base her opinions on facts, but this time? Might have to buy in.

She might also have to face the fact that time spent with Cruz destroyed her routine. On a normal day, her alarm would blare at 6:30, dragging her from what some might call sleep. She'd call it a battle between consciousness and not.

Being fairly regimented, the last couple weeks notwithstanding, she thrived on her morning routine. Up at 6:30, showered and walking out the door at 7:40, arriving at the office at 8:00 sharp.

Layla often teased her about knowing what time it was based on Cilla's arrival.

Today would be different. Since she was awake, she might as well get going.

She eased to the edge of the bed and sat up. Given Cruz's mass, an upgrade to a king might be in order. Assuming this whole thing worked out.

Which, yes, she apparently wanted since she hadn't ever considered a bigger bed for any other man who'd been in her life.

She glanced back at Cruz, realized this, too, was out of her routine. A man in her bed on a work morning?

Highly unusual.

Still, she couldn't help but smile and all thoughts of work vanished. Maybe, given the time, she'd snuggle next to him. If the last few times they'd made love were any indication, it wouldn't be hard to rouse him from sleep. She'd make it worth his while.

Sure would.

Already, her nipples tingled, pressing against the fabric of her soft cotton pajamas.

She shook her head. Wasn't this her problem? Allowing herself to get distracted? Today, up early, she could put a dent in her to-do list. And that's what she'd do.

Get it done.

"I feel you looking at me," Cruz mumbled.

She whipped off a smile he couldn't see but made everything inside her come alive. Happy. Somehow, after the hellacious night, she found herself happy. "You're easy to look at."

"Wanna come back to bed and I'll put a smile on your beautiful face?"

"You already did. You just can't see it."

"Good to know. Always room for more, though."

"My kinda fella." She stood, then bent over the bed, popping a quick kiss on his lips, morning breath be damned.

He lifted his hand from his chest, reached out for her and she grabbed hold, entwining her fingers with his. "Go back to sleep. I need to get to the office. If I stay here, you'll tempt me. Just pull the door shut when you leave."

"No," he rolled to his side and rubbed his free hand over his eyes. "I gotta get back home. I'm already on Zeke's shit list and he wants an update on my research yesterday. Mind if I grab a shower with you?"

Mmmm. . .this might be a lovely way to start the day with a bang. Literally. "Not at all. Maybe you'll put that smile on my face again."

"Honey, you know I will."

AN HOUR AND TWO ORGASMS LATER, CRUZ AND CILLA STEPPED out of the elevator on the parking garage level under her building. Beyond the security gate, a horn blared as a truck and a few cars cruised by.

The early crowd on their way to work.

If Cruz hauled ass, he'd be home by 9:15 and could brief Zeke on Cilla's case. Then he'd catch up on the other BARS projects in the hopper. All this time commuting back and forth to Charlotte and Asheville was definitely jamming him up. Which didn't play nice with trying to stay off Zeke's radar.

Beside him, Cilla, dressed to kill in a navy pantsuit and stilettos, shifted her purse to her opposite shoulder while they walked to the assigned space for her unit. The spaces on either side were vacant, leading Cruz to think either those units were empty or the owners already gone. Two down from her car, he'd parked his truck in a visitor's space.

He glanced around, counted half a dozen vehicles parked opposite of theirs. Overall, this area seemed quiet.

He paused at the rear of the truck, unlocking it. He'd toss his overnight bag in and walk her to her car.

"Do you have a lot to do today?" Cilla asked.

Still holding the bag, he paused. "Some. I'll get caught up. If you need anything, make sure you call."

"I'm not your responsibility. You have a job. I can't have you running to my rescue every time my father gets mad at me."

"I'd say last night was a little more than him being mad. Will you see him today?"

"Not unless he comes to my office. Which, I don't think he'll do. He's predictable when angry. The silent treatment is his principal weapon. He'll stay away and not call me until I call him."

"Wow," Cruz said. "That's rough. Will you reach out?"

She shook her head, sending her chin-length hair swaying. "Not today. The way I feel now, it may be a good long while.

"I didn't sleep much last night," she added. "It gave me time to think about needing space. Room to breathe away from my father. I'm under his thumb. My office is two floors below his. I never thought much about the symbolism in that, but it's as if he's on top of me all the time."

"It's a valid point. The new office should help."

She nodded. "I think so. It feels . . . good. Like freedom. Does that sound horrible?"

"Not at all. I live and work with my family. It's 24/7. I love them, but I like my alone time, too."

"Exactly."

She dug her keys from the outer pocket of her purse and gestured to her car. "I'd love to stand here with you all day, but I need to go."

That, he most definitely understood. He felt it too. The pull to be near her. Talk to her.

Touch her.

He ran one finger down her perfect cheek and then kissed the spot before easing back. "Call me later," he said. "Let me know how the day is going."

"I will. If nothing else, it should be interesting."

"Hang on," he said. "Let me put this in my truck. I'll walk you to your car."

"I'll be fine."

She turned, headed for her car and . . .

Boom!

22

A BLAST, LIKE A BOMB GOING OFF, NOT THAT CILLA KNEW what that felt like, but the sound, *my God,* the sound bounced off thick concrete supports and rammed her ears like a pickax.

Then she was airborne, her body lifting from the ground, an altogether surreal experience. Blood roared and her pulse throbbed—*buhm, buhm, buhm, buhm.* Then everything crawled, a movie in slow-mo as she flew through the air, her arms splayed in front of her while she peered at her car, her precious Quattroporte, fully engulfed in flames.

"Cruz!"

Ooofff. She hit the ground, landing flat on her back, her head bouncing off concrete like a coconut.

Ow.

What the hell?

A fierce ringing filled her ears. She winced, then lifted her hands above her face, trying to focus, but her fingers blurred and melded into each other. Pain ripped through her right shoulder and she dropped her hand, lifted the other to her ear.

What the hell just happened?

Everything hurt. Her legs. Her arms. Pain whooshed up and down.

Face. Her left cheek. Something warm oozed down the side.

She lifted her hand from her ear, moving it toward her cheek. Then Cruz's face came into view just above her and he grabbed her hand. His mouth moved, but . . . nothing.

Only the ringing mixed with that *wha, wha, wha.*

When his face distorted, she blinked once, twice, three times until he came back into focus. "Can't . . . hear . . . you," she said.

Wha-wha-wha.

His lips moved again. ". . . . hear me? Cilla!"

Yes. She peered at his mouth, focusing hard while panic slithered, circling on the edges of fuzzy thoughts. A weird darkness crept in. Like a narrowing tunnel, slowly fading. "I . . ."

She tugged, trying to release her hand from his grip. "My . . . cheek," she said. "Hurts."

"Don't touch it."

What?

She fought him, yanking hard, but he held on. What the hell was he doing? "Cruz!"

Lifting her free hand, she made a move to touch her face. He grabbed that one too.

"Cilla, please. *Stop.* I need to call nine-one-one."

Call 911. Yes.

"What . . . happened?"

"Your car blew up."

And then blackness creeped in, slowly dragging over her, calling her to sleep.

"Tired," she said.

"Cilla!"

She popped her eyes open and Cruz's face appeared again. "Stay awake."

At that, she snorted. "Too late."

And then the blackness swallowed her.

CRUZ STOOD OVER CILLA'S ER BED WONDERING WHAT IN THE holy fuck had just happened.

They wouldn't let him ride in the ambulance with her, so he'd grabbed an Uber and met them at the hospital. His truck was still parked near Cilla's car, but he hadn't been able to get close enough to either of them to assess damage. For sure, hers was toast. Having no time to ask questions, he had zero information, but how the sucker went up? The blast blowing the windows out and sending glass and metal and shards of plastic flying?

Had to be a bomb of some sort.

One that blew them both off their goddamned feet. Cilla, way lighter than he was, had gone straight airborne while the bed of his truck did a fine job of shielding him. He'd watched, helpless, as she careened through the air. Despite the truck offering some cover, he'd blasted backward, hitting the pavement for what seemed like a solid minute, but was probably only a few seconds before her.

Broken glass and plastic flew, some of it carving into her cheek. He'd only been grazed on the exposed side of his face.

Unable to access Cilla's phone, he'd told the cops who'd responded to the call who she was and that her father was Darren Randolph, but he didn't have a cell number for him.

Plus, after the night before, he never wanted to see or

speak to the son of a bitch again. Still, Cilla was his child and he deserved information regarding her condition.

The cop Cruz had spoken to on-scene assured him they'd contact Randolph. For now, Cruz stood next to the bed where Cilla lay, IV in her arm, eyes closed and half zonked from a concussion, a six-inch and violent looking gaping wound down her face and some sort of shoulder injury she'd need an MRI for because the X-rays showed no broken bones.

A dark-haired guy with chubby cheeks and freckles entered the ER bay. He wore a lab coat that said Dr. Tiles.

This guy was the doctor? He looked about twelve.

The man held his hand to Cruz. "I'm Dr. Tiles."

Cruz nodded and shook hands. "Cruz Blackwell. This is Priscilla Randolph."

"I understand she was involved in an explosion?"

"Yeah. Not in it but standing near her car when it blew. She was leaving for work."

He nodded like this news was nothing horrifying. Nothing out of the ordinary for an ER doc in a Charlotte hospital that saw all sorts of violence-related injuries.

Still, to Cruz? Big deal. Major big deal.

"All right," Tiles said. "Were you there? Can you tell me what happened?"

"Yeah. Her building has an underground garage. We were walking toward the car and it . . ."

Whoa. Cruz's head spun for a second, the room whirling around him. His breath caught and he gripped the bedrail, hoping to hell his legs didn't cave on him.

"Mr. Blackwell?"

Cruz blew out a hard breath. "Yeah. Sorry. I guess it all caught up."

Tiles studied him with the fascination of a scientist on

the hunt for a rare antidote. "Understandable," he said. "I see some scratches on your face. Were you injured in the blast? Hit your head? Anything?"

"No. I'm good. I got knocked down, but caught myself. Didn't hit my head."

Cilla had taken the brunt.

All he knew was they'd both been sent ass over elbow and by the time he'd gotten to her, she was flat on her back on the concrete with blood dripping from that canyon of a wound.

Cruz cleared his throat. "We, uh, were knocked off our feet. I don't know if she got hit with glass or some other debris," he pointed at her face, "but she's got that nasty gash."

"Let's take a look." Dr. Tiles moved to the opposite side of the bed. "Priscilla? Can you hear me?"

Cilla's eyes fluttered open. A good thing, considering she'd suffered a head injury.

"Hi," Tiles said. "You're in the emergency room. I'm Dr. Tiles. May I examine you?"

Her eyes drifted closed, the lids obviously too heavy for her. "Yes," she said.

The doc lifted the bandage, cocked his head one way, then the other and replaced the dressing. "It's a large laceration. We'll clean that up and I'll get it stitched."

Cruz nodded. "Here? In the ER?"

"Yes, sir."

Cruz peered back at Cilla and the unmarred perfection of the right side of her face in contrast to the gaping wound he'd seen on the left. For whatever reason, his mind kicked back to the *Charlotte Lawyer* covers he'd seen online after he'd first met her and had gone digging for info.

Not that she was a cover model for a living, but a

woman this freaking stunning? One who clearly cared about her appearance, given the care she took putting herself together, he had to think, wouldn't want her face butchered.

Would anyone want their face butchered?

Conjuring what little of a filter he could, he chose his words and faced the doc. "I mean no offense here, but I have to ask. Are you a plastic surgeon?"

"Me? No. We don't have plastic surgeons in the ER. Typically, we get patients stitched and then they follow up with a plastic surgeon if necessary. I assure you, Mr. Blackwell, I've stitched plenty of wounds. I'm good at it."

Good? He's *good*.

Cruz nearly laughed, because the gash on Cilla's face? Nasty. Right now, he'd pass on good. They needed great.

"I'm sure," Cruz said, tapping the browser on his phone. "But you don't know her."

He searched Cilla's name, clicked on the images tab and found the *Charlotte Lawyer* covers he'd been so enthralled with. On the latest, she wore a black pantsuit and her signature sky-high heels while standing in a courtroom in front of a judge's bench. Her hip-shot stance and crossed arms screamed badass and this doc needed to see it. To see her in action. So to speak.

He held the phone up for Tiles.

"This," Cruz said, "is Cilla. She's a lawyer. On the freaking cover." He pulled the phone back and enlarged the image. "Look at her face. She's . . . beautiful. No, more than that. Stunning. She gives pressers and sound bites like a rock star. The camera *loves* her."

He paused a second, glancing down at her. Jesus, she was banged up. That alone carved a hunk of his soul away.

And that? The sadness and worry he'd been feeling

since watching her sail through the air after some prick had blown up her car?

He'd never experienced it before. Not since his father died. And that scared the hell out of him.

Something squeezed in his chest, gripping so tight it stole his air. He held his breath a second, then blew it out before facing Tiles again. "*I* love her. I'll love her no matter what she looks like. But her?" He shook his head. "She's not lucid. She can't tell you what she wants, but I'm sure she doesn't want a giant scar down the front of her face."

"Sir—"

"Richards," Cilla croaked.

Both he and Tiles looked at her. "What?" Cruz leaned over the rail, got right next to her face. "Cilla? What did you say?"

"Doctor," she said. "Richards. Riley Richards. Client."

And who in the fuck was Riley Richards? And why was she talking about her clients now?

Unless . . .

Cruz went back to his phone and googled Dr. Riley Richards.

Bingo.

Plastic surgeon.

"Okay," he said. "Here we go. Riley Richards is a plastic surgeon. She must be one of Cilla's clients."

"Call her," Cilla croaked.

Cruz tapped on the link. "I'm on it."

"Mr. Blackwell," Tiles said just as someone picked up the other end of the line.

Cruz held a finger up, silencing Tiles.

Minutes later, after throwing Cilla's name around and explaining to the doctor's nurse what he was calling about, Dr. Richards got on the phone.

"Put the doctor on," she told Cruz in a no-nonsense tone that reminded him of Cilla. No wonder she liked her.

He handed the phone over, waiting patiently while Tiles offered a quick assessment of the situation and then said, "All right. We'll see you soon."

Tiles handed the phone over. "She has privileges here and is on her way. I guess y'all have some pull."

"Not me." Cruz pointed at Cilla. "Powerful family."

Then he paused and for the first time in nearly an hour, stopped moving and thinking and worrying and just dipped his chin to his chest and let out a breath.

This entire episode was straight out of hell.

One second they were standing in the parking garage and the next? *Boom!* Hunks of glass and various other debris raining down like tiny daggers.

"You okay?" the doc asked.

Probably not. He didn't have time to think about it. He needed to get Cilla squared away. See if she could stay awake long enough to tell him what the fuck she needed.

Did she want her father here?

After last night? Who knew?

He'd have to get her mom's number, though.

First, he'd deal with Doctor Tiles. He lifted his head, met the ER doc's eye. "I'm fine. Look, I'm sure you're great and we mean no offense by calling in this other doctor. Call it a second opinion, call it whatever, but Cilla needs to come out of this knowing we did everything we could for her."

"Well, obviously. I'd love to be the one to do that."

"I get that. Believe me. All I want is for her to not freak out when she wakes up and looks in a mirror."

"She'll still probably be upset."

He shrugged. "Maybe. But I'll be able to tell her we did

what she wanted. That we did the best we could for her. And that's what'll matter."

CILLA, DRESSED IN A HOSPITAL GOWN, LAY IN BED WAITING FOR Dr. Richards's arrival while doing her best not to think about her head and the pounding pain. It was as if a psychotic, caged gorilla rattled around in there. Being grateful for surviving only got her so far with King Kong doing his thing inside her skull.

She inched—that hurt—her head sideways to where Cruz sat in the crappy chair beside the bed, his thumbs hard at work on his phone.

Now that her initial mental fog had cleared and she realized that yes, her car had blown up right in front of them, she owed him a thank-you for not letting her touch her cheek.

"Hi," she said.

He whipped his head up and offered her his amazing smile. The full-wattage one that, if she were any sort of a decent judge, held a boatload of relief. "Hey, you. How's the head?"

"Hurts."

"To be expected. You have a concussion."

"I always wondered what those felt like. Now I know. Anyway, thank you."

"For?"

Everything? She lifted her hand and—ow—winced when the IV needle tugged. She lowered it and raised the other, pointing to her face. "Not letting me touch it."

He shrugged. "You'd have done the same."

Yes. She would have. He'd stayed calm when others

would freak and she appreciated it. Maybe even loved him for it.

Speaking of that little word, had she been dreaming when she'd heard him tell the ER doctor that he loved her? Did that actually happen or did she, in her concussed state, imagine it?

She couldn't be sure, but what a lovely thought.

Cruz stood, slid his phone into his front pocket and dropped a kiss on her head. "Richards is on her way. You're a beast thinking of that when you're half zonked."

"I defended her son on a vandalism charge. He's in college and was drunk. Carved his name in fresh cement on campus."

Cruz laughed. "Idiot."

"He's a good kid. Dean's list, tons of volunteer work. The university wanted to use him as an example and pressed charges. I got him off with community service."

"The ER doc wasn't too happy with us, but he'll get over it."

For a second, she considered asking for the mirror out of her purse.

Why bother?

Not only was the wound covered, but she was also in no rush to see it.

She'd long since accepted the fact that she had a sense of vanity. Growing up, she'd been aware of mother's beauty and her father had expectations of how they appeared in public. Never disheveled. For a time, jeans were prohibited. Jeans, for crying out loud.

After years of being critiqued before walking out the door, Cilla was anal about her appearance.

And a giant scar down the front of her face?

Not something she could deal with at the moment. She let out a breath and pushed her thoughts to more practical matters.

"Where's my car?"

"The cops said they'd have it towed. Want me to call them?"

"No. I'm sure they'll let me know. Did you see it? How bad is it?"

His lack of response or body language gave her the answer.

"That bad, huh?"

He reached for her hand, tangled his fingers with hers. "I'm sorry. I didn't get close enough to see the interior. From the interior fire, guessing it's not good."

"Well, that sucks. I love that car."

"I know. Good news is you can get another one."

True. She'd custom-ordered the first one, she'd custom-order the second.

"How about your truck?"

"Not sure. It didn't look too bad. I got out of there before the crime scene guys were done. I'm not worried about it."

"Oh. *Jesus.*"

At the sound of her father's voice, Cilla did that inching thing again with her head, peering left and trying not to send the room spinning.

Gaze glued to her, Dad stepped into the room.

Still holding her hand, Cruz stood, clearly ready for whatever might occur in the next minute. Cilla's pulse kicked up and she squeezed Cruz's hand, letting him know she was A-okay.

For now, anyway.

"Dad," she said, "you didn't need to come. Everything is under control."

He rushed to the bedside, opposite Cruz. "Sweetheart." He gripped the handrail. "I'm so sorry." He shook his head. "What happened?"

"Car blew up," Cruz blurted, his tone carrying an icy edge. "Interesting how that happens after your buddy Paul threatened her."

Dad's head snapped back, and a horrified, open-mouthed gawk took over his face. "You think *Paul* did this? That's ridiculous."

"Is it?" Cilla said. "Cruz is right. Paul is an executive at your company. If you remember, I helped you renegotiate his compensation package. He has certain incentives based on profitability. My digging around about forever chemicals could impede that."

"Cilla! You can't accuse the man with no proof."

Couldn't she? "Please, Dad. You of all people know how money changes things."

He stared at her for a few seconds until his gaze dipped to the bandage covering her face. "What happened to your face?"

"Flying debris," Cruz said. "Probably a hunk of glass when the windows blew out. She wouldn't know, she was unconscious." He cocked his head and narrowed his eyes at Dad. "I saw it, though. The way that car came apart. From what I hear, the cops think it was a pipe bomb." He pointed to Cilla's face. "This is *nothing* compared to what could have happened. She could have been inside that car."

Dad gave him his hard-nosed mutinous face. "What time did this happen?"

Cilla rested her head back. They were talking about her car being blown to bits and her father wanted to know timing? "Around six-thirty, but what does that have to do with anything?"

"A lot," Dad said. "Think about it. You like routine. You left for work today earlier than normal."

Cruz turned to her. "Who knows your schedule? The cops are going to ask you, so you might as well think about it."

She considered that. Layla, of course, knew her schedule better than most, but her assistant had no reason to do something like this. She wouldn't. Ever. Cilla believed that.

Her mother also knew her schedule. And her doorman. Aside from those few people, there weren't many others. Maybe a few friends.

None of whom would do this to her.

"Outside of my doorman," Cilla said, "my parents and my assistant. Only a few people."

"How about Paul?" Cruz faced Randolph. "Does he know her schedule?"

Cilla squeezed Cruz's hand again. As much as she didn't want to agree with her father at this moment, he was right. Cruz shouldn't be spouting off about suspects. "Hey," she said softly. "We're okay. I don't want us jumping to conclusions. Law enforcement will investigate and hopefully find whoever is responsible."

"I know. But we can narrow the suspects."

"It's not a secret I'm regimented. But my father's employees probably don't know what time I leave my house."

"Maybe a disgruntled client," Dad offered. "You've had threats before."

The bullet left on her car and now this, when she had a pending murder trial? It could all be connected.

Maybe.

"We need to see the garage's video footage," Dad said.

Cruz peered down at Cilla. "I'm already on it. I asked Rohan to look."

Ah, Rohan. Fantastic idea. "Has he found anything?"

"As of twenty minutes ago, still working on it. He's close, though. We may know before the cops who did it."

"That's good," Dad said. "I'll bury whoever did this. I promise you that."

Cilla let out a soft snort. She couldn't help it. "Last night you weren't feeling so protective. In fact, you told me you'd never forgive me."

"Sweetheart, I was upset. You know me. I don't mean half the things I say."

"You said hurtful, no, devastating, things I will never get over. Ever. This whole situation is stressful and, frankly, I don't need you adding to it. I'm waiting for the doctor to come in and stitch me up and I'd prefer you not be here. I'd like you to leave."

At this, Dad drew his eyebrows together, confusion seeming to take over his face. "You're throwing me out?"

King Kong kicked behind her left eye, so Cilla put her head back and closed her eyes. "That's awfully dramatic, Dad."

"She's throwing you out," Cruz said. "Leave."

"Who the hell do you think you are, talking to me that way?"

"I know exactly who I am. Your daughter has asked you to leave. Unless you have more to tell her about what happened this morning."

Now she'd had it. What she didn't need was these two screaming while her head came apart. She opened her eyes, but didn't bother lifting her head "Please," she said. "Just . . . stop. Dad, I need you to go."

Cruz shook his head. "Sorry, babe. I saw what happened last night. He said you betrayed him. And, this morning, your car blew up at a time he knows you're usually nowhere near it." He faced Dad again. "You yourself brought that up."

For a few seconds, Cilla was still, her body somehow completely numb. If only her head could be the same. Despite the pain, her thoughts whizzed.

Cruz had a point. But Dad? No. Couldn't be.

Could it?

Her father had always been big on revenge. On testing people and dealing out punishment when the results proved unfavorable.

He'd done it with her own mother. Someone he'd claimed to love.

Would he do this? Risk his own daughter's safety?

No.

6:30.

She'd broken routine. No, no, no.

Cilla sucked a breath, slowly turned her head, and met her father's gaze, holding it for a long few seconds before deciding to dive into what would more than likely send her father on a rampage.

"Dad? Did you have my car blown up?"

For a moment he stood still, his face like solid stone, refusing to reveal any reaction. What kind of man could be so calm when his daughter asked a question like that?

Chill bumps broke out on Cilla's exposed arms. Could her father be that evil?

"This is ridiculous!" Dad said. He spun on his heel and headed to the door. "I won't be accused of this! Once you're clearheaded, you'll apologize."

Not likely.

"Dad! Wait."

He stopped, angled back to her with a smug smile, but he wouldn't hear what he wanted. Not from her anymore.

When she didn't speak, her father's smile faded, and he held out his arms. "Either apologize or I'm leaving."

"Funny," she said. "We haven't heard you say you didn't do it."

23

THE ROOM FELL SILENT WHILE CRUZ STOOD BY, LETTING CILLA handle her father, but—holy hell—he wanted a piece of this asshole.

An enormous piece.

Just pound the fucker into the ground. His own father's words came back to him. *Know what you're doing, son. Don't be so rash all the time.*

If Cruz's suspicions about Randolph blowing up that car were true, the guy deserved whatever pain and suffering Cruz and the justice system could inflict.

Then the asshole turned to him, pointing his finger and sending a juicy surge of adrenaline roaring.

"This is your fault!" Randolph hollered, his face so red it looked about to burst. "You're filling her head with lies! You shut your fucking mouth!"

And, oh, oh, oh, Cruz knew the craziness he saw in the man's eyes. Had experienced it enough himself in the seconds before he lost his shit on someone. The rage. The need for release. The lack of control.

Yeah, with just a tiny push, Cruz might help old

Randolph over the edge. "No," Cruz said, his voice level and matter of fact. "Not until I hear you say it. That you didn't blow up your own daughter's car. Say it."

"She's my child!"

Un-huh. Still no denial. *Got him.* "Yes, she is. And you'll admit what you did. Tell her."

Voices from the hallway sounded. "Call security," someone said.

Randolph's fingers curled into fists. Oh, this fucker. Let him try it. Let him take a swing. Cruz would love nothing more than to beat the ever-loving shit out of him. And right now, he didn't give a crap that the guy was thirty-five years his senior. If he took a swing, Cruz considered it open warfare.

Besides, if anyone deserved an ass-kicking it was Darren Randolph.

"You're messing with the wrong person, son." Randolph said.

"I'm not your son." Cruz held his arms out. "And I'm right here. Bring it on."

"The two of you," Cilla said, "stop."

Randolph didn't bother looking at her. His gaze stayed glued to Cruz. "I'll ruin you and your fucking family."

Not likely. He might be powerful, but BARS had enough resources to do battle. Rohan alone could probably dig up wads of dirt on Randolph.

"Try it," Cruz said. "With what I know about your company and forever chemicals, you have way more to lose than we do."

"Cruz!"

He peered at Cilla. "I'm not one of his lackeys." Cruz faced Randolph again. "If we find out you had something to do with this, you'd better hide because I'll come for you. *I'll ruin you.*"

"Dad!" Cilla said, her voice rising and carrying a screechy edge. "Please, tell him you had nothing to do with this."

Randolph faced her, his gaze zooming straight to the bandage and then his head whipped back, as if someone had struck him. "My beautiful girl," he said. "My beautiful, beautiful girl. We'll get you the best. I swear to you."

Cilla blinked, then blinked again and her eyebrows drew together, giving her a puzzled appearance. As if trying to decipher a foreign language.

"That's what you're worried about?" she asked. "How I'll look? Dad, it doesn't matter."

Hold on. Whoa, whoa, whoa.

"Wait." Cruz faced Randolph again, his mind ticking back to minutes before. "You know her routine. What time she leaves. *You* said she'd left earlier."

Randolph's eyebrows shot up and another spurt of adrenaline fired.

Got him.

"You fucker!" Cruz cornered the bed, storming toward Darren Randolph, his finger stabbing the air. "You did this!"

Still by the door, Randolph pointed. "Stop right there."

"Cruz!" Cilla shouted.

Rage in full boil, Cruz blew right past that. This fucker may not have put that bomb in his daughter's car, but Cruz had a feeling he knew something about it. And he'd find out. Whatever it took.

Barely two feet away, Cruz stopped, let his hands hang at sides, refusing to touch Randolph, but ready for whatever the old man would do. "Who did it?"

"What are you talking about?"

"Your buddy Paul? He's been threatening her. You

know that, right? About the bullet left on her car? Or was it you? Maybe you wanted to scare her? The bullet is one thing. This? If she had been in that fucking car, she'd be dead!"

"You shut your mouth!"

Then Randolph did it, he raised his hands . . . and shoved Cruz.

"Dad! Stop it!"

"Shut up," Randolph said, shoving Cruz again.

Cruz fought for the control his parents had always begged for. Somehow, that control, all the lessons he'd learned growing up, vaporized.

Or maybe he just felt like punishing this guy.

Cruz squared his shoulders. "Don't touch me again."

Randolph put his hand on Cruz's chest . . . and shoved. One step back. That's all Cruz gave this fucker.

On his best day, patience wasn't exactly Cruz's strong suit. Now, he glanced at Cilla, ghostly pale, her green eyes giant orbs. "Stop it! Both of you!"

But Randolph? He lifted his hand again, set it flat on Cruz's chest and . . . shoved.

And now Cruz was done.

Bam!

He swung, ramming Randolph square on the jaw and knocking him back a few steps. The sight of blood offered a sick satisfaction Cruz hadn't experienced in years.

Randolph stumbled, lost his balance and windmilled his arms, grabbing for the door, but missing. He landed on his ass in the doorway.

Not being one to kick a man when he was down, Cruz stood in place, hands loose at his sides. "Get up," he said. "If you wanna finish it, get up."

"Cruz!" Cilla shrieked. "Stop!"

Randolph stayed on the ground, just set his head against the floor and lifted his hands to his face.

"Dad? Are you all right?"

Finally, the man dropped his hands, got to his knees, and peered up at Cilla.

"I'm sorry," he said, his voice shattering like glass in a hurricane. "It wasn't supposed to be this way."

"Dad?"

Still on the ground, he shook his head. "I never wanted . . . Cilla, you have to know, I never wanted you hurt. It was just a car. A lesson. That's all. You weren't supposed to *be* there."

"Oh, Dad."

A security guard flew into the room, spotted a bloody Darren Randolph on the ground and his gaze flew to Cruz.

"It was him," Randolph said. "Call the police. I want him arrested."

THE FOLLOWING MORNING, AFTER BEING BAILED OUT BY A none-too-happy Zeke and checking on Cilla, whose mother had flown in the night before to take care of her after she'd been released from the hospital that morning, Cruz drove his ass back to Steele Ridge.

Thankfully, he'd parked far enough from Cilla's car that his truck came through with only minor scratches and dents from flying debris. All of which he could repair.

That was the easy part. Cilla? Pissed at him. He got that message loud and clear when she'd said as much.

Hell, at least she was honest. A good sign, he thought.

Next would be his mother.

By getting locked up, he'd done the one thing his parents had spent most of his teenage years fearing; he brought embarrassment to his family. Plus, he'd been unavailable for Cilla.

Somehow, he'd time-warped back to the restless teenager who couldn't seem to stay out of trouble.

Helluva twenty-four hours.

Just after 1:00, he stood in the hallway outside the Friary's kitchen where Zeke had told him their mother was having lunch. Mom had texted him an hour ago informing him they needed to talk upon his arrival.

And he'd definitely gotten the impression it wasn't a request.

Time to slide into his big boy pants, explain himself, and apologize for his unacceptable behavior.

Gee, he might get a time-out after this.

Sent to his room.

He shook it off. Sarcasm wouldn't help him. Particularly since he'd caused this mess. Bad enough he had to deal with his own humiliation over the entire fucking episode, now he had to face Mom's disappointment.

Maybe that Asheville Craftsman wasn't such a bad idea.

"I know you're there," Mom said. "I heard your footsteps."

Dang.

Here we go. He drew a breath, stepped into the kitchen, and strode toward her, stopping a few feet from where she sat at the island, a plate in front of her with a discarded napkin sitting on top.

She swiveled, met his gaze, then shook her head. "Cruz Blackwell, if I weren't so happy to see you, I might have to kill you. How's Priscilla?"

Ouch. Cruz shrugged. "She's okay. Zeke dropped me at her place for my truck, so I stopped to see her. They released her this morning. Her mom is there."

"Good," she said casually. "Too bad you couldn't be there

for her. Considering you *spent* the *night* in *jail*. I thought you'd grown out of this nonsense."

Yeah. So had he. "Apparently not. I'm sorry."

"You should be." She stood, picked up her plate and walked to the sink where she set the plate down before turning back to him.

Then she did it. Folded her arms across her chest in that way she always did when about to hand one of them their heads.

Already his ass cheeks clenched.

"I don't understand," she said. "You attacked Priscilla's father. I won't bother asking what you were thinking. Clearly, you weren't."

Taking his life into his hands by moving closer, he walked to the island, dropped into the stool at the end. "Guessing Zeke filled you in?"

Across from him, Mom shifted and leaned back on the sink. "He gave me the highlights."

"Zeke said Rohan grabbed security video from the garage. Some guy drove up to the gate in the middle of the night, punched in the code and went straight to her car. He knew what he was looking for and crawled underneath. Probably planting the bomb. Randolph all but admitted he arranged it. To teach Cilla a lesson."

Mom gawked. "How a man could have his own daughter's car blown up, I can't comprehend. Pure evil. He'll be dealt with. Either in this world or the next. Now, I need to hear from you. What on earth possessed you?"

Good question. "I was mad. Lost it a little."

"A *little*?"

He threw up his hands. "Hey, it was a one-time thing."

"That landed you in jail." She shook her head, let out a huff. "I want to be furious with you. Part of me is. I'm . . . I don't know." She held up a finger. "Actually, I *do* know. *You* are a carbon copy of your father. In every way. When we met, he had that fire in his belly, just like you. He told me watching you was like watching his life play out all over again. It terrified him. We tried so hard to avoid this, Cruz. All he wanted was for you to live a decent life and not . . ."

She clammed up, folding her lips in and clearly holding something back.

Well, he was here and ready to face whatever lecture she'd level on him, so they'd might as well hash it out. He rolled one hand. "And not what?"

Finally, she shook her head. "We never wanted you boys to know. Ever. But I had to tell Ash. He wanted to join the FBI and I knew they did background checks. I couldn't let my child be blindsided."

What the hell was his mother talking about? "Mom? Why are we talking about Ash and the FBI?"

"Because when I met your father, he'd just gotten out of prison. He'd been paroled six months earlier."

Wait. What? *Parole?*

Cruz stared at her for a solid ten seconds.

"Breaking and entering," Mom continued. "He'd done two and a half years and swore he'd never go back."

"Dad was in *prison*?"

"How do you think he got into the repo business? For him, it was the legal way to steal. It gave him the adrenaline rush he needed. As long as it was legal, I didn't care. I loved him and saw beyond the not-so-good stuff. I promised him that if he stayed straight, I'd love him forever. Meant it, too. Then we had you boys and he didn't want any of you ending up like him. He wanted our boys to be solid citizens. And then you started acting out. Fighting and staying out past curfew and your father panicked."

Holy, holy shit. Suddenly, the whole of Cruz's childhood came into sharper focus. Like a filter had been lifted and everything appeared in full, vibrant color. All the smacks on the head and yelling. Mom intervening and sending a pissed-off Cruz to his room to cool down while Mom tore into Dad one floor below for being too tough.

"Wow," Cruz said. "That's why he was so hard on me."

Mom nodded. "Like I said, he recognized your fire. None of the other boys had it. Sure, they played rough, but you? You had that mean streak and he wanted it gone. He did it the only way he knew how."

Fairly gobsmacked, Cruz sat back, studying his mother's puffy eyes. Had he made her cry? Ack. That took the whole thing to another level of craptastic. "Mom, I'm sorry I disappointed you."

"You did. I'll get over it. You disappointed yourself, too, and I think that might be worse."

No kidding.

Mom shook her head. "What about Priscilla? If her father is bent on pressing charges, you could go to prison. I don't think Ash can help you out of this one."

"I wouldn't ask him to."

"Maybe Priscilla can help."

He shrugged. "I haven't thought that far ahead. She needs to rest now. She found me a lawyer. He said he'd talk to the DA about dropping the charges. Extenuating circumstances. What with her father blowing up her car."

"I imagine he'd want this dealt with as quietly as possible. Obviously, you care about her enough to take on a man like Darren Randolph."

This part was simple. He nodded. "I like her. A whole lot."

"I see. Do you think beating up her father is endearing?"

Having had just about enough of this flogging, Cruz held his hands up. She might be his mom, but he was also a grown-ass man. "I didn't *beat him up*. I punched him. Once. After he pushed me. *Three* times."

Mom shook her head again. One of those slow torturous ones. Back and forth, back and forth, back and forth. "I don't know what's worse. You being foolish enough to allow yourself to be lured into that trap or you actually hitting the man. How could you not see he was baiting you?"

"I was a little distracted after we almost got blown up. I mean, she could have been killed. And the idea of losing her? After finally finding someone who makes me laugh and doesn't get insulted when I'm at my unfiltered best, well, that's a gift, Mom. A freaking truckload of gifts. And I could have lost her."

Mom cocked her head, then twisted her lips, fighting a smile. Great. Now she was having fun? Seriously?

Yes, let's make this as painful as possible for Cruz and then wallow in the enjoyment.

"Cruz Blackwell," she said, "are you in love?"

Love. There was that word again. Somehow, the second time around, it didn't terrify him as much. Didn't make him feel so ... unnerved. This time, it gave him a buzz. A swarming, weird happiness that washed over him.

"I think so. It's kinda scary, but in a good way."

"Yes, it is. It's what happens when you let yourself be vulnerable. You're not that sort. Believe me. I was married to your father. I understand men with an aversion to vulnerability. Some never allow themselves to acknowledge it. It makes me proud that you're not one of them. I'm also thrilled for you."

Mom walked around the island. Instinctively, he swiveled to face her. She set both hands on his cheeks.

"You're my son and I love you. If you ever get arrested again, I'll kill you myself. Understood?"

"Yes, ma'am."

"Good." With that, she dropped her hands, smacked a kiss on his cheek and stepped back. "Now, who's this lawyer helping you?"

Cruz shrugged. "Some guy Cilla knows. She said he's good. She's gonna talk to her father. Get him to drop the charges."

"Oh, that'll be fun, I'm sure. Send me her number, please. I'd like to thank her."

Cruz slipped his phone from his pocket, sent Mom the number, then set the phone down on the island, spinning it round and round and round a few times before looking back at Mom. "So, about Dad. Are Ash and I the only ones who know?"

"That he was in prison? Yes. Since he wasn't from around here, we put it behind us."

"You gave him a chance."

She shrugged. "I saw the good in him. He deserved an opportunity to have a better life. I was and still am proud that he'd moved on from his past."

His mother. So forgiving. "A lot of women would run from a convict."

"I wouldn't blame them. Lucky for us, he figured out how to live an honest life."

"He knew you'd leave him, huh?"

"I made that clear. And, if I'm any judge of character, brace yourself because I have a feeling Cilla is going to set some boundaries with you."

"Like not socking her father?"

Mom snorted. "Something like that. I'll tell you the same thing I told your father. Figure it out or you'll wind up a lonely man."

He sat back, blew out a breath. Between the booze and now this, he'd turned his life into a shit show. At least he had the opportunity to fix it.

Since they were having this heart-to-heart . . . "Mom? There's something else."

"Oh, boy."

He laughed. "It's nothing horrible. At least, I don't think."

Mimicking his gesture from a few minutes earlier, she rolled one hand. How could he tell her, after they'd built her dream home, he wanted to leave it?

"You know," he said, "there have been a lot of changes around here with Maddy, Liv, Brodie, and Lena."

Mom nodded. "Indeed, there have. It's been hard for you. I've seen it."

"Not hard." When she gave him a heated look, he shrugged. "Okay. Yeah. It's been an adjustment. But it's been good, too. My brothers are happy. The house is full of life."

"A lot of life," Mom cracked.

Cruz snorted. "Yeah. Which brings me to my point. With all these people around, I realized something." He held her gaze. "I need space. Mom, I didn't plan it, but the other day I drove by a house in Asheville. It's for sale and it caught my eye. I'm going to put an offer in."

Before she could speak, he plowed forward. "Not full-time. I think it'll be a part-time thing. The house is close to downtown. I could use it as an investment property for vacation rentals. Then, when it's not rented, I'll crash for a few days when I need privacy. I can commute home for work. Plus, Cilla just bought an office close to there. I'd be close to her. Figure out where this relationship is going."

There. Said it. Just blurted it out. He sat back, dipped his head, and waited. When nothing happened, he looked back at his mother, found tears shimmering in her eyes.

Shit. He'd made her cry. Again.

"Mom, I'm so sorry."

"Don't you dare," she said. "Don't apologize for wanting to live your life. I told Ash the same thing when he moved out. I love having my babies in my nest, but I refuse to be the reason you don't chase your dreams. If this move will make you happy, I want you to do it. Life is too short, and opportunities don't always come. When you have them, and you want to grab hold, you should."

Relief landed on him like a ten-ton concrete block. His shoulders drooped and he let out a huge breath. "Wow," he said, shaking his head. "You're amazing. I always knew it. I didn't want to make you sad, though."

"That's the thing, my boy. I'm always sad when one of you leaves for even a day. Love does that. It's not a bad thing."

Yeah. He supposed it wasn't.

Mom stood tall and nodded. "You have my blessing to do whatever will make you happy. Now, go get cleaned up and get to work. We have a business to run."

24

THE SOFT CLUNK OF CILLA'S BEDROOM DOOR HANDLE sounded and she opened her eyes just as the door came open. A shaft of light from the hallway pierced the darkness. Mom had closed the blinds and drapes, ensuring not a smidge of light would enter. At first, Cilla considered it overkill, but given the stabbing whenever she opened her eyes, she welcomed the pitch-black.

Having never had a concussion, Cilla hadn't known what to expect. All she knew was her head hurt.

Badly.

That shaft of light? Might as well have been an axe splitting her skull.

Jeez. How long would this last? She had things to do and lying around in bed all day wouldn't win her a murder trial. Thankfully, Layla had offered to hold down the fort, including getting things rolling for the move.

Definitely a pay raise coming in Layla's near future.

"Darling?" Mom said, her voice so low Cilla barely heard her.

"Yes?"

"The doorman just buzzed. Your father is downstairs. I was about to send him away, but, well, I don't want to make that decision for you. What would you like me to do?"

Her mother. Always the reasonable parent. No matter her difficulties with Dad over the years, Mom had never—not once—used Cilla as a weapon.

As a sulky teenager, she hadn't appreciated it. As an adult who, on the daily, witnessed her father's annoying behavior, she wasn't sure how her mother had stayed with him almost fifteen years.

And now, after the scene in the hospital the day before and pressing charges against Cruz, he had the nerve to show up at her home.

"I can't, Mom."

"That's fine. I'll tell him. Try and sleep."

Cilla sunk back into her pillow and closed her eyes again. A vision of her father on his hands and knees admitting to conspiring against her plagued her mind. Absolute venom with no antidote.

And how long would *that* last?

No doubt, a long time. The idea of it eating away at her sent the marching band in her head into parade-mode.

She had to get rid of these thoughts. Move on and not let her father's betrayal tear her apart. But, how?

Before Mom could back out the door, Cilla opened her eyes. "Mom? Wait."

"Yes, dear?"

Slowly sitting up, Cilla peered at her mother, dressed in one of her favorite cashmere lounge sets Cilla had bought her for Christmas last year because she thought the charcoal shade would bring out the green in her mother's eyes.

She'd been right.

Those eyes, Cilla had noted earlier when they'd left the

hospital, now appeared puffy. Tired. Mom had to be exhausted. She'd flown cross-country the night before and had been playing nursemaid all day.

Probably the last thing Mom wanted was to deal with her ex-husband.

Maybe they simply needed to get it over with.

Cilla lifted her palms to her eyes and gently pressed. "Have him come up. I want to speak with him."

"Oh, Cilla. I don't—"

"It's fine, Mom. Thinking about it is worse than the headache. I'll say what I have to and then we'll be done."

"All right. Do you need help getting out of bed?"

Upon arriving home, Mom had helped her shower and throw on tights and a long-sleeved T-shirt. The ultimate casualwear her father would curl his lip over.

Well, too bad. He'd created this havoc, he could suffer over her choice of clothing.

"I can do it," Cilla said. "Keep your phone close. I'll call if I need you. Would you please crack the curtains though? Just a little so I can see?"

"Of course."

While Cilla sat up, Mom walked to the switch beside the windows and tapped it, allowing the curtains to slide open a few inches. Afternoon sun squeaked in, illuminating the room just enough for Cilla to navigate it without tripping on something.

"That's perfect. Thanks. I need to use the bathroom."

Mom, being Mom, stood by while Cilla levered out of bed, grabbed her phone from the nightstand, and made her way to the bathroom.

Before leaving the hospital that morning, Cilla had faced the mirror, seeing only a large surgical bandage with a few spots of blood, at which point, she'd asked a nurse to change the dressing. Intellectually, she understood twenty stitches currently held together her cheek. All done by her plastic surgeon client who'd informed her that they'd deal with the scarring once the stitches came out. One step at a time.

Cilla further understood that in the next few hours, based on doctor's orders, she'd have to remove the bandage and allow the wound to air. At which point, those stitches and the angry red skin would be on full display.

One thing at a time.

That's all she could do. For now, that one thing would be rest. The more rest, the sooner she'd be back to work.

Lucky her, the stitches were to be removed in five days. In less than a week, assuming the concussion didn't hold her down and she didn't need to request a continuance, she'd be back at work with a healing wound and scar that would completely distract a jury.

Can't worry about it.

Not now, anyway.

Cilla flushed the toilet and made her way to the sink where she focused on pumping soap—three pumps—into her hands and washing them. The rhythmic movement was a welcome distraction until she rinsed, dried off and found the nerve to face herself in the mirror.

Lying flat had mashed her hair in the back, but the top was lumpy and somewhat mangled compared to her normally sleek strands. Mom had washed her hair for her that morning. No easy feat when trying to keep her bandage dry and the roar of the blow dryer had nearly sent Cilla to her knees. They'd done their best to towel dry it and Cilla had gone to bed with a half-wet head.

Now she looked like a straggly mess.

Lord, this is what Cruz saw when he'd come by earlier.

Well, it wasn't as if he hadn't seen her first thing in the morning. Nevertheless, between the bandage and her hair?

Awful.

Despite being more than a little peeved at him for punching her father, they were still in the phase of her wanting to be . . . attractive. Pulled together.

Instinctively, she picked up her brush and held it.

She should do it. Run it through her hair and at least try to fix the rat's nest on top of her head.

Except . . . no.

Given what her father had done, he'd lost the privilege of seeing her at her best. Like her, he'd have to face the fallout of his actions.

The doorbell rang just as Cilla reached the living room. Spotting her, Mom halted on her way to the door, her gaze zooming right to Cilla's hair.

"I know," Cilla said. "I'm a mess. I don't care."

Mom shook her head. "You look fine. More than fine. Are you all right?"

"I'm as all right as I'm going to be." Cilla gestured to the door. "Let's get this over with."

"Do you want me to wait in your office?"

Since the divorce, Cilla could count on one hand the number of times her parents had been in the same room together. Mom had long since moved on with her life, finding happiness out west, while her father hadn't.

He'd spent the last twenty years serial dating women just old enough to drink. All of which Cilla felt fairly certain was some sort of twisted message to Mom about his ability to still attract young, beautiful women.

Of course, his money helped, but Cilla veered from stating the obvious.

"Please stay," Cilla said. "Let him squirm."

Mom let out a chuckle. "Good for you, darling."

While Mom opened the door, Cilla settled on the sofa, tucked her phone under her thigh, and pulled the throw blanket over her legs. Seconds later, Dad came from behind the cover of the entry hall. When his gaze landed on her, he paused, taking in the sight of her while his face pinched into a wince.

Cilla pointed at her cheek. "Lovely, isn't it?"

He moved toward her, arms extended. Oh, no. He couldn't think she'd welcome a hug from him after what he'd done.

Holding up a hand, she'd stopped him mid-stride. "Come sit down, Dad. I don't have much energy, so we'll say what we have to and be done."

He turned to Mom. "Would you give us a minute?"

"No." Cilla said. "She won't." She patted the spot beside her on the sofa. "Sit, Mom."

Her father's eyebrows hit his hairline, his forehead wrinkling despite the Botox he regularly pumped in there. "I'd prefer to talk privately."

Fury ripped into her already battered skull. "I'm sure you would. Too bad. Mom stays. She's been with me all night, trying to help me through a trauma. So, you will have to be a man and tell us what exactly you did. And you should know, a detective called this morning and told Mom he'd be coming by later today to update me on their investigation. You'll probably be contacted after I tell them about your little admission."

Still standing, her father unbuttoned his suit jacket, preparing to sit in one of the two chairs across from the sofa. "What admission?"

Always the consummate liar, her father sat, his features stiff, yet somehow relaxed leaving him completely unreadable. Total puzzle.

"Please, Dad. Don't do this. Look at me. Look what you did to me. For once, take responsibility for your actions. Including sabotaging my case."

He held his hands wide. "What I have I done?"

"Conspiracy to start with. You all but admitted you had my car blown up. You also used your influence with Nagle to get my plea deal rejected."

"Yes," Mom said. "Rosemary Nagle took great pleasure in sharing with me how our daughter was humiliated. Excellent work, Darren. You should be ashamed. Then again, you don't feel that particular emotion."

Dad gave her a heated look, then shifted his gaze to Cilla who offered a faux cheery grin.

"On that subject," she said, "in between bouts of vomiting this morning, thank you very much, I phoned Rick Bandy, the prosecutor on my case. I filled him in on what Mrs. Nagle told Mom."

Dad's eyes grew to the size of dinner plates. "Are you insane? You'll ruin a respected judge."

As if she cared? "Gee, Dad, what was it you told me after that hearing?" She peered up at the ceiling, replaying the conversation in her mind. "Oh, right. I remember." She met her father's gaze again, picturing burning a hole through him. "You said, 'Maybe it's what should happen.' In this case, I agree. Rick has assured me he'll take care of it. Judge Nagle should, at the very least, be recusing himself from my case any time now and we'll get back to giving my client a fair deal. Personally, I hope the Judicial Standards Commission investigates. *That* would be fun. As for you, tell me everything you've done and maybe you can convince me not to send you to prison. Did you send Paul to threaten me?"

Dad eased back, crossing one ankle over his knee. "Don't

be so dramatic. I asked him to talk to you about nosing around in Morgan."

Oh. Please. "You *are* clueless, aren't you?"

"Watch your mouth."

"No," Mom said. "*You* watch your mouth. If it were up to me, I'd lock you up for the rest of your life for what you've done to my child."

"Our child."

"Not in my book. After this, you're dead to me. I wouldn't blame Cilla if she never wanted to hear from you again."

Dad gave her a hard look and Mom laughed. "Darren, your intimidation tactics stopped working on me years ago."

Go Mom. Still, she needed to keep the discussion from derailing.

"So," Cilla said, "if I've put the pieces together correctly, you've been behind this the whole time. Were you the one who pulled my access to the Randolph server?"

When Dad stayed silent, Cilla slid her phone from under her thigh. "Fine. If you don't want to talk to me, I'll call the detective who'll be here later and give him a preview of what I intend to tell him. Let him get on it quicker."

Dad raised a hand up. "Put that phone down."

Cilla swiped at the screen. "Not unless you start talking."

She shot him a glance and he let out a sigh. As if the entire episode might kill him. "The day you found the reports on the plane," he said. "I spoke to Paul. I know you, Cilla. You're the curious sort. Always wanting to do the right thing."

"And that's bad?"

"I couldn't have you poking around. I had your access pulled. Clearly, it didn't stop you."

"Okay. When that didn't work, you sent Paul to see me. And when that didn't work?"

Silence once again hung over the room, but Dad shook his head. "All I wanted was to stop your inquiries. To show you that if you mess with my business, there are consequences. I wanted all your access shut down. That's all."

Her access. What did *that* mean? She thought back on the last weeks. The things that had gone sideways. *Oh, no . . .* He didn't.

But if he'd gotten to Nagle . . .

"Dad, please tell me you're not the reason my investigator suddenly can't get his contacts to return his calls."

Beside Cilla, Mom tsk-tsked. "So typical."

"I may have put a call in to the police chief. That's all."

"Dad! You're messing with my clients' freedom! What the hell is wrong with you?"

A stabbing pain pierced her right eye and she pressed her fingers against it. So twisted. All of this.

"Never mind," she said. "I'll be sharing that with detectives as well. Unless you'd like to call your buddy the police chief and fix this on your own?"

Dad met her gaze again, the flush of his cheeks indicative of his annoyance. "I'll take care of it."

"Excellent. Were you the one who put that bullet on my car?"

Mom bolted upright and swung her gaze to Cilla. "What bullet?"

Yikes. She'd made the tactical decision to not share that minor detail with her mother. Now, she'd have to deal with the fallout. "I was leaving the office one day and found an envelope on my car. It had a spent bullet casing in it."

"Cilla," Mom said, "why didn't you tell me?"

"Because you'd worry, and I didn't know exactly what I was dealing with. I wasn't sure if it was a disgruntled former client or what." Cilla went back to her father. "Was it you?"

Dad's silence told her everything she needed to hear. Typically, he'd be his bombastic self, spinning a tale, deflecting blame, and somehow making it her fault.

This time? Silence. Perhaps he had a soul.

How the hell did they get here? He'd adored her.

Or maybe it wasn't her. Maybe her accomplishments were what he adored.

"Fine," Cilla said. "When that didn't back me off, you had my car blown up. From what I've heard, it was a pipe bomb. I haven't seen the security footage yet—I'm guessing the police will show it to me later. Cruz saw it. The person who put the bomb in my car had the access code to the garage. Drove up at three a.m., punched in the code, parked across from my car, crawled under, and did something. We're assuming it was the bomb. Then he simply drove off. Who is he, Dad?"

Again, her father stayed silent. She should have expected as much. The throb in her head double-timed and she closed her eyes for a brief second before facing her father again. How she wished she had the energy to scream or cry. Something.

So tired.

Or maybe she was like Mom, and her father was simply dead to her.

"I could have been killed," she said, "and you won't give me the benefit of an explanation?"

Nothing. Self-preservation mode had kicked in. All he did was sit there and stare at her.

She knew him well enough to know she'd get nothing out of him.

Perfect. If he couldn't be man enough to admit what he'd done, she'd have no guilt over ending this useless conversation.

Slowly, Cilla pulled the blanket from her legs and folded it, aligning the corners the way she liked so the fringe would hang over the back of the couch. She set it back in place and smoothed the wrinkles before turning back to her parents.

"I'm tired," she said. "Going back to bed. Mom will show you out."

He reached for her, grabbing her hand. "Cilla."

She snatched her arm back, the movement too fast and sending her head spinning. "No, Dad. If you can't be honest with me, we have nothing more to say. Now it's up to the PD to figure out. I won't help you anymore. Do yourself a favor and drop the charges against Cruz Blackwell."

"Now you think you can threaten me?"

"Don't be so dramatic, Dad. I'm simply giving you legal advice. You pushed him. As I recall, three times. I saw it. I'll tell the police how you instigated that situation." She shrugged. "Or maybe Cruz will sue you. That would be a nuisance, wouldn't it?"

She moved, took three steps, and when she didn't get dizzy, kept going, moving away from her parents toward her bedroom.

"Cilla!" Her father thundered. "You don't walk away from me."

"Actually," she called without stopping, "it's my house. I'll do what I want. Goodbye, Dad. And good luck. You'll need it."

25

CRUZ DID AS HIS MOTHER SUGGESTED. GOT CLEANED UP, spent the rest of the day in the Theater with his brothers working on two fresh cases, and then, dog-tired, walked to his suite, called Cilla for what had to be the eighth time and dropped into bed at midnight.

Seven hours later, after taking in a fantastic sunrise that had to be a good sign for the day, he grabbed a quick shower and tromped to the garage where he climbed into the Stutz.

He'd texted Cilla last night, letting her know he'd be in Charlotte today and if she were feeling up to it, he'd like to get her out.

What he didn't mention was that he'd be driving the Stutz and ready to give her the promised ride.

Two hours into the drive, his phone rang. Cruz scooped it from the passenger seat, glancing quickly at the screen.

Tom Cleo. AKA his defense lawyer.

Pondering that, Cruz immediately returned his attention to the road.

A call from Tom so soon couldn't be good. Could it? Just seeing the guy's name made Cruz's skin itch.

The phone rang again and already distracted, Cruz checked his rearview, found a few cars about half a mile back and safely pulled to the shoulder, shifting to park before picking up the call. He tapped the speaker button. "Hey, Tom."

"Cruz, hi. Got good news for you."

Good news. Excellent. That'd teach him to prejudge a situation. In his mind, though, lawyers tended to be cynical. Tom's news might not be what Cruz considered good. "I could use some," Cruz said.

"I just spoke to the ADA handling your case. They dropped the charges."

Whoa. Cruz shook his head. Did he hear that right? "Come again?"

"The char-ges," Tom said, exaggerating every syllable as if they had a faulty connection. "Have. Been. Dropped."

The full power of relief bent Cruz forward. He rested his head on the steering wheel and let out a whooshing breath. "Wow. That's fantastic."

He sat for a few seconds, absorbing it. Letting the reality flow over him. Everything would be okay. He knew it. *Felt* it.

His mother—brothers, too—could hold their heads high when facing Steele Ridge's gossipmongers.

"It is," Tom said. "Mr. Randolph has decided he's not interested in pressing charges. A couple of detectives also spoke with Priscilla, and she confirmed that her father instigated it. The DA has bigger fish to fry."

Randolph dropped the charges? Cilla had to have had more to do with it than just narking on him to the detectives.

Either way, Cruz was a happy guy.

"Okay," Cruz said, letting out a hard breath. "We're good then?"

"We're good."

"Thanks, Tom. Cilla was right. You're a great attorney. Send me a bill."

"Oh, don't worry. I will."

They both laughed.

"If there's anything else," Tom said, "I'll let you know. Take care, Cruz."

"Yeah. You too."

Cruz clicked off and sat for a second while a truck roared by, followed by the whoosh of three speeding cars.

Since the second the jail cell door slid closed, he'd had a brutal tightness in his solar plexus. His entire body, actually. Between the idea of being convicted, prison time, disappointing his family, and having a criminal record, he envisioned his life flying over the side of a cliff.

Every good thing he'd worked for, blown to bits over one stupid mistake. Over losing his head. The one thing his parents had always warned him against.

And now, he knew why. They simply didn't want him winding up like his father.

Something he now fully understood in a way he couldn't have prior to knowing his father's history.

All of it. The screaming matches between he and Dad, his father constantly raging at him, nitpicking his every move.

He got it.

Finally.

"Jeez, Dad," he muttered, his body loosening. "You or Mom could have helped me out and explained it to me. Maybe it wouldn't have taken thirty-one years to understand."

Something flashed in the rearview mirror and he snapped his gaze up, expecting to see another car.

Nothing. No vehicles even close.

He swung his head around, peeking in the backseat. Nothing.

And yet, here he was, in his father's car, talking to the man and . . . had to be a sign. Since his father's death he'd always imagined him watching over them. In life, his father had had a huge presence. In the beginning, he couldn't imagine living without him. Without hearing his voice or his laugh or, yes, his hollering.

It was all too much. And then, when he was gone, the quiet became maddening. Like a giant hole had swallowed part of their lives.

Which, Cruz supposed, is exactly what had happened when they put their father into the ground.

Over the years, when bored, he'd done research on the spirit world and how the dead liked to play with electricity. Lights flashing, music suddenly playing, televisions switching channels.

All of it fascinating and a little woo-woo for Cruz, but maybe . . .

He shook his head and laughed. "Okay, old man. I got your car built and back on the road and you're fucking with me?"

When no response or additional flashes occurred, Cruz shot a message off to his mother and brothers in their group text letting them know the charges had been dropped.

Then he shifted the Stutz back into gear and merged into traffic. In another hour he'd be in Charlotte and would give Cilla the news himself.

A good day. That's what he had going right here.

A really good day.

. . .

CRUZ STEPPED THROUGH CILLA'S FRONT DOOR AND NODDED AT her mother, a woman who'd not only opened the garage gate for him but once again thanked him profusely for being with Cilla in the hospital until she could get there.

Oddly, Cruz and Marlena clicked from the get-go, both on board with whatever Cilla needed.

As opposed to Darren. *That* fucker focused on what Darren needed.

All. The. Time.

After entering the short entry hallway that led to the open kitchen and living room, Cruz turned back to Marlena. "How's the patient today?"

"Better. Her color is back and she said her head doesn't hurt as much." Marlena stepped closer and leaned in. "Fair warning. She's upset about the incident with Darren. Personally, I'll love you forever, but I can see why she's upset. She doesn't want your fighting with people to be, well, a thing."

Ach. The humiliation of his teenage years, Dad screaming, Mom jumping to Cruz's rescue, came flooding back.

Cruz let out a soft breath, pushed aside the memories and nodded. "I was wrong. I know it and I'll own it. It'll never happen again. I promise you. If Cilla will let me, I'll always take care of her. Without using my fists."

For a few seconds, Marlena studied him, then reached out and patted his shoulder. "Thank you. I believe you, but I'm not the one to convince."

She pointed toward the living room. "She's inside."

"Thank you for the warning."

"You're welcome. From what I've seen so far, I like you. You stood up to my horrid ex-husband. That alone earns you points. Now go. I'll be in the bedroom if anyone needs me."

Thankful for the support, Cruz walked to the end of the hallway and found Cilla sitting in the living room. They'd moved one of the upholstered side chairs next to the sliding doors so she could look out the window.

At least she wasn't locked in a pitch-black room anymore.

She wore a pair of baggy jeans with a gray V-neck sweater. Her feet were bare, but a pair of fuzzy white slippers lay on the floor. How cute was that? She hadn't struck him as the fuzzy white slipper type, but he kinda liked it. Enjoyed learning the silly, mundane things of ordinary life.

Slowly, she turned her head, spotted him and held his gaze while Cruz's pulse went ape-shit. Was she happy to see him? Not happy?

As body language went, she gave him nothing. Zippo. No wonder she was a crack lawyer.

"Good morning, Cruz Blackwell."

And then she did it. Her lips slid into a full-on smile that nearly sent him to his knees. It wasn't one of those you-poor-schmuck smiles. This was a I'm-happy-to-see-you deal.

At least, that's the way he read it and he was pretty good with that stuff.

He walked toward her, his body moving faster than he'd intended and in the short time it took him to reach her, his thoughts froze. Kiss her? Don't kiss her?

What would she expect?

Too much thinking. He shook it off. Paralyzed by his own thoughts, he went the safe route and dropped a kiss on top of her head. Gently, he ran one hand over her silky dark hair and the clean scent of her shampoo settled his rioting mind. "It's good to see you," he murmured. "Really good."

Then he stood tall, peering down at her. Her mom was right. She did look better. The pale zombie vibe had passed.

She still wasn't the vibrant Cilla he'd met months ago, but she looked more like herself than she had yesterday.

"I'm glad you came," she said. "We should talk."

Ugh. The words of doom. At least in his experience. Come to think of it, he'd usually be the one saying them. Now, suddenly, he realized just how much it sucked to hear.

Totally taking that phrase out of his repertoire.

"I know." He pointed to the other chair. "Mind if I bring it over here? That way you don't have to move."

"Sure. It has sliders. Just need to get it off the rug."

Quickly, he walked to the chair, picked it up by the bottom, balanced himself and then set it on the floor so he could push it.

Positioning it just across from her, he left a couple of feet between them and sat. Before she could speak, he jumped in. "I'm sorry I hit him."

He'd apologized to her in the hospital, then again yesterday when he'd stopped to check on her, but it couldn't hurt to do it again. Right?

"Cruz, you've apologized three times. I know you're sorry. What I need to know is it'll never happen again. With anyone. I don't want us to be out somewhere having a nice dinner and you explode."

He raised one hand. "My behavior was inexcusable. I know that. I let my emotions take over. You were hurt and he'd basically admitted to playing a part in it. I turned into a juvenile and lost it. I know better and will do better."

"You know," she said, "I finally found someone who's not afraid to stand up for me. Particularly with Dad. That means so much to me. Truly. It's also terrifying. Doing what I do, sometimes people say nasty things about me. Online, in person, doesn't matter. People take shots, Cruz. I can't have you punching prosecutors who don't like the way I question their witnesses. See where that can be a problem?"

In his own defense, he'd spent most of his adult life out of brawls. He'd matured, found other outlets for that form of aggression. He'd told her all this.

But, he supposed, he needed to do his penance here. Convince her to take a chance on him.

He jerked his head once. "I understand. It hasn't happened in years. I swear to you. This was different. Something snapped in me and trust me, a night in jail and facing criminal charges was enough to get my head out of my ass. Then I had to face my mother. I realize now how much I could have lost. I brought embarrassment to you and my family. Cilla, I swear to you, it will never happen again. I'll make sure of it."

She tilted her head and studied him. "Good. Because it's not something I can tolerate."

"I get it. I grew up disappointing people. No interest in going backward."

"I'm not disappointed. Or embarrassed. Not by you anyway. My father? Different story."

"He dropped the charges."

Her eyebrows shot up. "Whoa."

"Yep. I got a call from the lawyer on the way here. I'm in the clear. You seem surprised."

"Stunned actually. He never backs down. Ever. He was here yesterday. I advised him to drop the charges. He didn't take it well."

"Whatever you said, must have worked."

She let out a soft sigh. "At least something came out of it. The only thing I got from him was admitting he pulled my access to his company files. Other than that, he admitted nothing. So typical of him. We could have been killed and he's still all about himself."

"Most narcissists operate that way."

"I know, but I'd hoped his love for his child might make a difference." She waved it off. "Anyway, it's in detectives' hands now. They came by to see me yesterday. You'll probably hear from them. I told them everything I could remember about the explosion and the arguments with Dad. Threats from Paul. The Morgan contamination, everything. I also have Ed, my investigator on it. This morning he told me he spoke to one of his contacts at the PD. They'd gone dark on him—also my father's doing—but are now returning his calls after I called Dad out on it. Anyway, Ed heard from one of his contacts that Paul got nervous when questioned."

"He shit the bed?"

"Sounds like it. Ed's source told him Paul hired someone, at my father's request, to put the bullet on my car. Dad knows I've received veiled threats in the past. Somehow, he thought that was the way to, as he put it, teach me a lesson."

"That had to be hard to hear."

"Actually, not so much. I'm sad. Devastated, really, but not about what he did. About how I feel. I'm totally numb. It's like a switch flipped in my head. He'll always be my father and I'll always love him, but I don't want him in my life. I know that. I've had enough."

"Understandable. What about the bomb on your car?"

She nodded. "They hired someone for that, too."

"They have all sorts of lowlifes on the payroll."

"I suppose. Paul gave up the guy's name. They arrested him an hour ago."

Oh, man. That was the best news. With the guy locked up, she could put this mess behind her.

A buzzing noise sounded, and she slid her cell from under her thigh. "Sorry," she said. "I'm playing phone tag with Kayla."

"Not a problem."

"This is her. I'll put her on speaker." She tapped the screen. "Hi."

"Hey," Kayla's voice filled the room. "How're you feeling?"

"Better today. Thanks. What's up?"

"Things are moving. I have an update for you."

26

CILLA MET CRUZ'S EYE. THINGS MOVING MEANT GETTING beyond this nightmare and figuring out her new normal. Without her dad.

With Cruz.

"I like movement," Cilla said. "Just so you know, Cruz is here and you're on speaker."

"Good. Everyone will be in the loop. I spoke to my EPA contact first thing this morning. She's at the federal level, but has spoken with someone at state EPA. Your investigative reporter is shaking things up. Asking questions they have no answers for. My contact said the story will run either tomorrow or the next day. They're, as we speak, scrambling to get organized. Based on information provided by Allison Caplin, they've opened a new investigation into Randolph Industries. Not only in North Carolina. All the plants around the country."

Cilla set the phone on the arm of the chair and leaned forward, resting her head in her hands. "Wow."

"I'm sorry, Cilla." Kayla said, her voice softer, more

sympathetic than the direct lobbyist Cilla had experienced before.

Cruz reached over, touched Cilla's knee. "It needs to be done. Someone has to stop them. You did the right thing."

Whether from the concussion or the thought of outing Randolph Industries, sickness pooled in her stomach.

A vision of a bald Brittney Tate popped into Cilla's mind. How many other Brittneys might be out there?

You did the right thing.

Still, it stung. Weeks ago, she and Dad were a united front. Always having each other's backs. At that point, she'd never have imagined betraying her father. Then again, she wouldn't have imagined him betraying her the way he had.

She lifted her head and sat back again. "I know," she told Cruz. "It's just hard."

"If this EPA investigation goes the way I think it will," Kayla said, "you'll be out of it. You may have called it when you said North Carolina could sue them. The AG loves nothing more than a spectacle and rumor has it he's eyeing the governor's mansion. He'll take any opportunity to put himself on the news."

Great. Not only had she blown the whistle on her father, she'd inadvertently given a politician enough ammunition to crucify Randolph Industries in the press.

Banner day.

Cilla sighed. "I know this is good news. It sucks for me personally, but I understand it had to be done."

"Cilla," Kayla said, "you have my undying respect. Plenty of people, I can rattle off ten that I know of, would have done nothing. They sit back and watch their profits soar while people are sick and dying. It's disgusting."

"Yeah. I couldn't do that. That crosses the line."

"Oh, hang on." Kayla broke away, speaking to someone on the other end, her voice muffled as if she'd pulled the phone from her ear. "I'm back. Sorry for the interruption. I have to take another call. I'll let you know if I hear anything else."

"Of course," Cilla said. "And, Kayla, thank you. For everything."

"You're welcome. We've got this. Get some rest."

Leaving the phone on the chair's arm, Cilla tapped the screen, sat back and eyed Cruz.

"I'm sorry," he said.

"Me too. It shouldn't have gotten this far. My father knew people were sick and did nothing." She peered out the window at the bright sunshine, then came back to Cruz. "When you called, you said something about lunch. Can we do that? I'd love to get out."

"Absolutely. Want to invite your mom?"

A burst of something warmed her. Cruz and Mom seemed to be a united front. Probably because they both hated her father.

"I'll ask her, but she'll say no. She likes her alone time and would enjoy the break."

Twenty minutes later, as expected, Mom bowed out of lunch, opting to go for a walk and grab something on her own. Fine with Cilla. She adored her mother, appreciated the help more than she could verbalize, but the hovering over the last two days had been maddening.

Plus, she wanted time with Cruz, who'd just promised her he'd never punch someone's lights out again. Despite knowing he meant well, she couldn't have that. Couldn't live with the constant worry of when he'd pop off.

Time would tell, but down deep she believed him. Every instinct she possessed assured her they'd be okay. More than okay. She took comfort in that. In trusting herself and him. In grabbing his hand and curling her fingers into his as they stepped off the elevator at the garage level of her building.

Outside, street noise scraped against her ears, the concussion seeming to amplify every sound. Still, there was a normalcy to the engine noises and honking horns she suddenly appreciated a whole lot more.

"Got a surprise for you," he said.

She laughed and met his eye. "Well, I hope it's a good one. I'm kinda filled up with bad ones."

"It's good. At least I think it is."

They rounded the corner at the elevator bank and Cruz pointed straight ahead. Taking his cue, she looked in the direction he'd pointed.

The Stutz!

Still walking, she let out a tiny squeal. Silly as it might be, after the stress of the last week, excitement lit her up.

He must have fixed the leak. "You did it," she said.

"All better now. And, since I promised you a ride, here we are."

"Yay," she said, giving his hand a squeeze. "This car is so beautiful. I can't wait."

They stopped at the passenger door and Cruz used the key to unlock it. Old cars. No key fob. That alone sent her system humming, thinking back on simpler times when technology hadn't yet turned the world upside down.

He opened the car door and rested his hand over the window. "When you're feeling better, I'll let you drive."

"Oh, I'd love that."

"In fact," he said, "remember when you asked if you could buy it?"

As if she could forget? "I do."

He held up the key. "It's yours."

Wait. What? The guy who'd told her just days ago he'd never sell it, had just told her she could have it.

"Uh," she said. "I don't understand. You said you'd never sell it."

Flashing that classic Cruz smile, he tilted his head, keeping his gaze on her. "I'm not."

Her head must be seriously banged up because she didn't understand. "You just said I could buy it."

"I'm giving it to you. I want you to have it."

Now her mouth dropped open, shock temporarily paralyzing the rest of her. Giving it to her? This had to be some sort of guilt-inflicted peace offering. Had to be. She couldn't accept it.

No way.

"Absolutely not," she said. "I love that you want me to have it. It's an amazing gesture." She set her hand over his arm and squeezed. "But this was your dad's car."

"I know. And he'd want someone to love it as much as he did. I'm not sure that's me."

Now he was talking nonsense. "Of course, it's you. You rebuilt it. Just hearing you talk about that, I know how much you love it."

"I do. But a lot has happened. Not just with you, but with my family, and I've spent the last couple of weeks figuring some things out. I still have a ways to go, demons to get rid of, but the Stutz? I built it for my father. To somehow prove something. It wasn't for me. Cilla, I've spent ten years obsessing over this car, trying to get it perfect, chasing my father's dream. Chasing a ghost. When I was sitting in that jail cell, I was thinking about Zeke and how he'd rip into me and how he'd recently asked me if I'd ever finish messing with this car."

He broke eye contact, peered down at the car and blew

out a hard breath. "As long as it's in my possession, I will always find something wrong. I will always chase my father's dream. Trying to make it perfect." He met her gaze again and held it for a few seconds. "I need to stop chasing his dream and chase my own. I'm not exactly sure what that dream is, but I want you in it. Experiencing it with me."

Cilla opened her mouth, then closed it again. It took a powerful man to admit his feelings like this. To be vulnerable.

That alone stole her breath. That he trusted her, cared for her, that much.

How she loved him.

As sure as she was standing here, about to tell him she couldn't accept it, she knew she'd never want to be apart from him.

Ever.

She stepped closer, cupped her hands around his cheeks and kissed him softly, gently brushing her lips over his, allowing herself to take comfort in his warmth and forget about the chaos raging around them.

She eased back from the kiss and dropped her hands. "Wanting me to have it means so much to me. That you'd entrust me with something that's such a huge part of your life. Truly, I can't imagine a better gift."

"Well," he smiled, then dropped another quick kiss on her before backing away. "Spending time in a cell offers time to reflect and I figured some things out. The first being that I love you."

She gasped. Cruz, full of surprises today. "You—"

His hand shot up. "Wait. I don't expect you to say it back. I just . . . I wanted to be honest. So you'll know my intentions are to take care of you. Always. And try to make you happy. I won't screw up again." He laughed. "At least I won't be punching people. I'll screw up in other ways. That's just me. But," he glanced down at the Stutz, "the best way to show you how much you mean to me is to see you cherish this car as much as my dad did. That's what he'd want and that's what I want. For the woman I love to be driving Dad's dream car. It's kinda perfect if you think about it."

Yes. It was. Heaven help her if she wrecked this car, though. The guilt would destroy her. The responsibility might be too much.

But perhaps there was a compromise.

She held up a finger. "I'll make you a deal. I'll keep it, but it'll be ours. To share. You drive it when you want. I'll drive it when I want. It might get complicated with you living three hours away, but maybe I can store it somewhere near my new office. Then it won't be as long of a commute."

He pressed his lips together, clearly pondering the idea.

"About Asheville," he said. "I talked to my mom about the Craftsman."

"Wow. You *have* been busy. How'd that go?"

"It went well. She told me to do what I want. Which, you know, I shouldn't have been surprised. She wants us happy. Even if it means leaving."

"She's amazing. Total reverse of my father."

"That's for sure." He waved it off. "I don't want to talk about him anymore."

"Me neither."

"Good. So, the Craftsman. After talking to my mom, I put in an offer. Waiting to hear, but the realtor thinks it's a go."

He'd be in Asheville. Near her office. Her pulse kicked up and she didn't bother fighting the smile begging to be set free.

The universe worked in odd ways. Odd ways that

allowed Cilla to suddenly envision a life with a man she loved and a family of her own.

"Congratulations," she said. "That's fantastic. I'm so excited."

"Yeah? Me too. The house has that two-car garage. We can keep the Stutz there. Then when you want to drive it, you can grab it."

She bobbed her head. "I love that idea. Cruz Blackwell, you'll probably drive me to madness, but I'd love sharing *everything* with you. My life, my dreams, my heartaches. I know it'll all be safe with you. And that's way more than I ever expected."

"Cilla, I've never thought about the future. Never had a dream of my own. It was always the Stutz. Now? I see it. My dream. You, the house. Having someone to come home to. It's good. Exceptional."

"Yes. It is." She gripped his hands. "We'll build our dreams together."

———

Thank you for reading *Crash Course*. Keep reading for an excerpt of *End Game*, book 5 in the Steele Ridge: The Blackwells series. There's also an amazing special edition of *End Game* available. If *Crash Course* was your first Steele Ridge book, you may want to check out Steele Ridge: The Steeles or Steele Ridge: The Kingstons.

END GAME

BY TRACEY DEVLYN

As a savvy and successful lobbyist, Kayla Krowne knows all about deception. Each day, she swims in a vast tank of opportunistic sharks. But nothing prepares her for the downward spiral her life takes after witnessing the assassination of a high-profile public official. When the police suggest she may have been the true target, her only hope of rooting out the murderer lies with the one Blackwell brother she's never been able to win over. The one she's held a secret longing for since their first meeting two years earlier.

Special Agent Asher Cameron Blackwell's day started off bad and ended worse. Not only is he drowning in a swamp of paperwork, he now has two investigations involving none other than Kayla-effing-Krowne. One is a presumed assassination case and the other one he's compelled to keep from her because of a promise he made to his semi-estranged brother, Zeke

Forced into close proximity, Ash and Kayla finally give in to the passion they can no longer hide, forging an unstoppable union as they navigate an intricate maze of lies and betrayals, and uncovering a heartbreaking conspiracy that leads them to Kayla's doorstep. It's a life-and-death battle that they dare not lose.

Grab *END GAME* now!

ACKNOWLEDGMENTS

I love this part of writing a book. It reminds me how lucky I am to have fantastic people in my life.

Thank you to Tracey Devlyn, my collaborator and dear friend, for always listening to my whining when my characters don't cooperate. I'm so grateful we met at that Windy City RWA meeting all those years ago.

To Kristen Weber, editor extraordinaire, thank you for your guidance and encouragement when I'd written myself into a tizzy! Martha Trachtenberg, as I write this, *Crash Course* is in your amazing hands where you will catch errors that everyone else misses. Your attention to detail saves me every time. A huge thanks to Stuart Bache for yet another fantastic cover in the Blackwells series. I could stare at them all day.

Thank you to David Ellis, who never laughs (at least to my face) at my legal questions. You made sorting out the wranglings of plea agreements and "judge speak" a whole lot of fun.

I'm incredibly grateful to Linda Berlin, a pilot who didn't know me, but took the time to help a fellow author understand preflight checks. I hope to one day fly with you.

Heather Machel, all I can say is we'd be lost without you. Maureen Downey, thank you for everything you do. You're amazing. Tessa Russ, thank you for being part of the team that keeps me organized!

As always, thanks to Liz Semkiu for not only explaining

the medical procedures surrounding facial lacerations, but for doing an early read on *Crash Course*. Sandy Modesitt, you'll always be part of Team Steele Ridge. Thank you for the beta read!

With every book, I end my acknowledgments by thanking my husband and son. Without them, this crazy publishing ride wouldn't exist. My thanks are particularly meaningful this time. After years of traveling to baseball fields all over the country, my "baby" broke a bone in his hand just weeks before the start of his last college baseball season. When the first doctor told him the season wouldn't happen, my son proved him wrong by putting together the season of his life. All while my characters were busy being stubborn and unwilling to help me finish this book. Thank you to my husband and son, who showed me what it looks like to not give up. For that, I will be forever grateful. I love you.

ABOUT ADRIENNE GIORDANO

 **Adrienne Giordano** is a *USA Today* bestselling author of over forty romantic suspense and mystery novels. She is a Jersey girl at heart, but now lives in the Midwest with her ultimate supporter of a husband, sports-obsessed son and Elliot, a snuggle-happy rescue. Having grown up near the ocean, Adrienne enjoys paddle boarding, a nice float in a kayak and lounging on the beach with a good book. For more information on Adrienne's books, please visit www.AdrienneGiordano.com. Adrienne can also be found on Facebook (AdrienneGiordanoAuthor), Instagram and Goodreads.

Don't miss a new release! Sign up for Adrienne's new release newsletter!